CASCADE
CHAOS

By William Slusher

CMP Publishing Group, LLC

All inquiries, including distributor information, should be addressed to:

CMPPG, LLC
27657 Highway 97
Okanogan, WA 98840

email: **info@cmppg.org**
website: www.**cmppg.com**

Visit the *Cascade Chaos* website at www.cascadechaos.com!

ISBN13: 978-0-9619407-5-1

Library of Congress Control Number: 2010932707

Author's Forward

Cascade Chaos is fiction. It is entirely a product of the author's creative construction. Many readers may imagine they are or know characters in this story, but nay, all are either invented, or if real in name, history or public domain, are referred to in a wholly fictional context.

There is a gun and pawn shop in Okanogan run by two friends of mine from whom I have bought guns and ammo, but these men of good humor are absent from *Cascade Chaos* and their shop does not resemble Winslow's Gun and Pawn.

There is also a DMV office in Okanogan County, but, as far as I know, nothing illegal goes on there, and no one named Bailey works there.

For the record, the sheriff and the jailer of Okanogan County, also friends, do not put minors on chain gangs. In fact, they don't even put chains on chain gangs.

One of the many benefits of living in rugged, remote Okanogan County is association with our large American Indian population, a diverse people of passion, wit, art, and character. I am of the Redneck tribe, rather than any 'redskinned' one, and thus I can never fully understand what Indian life is like, but I have tried to represent natives as faithfully as I do understand them, to the extent that I represent them in *Cascade Chaos*. I beg the Tribes' indulgence, and hope their good people find a chuckle or two in how all the characters in *Cascade Chaos* are portrayed.

Likewise, I am not a grizzly bear—I don't even know any—but I have also tried to represent these impressive creatures as faithfully as I understand them as well. As far as I know, regrettably, there is no grizz named Tonny.

Thus it goes throughout *Cascade Chaos*. I'm just making it up as I go along.

This I'm not making up: The bear on the cover was photographed sans rose by professional photographer Ron Niebrugge of Seward, Alaska. Thanks to Janine Niebrugge for her patient negotiations. See their excellent work at www.wildnatureimages.com.

I photographed the rose, the zenith of my photographic acumen. My friend and graphic maestro, Chuck Gallup, so skillfully placed the rose in Tonny's mouth.

I would be remiss in failing to thank my industrious publisher, Edna Siniff, as well as fellow writer, Kim Freel, for prepping *Cascade Chaos* for printing; dear friend, Joyce Tarpley, for proofreading; and my ever indulgent, supportive, and dearly-loved wife, Linda Shields, a tireless, dedicated, country doctor and a lady of a vanishing genre.

I'd also like to thank Ms. Ellen Williams, the volunteer guide who gave me my very own delightful and wonderfully informative tour of the magnificent Washington State Legislative Building. To any extent that there is error in my representation of the Washington state capitol, it is entirely mine.

That's it. That's about as serious as *Cascade Chaos* gets. Enjoy!

—William Slusher - June 2010
Riverside, Washington

PROLOGUE

Washington (state!)

The rangy cougar knew that scent left in the rain by the big noisy truck, of course, it was the giant bear. Not the common black bear of these Wenatchee Mountains, but the great terrible monster from farther north, the one called grizzly. When you're a cougar, you do damned well to know these things.

What that bear was doing in some two-leg's giant machine, the cougar didn't even want to think about.

Chapter One

Okanogan

"Jesus Christ, would you look at the size of that thing!"

Okanogan County isn't.

There is no county in Washington pronounced oh-can-*no*-gan. The county pronounced oh-can-*nah*-gan, however, is bigger than some American states, yet it is spiced with fewer than forty-thousand human residents. These include twelve Indian tribes, several Seattle weekenders who own escape homes in the county, some Hispanics, and a dozen Koreans smuggled across the Canadian border last night. There are many whites, of course, and some blacks, but both of the latter are fishing in Alaska at the moment. If you have to ask why the county isn't pronounced like it's spelled, you probably wouldn't be happy living here.

There are virtually no grizzly bears in Okanogan County, which is in the center of the state, snuggled warmly against Canada. A pittance are known to hang around the border in the remote, North Cascades wilderness areas, but they think of themselves as Canadian grizzlies out for a hike.

Okanogan County is high, rolling desert, towering forests, snow-capped mountains, sagebrush plains, beautiful lakes and rivers, and numerous pot patches. The county seat is also named Okanogan, and was once a bustling river-boat hub. It is now a pleasant little town by the—surprise— Okanogan River with several dozen homes, a post office, the county courthouse and jail, a large western emporium, convenience markets and, of course, the requisite gun store doubling as a pawn shop.

It is an altogether splendid place to live and foment revolution.

Winslow's Gun and Pawn was owned by Hogan Winslow. At seventy-two, Hogan was half deaf from Vietnam service and ten years as a soldier-for-hire in Africa, with the commensurate lifetime of gunfire. Hogan also had the personality and warmth of a constipated wart hog, which he knew and didn't give a damn about, so for the last two years he had left the running of the gun and pawn shop to his granddaughter, Loverly.

Loverly had been raised all her fifteen years under Hogan's exclusive tutelage. Hogan's unofficial daughter-in-law, Nadine, had demanded Hogan pay for an abortion after finding herself pregnant by Hogan's ne'er-do-well son. She'd enjoyed a one-nighter with the son during his brief parole, before the latter was killed six times by a cranky deputy for pulling a gun on a traffic stop. Deputies are fussy like that.

Hogan, never a crusader for women's rights, actual or assumed, reasoned with Nadine. He said that if she killed his one and only grandchild, ending his bloodline forever, he would bury Nadine in an unmarked grave two-days pack-horse ride into the Pasayten Wilderness. Nadine was alert to this sort of discourse. After all, there were those stories about the two Seattle lawyers who poached an albino fawn on Hogan's upper Tunk property. They'd been found strung up by their heels and gutted like trophy elk. The sheriff never did figure that one out.

Hogan had that cracked ice look in his eyes.

The day Nadine was discharged from the Tonasket hospital maternity ward, where Hogan had paid her bills, she placed the child on a blanket in a plastic laundry basket. She deposited the basket on the doorstep of Winslow's Gun and Pawn with a poignant note that read "Fuck you, you old fart!"

Nadine thence wisely disappeared from Okanogan County for the duration.

Hogan had looked down at the basket with its wailing contents, and promptly took same to the little market nearby for formula and throw-away diapers. Fuck it, he thought. What's so tough about motherhood? Clean 'em up, fill 'em up, and teach 'em to shoot. Big deal.

The only musical Hogan had ever seen, briefly while channel surfing, had been My Fair Lady. He'd identified with ornery old Doolittle, and he thought there could be no finer name for a little girl than Loverly.

Hogan was tall, scarred, sun-cooked, gray and bony. He was also a sour-minded, right-wing asshole, but he was no dummy. He knew that once guys learned that Loverly knew more about guns than half the life members of the NRA, they'd buy more blasting irons from the charming, Lolitish Loverly than from a crabby, bone-headed old pawn broker. So Hogan had gradually shifted more and more of the after school operation of the shop to Loverly as she had grown, until he now did little more in the afternoons than play chess, gossip, and drink with the locals who orbited around Winslow's Gun and Pawn.

This business model ran somewhat contrary to Federal Bureau of Alcohol, Tobacco, Firearms and Explosives guidelines, not to even mention child labor laws, but the BATFE was one of many official entities Hogan didn't give a happy damn about.

Hogan liked to think he hung around the store to protect his granddaughter in case of a robbery, but in his heart he knew that Loverly could shoot her way out of a Congolese coup. He had given her a .45 caliber custom 1911 automatic pistol when she was ten. Loverly was delighted and, under supervision, had put a thousand practice rounds a year through it. She could field-strip, clean and reassemble it in two-and-a-half minutes, ten seconds less without the blindfold.

Loverly often felt sad for her classmates who did not have a retired mercenary for a paw-paw.

Between advancing palsy and fading vision, Hogan himself could no longer hit a barn with a gun if he were locked inside it. Loverly had taken to hiding Hogan's truck keys as he was basically driving by braille anymore. When he subsequently drove his John Deere tractor to a gun show in Omak, Loverly shook her head and took the starter motor off the machine.

Country gun shops have their standards. They must be in rustic old buildings built of raw wood with rusty steel bars on the windows and doors. They must concurrently be pawn shops littered with air compressors, construction tools, military surplus detritus, and just about everything else.

Country gun stores must also have stacks of dog-eared gun and hunting magazines and one called Soldier of Fortune, a sort of worldwide journal for the mercenary profession. Ancient to recent photos of hunting kills must be tacked up everywhere. These are usually taken from a low angle with the hunter about ten feet behind the carcass, so the average late trophy animal looks like a record Boone and Crockett dinosaur.

It's also customary at country gun stores to have new and used guns, lots of them, of every description, and enough ammunition to keep a Wermacht division at bay for week. You don't want to be near a burning gun store.

BATFE regulations also required at least one dog. Winslow's Gun and Pawn had an enormous, overweight, brown ranch dog named Ronald Reagan. The dog was a boxer/rottweiler/husky/pit-bull/beagle mix, graying at the muzzle like Hogan. Ronald Reagan was also a female, but Hogan hadn't noticed until two days after he'd named her for The Big R, and he didn't feel like changing it.

Ronald Reagan had just shown up one frigid winter. She was sick and starved to her ribs, and suffered a length of jagged, bent-wire chain secured around her bloody raw neck with a rusty padlock.

Hogan had posted an ad in the Chronicle saying anyone who wanted to claim the old dog could come get her, and he vowed to chain them by the neck to a tree if they did.

Fortunately for all concerned, no one showed.

Ronald Reagan was all but lifeless unless she perceived a threat to Loverly at which time she made Cujo look like the Taco Bell mascot.

Hogan's deceased punk son hadn't been entirely without taste in women. Nadine had been the same busty, pretty, short-haired blonde that Loverly had become. When Loverly had asked Hogan if she could get her ears pierced he'd said OK, one lobe hole each ear, but if he caught her with anything else pierced, or if he ever saw any tattoo anywhere on her, he'd burn it shut or off with a hot screwdriver. Loverly had never quite been sure if Hogan was being metaphorical, and she'd elected not to test him.

There were some old wooden tables and chairs in the rear of Winslow's Gun and Pawn, and in a side room were refrigerators with beer and soft drinks, and what amounted to a small but well equipped bar.

Membership to the Winslow's Gun and Pawn social club was exclusive, by invitation only, subject to revision, and curiously eclectic. Hogan hated everybody so he drew no sexual, racial or cultural lines, although he wasn't quite up to speed on the gay, lesbian and transgender front as yet. 'Don't ask, don't tell' was still a good idea at Winslow's. Hogan also threatened to shoot smokers on site.

The first to arrive this momentous evening was Alexie Ledbetter, an alcoholic ex-stripper and former call girl from Seattle. When 'Sexy Lexie' had aged out of the Seattle sex business two years ago, she'd crawled into Okanogan County where she could find a cheap isolated trailer to live in on what she could earn cleaning houses.

Lexie had been a bitter, withdrawn woman strung out on just about every illegal chemical in the cabinet, but in the last two years she'd weaned herself down to booze in a way no one had expected. When Washington went 'no smoking' in all public places, Lexie damn near died for the umpteenth time, but it had reduced her addictions now to only legal alcohol, which she drank mostly at Winslow's between seven and nine.

No one who'd known Lexie when she arrived in
Okanogan County would've given her a year to live, but
she'd evinced a strength and survivability no one thought
she possessed. Some of her youthful attractiveness had even
reblossomed. She now wore her sandy hair tied back in a
ponytail.

"Damn, Lexie," Hogan said, hobbling bent for the tables,
"you look like forty miles of bad road today!"

"You silver-tongued devil, you," Lexie said, sitting
wearily. "You got such a way with words. You look like a
new set of golf clubs for Wayne Clement, you ask me."

Wayne Clement was a mortician in nearby Omak.

Hogan laughed and coughed violently, drawing a worried
glance from Loverly. He got his breath, and sat at the big
round table across from Lexie. Loverly set drinks before
them both.

Lexie lifted hers. "To your health, you smelly fossil!"

"To your tits!" Hogan answered, spilling some of his
drink as he clinked Lexie's. He laughed with raspy effort
again.

"It'd take twenty court clerks six months just to tally up
all the laws we'd be breaking."

The clatter of a diesel pickup truck drew near out back,
then went silent. Heavy feet thumped on the back porch
and in walked Boot Colhane, a tall, widower cowboy with
weathered eyes and not a spare calorie in two-hundred-
twenty pounds at forty-two years of age.

Boot sat down heavily in a light cloud of dust, and
turned up the dewy Corona Loverly handed him. "I'm
getting outta cows!" he growled. "Them goddamned, three-
piece suit, momma's boys in Olympia are running me outta
business! Their damn land grabbin' and regulations gonna
have us all as dependent on foreign food soon, like we are on
foreign oil now."

"What's it like in a cow?" Loverly said, bumping Boot with her hip.

"Comere Darlin'," Boot said, "and I'll show you like you'll never forget."

"In your perverted dreams, creepo."

"Hell, you always say yer quittin' cows!" Hogan said. "You a cowboy and a farmer, and you ain't gonna make it on alfalfa. You'll be punchin' cows when you topple out of the saddle twenty years from now."

"Yeah. Probably." Boot said. "If the—"

"Goddamned liberal assholes don't run you out first, yeah, yeah," Lexie said.

"Oh I didn't know you loved liberals so," Boot said.

"Kiss my—no, never mind. I hate 'em and you know it. Those Seattle prigs never got enough of tryin' to outlaw my trade too, you know. Christ they were forever comin' up with new ordinances about how close we could dance, what we could take off, where the clubs could operate. But, buddy, I did lap dances for half the goddamn state legislature at one time or another, including some of the women. Liberals just hate all people havin' any fun, even themselves. They're sick that way."

This unassailable gospel was roundly drank to, though Hogan insisted Loverly drink Sprite. "No caffeine!" Hogan had proclaimed long ago. "No drugs the doc don't say you got to have. No booze 'til your eighteen! And no smokin'...or I'll kill ya!"

Concerns about overparenting did not keep Hogan awake at night.

The back door opened again, this time to a fiftyish Native American man of the Nez Perce tribe, replete with a gray buzz-cut, a long, hooked nose, and a squinting, leathery face. He wore a faded western Stetson, jeans, boots and a sweatshirt with a gun-shaped lump at the waistband.

Dr. Runs With Rivers was a veterinarian on the nearby Colville Confederated Tribes Reservation. He had once considered having his name changed to Hell-no-I'm-not-that-guy-in-Dances-With-Wolves, but it proved too awkward. His real name was of the Salish native American language, but it was damned near impossible for stupid white people to pronounce, let alone spell, so he'd had the name changed to its literal English definition, runs with rivers.

"Runs!" Everybody toasted on his entrance. Today Runs had a huge, frowning Indian kid behind him.

Runs had figured out as a child that reservation life could have it's uncharming qualities, and, if he had any hope of becoming more than the tubby, diabetic drunk his unknown father had probably been, he had to get educated. He applied himself at school, and joined the US Marine Corps at seventeen. After combat service in Grenada and Panama, Gunnery Sergeant Rivers resigned the Corps, much to its lament. With his government benefits and two jobs on the side, he worked his way through college and veterinary school.

Runs raised his hand like Tonto. "How," he said.

"How!" everyone replied, showing their palms.

"Red man want firewater?" Loverly said, moving for the side room.

"Is a duck watertight, little paleface?" Runs answered, taking a chair.

Everybody peered curiously at the tall, fat Indian boy who dwarfed Runs. He wore long, baggy, red nylon basketball shorts, and a red headband around shaggy black hair. His fashionable red T-shirt said "If you ain't Tribal, you ain't shit!"

"This here's Blubbo," Runs said. "He's with me."

"Blubbo?" everybody said at once.

"Yeah. Tell 'em why, Blubbo."

The enormous Indian boy sighed and rolled his eyes. "Cause I'm a fat assed punk, gang banger, druggy, car thief, rez monkey on loan to Runs from the sheriff," the boy recited, mechanically. "My name is Blubbo 'til I lose twenty-two pounds so I can join the Marines so I won't become just another dabestic fat drunk in jail and shame my people."

"Di-a-betic, dammit," Runs said. "Not dabestic!"

9

"Diabetic," the boy said.

"Damn, Runs," Lexie said. "Ain't that a little insensitive?"

"Fuck sensitivity," Runs said in an oratorical milestone of succinctness. "Sensitivity is overrated. Sensitivity don't make fat boys lose weight. Discipline and exercise do. Blubbo's six-five and weighs two-fifty-two. Sarge says they won't take him til he's down to two-thirty."

"He another jailbird?" Boot asked.

"Yeah. Ever once in while the sheriff gets one he thinks is worth saving, so he gives him to me. It's that or a striped suit and pullin' weeds on state right-of-way in hundred degree heat with a shotgun pointed at you. And his name ain't 'he.' It's Blubbo."

"Excuuuse me." Boot stuck a calloused hand at the kid. "Blubbo, I'm Boot, This is Lexie, and this is Hogan, the ugliest white man on earth."

"Up yours, Sleeps With Sheep," Hogan rasped.

"And," Boot said, indicating Loverly who was setting a straight rum before Runs, "this is the dee-lectable Loverly herself."

Loverly nearly spilt Runs's drink, for she had found her true love at last. She stared coquettishly at Blubbo who scowled and harumphed.

"Heyyyyy," Loverly said. "He's cute! I think I'll marry him."

Everyone but Blubbo laughed, which embarrassed the boy. He frowned and pursed his lips.

"Better be fond of the cowgirl position," Lexie muttered, studying Blubbo's bulk.

"I don't need no girl!" Blubbo protested. "'Specially not no white girl. I'm Native blood!"

Loverly winked at Blubbo. "Ah. Racist, sexist, and afraid of girls. I can fix all that."

"I ain't afraid a nothin'!"

"Son," Boot said, "if a man ever stops bein' afraid of cars, motorcycles, tractors, horses, guns or women, he better step back and rethink himself, 'cause he's about to git hurt bad by one of them."

"Amen," Runs said.

"Damn straight," Hogan agreed.

Blubbo sulked. Loverly stared at him with a smitten smile.

"How would we even *get* a goddamn grizzly bear? We'd get eaten before we ever got to Olympia."

The last current member of the Winslow's Gun and Pawn Shop social club arrived in a huff. He blew through the door in running sweats and shoes, and a red t-shirt emblazoned with the famous quote attributed to Winston Churchill: "Any man who is under thirty, and who is not a liberal, has no heart. And any man who is over thirty, and is not a conservative, has no brains." There was no hard evidence that Sir Winston ever said that, but the irrefutable truth of it was no less profound to the group.

"Here comes light loafers," Hogan mumbled.

"Paw-paw," Loverly warned.

The newcomer's name was Nerves, just like it's spelled, because he made hysteria look like sloth. He was Hispanic, in his forties, had straight black hair and was as fit as the marathon runner he was. Nerves was also gay as Harvey Milk, and didn't care who knew it. The latter bothered Hogan, who was about as enlightened as a plantation overseer.

Nerves was waving a newspaper in the air. "You won't believe it! You absolutely will not believe it!" Loverly brought Nerves a tomato juice with ice. He was a preachy gay health nut, but he was the Winslow Gun and Pawn Shop social club's preachy gay health nut.

"You will not believe it!" Nerves repeated with his Mexican Joan Rivers voice, dropping delicately into a chair with his knees neatly together, chin up.

Loverly studied the pulsing veins in Nerves's high forehead, his bulging eyes, and the spittle on his lips.

11

Hmmm, call 911, lay the patient flat, check for breathing, thirty compressions, one breath... Nerves slapped the newspaper onto the table. "They've finally done it. Those insipid cretins have finally done it!"

"*What!?*" Everyone but Blubbo said with an edge.

"Grizzlies!" Nerves roared, inasmuch as a preachy gay health nut could be said to roar. "That porcine state senator Lisa Belle has introduced a bill to 'restore' grizzly bears to Okanogan County!"

This was cause for a round of eloquent rejoinders.

"Shit!

"Grizzlies?"

"In *our* county!?"

"That dumb bitch!"

"God...damn!"

"As God is my witness," Nerves said. "There it is on page three of the Seattle Times: 'State Senator Lisa Belle proposes to restore grizzlies to Okanogan County.' She says that 'Washington should fulfill its environmental debt to Mother Nature and return the noble grizzly bear to its historic habitat.' She wants to have the state release a total forty-five sows and fifteen boars in Okanogan County over a two-year period. Our district senators have objected, of course, but those democrat simpletons in Olympia ignored them as always."

"Big surprise," Boot said.

"*Sixty* grizz..." Runs said.

"Sixty! Belle's bill actually requires the Washington Department of Fish and Wildlife to implement the recovery on state lands, because the Washington state legislature can't dictate policy on US forest lands. Everybody knows the bears would quickly move into the Pasayten Wilderness and the bordering ranch lands."

"The old end run," Hogan growled.

On the eastside of the Cascades, nothing was so despised as the numerous outlander covens of liberal know-it-alls anxious to foist policy they didn't have to live with onto people who did.

12

"The bill has zipped through committee—another big surprise, Senator Belle swings a lot of punch in Olympia— and it comes up for a senate floor vote in a couple of weeks."

"Jesus Christ," Boot said with a sigh. "I bet that dizzy broad's never seen a grizz in a goddamned zoo."

"How can they do that?" Loverly cried. "This is our home! Senator Belle lives on Vashon Island in Seattle. It ain't her who'll have to look over her shoulder when she's in the woods. It ain't her calves and lambs that'll get eaten. Who does she think she is?"

"She don't 'think', darlin'," Lexie said, "She knows she can get away with it. Same way the legislators got away with lowering the super majority for raising taxes last year. You got the might, you got the right. That's how that woman thinks."

"But it's not right!" Loverly said. "It's us got to live with the largest meat eater in North America, not her. It ain't her kids she'll be havin' to keep close to the house. It's ours."

"Right ain't got nothin' to do with government, Loverly," Runs said.

"Got that right," Blubbo muttered, rolling his eyes.

"But grizzlies are dangerous!" Loverly said. "Doesn't she understand that?"

Nerves snatched up the paper and opened it to the article. "Oh no, no, no," he said. "Listen to this: 'I have been assured by my good friends with the Washington Alliance For Nature'—"

"That bunch a' university cone heads wouldn't know a grizzly from a pink chipmunk," Boot said.

"I was a 'university cone head', thank you." Nerves scowled at Boot, then continued. "Belle says she is '...assured by the Washington Alliance for Nature that the rural public conception of the risk to people and livestock from grizzly bears is greatly exaggerated, and we may look forward to sharing nature in complete harmony with this most magnificent of God's beautiful creatures'."

"That pompous bimbo is dumber than a muck tub," Runs said. "A grizz is an eating machine. See it. Eat it. And it eats a lot."

"Oh noooo," Nerves said. "Why, Senator Belle says right here: 'Washingtonians are in more danger of being struck by lightning than being attacked by a grizzly bear.'"

"That is such an asinine comparison," Runs said. "Okanogan County has almost no grizzlies at the moment, but we get a quarter-million lightning bolts every year. Does that ditsy debutante have any idea how that analogy would change if we had a quarter-million grizzlies roaming around Okanogan County?"

Nerves read on. "'Hikers need only wear little bells when in the wild so as not to surprise the gentle grizzly. Any bears who venture too close to humans may be easily repelled by a simple can of pepper spray.'"

"Hey," Boot said, "you know how you can tell grizzly shit from black bear shit?"

Everyone but Nerves had heard this joke. They tittered.

"How?" Nerves asked.

"Because it's full of little bells, and it smells like pepper spray!"

Everyone cackled, including Nerves.

Everyone but Hogan.

"Goddamn it!" he suddenly bellowed. Everyone instantly stopped laughing and stared at him.

Ronald Reagan jerked awake. The old man was courting coronaries again.

"Historic habitat?" Hogan croaked.

"Easy, Paw-paw," Loverly said, bringing the old man another beer.

"Historic frigging habitat, huh? Well guess what. The original natural habitat of the grizzly included Seattle and Olympia. I don't hear 'em callin' for grizz to be 'restored' to that part of their natural habitat!"

"Grizz ran the whole west coast as late as 1850," Runs said.

"So what's the problem, man?" Blubbo suddenly interjected. "You just 'restore' a grizzly into the statehouse in Olympia when they vote. See how they vote then."

Everyone whirled and stared at Blubbo, then broke into gales of hysterical laughter.

"Yeah!" Boot howled, slapping his knee.

Perfect!" Lexie said, her eyes watering. "That'd teach those silly idiots."

"I love it!" Hogan roared, choking on his laughter.

"Maybe you ain't as dumb as I thought," Runs said, wiping his eyes.

"Shove a grizzly right up their arrogant twinkies!" Nerves cried. "See what kind of 'harmony' they live in then."

Everyone laughed again.

Loverly ran around the table and hugged Blubbo. "You're so cute!" she said.

"Aw, git offa me, white girl!" Blubbo grumped, freshly embarrassed by all the laughter. He shrugged the undiscouraged Loverly off, and scowled at the group. "Well, what's so damn funny? They gonna stick sixty grizzlies up our asses, right? Why *not* stick one live grizz up theirs?"

There is a point in every great movement that may in retrospect be called its genesis. The laughter of the group slowly coasted down to chuckles, then to snickers, then to 'ahem's, then to nervous glances at Blubbo and each other. A long, pregnant silence passed while eyes flicked back and forth one person to another. Smiles faded.

At some point in the scary quiet, all mirth drained from the group, and a sense of deep, righteous resolve moved into the roots of their souls.

The Free Okanogan County Movement was spawned.

CHAPTER TWO

Western Montana

The grizzly was not the 'largest meat eater in North America', as Loverly had said, though the distinction is a thin one when confronting either the grizzly or the usually larger Kodiak and Polar bears. Moreover, rather than being a strictly meat eating carnivore, the grizzly is an omnivore, an industrial grade, self-propelled, organic garbage processor that eats everything edible and much that isn't. This was also was a specious detail for folks within smelling distance of either creature.

The bear that was in for the adventure of his life was overweight like the rest of America and thus was soon to be named Tonny by Loverly Winslow, so we'll just call him that now.

All species have their Blubbos, and Ursus Arctos Horribilis was no exception. Tonny had sprung from a long line of fat grizzlies in southern British Columbia who themselves had ancestors of the Kodiak tribe. Tonny's forebears had migrated down from farther north for a hundred years. Tonny's ancestors, including his parents, had enjoyed all the elk, caribou, moose, deer, fish and discarded Big Macs they could stuff down themselves for several generations. They were thus much bigger than average for grizzly, which is to say about a thousand pounds.

By whatever genetic anomaly that occurs, Tonny had grown to dwarf both his already large parents. In his well fed prime of about ten years old he weighed eighteen-hundred-ninety-six pounds. He was nearly six feet high at the top of his shoulder hump, but stood almost thirteen feet when he rose up on his hind legs to sniff the air for his favorite indulgence, poontang. Tonny had feet as wide as a large man's shoulders, a nose the size of a dinner plate, a skull the diameter of a garbage can and a blubberous butt the as wide as a minivan. His claws protruded nine inches beyond the leading edges of his front feet, his canine incisors were five inches long, and his poop looked like black basketballs.

When hunters observed Tonny's droppings on the trail, they hurried back to their trucks fervently vowing to bring bigger guns on their next trip into the snow capped Rockies. To hell with pepper spray and bear bells. Better to risk prosecution by the feds than to become one of the enormous crap clods Tonny left in his brush-busting wake.

Tonny was a simple soul in theory. He only asked to be left alone to eat, sleep, and make little bears with accommodating sows. In practice, however, this got more complicated. It meant killing and eating whatever got between him and these endeavors, which entailed a lot of fighting with other male grizz, intimidating wolves off their hard earned kills, and even killing another male's sired cubs so the sow might more speedily reacquire her sexual appetite. Tonny was the ultimate pragmatist. Fighting was Tonny's third most favorite indulgence behind poontang and eating. Fighting tended to generate a good appetite for both.

As the previous winter had been severe, the herds of elk and caribou and the clusters of moose had moved down in altitude and latitude. Tonny, theretofore one of the few Canadians who didn't say ey? in every sentence, decided he'd see if the US was all it was cracked up to be. After all, how could fifteen-million illegal immigrants be wrong?

So Tonny crossed the border high in the Rockies and made his way to the Flathead National Forest of northwestern Montana.

If he'd had any idea of the events that lay before him, he'd have said screw these crazy Americans and returned to Canada, home of proud, brave Canadians, and Americans suddenly made anti-war saints by the possibility that they might actually have to serve under fire.

Initially, Tonny found America to his liking as the

discarded fast food rate in the lower forty-eight far exceeded that of Canada, though American parks did use those annoying anti-bear trash cans. Tonny had learned to rip the cans entirely from their posts and mangle hell out of their shape, but as the damn things were welded steel they were devilishly impossible to open without an acetylene torch, which he had no training in. What a tragic waste of good leftovers, Tonny had often groused.

In their famous devotion to nature's wondrous creatures, however, Americans more than made up for the trick garbage cans with the prodigious quantities of food they thoughtfully threw into open dumpsters and out of car windows, not to mention all the delicious gut piles they left after deer, elk, cariboo and moose kills.

Tonny's brief American sojourn had to date brought him into contact with but one two-leg, and he couldn't say he liked them worth a damn. Though he'd yet to catch one, there was apparently very little meat on them. Worse, they seemed to carry sticks that emitted loud, sharp noises, immediately upon which a bear minding his own business got a searing pain in his left front paw.

The two-leg species had not enjoyed a sterling ambassador in the meth-tooting poacher named Arliss Bernall who happened upon Tonny in the Flathead National Forest. Arliss had fired one panicky deer rifle shot in Tonny's direction before dropping the rifle to run screaming down the trail. The loud noise had startled Tonny, but the bullet that hit him in the left front paw stung like a thousand hornets and gave him throbbing pain that had only become worse. Tonny nursing his hurt paw was probably the only reason Arliss Bernall lived to be the town drunk exaggerator for his wide eyed tales of a twenty-foot grizzly, instead of becoming processed into a half-dozen large black balls of steaming dung.

Forest Service law enforcement officer Packwood Rudd was another matter. Packy had been an enforcement ranger -

called a LEO in the service - for nineteen years and had been assigned to the Flathead National Forest for the last eight of them.

Packy had seen a lot of bear damage and scat. He had also been a structural engineer for a year after college, before he left the rat-race for the woods. He was thus perhaps uniquely qualified to estimate the physics involved in tearing the anti-bear refuse container now before him clean off its concrete post and squashing it like a beer can.

Damn, Packy thought, studying the crumpled, scratch-streaked garbage can. As if having to endure all the summer tourist vermin weren't pain in the ass enough, he was now going to have to notify his ditzy boss of his suspicions about a dangerous bear.

Packy despised the area special-agent-in-charge, Melony Gaynor, PhD. He had once been sanctioned for calling her Princess Affirmative Action. Packy regarded Gaynor as lower than the detested tourists who polluted his beloved wilderness with their pop and beer cans, boom boxes, stinkweed butts, diapers, graffiti and fast food wrappers. The less he had to do with "Doctor" Gaynor, as that pompous, puffed-up pretender insisted on being called, the happier they both were.

Packy looked warily into the woods around him knowing that he had a new, uncatalogued grizz this season, and while it probably wasn't the twenty footer that stupid crankhead Arliss Bernall claimed he saw, it was still big.

Like...really big.

CHAPTER THREE

Olympia, Washington

Washington State Senator Lisa Belle was a short, dumpy white woman with short hair who wore shorter business skirts than she probably should have for her chunky calves. Regardless, her legendary rich-bitch-witch demeanor made her feared enough to offset several feet of height. She saw herself as the new, improved Hillary. Lisa Belle's three previous marriages had been shorter than most football seasons. Her current marriage to a much older, philanthropic shipping firm owner was barely months old.

In her office in Olympia, before her entire staff in the conference room, Lisa was in true form.

"Listen to me, goddamn it!" Lisa snarled, slamming a curled up newspaper onto the big mahogany table for emphasis. "I didn't claw my way up from poverty in a small country town to where I am today to be put off of this grizzly bill by a bunch of whiny, inbred, eastsider peasants and their boogeyman tales about the noble grizzly bear."

Lisa had actually been a doctor's daughter in Bellingham which, though a smaller municipality, was basically a bedroom suburb of the greater Seattle megalopolis, so it wasn't like she was Daisy Duke cum Nancy Pelosi. Notwithstanding, no one at the conference table was about to mention that.

One staffer, a ruggedly handsome black man who was Lisa's private security escort, now stood at the door end of the conference room in a well tailored suit. He might have brought it up but he didn't. His name was Perry Dinwiddie, a name one might not expect for a former Navy SEAL who had worked three years in Iraq for the muscle firm formerly known as Blackwater before getting hired by Lisa Belle. Lisa had richly earned more than a few death threats for her many ill-considered legislative inspirations, most of which never made it out of committee, even in Democrat dominated Olympia.

Lisa had become famous for her lawsuit before the Washington Supreme Court to lower the voter referendum mandated two-thirds legislative majority required for raising taxes to merely fifty-one percent. Lisa felt she and her liberal colleague legislators needed less embarrassment as they plundered the taxpayers, and less accountability for doing so.

The Washington Supremes, in their building across a grassy parking loop from the Washington statehouse, told Lisa to put her voter screwing idea where the sun don't shine, but she and her colleagues raped the people's will anyway a year later by legislative overturn of the tax limiting referendum. The people's will was such an annoyance to Washington's predominantly democrat legislature.

Lisa was pleased because she knew the vaunted American people were dumber than used cat litter. Left to themselves, the self-obsessed idiots would die from collective ignorance in five years. Washington voters west of the Cascades were stupid enough, but those Deliverance-reject, cro magnon, eastside country clod busters were even worse.

Lisa had busted her hump trying to craft a real piece of legacy legislation she could point to when she ran for the US Senate the next year. The Senator Lisa Belle Noble Grizzly Bear Restoration Act was one of only four items of legislation she had written in seven years as a state senator that had ever cleared committee. This one, Lisa was convinced, was guaranteed to catapult her into the US Senate.

The Senator Lisa Belle Noble Grizzly Bear Restoration Act had all the necessary legislator promoting elements. It was greener than green, and it would bring in millions of campaign dollars from nature groups and the rest of the greenie religionists from her state when she ran for the US Senate.

21

The only people who might object would be those
dim witted troglodytes in Okanogan County where her
bill proposed to install just sixty breeding grizzlies in two
years, for Christ's sake. Those ignorant simpleton farmers,
cattlemen, sheepherders and wild Indians were among only
38,000 residents in a distant flyover county bigger than
some states, and they wouldn't open their hearts to a few
adorable, big, furry teddy bears? Besides, it wasn't like those
Jesus cult morons didn't sleep with enough guns to kill any
grizzly that got off the reservation a hundred times over.

Lisa had had an adorable, big, furry teddy bear right up
until she was shipped off to boarding school at fourteen. She
was still pissed at Mommy for hiding Foofie that year.

She scooped up the paper and held it open toward her
nervous staff, except Perry who, having been shot on two
different occasions, required considerably more than Lisa's
intimidation to make him nervous.

"So get off your asses and show me some hustle!" Lisa
bellowed, her nostrils flaring. "Don't make me wonder what
I'm overpaying you people for! Get onto every contact we
have in the media, pronto. I want to see magazine, TV,
and newspaper stories about how harmless the grizzlies are
and how cruelly man has ejected them from their rightful
habitat. I want to hear about how balanced predation
promises to restore our threatened elk, deer, and moose
populations. Get on our people in the universities. What
are we paying them for anyway? Most of all I want to reach
out to all our friends in editorial positions to quash these
goddamned whiny yak-yak articles about some aberrant
grizzly who ate some Alaskan kid fifteen years ago. And I
want all those horrid photos of grizzly-kill human carcasses
off the Internet, or at least made out by our friends in the
media to be fraudulently staged."

Lisa stood breathing hard, shifting her buzzard eyes from
one staffer to the next. "Are you people still here!? Actual,
aggressive *action*, pronto!" Everyone grabbed their little
push-button brain devices and hurried for the door.

"Mr. Dinwiddie, you may remain. I have some security

issues to discuss with you."

Perry Dinwiddie eyed the ceiling. When he closed the door he locked it and shrugged out of his suit jacket. Lisa told her secretary on the phone that she was not to be disturbed for twenty-minutes, under penalty of rendition to Yemen.

Lisa strode around the desk scowling at Dinwiddie who looked back at her through narrowed eyes. She threw a hand to the back of Perry's neck and slammed her lips onto his for thirty slurpy, groping seconds before slapping her other hand onto his crotch.

She zipped Perry's fly all the way down.

"So, what do you think, big boy?" Lisa breathed like a panda with asthma. "Can Mr. Binkie come out to play?"

Chapter Four

Okanogan Township, Okanogan County, Washington

The laughter in Winslow's Gun and Pawn Shop had faded for several screamingly silent seconds.

Hogan, the aging mercenary, Boot, the cattleman, Lexie, the ex-stripper/call-girl, Runs, the Native American veterinarian, Nerves the gay law professor, Blubbo, the errant and enormous rez punk, and Loverly, the adolescent gun shop manager, looked at each other.

Each knew that they were on the cusp of making history, that a window into greatness had opened, and that a once-in-a-lifetime opportunity to strike a blow for freedom had been put right on the table before them. It was frightening as hell.

Centennial seconds ticked by.

"Nahhhh," Nerves finally blurted, to the monstrous relief of all sitting at the table. "It'd take twenty court clerks six months just to tally up all the laws we'd be breaking."

"Nahh," Boot said. "We'd all go to jail."

"Nahh, Insane," Lexie said. "How would we ever get a goddamn grizzly bear? We'd get eaten before we ever got to Olympia."

"Nahh," Hogan said. "It'd take too much money."

"Nahh, Crazy," Runs said. "Even if we brought it off, we'd get juiced for murder when the bear chewed somebody up."

"Nahh. They'd kill the poor bear," Loverly said, shaking her head.

"Pussies," Blubbo muttered.

"Drop and gimme twenty, big mouth!" Runs snarled. Blubbo rolled his eyes, got to the floor, and started pumping out the push ups.

Everyone stared at the table while Blubbo finished.

"...eighteen...nine...teen! Twuh-twenty!" Blubbo gasped. He stood, heaving for breath. "You're all still pussies. I don't know...how the hell...your ancestors...kicked the shit out of mine. I really don't."

"Blubbo, you want twenty more?" Runs said.

"No sir," Blubbo said, already on a coronary threshold.

A glum silence resumed, and again it was Nerves who broke it.

"Buuuuuut..." Nerves said, now commanding everyone's undivided attention. "I mean, well, of course it's crazy and impossible and all, but just for discussion's sake, you know, just, you know, like, *theoretically* speaking, we wouldn't exactly have to turn the bear loose in the statehouse. Nobody would have to get hurt, not even the bear."

Nerves ruled. Everyone focused on him. He savored the attention for several long seconds.

"What's our goal here?" Nerves said. "We don't actually want to have the grizzly bear eat or even injure anyone, right?"

"I do," Blubbo said.

"Shut up, Blubbo," Runs growled. "You ain't got a vote here."

"Story of my fucking life," Blubbo mumbled.

Nerves continued. "I mean what we actually want is for this imbecilic grizzly bill to go down in flames when it comes to a vote in the state senate, right?"

"Yeah," Boot said. "So?"

"So all we'd really need to do is take the bear over there in...what, I don't know, an old horse trailer or something, and park it in front of the statehouse on the morning the bill is to be voted on, and leave it there. We call the news media—anonymously, of course—and tell them to bring their cameras and come see what that silly Lisa Belle wants to drop in our back yards. Say we, like, starve it for a while first, and it'll be meaner than a...well, meaner than a starved grizzly. It'll be snarling and lunging at the bars and roaring.

Picture that going out to the wire services and hitting the Internet! Pow! Who's going to vote yea then?"

Everyone stared at Nerves.

Finally Boot raised a calloused hand, slammed the table, and leaned back in his chair. "By God, I like the hell out of that. I'm sick to death of politicians kicking my ass!"

"We ain't starvin' no bear!" Loverly said, emphatically.

"Yeah," Lexie said. "I'm not starving any animal. Besides, we don't wanna be seen as animal abusers. That'll just turn public sympathy to that fat twat and her bonehead grizzly scheme."

"Aw, we wouldn't have to starve it," Hogan said. "By the time we catch a grizz and haul it to Olympia, it'll be growly enough for TV cameras anyway, even if we keep it fed."

"Oh we'll keep it fed alright," Runs said, exasperated. "It'll be the fattest bear in North America after it eats all seven of us. Do you hear yourselves? Do you have any idea what it would take to find, let alone capture, let alone transport to Olympia, a goddamned grizzly bear? An average adult grizz weighs five-hundred to eight-hundred pounds!"

"Well," Lexie said, "the park service traps them all the time."

"Yeah," Blubbo said. "Dart the bastard, like they do elephants on Animal Planet!"

Runs gave Blubbo a withering look. Blubbo sighed and watched the ceiling.

Hey," Runs said, "correct me if I'm wrong, but I think I'm the only large-animal vet in the room, ergo I probably know more about darting and trapping than you geniuses! It isn't that simple. We have to find it first. We have to get close enough to dart it or trap it. Any of you ever tried to sneak up on a grizzly with a dart rifle, let alone with a truck and a pipe trap? Forget darting it. Even if we find him and hit him with the right dose—and who knows what that is, and we could kill it with the wrong dose—the thing will run a thousand yards through brush in the time it takes the drug to drop him. How we gonna move 600 pounds of unconscious bear blubber uphill through dense brush or trees without injuring it?"

"Yeah," Hogan said. "Besides, pipe traps and shit cost a boatload of money. Where we gonna get a bear live-trap that can't be traced?"

"And another thing," Runs said. "What're we gonna do, just mosey down I-90 with a live grizzly in our horse trailer? You don't think people might notice? You don't think we'd have fifty cops on us before we got ten miles? Reckon the security around the statehouse is just going to ignore the Okanogan Idiots Tribe when we pull up with our kidnaped endangered species? How we gonna get food in and manure out of the trap without becoming food and manure ourselves?"

The group grew morosely silent once again. Loverly circulated, filling everyone's drinks or replacing their beers.

"Welllll..." Boot finally said. "I been thinking about that."

All eyes swung to the big, tanned cowboy.

"Say we use an old cattle trailer. The new ones have two decks but we'd only need some old single decker. The trailer's got partitions side-to-side at two points, to divide the interior into three compartments, a big one in the lower middle bay, and two, raised smaller boxes over the axle pairs. All three compartments got sliding passage doors in the partitions and outside walls so certain cows can be delivered or loaded at certain places without having to unload the whole bunch or mix lots. The partition doors crank open and shut by cable cranks on the outside of the trailer. The outside doors are on overhead sliding tracks. You just unlatch 'em and slide 'em open and shut.

"So we actually got three separate cages on one trailer when we need 'em," Boot expounded, waving his hands to illustrate. "Come time to clean Mr. Bear and feed him, see, we just bait him or draw him to one of the end boxes, and crank the partition door shut. Then we go in the middle section down close to the ground, clean it out, leave his food and water. Then, back outside of course, we open the partition door again, he goes to the middle bay to get his food, we wind the partition door shut. We just keep shifting him from one section to the other to feed and clean him."

Everyone stared at Boot, their eyes wide. They couldn't really see any kinks in this idea.

"Is this rig and them swing walls strong enough?" Hogan said.

"Bet your ass," Boot answered. "It's heavy aluminum bar stock made to keep twenty-five tons of live cows in, most of which weigh more than a grizzly. I reckon ain't no bear gonna get out of it."

"Brilliant!" Nerves suddenly cried, clapping his manicured finger tips.

"Brilliant, my ass," Runs said. "How we gonna keep a six-hundred pound grizzly outta sight in an open livestock trailer? They have hundreds of ventilation holes in the side walls."

"Well, the old cattle pots have horizontal slats even more open to view," Boot said immediately. "But we use tarps. Hang 'em on with trucker bungees. We'd only have to tarp the central chamber, twenty-feet or so, 'cause we'd only have the bear in the end boxes over the axles just long enough to clean the middle one and put food in it."

Runs frowned but couldn't immediately trash this idea.

The muscle bound marathoner, Nerves, leaned back in his chair, raised his tomato juice glass, and smiled broadly. "Begorrah! I've fallen in with scoundrels!"

"You've fallen in with idiots," Runs said. "They'll see Boot's truck and livestock trailer, including his tags, on a million surveillance cameras. Not to mention that his road tractors all have Boot Colhane Trucking, Inc., Omak Washington, painted on the goddamned doors! Reckon CSI can work that one out in a year or two?"

All eyes swivelled again to Boot. He was lost in thought.

"Welllll...I been thinking about that, too," Boot finally said.

Everybody sat up. Blubbo leaned forward slightly.

"There's this old ex-hippie up in Ferry County, Sol Pickering. Drove trucks since the seventies when he found out that man can't live on pot and LSD alone, after all.

Hauled cattle and logs. There's an old '77 possum-pot trailer on his place and a solid old '89 Peterbilt long-nose we can pull it with, that ole' Sol don't use no more."

"So..." Hogan said, "we steal this Sol guy's truck?"

"*Steal*...a trailer truck?" Lexie said.

"Noooo problem," Blubbo said.

"Can it, Blubbo!" Runs said. "I'm tryin' to keep you outta jail!"

"Can we all say 'felony,' boys and girls?" Nerves said.

"We ain't truck thieves," Loverly protested.

"Yeah," Lexie said. "Besides, what happens to old Mr. Pickering when the cops come knocking 'cause his truck was used in the crime of the century?"

"Well, that's a bit of an overstatement," Nerves said.

"Oh yeah?" said Lexie. "So you got no problem with some poor, clueless old man getting hauled off to jail for grizzly rustling? Having his means of living impounded as evidence?"

"Nobody's locking up Sol Pickering," Boot said.

"Now how would you know?" Lexie demanded.

Boot leaned back in his chair and picked nacho-chip residue from his teeth with his knife.

"Because they'd have to dig him up. Literally."

Everyone now stared at Boot.

"Sol Pickering croaked deader than Bill Clinton's fidelity late last year. His place was willed to his sister, wife of some fat-cat banker in California. She ain't even been up to see it, probably because it's a hermit's hideout on propane and solar, way up off the grid. It's so far back in the Ponderosas up near the Canadian border that God couldn't find it with GPS. It ain't worth a whole lot, especially to some rich woman in Califreakingfornia. Old Sol was poaching mountain sheep the day he rolled his ATV over a cliffside trail. His place has sat vacant for months, and probably will for a long time. I'd bet the tags on both that Pete and that old cattle box are still valid, though."

"Oh I like it!" Nerves said, fingers to his lips. "That's truly precious. The truck will get impounded, but eventually the police will have to release it back to Mr. Pickering's estate. Nothing's lost!"

Hogan said to Boot, "You sly dog, you. So when the state police come knocking on Sol's door, nobody will be answering. Their investigation will slam into a dead end as long as nobody connects us with his truck and trailer, which, conveniently for us and ole' Sol, he ain't using no more."

Slowly all eyes rotated to Runs, who had been the antagonist, and was thus expected to voice an objection. Runs met each gaze but didn't say anything.

"Come on, Runs!" Nerves said. "Think what a great thing this is. Nobody gets hurt. It'll go nationwide on the news. We'd be holding the modern day equivalent of the Boston Tea Party. We could post signs on the trailer, 'Don't tread on us with your savage man-eating bears! Eastsiders have rights, too! No bearation without representation! An eastsider's right to choose! Mr. Grizzly goes to Olym–'"

"Yeah, yeah," Runs said. "I get the picture."

"Yeah, Runs!" Lexie said. "Think of the media coverage we'd get. 'Mysterious freedom activists bring giant bear to statehouse.' Imagine Lisa Belle trying to babble on about how harmless grizzly in Okanogan County would be with a big, hairy, smelly, snarling, eight-hundred pound monster right there on the street roaring right in front of the state capitol! What a statement we'd be making for eastside independence! That bear bill will die like John Edwards had endorsed it. Shoot, while we got the media's attention, we might even be able to issue a demand for secession from Olympia!"

The group sensed this was a time to shut up and let Runs think. After all, everyone knew he would be essential to the mission. Agonizing seconds ticked by.

Runs's veins throbbed as he wondered how he'd gotten himself into being the deciding vote for a lunatic scheme like this. Still...if they could bring it off, it would almost certainly kill the bear bill, which needed killing, and, yeah, it could theoretically become a publicity jumping off point for East Washington statehood. Then we'd be done with those clueless liberal ding-dongs and their inane meddling for good. Besides...let's face it...it would be a fun way to break it off in the white man.

"Well..." Runs finally said. "It might work with just a small bear."

Uh oh, Ronald Reagan thought.

"Yeah!" Everyone yelled at once, and high fives smacked about the table. Even Blubbo smiled, which endeared him yet more to Loverly.

"Listen up!" Nerves cried. "Everybody listen up!" The revelry faded.

"Alright look. Best case scenario, we're going to be breaking a whole penal code book of laws, some federal, and you can get more jail time for breaking a game law in this country than you get for murder. We're kidnapping a federal endangered species—a threatened species technically—that can't legally be trapped or transported without government permits. Not to mention that we're going to temporarily have to steal a trailer truck. And we're probably going to be violating a boatload of ordinances about leaving a dangerous animal in public, even secured in a cattle trailer."

"So," Lexie said, "you're saying it's too risky?"

"Not exactly, Lexie. If it goes right—and that's a goddamned critical 'if', here, people—then none of this rises to the level of terrorism or even serious crime. The bear stays safely contained. The state will transport the bear back to its habitat unharmed. We're, um, borrowing a truck, but there won't be much of a complainant there, because the late Mr. Pickering's estate will eventually get the truck back. And the rest of it is misdemeanors and non-moving traffic offenses. Lisa Belle and her crowd of lefty loonies will scream for our heads on a silver tray, but that'll get offset by the hoopla in the media. Some of the public, like the Tea Partiers and others, will see us as innovative political heroes. My guess is, the cops will make a token effort to find whoever did it for about a week, and then blow it off. The whole state law enforcement community hates that wretched Belle shrew as much as we do because she's fu–ah, screwed them too."

"And the other shoe?" Hogan said.

"The other shoe is we have to bring it off exactly as planned, people. Nobody can get hurt—including the bear—and no property can get damaged. If we screw this up, we could all be wearing prison orange for a long time, except for Loverly and...um, Blubbo, who are minors. But even they would be in big trouble."

Runs hit the table with his fist. "Blubbo and Loverly ain't in this," he declared. "I ain't 'contributing to the delinquency of a minor'!"

"Ditto!" Hogan grunted. "Loverly's out."

"But I'm *already* a delinquent!" Blubbo objected.

"That's what I'm trying to *fix,* not foment!" Runs said. "The sheriff will never give me another kid to straighten out if I get one involved in a deal like this. And you'll never get in the Corps with a serious criminal record! No way, Blubbo!"

Blubbo was outraged. "You can't cut me outta this man. This is my big chance to stick it to whitey! You can't take that away from me. I'm in!"

"Watch my lips: No chance. No way. No how!" Runs said.

Loverly piped up. "Me and Blubbo are in, people. Get used to it."

"When Jane Fonda's buried in Arlington," Hogan said. "You and Blubbo can't have anything to do with this."

But Loverly didn't run a successful gun and pawn shop at fifteen without knowing how to play her odds in the adult world. Hogan knew this, and the fact that Loverly hadn't gotten angry, but just smugly surveyed the group told Hogan she was holding a couple of aces. He squinted at her.

"Too late," Loverly said with a smirk. "If you geriatrics were gonna cut me and Blubbo out, you had to do it before we knew the game. Now...we're both in all the way or we blow the whole thing to the state police. Shoot, I bet you could all be locked up for conspiracy right now."

"Yeah," Blubbo said, with sudden new interest in the crafty little white chick. "We're in or nobody's in!"

"Shit," Runs said.

"Shit," Boot said.

"Shit," Nerves said.

"Nice work, parent of the goddamn year!" Lexie said to Hogan. "Did you teach her to be a blackmailer, too?"

Hogan was beaming at Loverly with newfound pride. "Hell naw. She done that all on her own. Nice going, little darlin'!"

"Aw, thanks Paw-paw," Loverly said, blushing and studying her toes.

Lexie massaged her brow. "I don't believe this."

"Alright! That's how it is," Nerves said. "It's all settled. Now listen, people. As the treacherous Miss Loverly has just thrust in our faces, if this gets out to anybody - I'm talking anybody, here - we're screwed. That means nobody outside the seven of us and Ronald Reagan can know about it, ever. Nobody, especially not that one treasured confidant we all think would never tell. Nobody! Anybody here got any problem with that?"

Heads shook all around.

"Alright then," Nerves said, slapping his hand flat on the table. "Everybody swears an oath to secrecy!"

"Damn straight," Boot said, pounding his scarred hand down on Nerves's.

"Hell, yeah!" Hogan said, and his wrinkled hand hit on top of Boot's.

"My lips are sealed," Lexie said, placing her hand on Hogan's.

"Yep," Runs said grimly, adding his hand over Lexie's.

"Me, too!" Loverly said with excitement, plopping her little hand on the stack.

"Fuuuck whiteyyy!" Blubbo cried with passion, and everyone winced as he slammed his ham hock mitt down on the hand pile. The table bounced and beer bottles fell over.

Chapter Five

Western Montana

"This is Special Agent, Dr. Melony Gaynor, PhD. How may I help you?"

You insufferable twit, Forest Service enforcement officer Packy Rudd choked back.

"Boss," Packy said on the phone, "I think we got a problem."

Melony's face took on that expression she got when her cat...passed waste in the flower planter. Why on earth the Forest Service wasted so much money on neanderthal campground Nazis like Officer Rudd was beyond Melony. Forests were the people's playground.

"Packwood Rudd," Melony said, her voice oozing sarcasm. "To hear you babbling to the local press all the time, we always have problems. And I keep telling you, don't call me 'boss'. My correct title is Dr. Gaynor, or at least Special Agent Gaynor."

Temperrrr, Packy thought, sizzling. One more year to retirement. Then you can tell Princess Priss to go sit on Devil's Tower.

"No, I mean I think we got a freak."

Melony sighed, "You're always referring to the great American people as freaks, Packwood. They pay your salary. Remember that."

Tourists in flip-flops falling off mountain cliffs; tourists wrecking their motor palaces; tourists tramping off the trails; tourists crapping in the open; tourists spraying their dimwitted graffiti everywhere aren't 'great Americans,' Packy raged to himself. Great Americans come to the wilderness and treat it like a national treasure, not some Woodstock landfill, and when 'real Americans' are gone you can't tell they were ever here.

Heaven, Packy thought, is sitting up on a rise with a scoped Remington .308 and a cooler of beer, listening to ZZ Top, and shooting litterbugs on sight. The parks would suddenly stay cleaner than the Hadron Super Collider, and bears and wolves would be happy to police up the bodies. I'm not seeing a downside here, Packy mused.

"Hey," Packy said, "I'm the one who has to babysit 'em, remember? But I ain't talking tourists, here...boss." Packy would live out his days in a Norkie gulag before he'd call this arrogant Steinemite 'Dr.' anything. "I think we got a freak bear. A big grizz."

Melony paused. "Meaning what exactly? You've seen it?"

"Nope. But look, something big has been tearing up the refuse containers at the Widow Creek Campground."

"So? No big deal. Nobody ever goes there anyway except kids to do the backseat boogie. I'm taking that facility off the maintenance budget for next year because so few people use it."

"Boss, this thing has ripped specifically designed 'bear proof' refuse cans made of eighth-inch steel, from steel brackets off concrete posts."

"Oh nonsense, Packwood. No bear could do that. That's just drunk punk kids pulling them off with trucks and chains like the little redneck vandals did a couple years ago down at the horse camp."

"It don't look like chains and trucks, boss. Whatever did it stomped them and twisted them up. It also tore the door off the crapper. I think we got an uncatalogued grizz, and he's big, real big."

"Tracks?"

"Not in an asphalt parking lot where those cans are set so the garbage trucks can reach them. I looked around in the woods, but it's been raining pretty hard up here for two days. Everything off the pavement is mush."

Melony sighed with irritation. "Packwood, you've been bear paranoid ever since a rogue grizzly attacked that jogger girl up by the border. I know you found her that year–"

"What was left of her."

"Alright, already. But that doesn't mean we have some Jurassic grizzly in the system. The biggest grizzly ever catalogued in the Kootenai or the Flathead was estimated at fourteen-hundred pounds. Even it couldn't rip refuse bear-proofs off their mounts. It's the local inbred mountain kids with chains and those noisy, jacked up pickup trucks. Their people have been illiterate trolls for decades. Just submit it all in a report. The super is going to close that site for budget reasons anyway, so we won't even have the cans replaced. That's all, Packwood."

Packy Rudd sat in his park service truck, in the rain. He folded his phone shut, then looked again across the parking lot where one of the mangled refuse cans lay. He reached between his knees to reassure himself that he'd slid his Marlin 444 rifle into the scabbard mounted in front of the seat.

"One more year," Packy muttered.

Son of a...*bitch*! Tonny thought the grizzly equivalent of, standing in the rain with his throbbing left front paw off the ground. *If I ever find that the two-leg that stung me in the foot I'm gonna have him with some fava beans and a fine Chianti. Damn, my foot hurts!*

Sanitation, like erudition, isn't what bears do best. Grizzlies will eat anything, no matter how long it's been dead. They're notorious for stealing rancid elk corpses from wolf packs, burying them, and digging them up days later to feast on. Bodies evidently taste better to bears when they're full of worms, maggots, and beetles.

Arliss Bernall's unaimed bullet had seared across the top surface of Tonny's paw with relatively little tissue destruction and no bone damage, but the open, festering gash it had left was becoming severely infected. The paw was painfully tender, and was swollen so it looked like the head of a garden rake sticking out of a big, brown, hairy balloon.

Tonny had thought that tearing up the camp ground refuse cans and the two-legs' crapper would relieve his anger, but it had only made his foot hurt worse, and deepened his now raging contempt for two-legs in general, especially ones that smelled like methamphetamine and screamed holeeeee-shiiiiit!!! when they ran. Must be some kind of two-leg warning call to the rest of the pack, Tonny figured.

I find me any more two-legs, they're gonna *need* a goddamn warning call...

CHAPTER SIX

Olympia

Joe Kirksey was the Washington State Senator for District 7, which included Okanogan County. Except for the western Methow Valley, which was essentially a weekend campground for rich Seattle liberals, Okanogan County was red as a fire truck. It was also where State Senator Lisa Belle proposed to seed sixty fuzzy land sharks. She was thus micro-thrilled to hear from her secretary that Senator Kirksey was on the phone.

Still, Kirksey had the fanatic loyalty of those redneck eastsiders, and worse he had the backing of those lunatic, gun-in-every-crib, NRA über patriots, many of whom were even westside voters. Those gun freaks had given Kirksey an A-plus in their stupid little politician rating system, while giving her an F-minus. Lisa despised those racist, sexist, closet-militia rednecks, but the NRA swung a lot of weight at election time, as she'd found out after she introduced her Noble Gun Free Washington Bill four years ago. Christ in a jumpsuit, all she'd tried to do was ban handguns statewide including for police officers.

After all, what kind of image of a free, democratic America was conveyed by uniformed, gun-toting thugs everywhere? Lisa had decided that Washington needed to lead by example so she'd just proposed a simple statewide ban on handguns. She shook her head even now. You'd have thought she'd tried to outlaw the death penalty the way those NRA Nazis smoked her in the media for six weeks. It had damn near cost her re-election.

"Put the fat bastard through, Caroline."

"How's life in the big city there, Lisa?" Joe Kirksey

sounded like a bear in a cave.

You oughtta know, you calcified muff diver, Lisa said to herself. You've seen the VIP rooms in every strip club in King County.

"Why, it's horribly lonesome without you, handsome. You and Cathleen just have to join Griffin and me for dinner at Twelve Elms the very next time you're in town."

Fat chance, Joe Kirksey thought, and how pretentious of you to give your fourth husband's gaudy Vashon Island mausoleum on three acres some pretentious Gone with The Wind plantation name. Writer Pat Conroy once said there was an inverse relationship between the number of white columns on one's house and the IQ of the residents. Conroy must've known Lisa Belle and that old shipping zillionaire she married.

"Well now, thank you kindly, Lisa. We'll look forward to it!" That and Ebola Zaire.

"What can I do for my best friend in this great state of ours, Joe?"

A pause ensued.

"Lisa...have you ever seen a grizzly bear?"

Ah ha. That's what this is about. Lisa thought fast. "Of course, Joe. Hundreds. Well...a dozen anyway." In fact, Lisa had never seen a grizzly, but she'd seen that television series about the late grizzly cuddler Timothy Treadwell and his late girlfriend. It had been enough to convince her that she would never get near a live grizzly if it chased her to Myanmar.

"Now, I'm talking up close and personal here, Lisa. Smelling distance."

Lisa's infamous temper began to gurgle. She wanted to say I'm going to break this grizzly bear bill right off in you and the rest of those incestuous outback desert neanderthals you represent, but Joe Kirksey was no freshman, and besides, anyone in the public eye had to be damned careful lest they become a hit freak on YouTube an hour later.

"Joe, I've conducted extensive research into our noble friend the grizzly bear, working closely with noted experts."

Balls, Kirksey thought. You probably worked directly
under a couple of UW biology professors, possibly together.
I bet you promised them a new look at their grant aps
if they'd tell the public the grizz was just America's own
answer to that Peter the Gay Possum cartoon character the
anal astronauts were trying to shove into new first grade
textbooks.

"Well Lisa, I've been reading this..." Kirksey struggled
not to choke, "'Noble Grizzly Bear Restoration Act'...you've
hustled through committee and have scheduled for a fast
track vote in a few days. And...well, Lisa, a grizzly bear
generally leaves man alone, but when it don't, the results
are catastrophic. Why, there are pictures on the Internet of
people killed by grizzly that would turn your–"

"Now, Joe, I have it on good authority that those pictures
are just digital fakes contrived by those anti-bear nimbies
in your district to paint a dreadful misrepresentation of
the noble grizzly. When are you Republicans going to stop
trying to frighten the public with scare tactics?"

"Nuts, Lisa. Democrats invented scare tactics. It's the
whole essence of the global warming hysteria. And can we
pass on the 'noble' bullshit? It's like saying 'common sense'
gun control when there ain't no common sense to disarming
the law abiding public while leaving criminals with their
guns."

Blood squirted out Lisa's ears, but she brought it under
control.

"Another argument for another time, Joe."

"Here's one for now. The grizzly is a land shark, Lisa.
Suppose I wanted to 'restore noble great white sharks' off
Miami beach. How do you think Floridians would take to
that?"

"Sounds like a Jewish/Cuban problem to me."

"OK. Suppose I want to 'restore' alligators in Puget
Sound off, say, the dock where your nieces and nephews
swim and water ski?"

"Grizzlies are an endangered, displaced species, Joe.
Alligators aren't."

40

"Says who? Grizzlies are proliferating so well the feds are going to de-list them."

"That's questionable now because of the climate change threat to habitat."

"Crap. Climate change threat is the power lever of the moment for you folks who want to foist dangerous animals where other people live. Climate change threatens a couple million Haitians a lot more than it does grizzlies. You gonna, say, invite some Haitians to move into those nine bedrooms you don't use?"

Lisa steamed, but she stuffed it in.

"Come on, Joe. Be serious. Haitians aren't native to Washington. Grizzlies are native to the North Cascades."

"Once upon a long gone time they were, yeah. There was also a time when they roamed all over what is now Seattle and Olympia, but, gee, correct me if I'm wrong here, Lisa, your bill neglects to restore grizzlies into the Seattle City parks. An oversight when you drafted the bill, no doubt."

"That's ridiculous, Joe and you know it. Seattle is a thriving hub of commerce, education, the arts, and science. Okanogan County is, well, forests, sagebrush, and farmlands."

"What about me and my people who live in those forests, sagebrush, and farmlands?"

Lisa snorted trying to hold in a snicker. "Joe... we're talking a productive, progressive urban center of enlightenment over here. You...Okanogan County, Jesus Christ, you're mostly Native Americans for one thing— Indians—and the rest of you are...well, let's just say Seattle serves humanity on a much greater scale."

"You've been getting high on your own supply of propaganda, Lisa. Without farmlands and forests, cities would drop dead faster than the spotted owl. And I got news for you. The Indians in my district, not to mention my other constituents, have no more enthusiasm for a grizz eating their kids than you would, if you had any kids."

"Grizzly kills are rarer than lightning kills, Joe."

"That stat's about as valid as a Democrat defense strategy.

You put as many grizzly in Washington as there are lightning strikes every year, and they'd eat us all."

"Joe, this grizzly bill is my ticket to the other Washington in next year's election. There is no way in hell I'm letting you or anybody else sabotage it. Take that to the bank."

A silence hung on the phone. Lisa broke it.

"So Joe, I think we've covered about all the common ground we're going to on the Belle Noble Grizzly Bear Restoration Act, and I'm sure you have other work to do, as do I. My bears are going into Okanogan County. It's a done deal. Get used it."

Joe Kirksey broke the silence now.

"Hear anybody singing, Lisa?"

"Singing? What are you–"

"I mean any fat ladies singing. You hear any fat ladies singing? Neither do I. See you in the senate chamber, Toots."

Lisa heard a dial tone. She slammed the phone into it's cradle. Conservatives! Lisa snarled to herself. What a sick blight on humanity!

CHAPTER SEVEN

Okanogan County

NORAD was never as busy as Winslow's Gun and Pawn Shop after it closed for business. The social club was charged with new hope, new excitement, new dedication, and a boatload of beer and liquor for all but Blubbo and Loverly. Loverly drank pop, but Blubbo was condemned by Runs to nothing but water. Lexie had brought in pizza and nachos. When Blubbo reached for same, Runs smacked his hand.

"Git away from that! You've eaten already."

"Ow!" Blubbo howled, jerking his hand back. "Ffffu–come on you old–uh, Runs. Nobody can live on salads and that ground up wheat shit!"

"By God, we're gonna find out. In the meantime keep your hands outta the snacks or it's back to the chain gang."

This evening's strategy and planning session had kicked off when Runs and Blubbo had walked in.

"Hi Blubbo!" Loverly said. Blubbo harumphed. Dumb white girls.

Lexie whistled. "Wow, Blubbo. Big boy ain't so big anymore!"

The group was dumbfounded to note that, in the week since the grizzly plot was hatched Blubbo had visibly lost weight, and toned up.

"Hey, Tonto," Boot said. "You done shucked some pounds, boy!"

Runs was clearly pleased. "The boy's dropped from two-fifty-two to two-forty-four in eight days. Fourteen pounds to go, and it's off to Paris Island. From the halls of Montezuuuuuma, to the–"

"–shores of Tripoleeee!" the group sang.

Blubbo was struggling to keep from smiling with pride and maintain his grumpy demeanor. He was still fat by any account, but 8 pounds in 8 days was an achievement and he knew it.

"I'd shake hands with Columbus for a milkshake," Blubbo snapped.

"When Sarah Palin marries Barney Frank," Runs said.

Between calisthenics, Blubbo had run increasing mileage each day on a gravel fire trail while rope towing an old ATV with the motor removed. Runs rode astride the ATV, reading a veterinary journal. This was more or less how the locals trained racing sled dogs when there was no snow.

"Ahh," Blubbo grunted. "This old brave's gonna kill me with all the shit he's making me do and eat. When I croak, I hope they lock him up for child abuse. Obama outlawed torture."

"Boo-hoo," Runs said.

"Hell, boy," Boot remarked. "You keep this up and you'll be havin' to beat the girls off with a stick. Like me."

"Oh it's gettin' deep now," Hogan said.

"Dramamine!" Lexie groaned.

"Sounds kinky," Nerves said.

"I can hardly wait," Blubbo said.

"Hmmmmm...," Loverly said, studying Blubbo with a smile.

Nerves had demanded the group have a name. The Free Okanogan County Movement was his suggestion.

"F - O - C - M." Lexie spelled.

"Fuck 'em?" Blubbo said. Phonetics weren't his strong suit.

"Yeah!" everybody said.

It was further agreed that the great mission would be code named Operation Grizz. The Free Okanogan County Movement was on a roll.

The table and several of the gun display counters were strewn with maps, website printouts, sketches, lists, books on grizzly bears, schematics of cattle trailers, and aerial/ground photos of the Washington Legislative Building, as the state capitol was officially called. The printer for Loverly's computer in the side room was whirring. Loverly and Blubbo took a 'virtual tour' of the capitol on the computer. Loverly took copious notes, and Blubbo sneaked glances down Loverly's cleavage. Some revolutionaries were more dedicated than others.

In two hours the Free Okanogan County Movement had decided several things.

Operation Grizz would require at least three vehicles, five if you counted trailers as separate vehicles.

The cattle rig was necessary to transport the bear safely, but in a container that could not easily be moved from in front of the Legislative Building after a few sabotage adjustments. Someone in a smaller vehicle would be needed to act as a reconnaissance unit to scout ahead for roadblocks, low overhead, traffic jams, cops or anything else that could stop the trailer truck. Even with the trailer tarped, a grizzly might make enough growling noise to raise suspicions if they had to stop near any other people. The scout car could also fetch essentials such as food and beer and tomato juice..

A third vehicle—Runs's crew cab, dually pickup—would be needed to follow along carrying tools and equipment in case of a break-down. The pickup would tow Boot's thirty-foot, gooseneck horse trailer containing large drums of diesel for the semi that it need not stop somewhere public for fuel. The trailer would also carry water cans, shovels, chunks of cow, and whatever else was required to sustain a stolen grizzly bear on a road trip.

Everybody agreed that Boot's idea for transporting the bear in the old cattle trailer was sound, but Nerves put icing on the cake. He was about to blow a vein to talk about it.

"I've figured out how we get a grizzly bear trap, and it won't cost us a dime extra!"

"I can't wait to hear this brainstorm," Hogan said.

"We don't need a separate trap. We use the trailer. We open up the back, put the bait in the front of the cattle trailer, and when the bear goes in, we slam the door!"

"Neat." Loverly said.

"Cool." Lexie said.

"I like it." Blubbo said.

Boot sighed. "I hate to rain on the parade here, but who's gonna stand by the trailer, to close the door when eight-hundred pounds of hungry grizz walks by? You, Nerves?"

"Yeah," Runs agreed. "Besides, it's damned unlikely that a grizz is gonna come around with people present even if the door closer person is on the roof. Most of 'em are still instinctively leery of humans. Besides, it could take hours. Days. We might draw a cougar or wolves instead."

"Oh ye of little faith!" Nerves said with a smirk, and he took a tantalizingly slow slurp of his beer. Then he tossed a sketch on the table and all heads leaned in. "Behold."

The late Sol Pickering's cattle trailer was already not unlike a bear live-trap in that the rear entry roll-up door, half the width of the trailer and on an overhead horizontal track, opened and closed by an exterior cable and hand-crank.

Boot slipped his glasses on.

Nerves's precise blueprint-like sketch depicted a fairly simple arrangement of trip-line, pulleys and drop weight which would slam the rear trailer door shut, fast, by falling from the trailer roof. A monofilament string inside the door would act as a trigger.

The group awaited Boot's judgement. He tossed the sketch down, leaned back, and whipped his glasses off. The suspense was excruciating.

"It could work," Boot ruled. The group released a collective sigh. "I even got a old jeep engine block and a truck brake disc that'll work for the weights. We'll have to do some testing to see what weight of clear fishing line is right...but dang if I don't think it can work!"

Boot stuck his hand toward Nerves. "Nice work, professor!"

Everybody then looked at Runs. He pushed the sketch back, raised his hands, smiled and began to slowly clap.

The FOCM cheered a beaming Nerves, and he was, of course, drank to by the adults, who would drink to just about anything anyway. Even Hogan, who thought swishies were sick in the dick, had to admit the plan was pretty smart.

Loverly gave Nerves a kiss on the cheek. He wasn't such a goofy pinhead after all.

"Humph," Hogan said, not wanting to encourage this sort of faggy genius. "So, where we gonna get a grizzly bear?"

"Excellent question," Boot said. "You don't see many in pet shops."

All heads turned to Runs.

"Me?" Runs said. "Why me?"

"Because," Lexie said, "as you pointed out, you're the animal expert in the Free Okanogan County Movement, and it was you who said we'd have to move it four-hundred miles."

"Well that was just because I was thinking we'd have to get it out of northern Idaho or northwestern Montana. The Kootenai and Flathead National Forests are crawling with them I hear."

It was also agreed by the FOCM that all the photographs and websites and virtual tours and guesstimates weren't going to cut it. An in-person recon mission to reconnoiter the statehouse and grounds in Olympia would be necessary. So would a field trip to wherever they were going to get the bear, so the inevitable problems there could be addressed. The question of who would perform these crucial missions sort of hung in the air in the rear of Winslow's Gun and Pawn Shop.

Boot broke the silence. "Count me out of the capitol visit. I'd rather go to hell than go to the westside."

"Me, too," Hogan said. "I'd rather listen to reruns of Jesse Jackson speeches."

"City hives give me hives," Runs said.

"I'll go!" Blubbo said, raising his giant porky arm.

"Forget it, fat boy," Runs said. "You're in training. I let you outta sight, you'll eat enough Whoppers and french fries to feed sub-Saharan Africa."

Blubbo sulked.

Lexie raised her hand. "That means Runs has to stay and babysit Blubbo, so–"

"I ain't no baby!"

Lexie sighed. Men and their impossible egos. "Figure of speech, oh great warrior. White squaw mean no insult. Peace. Ugh. It's better that me and Nerves go to the westside, anyway. We're from over that way. We know the neighborhood, the roads, the traffic, the assholes, yada, yada."

"Oh, how devine!" Nerves trilled, "I'll go with Lexie."

Loverly had wanted to go to Olympia, too. She'd barely been out of Okanogan County in her short fifteen years, and cities had a certain exotic appeal to her despite all the loopy liberal dorks who lived there. But she kept her peace. Paw-paw needed her to run the shop, and she was afraid to leave him. He might forget to take his heart meds again, or fall down or something. Or worse, he might try to drive somewhere. No. She had to stay close to Paw-paw.

Boot sat forward. "Look, somebody's gotta help me get old Sol Pickering's Pete running and pull that old cattle box outta the woods and down to my barn. The trailer's been there so long it's all grown up in brush. Ain't no telling what shape it's in, and it may take some work to get it roadworthy."

"OK," Runs said. "Me and Blubbo will help Boot."

"Be still my beating heart," Blubbo said.

"Great," Loverly said. "Paw-paw and me will go find a bear!" Loverly was fond of bears; they were like big puppies.

"The hell you say!" Hogan said. "Do I look like Tarzan of the goddamn jungle?"

"Come on, Paw-paw. Somebody's gotta do it. It'll be fun. I love bears!"

Hogan looked around to find everyone staring at him.

"Ahh...shit," he said.

"Yeaaaaa!" Loverly cried.

"FOCM!" the Movement cheered together, high fiving. The meeting was adjourned.

48

Oh marvelous, Ronald Reagan thought. I'm going bear hunting with a child and a blind fossil.

CHAPTER EIGHT

Western Montana

Forest Service enforcement officer Packy Rudd had continued to keep an eye peeled for whatever tore up the Widow Creek campground's bear-proofs and crapper. That jogger girl had been ripped eight ways from Sunday when he found what was left of her buried in a shallow pit two years earlier. It wasn't a vision one ever forgot.

Grizzlies generally minded their own business, but humans rarely did. Grizz were basically organic shredding machines and were more territorial than the Bloods and Crips. Aside from not wanting anyone hurt again, Packy didn't see a human kill by an uncatalogued mega-grizz in his area of responsibility as being a real career booster.

Worse, in a sense, was that another human kill would inflame the already anti-bear local public, which would clamor for removing grizzlies from the threatened species list, and for expanded hunting rights for the big shaggy bears.

At a minimum, he would be tasked to lead a team to hunt the killer bear down and kill it, lest the animal acquire a taste for humans once sampled. Packy's profession was to protect his beloved creatures of the national forests, not be their exterminator.

Packy closed and locked the steel gate to the access road for Widow Creek campground, for Melony had been right about one thing. It was only rarely used, and congressional attacks on the Forest Service's budget were requiring widespread belt-tightening measures.

Packy regarded Melony as a prissy affirmative action shill who had too many letters behind her name and too little field experience. He was convinced that she was dead wrong about the campground damage being caused by kids with trucks and chains.

But so far it was just a hunch. Packy needed evidence. So he threw a ripe, fragrant road-kill doe into his state pickup, drove to Widow Creek and dumped it in a clearing a hundred yards from the campground crapper that had had a steel fire door on it until...something...had ripped it off.

Nearby, Packy set a metal stake in the ground on which was mounted a night-vision trail camera on a motion-activated trigger. He used its laser to aim the lens at the doe corpse, switched it on and closed its camouflaged protective cover. At the last minute he decided to chain the deer's neck to a tree, so wolves might not drag the corpse away, nor might the bear until the camera could take a few shots.

Packy would drive back up and check the camera in two days.

For now, though, he would to pay a visit to Arliss Bernall, the Great White Hunter and nutcake meth tooter, to talk about his bear sighting.

Tonny hadn't slept well. His left forefoot remained swollen and painful. The necessary limping had strained muscles not designed for it, and he was sore all over. This made fishing damn near impossible, though standing in the cool mountain river waters did temporarily reduce the swelling and pain in his foot.

Regrettably, there were no two-legs around to eat, Tonny groused to himself. He'd never had any two-leg, but their meat appeared less hairy than deer, caribou and the like. Hair in your chow was a bummer. Besides, two-legs couldn't run so damn fast, or kick your eyes out, or stick you with their head claws. Granted, some two-legs could sting like a son of a bitch from a long way off, he'd learned, but, then, they seemed to have illogical pack rules that kept them from carrying their stingers with them most of the time. How stupid was that?

51

Surprisingly, Tonny could haul blubber as fast as a horse for short distances, but he preferred to steal other animals' kills rather than hunt his own, so he sat up and raised his big snout higher than a bus and sniffed the breeze that had borne him an interesting scent. He could hear it now, too, the alpha wolves in a distant clearing snarling at the submissives who were forced to wait hungrily and eat the leftovers when the dominants were satiated.

Hmmm, Tonny thought, twitching his leathery, plate-sized nose. Ding-dong. Avon calling!

The wolves didn't give up their doe generously. After all they'd just found it. They'd been delighted that it was already dead. A ripe ditch-bitch always trumped having to gang-drag the doe down. No running one's self ragged trying to catch the zippy thing and there was no risk of getting one's balls whacked off by a slashing hoof or getting stuck by long head claws. What's not to like, the wolves reasoned.

The wolves were outraged when Montana's answer to King Kong limped into the clearing, growling and drooling. On his way in, Tonny swiped some kind of stalky plant out of his way and when it hit the ground its shell split open and some black thing bounced out. The wolves circled, darted, and snarled viciously.

Grizzlies were never famous for their manners, but...there was something wrong with this one. It walked funny.

Instinctively, the wolves sensed a crippled prey, but Tonny adjusted their collective attitude by whirling on Lupo, the alpha male who rushed in from behind to bite him in his haunch. With a slashing sweep of a right fore paw as powerful as the business end of a back-hoe, but much faster, Tonny swatted the 90 lb., formerly dominant wolf, spinning it dead through the air into the trees where it hung impaled on a jagged tree limb shard, 17 feet above the ground.

Jesus fuzzy Christ, the wolves thought the wolf equivalent of. Gentle Ben's a little PMSie today. There were other deer in the mountains; no sense dying over this one. Besides, there was now one less alpha pack bully to have to fight for dinner since that asshole Lupo had gotten himself tacked to a tree. The wolves gave Tonny some ceremonial snarls and a few demonstration lunges—they had an image to uphold—but they soon split to find another prey.

Hope you choke on it, you fat prick! the wolves howled.

Moreover, the wolves knew the truth of the wild. Cranky ole' Darth Vader would get injured, sick or old someday. When he did, he'd also get slow and weak, and then some wolf pack would make dinner out of *him*.

That was how it worked out here.

Hot damn, Tonny thought. A nice, fat, bloated, ditch-bitch! I'll drag her off so those pencil-dick wolves don't come back to re-steal her. Then I'll pig out on her vitals before I bury her to ripen. Bon appetit, mon cherie! Tonny thought in his best French accent, which wasn't going to get him into any Québécois country club.

Tonny seized the doe by her haunch and beat it for the trees. He only got ten feet when the corpse was violently yanked from his mouth, nearly making him fall. Tonny roared in anger and pawed at some kind of shiny vine-like thing running in the grass from his doe's neck to a tree.

What the frigging Sam Hill is *this*!? Tonny thought the bear equivalent of. Two-legs! he thought. Only a stupid two-leg would fasten a good ditch-bitch to a tree! They get their dead meat from white pouches with little golden arches on them without having to fight off a single snarling wolf, and they want to steal *my* stolen ditch-bitch!? Wait'll I find one of those meddling two-legs!

Arliss Bernall nearly choked on his beer when he saw what looked like some kind of government pickup pull in behind his old stolen Chevy pickup in the dirt before the ragged trailer home he lived in. The white truck had a green stripe down its length, and antennas and a blue-light bar on its roof, which was all Arliss needed to know. It was the big one, Louise. The feds had finally come for him. Back to the joint again. Fuck *me*! He spat his mouthful of beer across the small room.

Arliss's heart went spastically arrhythmic as he hurled himself from the tattered, food-stained easy chair. He snatched up his crystal meth stash, then fell over an ottoman trying to run to his bathroom. He crab-scurried across the worn, faded carpet on his hands and knees, whimpering with the strain, praying the toilet would work this time. He'd just have to take his chances with the pot on the kitchen counter. He crammed the bag into the yellow mess in the toilet and hauled on the flush handle.

There is a God after all, Arliss thought, as the little plastic bag of smokeable methamphetamine swirled out of sight. He gasped for breath, his heart pounding so loudly he barely heard Packy Rudd's knock at the door.

"Slide the warrant under the door, motherfucker!" Arliss gasped by way of welcome.

"I'm with the Forest Service, Arliss. I just—"

"Bullshit! All you drug feds say that!"

Packy sighed. Maybe this hadn't been such a good idea.

"I'm a goddamned Forest Service enforcement officer, you idiot! Read the logo on the truck door. We ain't in the forest. I'm not here to lock you up."

Fuck, fuck, fuck, fuck, *fuck*! Arliss screamed to himself. I just flushed all the crank I had to my name for a fucking *tree* pig!? Fuck!

Arliss staggered to the trailer door and opened it. Packy's eyes watered at the stench. He backed up several feet.

"Well, like, what do you want, man?" Arliss said, his voice cracking.

"Chill, Arliss, I just want to talk to you about that grizz you say you saw last week."

"No shit, man?" Finally, someone believed him about that monster he'd seen. Someone who didn't think he'd made it up, or that he'd just seen an ordinary grizz and freaked out.

"Hey cool, man. Come on in! Want, like, a beer, man? It's a little warm on account of, like, my fridge don't—"

"Nooo thanks," Packy said quickly, observing Arliss's

scabby, pale, drawn face. He looked like Dracula at high noon. Packy knew meth-mouth when he saw it. He wouldn't go in that trailer with a chemical warfare suit on. "No, I can't stay long. How about you come out here?"

Arliss peered suspiciously about for feds in the bushes, then stepped out.

"Arliss, I need to ask you about this...bear you say you saw up–"

"I did see it, man, swear to god! Like, the size of a motherfucking elephant, man. Nearly killed me, man, but I, like, got away."

Bear ought to be fired for negligence, Packy thought.

"Look, Arliss, how big did you say it–"

"Twenty feet tall, man! Swear to God. Like, it musta weighed five-thousand pounds! Christ, it was...like...*big*, man!"

"Mm-hmm. Arliss, see that tree? It's right at twenty feet tall. You telling me this bear you saw stood that high?"

Arliss suddenly got sly. This tree pig wouldn't have driven all the into Whitefish unless he really wanted to know about the bear.

"Like, what's it worth to you, man?"

Packy sighed, shaking his head.

"Well, fuck you, man," Arliss said with a sneer, and turned for his trailer.

"You know, Arliss, maybe you'd be more comfortable if I dimed Sheriff Petree over here, so I don't violate your rights or something. Did you know they have all kinds of new forensic tricks now to get evidence out of septic tanks?"

Arliss wanted the county sheriff in his trailer like Osama wanted a SEAL convention in his cave. If he knew anything, Arliss Bernall knew when he was screwed because he had lots of experience at it.

"Look...ranger man...we both know I'm a crankshaft, and yeah I was tootin' the day I was hunting. But I wasn't...like... *that* fucked up, man. Swear to God, I saw what I saw."

"Tall as that tree?"

Arliss eyed the tree. "Well...OK, maybe not."

"Tall as your trailer?" The trailer's roof was about nine feet high.

Arliss turned around, then back.

"Listen to me, man...like...for the sake of some stupid fucking bird watching old lady hiking up in the Flathead. I swear on my, like, soberest moment that if that bear was standing up behind my trailer right now, he'd, like, be looking down at us, and his head would be, like, this wide." Arliss held up two hands three feet apart. "I hunted these mountains all my life that I wadn't in the joint, man. I seen several grizz, and I'm telling you, this damned thing will go a solid ton if he's a ounce. Two-thousand pounds plus. Swear... to...God."

Packy stared at Arliss.

Arliss wiped his face. "Look, your ears only, man. I was carrying a hot Weatherby custom 7mm with a Leupold scope. I boosted it from some Seattle fawn sniper's SUV last month. That rifle's worth three grand in any gun shop in Montana...but I dropped it when I saw this bear so I could run faster, and I ain't gone back after it, even though I got more stol–, uh, more guns." Arliss indicated his trailer, then himself. "Look at me, man. Don't it, like, tell you something that I'm afraid to go back after that expensive rifle, even with another gun?"

"Why didn't you shoot this...monster bear with the hot Weatherby?"

"Yeah, *hello*? I tried, man! Got off one shot before I figured out that damned thing could, like, eat all five rounds and me, too!"

"Did you hit it?"

"He didn't go down. After that, who the fuck knows, man? I'm gonna stick around to EMS a grizzly that would give Boone & Crockett a hard on?"

Packy took a business card from his uniform jacket pocket and scribbled a phone number on the back of it. He handed it to Arliss.

"That's the number of a recovering cranker I know. He's a gifted fuck downer."

"A...fuck...*downer*?" Arliss said. It had been a tough week.

"Yeah, you know, like when somebody is fucked so far up that God can't reach them with a ladder? Well this guy can fuck them back down again. Try him."

Packy turned to his truck.

"Hey man," Arliss said.

Packy faced him.

"How *do* those forensic guys, like, you know, get that evidence back out of a septic tank?"

CHAPTER NINE

Olympia

State Senator Lisa Belle patted her hair into place. Two of several photo frames of loving family on her desk were actually mirrors. Senator Belle rechecked her make up in one, then keyed her intercom.

"You may send the professor in, Caroline."

"Yes ma'am," Caroline said in the outer office. She scowled at the Cheshire Cat look on Perry Dinwiddie's face as the senator's bodyguard exited the office straightening his tie. Well, she sure couldn't blame the senator, Caroline thought, watching Perry's chiseled butt disappeared into the hallway. The brother was prettier than Denzel Washington.

"The senator will see you now, Dr. Windgate."

Ten minutes earlier, Perry had just finished guarding Senator Belle's body about as closely as physiology permitted. He tucked both Mr. Binkie and his shirt back in his pants while his boss and lover sorted through her purse looking for a lipstick. As she did, an anodized-carmine, snub nosed revolver fell out and bounced to the carpet.

"What the hell is that?" Perry said jumping to get out of the bouncing weapon's trajectory.

"What's it look like, Perry, an IUD?"

"You know what I mean. What're you doing with it?"

"The blessed all holy Second Amendment, darling. It says any breathing primate can own and carry one. The imbecilic Roberts Supreme Court just said so."

Perry picked the weapon up and examined it.

"Not exactly. What possessed you to get a pink gun?"

"Haven't you heard? The NRA thinks pink guns will draw more women members."

"My ass. I'm an NRA life member, and all the NRA babes I know shoot the same guns men do."

Miffed, Lisa tried to snatch the gun from Perry, but he'd been trained both in disarming techniques and anti-disarming techniques. He grinned and stepped back as Lisa reached in vain again.

"Exactly what are you going to do with this, Lisa? Guns are my department, and you couldn't hit the statehouse with one anyway. You're more likely to get yourself—or, worse, me—shot."

"Give me my gun!" Lisa hissed, steaming.

"Not until you tell me why you're packing it. You think I can't do my job?"

Lisa sighed. Men and their lame egos. All their brains were in their dicks.

"Because you can't be with me every minute of the day, Perry. Suppose one of those red-neck mountain gorillas from the eastside tries to make good on their threats while you're sniffing up my secretary in the Space Needle?"

"Threats, schmeats. Those emails are from dickless cyber wieners. Believe me, the doers in this world don't talk, and the talkers don't do. Nobody who has any serious intent to make your ashes into dust is going to pre-announce it over the goddamned Internet. And let me guess. You haven't even applied for a concealed carry permit to tote this pimp popper, right?"

"Oh, for God's sake, Perry. Permits are for Roosevelt slum scummies and those ignorant, eastside, cowboy wannabees. I am a Washington state senator!"

"Oh yeah. A Washington state senator who crusaded to ban handguns statewide, including cops. That was a brainstorm."

"I am different. I'm a...I, uh...serve the public at great risk to my life. Laws are for the public, anyway, not the...the ah...well, the ruling class."

"Spare me, Czarina Belle. Can you imagine what a

field day even the liberal press will have when some metal detector finds this thing in your purse, with or without a permit? If you think the NRA has been on your ass before, you ain't seen nothing like what they'll do then. They'll fry you crispier than Rosie O'Donnell."

"Alright! Then tell Caroline—you do remember my boobsie little black secretary with the masters degree in poly-sci who wears the red come-fuck-me pumps, right? Yeah, I thought so. Tell Caroline to make application for me. Now give me my—"

"Lisa, listen to me. They run an FBI background check on you when you apply for a CCP. Now I barely got your last DUI thing in Seattle handled, but cops, including the FBI, love you about as much as they do Roman Polanski. I guarantee you that any FBI computer will flag your name just like every other elected official in America. You can't afford to have some enterprising clerk who digs a little deeper than she needs to and dimes your DUI stop out to the Times."

"But, bu—" Lisa sputtered, "but that's an abuse of the permit process! That's government illegally using the permit requirement to keep a lawful citizen from carrying a gun!"

"No shit, Sandra Day. Why do you think the NRA is against a government permit to exercise a constitutional right?"

"Oh don't give me that neo-con bullshit, Perry. I have a *right* to defend myself!"

Perry smirked until Lisa got the pregnant irony of her last remark.

"Fuck you!" Lisa snarled and stormed into her private bathroom.

Senator Belle eyed Dr. Ermintrude Windgate who sat on the leather office sofa sipping the coffee Caroline had brought in. This self impressed wizard with a wedgie hasn't been laid since the Carter administration, Lisa thought.

"And so, as you may plainly see, Senator Belle," Dr.

Windgate continued smugly, "given my studies, my awards, and my long and stellar academic career, I am, shall we say, uniquely qualified to act as your expert witness on our magnificent grizzly bears."

Lisa pursed her lips. "Yes, well I can see that. But Dr. Windgate...um...may I call you Ermintrude?"

Now Dr. Windgate pursed her Bette Davis prunes. "Certainly not. Most people address me as Dr. Windgate, but as you are a distinguished legislator–"

Who swings a lot of dick where your grants come from, Toots, Lisa agreed silently.

"—my many dear friends call me Ermie."

Ermie? Lisa thought, like that marine corps Nazi who played that horrid drill sergeant in Full Metal Jacket? Charming.

"Mm...Ermie...let me be frank."

"Oh by all means!" Ermie could feel the grant cash rolling in.

"I have all the statistics quoting, data babbling 'experts' I need. What I'm looking for in you is a demonstrably bulletproof-documented authority who won't just tell my colleagues and the media what grizzlies eat and when they... um, do that sleepy thing..."

"Hibernate," Ermie said helpfully. How do two-digit trollops like this dimwit ever get elected? This woman was a poster child for term limits.

"Ah, yes," you overpaid bag lady, Lisa thought. "Hibernate. Thank you. What I need is someone who can sell my colleagues and the media a grizzly, someone who can make them want one for a pet their kiddies can ride on. I want the nation's top grizzly salesperson, like that Hollywood guy who plays with grizzlies on TV and rents them to the movie people.

"Um, actually he was killed by his grizzly not long ago, Senator."

"Oh wonderful! That's just fu–ah, wonderful! Well we won't be mentioning that when we discuss the Belle Noble Grizzly Bear Restoration Act on NPR tomorrow, will we?"

"Of course not, Senator. Remember, I was the inspiration behind the university's recent endorsement of placing the noble polar bear on the endangered species list. I assure you without reserve that I will present a splendid, award winning presentation, including hi fidelity sound images, to give the full impression of bear communications in the wild. No, no. I guarantee you, Senator, my program on our natural friends the grizzly will ensure that your senate colleagues and the media—"

"Fine. There isn't a lot of time here. I'm fast tracking the vote next week in among several yeoman pieces of legislature the press doesn't care about. The public is too du—um, too busy working to support their families in a Republican destroyed economy to truly understand the vital advantages to be had in restoration of the noble grizzly."

"Yes, of course. My program on the grizzly tomorrow will ensure that everyone understands that these gentle, private creatures are not to be seen as yet another Republican scare tactic. No, no. After all, our friends the good-natured grizzlies are not...'orange alerts!'" Ermie chortled like an NPR host fawning over Hanoi Jane Fonda.

Lisa forced a smiled. Get on with it, you congenital windbag.

Ermie snorted and continued. "When humans selfishly encroach upon them, grizzlies may rarely become...briefly problematic, but just a teensie puff of organic bear spray is all that's needed to send them on their merry way."

Lisa thought, get on your merry way Sergeant Ermie, before I have to spray you.

Dr. Windgate stood. "With supreme confidence, Senator Belle, I can assure you that, after my program on NPR tomorrow, the public and your colleagues will be thrilled to support the Belle Noble Grizzly Bear Restoration Act."

Icebergs, Captain Smith? Lisa thought. What icebergs?

CHAPTER TEN

Recon

Determined sub committees of the FOCM set out on their assigned missions with the excitement and sense of purpose only revolutionaries can know. They were having more fun than a democrat at a U.S. surrender.

Secretly, each was vicariously living his or her own image of favorite movie characters.

Loverly was Keira Knightly in *Pride and Prejudice*. She wasn't as erudite, she knew, but she suspected that her wind breakers more than made up for it in most modern scenarios.

Hogan was John Wayne, of course. No other stupid, pansy assed, dick brained movie star before or since was worthy of shoveling up after The Duke's goddamn horse.

Lexie was Helen Mirren, famous for playing Queen Elizabeth and thus having naught to do with a former stripper and call girl, but that was why Lexie chose her. Mirren was class.

Nerves was James Bond's boyfriend, giving whole new breadth to the expression, polar opposites, and glossing cleanly over the inconvenient truth that James Bond didn't do boyfriends. Nerves had a slave/master thing for Daniel Craig. Go figure.

Boot was Jean Reno in the great action film *Ronin*. Reno may have been a Frog, and he wouldn't have known a cow from a condor, but he was tough and cool, and that's what mattered.

Runs was the late, great Paul Newman despite wildly divergent politics. Newman was dignity walking.

Blubbo was the hugely underrated Wes Studi playing

Magua in *Last Of The Mohicans*. Blubbo just loved the romance of cutting the hearts out of white people.

With Hogan Winslow for both ersatz father and mother, one might think Loverly would have acquired a vocabulary and mannerism unique among young ladies, and one would be dead right. As a child, Loverly's colorful colloquialisms had gotten her into occasional hot water with her teachers, and by extension, Hogan. But lately, Loverly was not unaware of her unique circumstances. She deeply loved her Paw-paw with all her heart, but she wasn't confused that she was profoundly a girl and Hogan was notoriously an old bull crank.

Loverly had taken to watching videos of Jane Austin stories. She was enormously struck by the beauty, grace, femininity, and wit of the heroines. She promptly initiated her own run on Austen books at the Omak Library. By golly, Loverly decided, if Miss Austen can create such a dignified lady among all those snotty, limey assholes, then I can be one too, even growing up with Paw-paw.

Loverly had been confronted with this challenge just the previous day. She had roared over the gun shop hubbub to rotund Colleen Framer who'd brought her Winchester rifle into the gun shop among the other customers. "Open the action on that goddamned '94, Colleen!"

"Aahooooogh!" Ronald Reagan agreed from her saddle blanket in the corner. She had no idea what was up, but it was part of her job to back up Loverly.

Loverly winced, retro-considering that Jane Austen probably wouldn't have addressed a fifty-eight-year-old woman quite so forthrightly. "It's cocked," Loverly said, more gently now.

"Aw, it's alright honey," Colleen said, a smile across her plump red face. "It ain't loaded. I just need some ammo fer my old Winchester. The coyotes up my place is—"

"Famous last words, Colleen. You open that action right now, or open that door and carry your, um, rifle outta my gun store."

Colleen's face deflated. "Well...awright, Loverly, but it ain't loaded!" Colleen swung the rifle's cocking lever out, and a shiny 30-30 live cartridge spun out and clattered across the floor.

Loverly stormed around the counter and snatched the rifle from Colleen like a drill sergeant. "Gimme that!" She stabbed a finger at the bullet on the floor. "Ain't *loaded*! Ain't fu–uh...isn't loaded, huh?"

"Aaaooooogh!" Ronald Reagan said, struggling up from her saddle blanket.

Colleen stared at the ejected round, aghast. "Well... honey, I didn't know that was in there! I coulda swore—"

"What's that sign on the front door say, Colleen?"

"Well...it says to unload and open–"

"*All* guns are loaded, you–" Loverly, broke off her sentence, considering that Jane Austen probably wouldn't actually call Colleen a dumb cunt. "You coulda got somebody shot, Colleen. Maybe even my Paw-paw!" Loverly now stabbed a finger at Hogan who sat leaning on his cane in the rear of the shop observing Loverly's innovative consumer relations finesse with great content.

Hogan grinned at the shop full of gawking customers. "Taught her every goddamned thing she knows!" he announced with glowing satisfaction.

Hogan and Loverly closed the shop. Loverly dropped the keys in her purse, and checked that the .45 pistol in her backpack was loaded, cocked and safetied. She drove her grandfather east in Hogan's old Suburban, struggling to see the road through the steering wheel loop. They towed Hogan's ancient twenty-foot camper trailer.

Sitting up in the back seat was Ronald Reagan, who was always up for a road trip. The old hound hung her head out the side window when Loverly buzzed it down as they traveled through small towns at low speeds.

On the other side of the nine-seat SUV, Hogan checked

that his 12 gauge, Remington 870 police riot blaster was *not* loaded, and that the thunderous sabot slugs for it were in their box under the seat. It was embarrassing to accidentally blow a hole in the roof of your Suburban. Your ears rang shrilly for hours and those assholes at the Bodene's Body Shop never let you live it down.

At fifteen, Loverly was as legal to drive as the AFLAC duck, of course, but Hogan had that handled.

Hogan had been distressed when weakened eyesight threatened his driving. Independence and mobility meant a lot to him, but that near miss with that tour bus had been the clincher. Hogan had sent fifty-eight elderly Canadian casino gamblers and one puckered-up east Indian motorcoach driver on the ditch ride of their lives before he'd fled weaving down the road in the dark. Hogan had gotten God's loving message that night: You endanger any more of my flock again, you stubborn old bastard, and next time I'll give you fifty tons of Kenworth right in the kisser. Amen.

Hogan was weighing all this a year ago when he went fishing as all troubled people do, and, as so often happens to men who live right, he found his miracle.

Rolling quietly down a remote Pasayten Wilderness fire trail, Hogan had come upon a silver Mercedes sedan he knew belonged to one Bailey Waddell. Bailey was a short, tubby, married father in his forties who, in a gravity-defying miracle of physics, combed his hair up from his left ear and over his bald pate. This required enough hair-spray to harden the Okefenokee Swamp.

The Mercedes was memorable because nobody knew how Bailey could afford an overpriced kraut status symbol on a state clerk's paycheck.

Among other pursuits, Bailey Waddell led the Omak Church of Our Savior's youth bible study group, and chaired the Republicans of Faith for a Better Okanogan County. You can see it coming, can't you?

Hogan peered as he rolled past the Mercedes on the dirt

road. He was amazed to see Bailey Waddell's pale bare fanny bobbing up and down in the back seat, something akin to an albino walrus doing the forty-yard dash. Bailey's terrified face whirled around and he met Hogan's eyes. Hogan's eyes also met the ecstatically closed eyes of Merrilee Huntington. This remarkable scene was the more remarkable for Merrilee being one of Loverly's classmates. She had recently been suspended from school for seducing her algebra teacher, who was now giving English classes to call center workers in Bangladesh.

Hogan followed the First Commandment of Okanogan County: Mind your own business, but never forget.

The next day Bailey Waddell waddled into Winslow's Gun and Pawn Shop looking about two fibrillations shy of a cardiac crash. They went into Hogan's cluttered office, and Bailey closed the door.

"Alright, what's it gonna cost me, you old son of a bitch?" Bailey hissed.

Hogan had given the Bailey Waddell matter some thought.

"Why...whatever do you mean?" Hogan said, innocent as a pit viper.

"Don't jerk me around, Winslow! You know damn well what I mean. What I want to know is how much it's going to cost me to keep you quiet about what you saw yesterday."

"Why shoot, Bailey," Hogan said, all wide-eyed and perplexed, "I don't know what you mean. These old eyes of mine ain't what they used to be. I can barely see to get around anymore."

Bailey studied Hogan.

"So...you didn't notice anything...unusual, yesterday?"

"I was off fishing way up toward Palmer Lake yesterday Bailey. Hell, I could barely find the goddamn lake."

Macro-relieved at his incredible luck, Bailey said, "Well never mind then. I must be mixed up. See ya."

"Say, Bailey," Hogan said as Waddell opened the door, "Didn't I just read in the paper how you been promoted to office supervisor down at the DMV?"

So it had come to pass that, in only 24 hours, Loverly Winslow miraculously aged 3 years, conveniently bypassed the traffic safety education course, the instruction permit phase, and the entire driver's exam, and received her new Washington driver's license, hand delivered by the office manager of the local DMV.

With his normal flair for subtlety, Hogan had told Loverly that if she drove without him before he signed her off as safe in a year or so, he would make *Silence of the Lambs* look like *ET*.

Loverly got the eastbound Suburban with the welded patch in the roof up to highway speed, set the cruise, and began texting a girlfriend to tell her they would be gone to Montana for three days.

Hogan felt that a .45 automatic pistol was an appropriate accessory for a debutante, but these cell phone typewriter gadgets were the fucking scourge of society.

"No toys while yer drivin', Loverly!" Hogan snarled. "I see that stupid ding-dong brain pacifier out of your purse while you're behind the wheel again, and it'll be in the wood chipper right next to your driver's license!"

"10-4, Paw-paw!" Loverly said, snapping the phone shut.

Loverly treasured the rich, affectionate communication she shared with her grandfather.

It takes more than a big hat to make a cowboy. It takes a unique state of mind coupled to an equally unique set of skills. Boot Colhane was a real cowboy despite the New Orleans Saints ball-cap on his head.

Someone once asked Boot why he wore a hat that named a southern pro football team. "Anybody who can beat the goddamned Seahawks," Boot had answered. "Hell, I'd wear a *Brokeback Mountain* cap if those two fairies could whip the Seahawks, and they probably could."

The Seattle Seahawks were a good bunch of guys, Boot

knew, and most of them had never seen Seattle before they were hired, but damn it, they were now westsiders, collectively the silliest pack of liberal nitwits this side of San Francisco. Boot hated state and federal liberal legislators for robbing cattlemen of ever more federal land grazing rights with their goddamn wilderness bills. He was even more pissed than usual at Seattle because the state legislature had just passed another cougar-hugging, wolf-kissing goddamn law to keep ranchers from shooting those predators.

There were maybe twenty wolves in all fifty-four-hundred square miles of Okanogan County, and while there were many cougars, they were only rarely a problem. Nonetheless, liberal largess with game laws that impacted other people had given rise to a popular philosophy in Okanogan County called the 'three S rule'. Shoot, shovel, and shut up.

The state legislature met in Olympia, not Seattle where the poor Seahawks played, but they were all of a westside liberal asshole lot in Boot's mind. Thus the Seahawks had to take it on the chin in his hat wardrobe.

It had taken jumper cables and a quart of starter fluid, but Boot, Runs and Blubbo had gotten the late Sol Pickering's Peterbilt road tractor running.

They looked downright odd, wearing the yellow Walmart galoshes, rubber gloves, and surgical hairnets Runs had provided.

Blubbo whined over the ridiculous look this gear gave them all, but Runs was adamant that they don the equipment before even turning off the highway onto the long dirt trail up to Sol's isolated ranch. Nerves had driven everyone nuts with his anal paranoia about DNA and fingerprint tracing, but they knew he was right.

Dr. Runs With Rivers had dreamt of being on the faculty of a prominent equine hospital, researching horses, which he'd adored since his youth. Because of his exemplary student record, Dr. Runs With Rivers was readily admitted to residency at the prestigious Ordington Equine Center near Seattle. He was soon to learn however that he was hired partly for his record but mostly because he was so obviously and handsomely Native American. This lent false diversity credentials to the Ordington Center, which wouldn't have hired a black DVM if he were the Stephen Hawking of veterinary medicine.

In only a few months at the OEC, Dr. Rivers found the entire clinical staff to be arrogant, self-impressed, overrated, and brain locked. Indians had a quaint expression for this: Assholes.

Runs began to accidentally overhear conversations among faculty members about parties, weddings, staff get-togethers, and even faculty meetings which he had not been informed of, let alone invited to. He finally overheard Chief of Staff in the next recovery stall remark that, while 'Geronimo' was a superb clinician, he simply lacked the 'breeding gravitas' to practice in a leading equine medical institution. The other two senior vets in the stall had chuckled and nodded.

Runs walked into the stall, startling his colleagues. He plucked off his Ordington Center ID card, and frisbied it at the Chief of Staff. He told her she had a little too much gravitas of her own to attract much breeding.

Dr. Runs With Rivers had enjoyed all the distinguished academic professionals he could stand. He finished his residency at another clinic, then returned to the Colville Confederated Tribes reservation in Okanogan County to set up a private practice.

Runs's transition back to the reservation had its distinct disadvantages from a career standpoint because many Indians didn't have any money to spare for vet bills. So Dr. Rivers established a sort of barter system that allowed the horse crazy Indians to pay with fine colts and fillies and prime cattle which Runs sold off the rez at decent profit.

If America ever gave Washington back to the tribes, Runs would be elected chief-for-life, but neither was likely.

"Nobody goes near this rig unless their face is shaved and they're wearing their boots, gloves, and hairnet!" Runs repeated. "Eventually, the cops are gonna go over this rambling wreck looking for fingerprints, DNA, and any other clues to who was in it. Nobody sets anything down in the rig, no glasses, no tools, no chewing gum, no nothing. Nobody spits tobacco, blows snot, pees or drips sweat in the rig. Serious here, we can't leave any trace or we're all going to jail."

"How come we gotta wear these farmer fudd boots?" Blubbo demanded.

"Think, shit-for-brains! They'll trace the rig to Sol's Ranch, then they'll be looking all over for traceable footprints. Wal-mart sells Chinese trainloads of these galoshes every year, so they won't be traceable. When we're done, we'll burn all this stuff somewhere and throw the ashes in the river to eliminate any DNA trace that may get left in them. When we leave here, we'll be sweeping our tire tracks with a pine bough bundle as we go, all the way to the pavement. You get to walk behind and hand sweep what gets missed."

Blubbo began to suspect there may have been something indictable in old man Rivers's distant past.

The old Peterbilt truck tractor belched black smoke as Boot drove it up a cliff side goat road to a high plateau to retrieve Seth's ancient cattle trailer from the woods bordering the north flat of the remote, abandoned ranch.

All three men marveled yet again at a view they'd enjoyed all their lives. One could see all the way to the distant snow peaked Cascades nearly a hundred miles west. The view alone from the high range was worth the drive up the narrow dirt road. It was like the opening scene in *Sound Of Music*. You could almost see Julie Andrews whirling about, singing: "The hilllls are aliiive..."

Such plentiful, stunning vistas made a daily gift to Okanogan Countians of a profound communion with nature. This majestic beauty, together with a rugged remoteness that lent itself to meth labs and pot nurseries, were why life in Okanogan County was so superior to anywhere else.

The lads waded into the brush and small trees to check out the old gray aluminum cattle trailer's tires.

Lifelong westerners though they were, it had not occurred to them that, in the months of the trailer's abandonment, some tribe of hornets might have built a gray, paper mache nest the size of the port anchor on the USS Reagan next to the brush obscured lynch pin on the trailer.

Now the hills really were alive with big, yellow and green striped hornets and much colorful rhetoric as the cowboy, the veterinarian, and the not-so-fat-anymore Indian boy ran flailing and screaming from the woods.

The trio went forthwith to a hardware store in the distant, small town of Republic, bought a case of long-throw wasp spray cans, and returned with a vengeance, to say nothing of numerous red welts all over their exposed skin.

Back on site, Blubbo donned a pair of Sol Pickering's jeans. They rolled down and buttoned their sleeves, buttoned and turned up their collars, pulled the surgical caps down over their ears, and donned bandanas about their faces. With a can of wasp spray in each gloved hand, and Boot's shotgun slung about his shoulder, they looked like a hellish cross between a HAZMAT response team and the Three Stooges.

"One! Two! Three!" Boot said, and, roaring "Yaaaaaaah!" they charged. In seconds the trees, trailer, and beach ball sized hornet's nest was dripping with bug spray. The hornets went to DEFCON-1 and launched all their surviving air superiority assets, which counterattacked bravely.

This resulted in six, 30-foot streams of bug spray arcing about like the New York Fire Department at a five alarmer, only the NYFD aims.

Hornets still poured from the soaked nest, so the nature boys fell back on Plan B. Boot dropped his spray cans and racked his birdshot-loaded shotgun. Squinting against the swarming hornets, he took fast aim from ten feet away at the nest suspended beneath the trailer's overhanging front section. Prudently, he fired from an angle so as not to have bird shot ricochet back all over the Three Musketeers.

Plan B could be said to have had mixed results. The shotgun decimated the paper hornet's nest, but sparks from the blast ignited the petroleum-based bug spray which had now saturated the nest and the surrounding brush. With a truly impressive *whoof!* the nose of the trailer and much of the nearby brush lit off like that napalm strike in *Apocalypse Now.*

Wildfire was the number one natural hazard in dry Okanogan County, and residents—not to mention the law—took a dim view of anyone careless enough to torch off a couple hundred-thousand acres of prime forest dotted sparsely with houses, barns, churches, businesses, schools, orchards, meth labs, and pot gardens. Wildfire was damned dangerous for hundreds of county folk, and cost millions of dollars in people, water-bombers, helicopters, and vehicles to fight. It hacked off the animals too.

"Holyyy shiiiiit!" Boot, Runs, and Blubbo explained as they stampeded to retrieve the truck's fire extinguisher and two horse blankets Sol Pickering had used for floorboard mats. In an exhaustive, gasping effort worthy of a presidential citation, they finally foamed and flogged out the last remnants of the fire.

Residual smoke, yards of blackened brush, charred horse blankets, fire extinguisher vapor, and one scorched trailer made for a scene reminiscent of the Tunguska meteorite hit on Siberia.

Boot dropped the spent fire extinguisher, staggered to a log, sat and hung his head. He coughed painfully. Runs dropped to all fours and panted. Blubbo fell over backwards in a cloud of ash, and gasped like a beached grouper.

"I—unh, unh, unh—got to—unh, unh, unh—lose some—unh, unh, unh—more weight!" Blubbo said.

Like the nineteenth century American Indians, the surviving hornets said there goes the neighborhood. They cut their losses and moved on to rebuild elsewhere.

Boot, Runs and Blubbo backed the roaring road tractor up to the old trailer, and dragged it out of the woods. They were pleased to find that, other than a soot-blackened fore-end, the trailer was serviceable. Even the air brakes and lights worked.

They then took a cooler of beer and hotdogs from Runs's pickup, built a fire, and sat down to await darkness to cover their...borrowing of the Pickering cattle rig.

It had been a long day.

Lexie and Nerves now sped westbound on I-90 for Olympia in the latter's white Porsche.

Drunk deer hunters from Seattle, one of whom recognized Sexy Lexie, had shown up at her trailer two years ago and beaten her badly for her lack of enthusiasm for rape. She was a whore, right? So what was the big deal? Shortly thereafter, Lexie walked bruised and battered into Winslow's Gun and Pawn and asked for a used pistol and the training to use it. Within a month of practice with Loverly, Lexie become a fast, controlled draw, and a deadly shot.

When the hunters returned the next season, again holding up the stock in the American distillery industry, the driver's door mirror on their Excursion exploded in a shower of glass and plastic as they turned into Lexie's driveway. Sensitive to this form of expression, they made the jump to light speed in a cloud of gravel dust.

Lexie watched the white center stripes zip by in a blur. "Some spies we are, doing 90 miles an hour in a car about as inconspicious as a ghetto pimpmobile. Slow down, before we get locked up without having to steal a bear!" Nerves prissed with irritation, but he blipped the cruise down two clicks.

Unlike Bailey Waddell, who had 'earned' his $60K

Mercedes by selling hot drivers' licenses to employers of illegal immigrants, Nerves had come by his white, $136K Carrera legitimately, for he was independently comfortable by family fortune. His hard-core hetero Jewish father still regarded homosexuality as a moral atrocity on a par with buying a German car, which is why Nerves had never come out of the closet on either with his father

T. Larchmont Nuerves III, JD., PhD., was called 'Nerves' by default for a couple of reasons. His last name was Spanish and was pronounced Nwer-vay, but the spelling was just too much trouble for Okanogan Countians to sort out. The clincher was that Nerves was always about two synapses short of a stroke. He was born bug eyed, overwrought and short fused, and a lifetime of homosexuality hadn't improved this a lick. Nerves hated the butchering of his name, which nearly gave him a blood pressure blow out, but he accepted it because the Winslow's social club were the only folk in Okanogan County who didn't think he was a raving nut. Actually they did, they just didn't care. For Nerves, it was the same thing.

Nerves was a UCLA-trained environmental lawyer. Until last year, he had been an associate professor at the University of Washington in Seattle, and a card carrying über liberal with a California blue blood pedigree. Ten months earlier, Nerves had told the university to put its tenure where the sun don't shine, he never wanted it anyway, and he quit. At forty-one, he was now an excellent—albeit monumentally overqualified and underpaid—English teacher for Okanogan County High School, a pay cut somewhere in the range of $100,000.

Actually, Nerves had wanted tenure so bad his teeth ached, but he'd made the fatal error of not getting on the happy global warming band wagon like the rest of his liberal colleagues. At a faculty meeting, senior professor Dr. Ermintrude Windgate, Chair of the Ecology Department, had proposed that the academicians publically endorse a bill before congress to place the polar bear on the endangered species list for the 'threat' to it from global warming. Nerves had been the sole dissenter. He had stood and demonstrated the gauche audacity of challenging not only the famous Dr. Windgate, but–gasp–the whole notion of global warming as a man-caused, man-curable travesty.

"Hold it," Nerves had said at the faculty meeting, standing. This drew gasps of astonishment from his colleagues and a beady-eyed frown from Dr. Windgate. "There is no question the planet is warming, as it has done in numerous cycles before, and certainly I champion intelligent conservation. But I submit that even the most avid proponents of climate change theory among us remain unprepared to demonstrate a conclusive link to man. Yet now, in the name of an unproven theory, we are proposing to endorse the placement upon the endangered species list an animal the population of which has grown steadily for 90 years. Friends and respected colleagues, am I the only one here who thinks it a bit odd to call an animal endangered which has proliferated steadily for a century?"

The screaming silence that ensued told the notoriously overcooked Nerves that, why yes, he was the only stupid asshole in the auditorium who thought that.

In fact, he wasn't. He was just the only associate professor on the tenure list who had the cojones to admit his concerns. Dr. Nuerves was the only academician in the auditorium who still thought fair and rational consideration, independent of rabidly liberal politics, was the hallmark of a university. Unfortunately, no one else at the faculty meeting was sap-headedly naive enough to believe they'd be remotely considered for tenure if they dared question the New Holy Grail of academia, let alone publically confront the powerful Grand Dame of UW, Dr. Windgate herself. One could have done one's career at UW as much favor by getting caught in a child porn sting.

Dr. Windgate removed her glasses and displayed a smirk of amused condescension. "Ah. Yes. The estimable Dr. Nuerves graces us yet again with his...quaint...observations." The assembly, sans Nerves, tittered. Dr. Windgate glowed with satisfaction. Nerves approached critical mass.

To Nerves, Ermintrude Windgate was the personification of the disconnected, self-impressed, liberal academician who'd long lost the ability to separate science from politics. She represented, in Nerves's view, the very worst of politically bigoted, post-modern American academia. Well, by God, T. Larchmont Nuerves III, JD., PhD., of the San Francisco Nuerveses thought, steaming, he hadn't come from a long and proud line of distinguished—not to mention staunchly liberal—lawyers and professors to be ridiculed by an intellectually incestuous, bipedal sow. Cautious forethought had never been what Nerves did best, but now he struggled as never before.

"I meant no disrespect, certainly, Dr. Windgate. I'm merely searching for the logic behind labeling a consistently growing species endangered."

"Fortunately," Dr. Windgate replied, still smirking, "the balance of us here at this great university can appreciate the grave risk the noble polar bear faces from the wanton destruction of its habitat by man's corporate folly."

Most of the faculty present murmured ascent and nodded heads. The few who shared Nerves's doubts held their water. If Dr. Nuerves was hell bent on professional suicide, he would have to go it alone.

"On the contrary, Dr. Windgate," Nerves said tightly, his hot wires humming. "I submit respectfully that the alleged folly itself is unproven, let alone its hypothesized effects. Indeed, I submit respectfully that the very endorsement you propose this august faculty make poses a 'greater' threat to the 'greatness' of this 'great' university than climate change does to the one of the largest land carnivores on the earth!"

What Nerves had begun in a professional monotone ended as scorchingly as Col. Jessup's testimony in *A Few Good Men*.

The gasp in the auditorium was dramatic.

Dr. Windgate's smirk faded fast, but it spread again across her saggy jowls as she recovered. "Next...one assumes, Dr. Nuerves...you will no doubt be enlightening us on the scientific virtues of...intelligent design?"

The faculty left wing, which was about two-thousand feathers to maybe twelve-or-so on the stunted right wing, chuckled dutifully. The twelve-or-so crossed themselves in grim silence.

Nerves boiled silently, letting his colleagues' ridiculing laughter subside. All heads turned to him.

Nerves took a deep breath, then let it seep slowly out. "It is...the indelible mark of a pathetically weak mind, of course...Dr. Windgate...to flee to irrelevant trivia when reason and logic abandon one's original premise. But as you bring it up, let me say that, without an iota of doubt, you personally remove all suspicion of any intelligence in the human design, so that theory may be lain...*forever to rest, you bloviating rectal cyst!*"

Thus did T. Larchmont Nuerves III, JD, PhD, come to teach tenth grade English at Okanogan County High School, and how liberalism gained another fanatically dedicated enemy.

"I'm a highly skilled driver, I'll have you know!" Nerves snapped at Lexie in his Porsche on their way to Olympia. "Cops can tell that. They never bother me."

Which, of course, was when blue and red lights came on behind them and something went whoo!-whoo!-whoo!-whoo!

Lexie looked in the vanity mirror. "Oh, congratulations, Dale fucking Earnhardt. We're busted!"

"Cops always roust guys with nice cars!" Nerves said, his voice rising in pitch, his eyes flicking from the rear view mirror to the road and back. "They're just jealous jackboot Nazis!"

"Oh yeah, and you doing speed limit plus thirty had nothing to do with it. Pull this thing over before super trooper back there starts shooting!"

"I'm stopping, already! Fucking storm trooper cops! A law abiding citizen can't own a nice–"

"Just zip your mouth, Nerves. Take the ticket and let's

be on our way. There's already going to be a record of this car and your name here at this time. Don't give this cop any other reason to remember us!"

"I know what to do!" Nerves said shrilly. He buzzed his window down.

The Washington state trooper looked a little like a grizzly himself. Despite his meticulous gray uniform with a sergeant's stripes on the sleeves, he was huge, thick, and hairy, and had a deep, don't-mess-with-me voice.

"Sir, can I see your driver's license, registration and proof of insur—"

"Awright, already! I'm getting them, aren't I?" Nerves was quivering.

"Cool it, Nerves!" Lexie hissed.

"Here!" Nerves said, thrusting his documents at the officer. "You know I pay your salary, Officer?"

"Mmm-hmm," the trooper said. "Well, I need a raise, boss."

"You need to be fighting crime, officer! Not harassing honest, law aaaach!"

Lexie had sunk her claws into Nerves's thigh. She leaned over to look at the trooper's face and curiously noted two small, star shaped scars, one on each of his cheeks. It wasn't a face one forgot.

"Law abiding taxpayers," the trooper mechanically recited, finding Nerves's documents in order. "I know, I know. Well sir, how about you just slow—"

"You know, darling," Nerves prissed, flipping his wrist, "it's so comforting to know that if we ever have a retarded son, he can always make a good living...as a policeman!"

"Oh Christ," Lexie said, shading her eyes.

A pregnant silence passed, which the trooper broke, saying "You know, sir, I was about to let you go with a warning, but..." He tapped Nerves's document's against his other hand. "Wait here, sir." The big sergeant returned to his flashing car.

"You pea brain!" Lexie seethed. "If they gave medals for stupidity, you'd look like a Guatemalan field marshal!"

Nerves's eyes gimballed about like C3PO's. He was about to cork off a vein.

"Stay here, dumbass!" Lexie said. She got out, slammed her door, and strode back to the trooper's car.

Trooper Ron Halloran looked through his windshield when he heard the Porsche's door thump shut. Normally he hated it when citizens came back to his patrol car uninvited. Every Tom, Dick, and Harriet carried guns anymore. Very few of them ever broke a law with a gun, but they who did were a constant worry to road cops.

Ron didn't think he needed to be too concerned this time, though. It was the driver's wife or girlfriend or whatever, and she was a stunner. Her hands were empty and it was pleasantly obvious to the sergeant that there were no concealed weapons under those shorts or that tight halter thing.

Lexie got in the passenger seat and chemoed the sergeant with a beauty queen's smile and some truly healthy cleavage.

"Do you mind, officer?" Lexie said, breathlessly. "I've never seen the inside of a real police car."

My kinda woman, Sergeant Halloran thought. All tits, no brains. "Suit yourself," he said, and went back to writing a citation for reckless driving.

"Can I ask you a question, sir?"

"Yeah, but if it's will I let your husband, there, go with no citation, the answer's not a chance."

"Oh God no. He's not my husband. Besides, he's right off Capitol Hill. He's just my ride, and he's too stupid to get a break. I was just wondering, who's your scartist? He's really good."

"My what?"

"Well, you know, tattoos and piercings are so passe now, so the really cool guys are getting cosmetic scars like those neat little stars on your cheeks. The cutters who do them are called scartists on the street. I'm just wondering who yours was, because those little stars are too cute."

Trooper Halloran's eyes narrowed. "Lady, my 'scartist' was some coked up little maggot who shot me through both sides of my mouth with a .22 about ten years ago. I didn't pay for it. But he did."

"Oh. Well, I still say they're sexy. I used to be in the Seattle skin trade, you know, and I hired out to do bachelor parties and birthdays and all. I was dancing for a party one time and there was a guy there, looked a lot like you. Even had those little cheek scars."

Trooper Halloran began to uncomfortably suspect that the titsy bimbo was nowhere near as dumb as he'd thought. He paused with his pen and looked carefully at Lexie.

"So?"

"Oh nothing," Lexie said, looking at the trooper's name tag, "officer...mmm...Halloran. I'm sure it wasn't you because this guy was doing lines of coke."

Halloran remembered the party. He'd been going through an Auschwitz divorce at the time, and Helga, Bitch Queen of the SS, was taking his kids, his house, and most of his future paychecks. He had briefly drank too much and used a little, but he'd been dry and clean for two years. This woman couldn't prove what she saw on the word of an ex-stripper-whatever, but she wouldn't have to for Internal Affairs to get real ugly. At a minimum, the brief drug use could cost him his stripes.

"See," Lexie said, "I used to give a lap dance that would have guys coming in the club the next day asking me to marry them. Sometimes they'd even bring little memento photos from the party, you know? You'd be surprised what some of the guys in the background are sniffing off the top of the bar. I kept all those photos. In my line of work then, you never knew what might come in handy."

Trooper Halloran stared at Lexie who looked back like Shirley Temple. He steamed, but he knew he was dealing with a player. Besides, the big mouthed turkey in the Porsche had just been fast on a clear, dry, interstate highway in broad daylight in a car made to do it. He really didn't qualify for reckless. Sergeant Halloran tongued his cheek and squinted at Lexie.

"Ma'am, are you gonna see to it the space cadet up there

slows down?"

"Count on it, now and later," Lexie said.

"And are you gonna fine-tune his mouth a little?"

"Well I won't cut his tongue out with rusty garden shears, officer, but when I'm done with him he'll wish I had."

Halloran studied Lexie for several long seconds. Then he handed her Nerves' documents. "Have a good day, ma'am."

Lexie smiled genuinely now, leaned across the car, and gave Sergeant Ron Halloran a kiss he'd never forget. Now *he* almost blew a vein.

Halloran watched Lexie's fanny wiggle as she stalked to the driver's side of the Porsche. He was amused to see her open the door, grab the driver by his sport coat lapels, and haul him out of the car. She pointed to the passenger side of the car, told him something that pinned his ears back, then got in behind the wheel herself.

The space cadet looked like an overripe beet, but he complied without comment.

CHAPTER ELEVEN

Flathead National Forest, Western Montana

Forest Service enforcement ranger Pack Rudd was shaken.

He stood on the edge of the clearing in which he'd set a bait doe and a trail camera barely two days earlier. The formerly grassy clearing was gouged up. There was the smell of a decaying corpse in the air, but Packy couldn't see any source. Maybe the grizz had just recently dragged off the doe.

Or worse, maybe that bear was still nearby. Packy levered open the bolt of his rifle just enough to ensure yet again that a live round was chambered, and closed it. He kept his finger tip on the safety as he looked around.

What really made Packy nervous was that the light chain he'd fastened that doe to a tree with was snapped off clean. Packy found the parted link in the dirt. This chain wasn't bolt-cut, hack-sawed or shot through, he thought, examining the link. Something put enough stress on this chain to break it.

Packy looked around at the woods wondering if his .444 was enough gun for what broke this chain and tore an expensive trail camera right out of its hard plastic case. He knelt by the camera debris, and removed the memory chip. Maybe it got some kind of decent shot before it got smashed.

When Packy stood, a great horned owl sailed silently through the trees, across the clearing and landed on a limb maybe twenty feet above the ground. As Packy's eyes followed the huge bird, he realized to his shock where the death stink was coming from.

The owl pulled a strip of desiccated flesh from the pecked up carcass of a large wolf hung in the tree on a jagged, broken-off limb.

Thirty feet away. Maybe fifteen feet up.

Bigger gun, Packy thought, looking around. I need to get a bigger gun. He hurried back to the campground to his truck. He wanted to get to the computer in his office to view the trail camera memory chip in his pocket.

As Packy got out of his truck to lock the Widow Creek campground gate, an old maroon Chevy Suburban towing a camper came down the park road and stopped. It contained an old man and a pretty young girl. She didn't look old enough to drive, but traffic enforcement wasn't high on Packy's agenda at the moment.

The old man glowered, but the young girl smiled and said "Hi, sir! Can me and my Paw-paw camp here tonight?"

"Um, sorry, miss, this campground's closed. But there are several informal sites by the creek about a quarter-mile up the road. No facilities, but the creek water is clean."

"Thanks!"

"Say...uh, our other campground is open about ten miles south of here. Full facilities, and some other nice campers. Sure you wouldn't prefer to camp there?"

"Naaah," the old man said. "We come out here to get away from backward-ballcap, underbritches showin', cell-phone yappin' dumbasses with their boom-boxes, hot wheels, barking dogs, little colored lights and screaming brats. We'll stay up the road here."

"Mmm. Can't say as I blame you, but...y'all know about camping in bear country, right? No food—not a piece of candy, not even food smells—in your camper or vehicle, right?"

"Yes sir!" the girl said. "We're experienced campers. We'll string our food a safe distance from our site, and we won't have a crumb in our vehicles. We got bear mace too!"

We also got enough firepower to drop the fucking White House Christmas tree, Hogan refrained from mentioning.

"OK folks," Packy said, stepping back. "Y'all watch out

84

for bears, now, this is...really...bear country."

The old man coughed and cleared his throat. "Actually, officer, we was hoping to find some grizz, we're big photo freaks, see?" Hogan held up the Canon digital camera with the zoom lens that he'd given Loverly for her last birthday. "Could you tell us where we might sight some?"

In your lap, if you aren't careful, Packy thought.

"Well, almost anywhere, sir, but if you drive a few miles up fire trail C-6, up beyond those informal campsites during the day, there's a good chance you might see one crossing that trail. But leave your camper at the campsite, make sure you got plenty of gas in your car, and stay close to it. You don't want to be on foot up there, especially at night."

"You got it boss," Hogan said. "Mucho thanko."

As the tourists drove away, Packy reflexively thought to check their tag number but the Suburban's tag was blocked by the camper, and the tag on the camper was bent and unreadable.

Heck with it, Packy thought, I got to get this chip in my computer, pronto. Besides, some old geet and his teenie granddaughter; what harm could they be to anyone?

Ten minutes later, Packy shoved the memory card into his office computer, and clicked up the photo management program.

Nearly a hundred thumbnail photos appeared on the monitor. As the camera had been triggered by an infrared motion sensor, it had taken many shots of the occasional deer wandering past in the distance, a stray rabbit hopping by. A fox appeared in a greenish night-vision image to gnaw at the doe carcass for a while. Packy raced through the thumbnails. Most of the pictures were simply of the dead doe, since even a bird or a blowing limb could set the camera off.

Packy became more disappointed as he clicked through the thumbnails. Nothing. Then there appeared some day shots of a pack of wolves discovering the corpse shortly after dawn. He recognized the big rangy dominant male of a pack he was aware of.

The camera had taken several shots of the arriving pack and their circling and snarling as the dominants moved in to eat, warning off the submissives who ranged about looking for an opening.

Then Packy leaned forward. Suddenly the wolves had all swung their heads to look at something evidently above and behind the camera's position. In the next shot the wolves had retreated, snarling, and an enormous, early morning shadow was cast across the wolves and the doe. It was the last shot the camera took.

Packy stared, trying to gauge the scale of the shadow.

"Holy shit," he whispered.

Tonny was sick and getting sicker. He dug up what was left of his stolen ditch-bitch and ate it, but he still felt like hell. The digging had been agonizing, since Tonny's left-front foot was so swollen he was limping awkwardly, and even standing in the cold mountain creek no longer helped. His foot throbbed with growing pain, but worse, now he was feeling queasy, hot and dizzy. Now, instead of being able to bully the wolves off their kills, he was growing rapidly closer to becoming one of same.

Tonny sat hard in a cloud of dust, and swung his massive head to relieve his headache and stiff neck. He raised his left front paw to lick it, but the effort hurt too much.

Bear, Tonny thought the bear equivalent of, I am one hurtin' cubby...

Forest Supervisor, Dr. Melony Gaynor, PhD., was madder than usual with her unwanted park-Nazi LEO, Packwood Rudd. He'd ignored her secretary's protest, just barged into her office, and thrown down some stupid trail-cam photos he claimed proved a giant bear.

"Packwood, I've been as lenient with you as any highly skilled manager could be, since I know how traumatizing for you it must have been to find that dead girl the grizzly got. Perhaps next time, you won't ridicule post-event counseling. But that was nearly two years ago, and my patience is expired. This...whatever this is, is certainly no proof of anything, let alone a monster bear! It's a damned tree shadow!"

Packy sighed. "Melo–"

"Doctor Gaynor, if you please."

"Boss! Look at that shadow. Those two little lumps at the top of the shadow—behind the wolves—are ears, I'm telling you! And I interviewed a witness. That's a bear! The damned thing will go twelve feet or more standing."

"Nonsense! Your witness is a retarded drug addict in a different place and time, and I don't see any ears in this shot, I see a simple tree shadow!"

"So...what, Melony...a tree just, what? Just shinnied in there between shots, or was it just a fast grower?"

"The sun is rising!"

"That would make the shadow shorter, not bigger! And, what, those seven wolves are suddenly scared shitless of a *tree*?"

"The camera startled them!"

"Nuts! Look at those pictures. How could they be reacting to the shot they're actually in? And you're saying some tree broke a chain and dragged off a full grown mule deer doe?"

Melony sprang up from her chair.

"I don't know! And what's more, I don't give a damn! Even if it is an aberrant grizzly, so what? Grizzlies *live* here, Packwood, they're our neighbors and our clients. What do you want me to do? Shoot it? Close the Flathead National Forest? Post skull-and-crossbone signs at all the entries? 'Beware of the dinosaurs'?"

"Of course not. Just close that sector between Widow Creek and the border until I can find or photograph this thing and get some handle on how dangerous it may be."

"Oh sure, Packwood. I'm going to tell my boss in Washington that I'm closing part of a public park noted for its grizzly bears, in the height of tourist season, because one of my...LEOs thinks there's a grizzly bear about? Right! I can see it in the papers now: 'Panic stricken special-agent-in-charge warns of giant, killer bear!'"

"Suppose this thing eats another tourist, while you knew it was an uncatalogued rogue? You want to explain that to your boss in Washington?"

"I don't know any such thing about any uncatalogued rogue bear!"

"I do!"

"Enough! I've been the soul of patience and sensitivity with you Packwood, but you have killer bears on the brain. You need a rest from the pressure, and God knows I need a rest from you. You have accumulated over twelve weeks of unused leave time. Go use at least two of them, effective right now! And use them somewhere outside my forest!"

Packy wanted to slam the door on his way out, but he remembered that special-agent-in-charge, Dr. Melony Gaynor, PhD., absolutely hated it when anyone left her office door standing open.

"Close the–. Damn!" Packy heard her say as he stormed down the hall.

Back at his office, after dark, Packy was tapping away at his computer emailing people who needed to know that he would be on vacation for two weeks. To hell with it. He wasn't getting scorched by his bimbo boss for doing his job. Let her deal with this bear.

A little flag on the screen rose to advise him of an inbound email. He called it up:

> From: FBI, Salt Lake City
> To: All US Forest Service Personnel
> Subject: Escapees
> FBI/SLC advises all addressed of the escape
> from the US Marshals Service, Boise Idaho, of the
> following subjects:
> Dwight Calvin Markus, AKA Calvus, BM, 34yoa,

73", 208 lb. Multiple prison and gang tattoos, scar on left cheek, multiple piercings: lips, tongue, nose, ears, nipples, naval, penis, and scrotums.

Mogo Ushwad Mawhani, AKA Cutt, Cutthroat, Cutter, Mogo. MEM, 36yoa, 68", 245 lb. Multiple tattoos of nude women, arms and chest.

Subjects escaped following traffic accident of government automobile while being conveyed by USMS to arraignment for assault, rape, burglary, stolen auto, and armed robbery. NOTE: Subjects have been known to prey upon campers in remote campsites of US, state and local parks and campgrounds, midwest and west. Detain for USMS. CAUTION: Subjects considered armed and dangerous.

Scrotums? Plural? Packy thought, studying the scurrilous looking mug photos of the two sullen escapees. Wonderful. Now I got these two altar boys to worry about.

Fortunately tourist attendance was light because it could still get damned cold up here at night. There were campers at the south campground, but there were a lot of them, and the site was near the headquarters complex. Not much risk there, even if these two felons came this way.

Hmm, Packy considered. There's that girl and her granddaddy way up north of Widow Creek.

What were the odds of these bad dudes going that far out off the beaten path?

Still, Packy thought, these dicks are old for gangers and they'll be looking for soft targets. They're already wanted for rape, so that girl is a factor. I'd feel awful if something happened to them.

Packy sighed and looked at his watch.

Damn. I better drive up there tomorrow and warn them, before I leave. That crabby old geet and the boobsie little teen would be helpless if these two career predators showed up.

CHAPTER TWELVE

Seattle

After lunch, Perry Dinwiddie drove his boss and co-merrymaker Senator Lisa Belle to a studio of North West Public Radio on the UW campus in Seattle. They were met by NWPR personnel and ushered to an anteroom outside the studio where sat Dr. Ermintrude Windgate and the oddest looking girl Perry had ever seen. And that was no small sampling.

"Ah!" said Ermie Windgate as Lisa and Perry walked in. "There you are!"

Nothing gets by you, does it, Lightnin'? Perry thought.

I hope this self-impressed old bat is prepared to back up my interview, Lisa thought, then: Who the weird hell is this?

"Senator Belle," Ermie ignored the Senator's...servant, "I'd like to introduce my best little research assistant, Ms. Bear-Daughter Lowenstein."

Bear what? Perry thought.

Thank Christ this is radio and not TV, Lisa thought, surveying the girl.

Bear-Daughter Lowenstein looked like the Chief's prized daughter, Princess Little Dove, in every B-grade Indian blaster ever filmed, only she wasn't little and she had enough rivets through her lips, ears and classic Jewish nose to get her head ripped off by an MRI machine. She had her red hair in Native American style with feathered braids. She wore a richly beaded, doeskin dress replete with fringes and some sort of beaded leather purse made in China hanging from a plaited leather belt. She also wore knee-length moccasins, which were also heavily beaded, and she had about two pounds of silver-and-turquoise bracelets on each wrist.

"Peace, my sister," said Bear-Daughter Lowenstein, sober as a judge. She held up forked fingers before shaking the senator's hand. She too wrote off Perry as the chauffeur, despite his Obama bearing and his $1400 suit.

Aleah Golda Lowenstein had entered the University of Washington five years ago the expensive private school graduate and only-child daughter of two blind-rich, hopelessly liberal, Mercer Island Jewish lawyers. She had been the quintessentially spoiled-silly, Jewish American princess whose chic designer threads cost more than some of her classmates' cars.

Aleah was, of course, to have studied pre-law, but that lasted about as long as it took Aleah to realize that lawyers, like, really had to, like, you know, study and shit, and actually pass that, you know, like, bar exam thing, before they drove their lavender Mercedes 550 Roadster convertibles to the Galleria to wile away the day shopping for Prada originals. Helloooo? All that, like, reading, you know? I don't think soooo!

So Aleah did what all vacuous freshman girls who can't do anything else do, she changed her major to women's studies. She threw herself into such cutting-edge courses as The Steinem Theory Of Menstruation In Men, and Gender In The Context Of An Excuse For Failure, and White Men As The Anathema Of Society. Predictably, she also stopped shaving anything, swore off deodorant and make-up as oppressive, dressed like a bag lady, pierced nearly every part of herself a needle could penetrate, and generally looked like an extra in *Zombie Witches From Hell*.

Still, God knows how, fulfillment had escaped Aleah Golda Lowenstein. It was then that she accidentally discovered the peace-loving, agrarian, American aboriginals who had been so shamefully, like, genocided by those very same, like, anathemoratic...you know, white male oppressors, man!

So UW's American Indian Studies Department gained its

most devoted, if slightly wattage challenged, student.

To the shock of her mother and the incendiary apoplexy of her father, Aleah legally changed her first name to Bear-Daughter, and gave away all the horribly overpriced designer symbols of her unenlightened life to an ecstatic Goodwill. She now began dressing as a 50s, Hollywood western Indian princess, or the star of some kind of racist porno flick, it could be hard to tell.

Aleah kept her Ferrari, though.

It was when Aleah took that advanced course on The Sow Bear As Metaphor For The Inferiority Of Men, that she devoted herself to the noble grizzly bear.

Perry Dinwiddie thought, man, a mind really is a terrible thing to waste after all.

Lisa wiped her hand on her skirt.

Ermie Windgate said, "I should think it is readily apparent that Ms. Lowenstein is my brightest graduate assistant on the subject of the noble grizzly bear!"

"Ms. Lowenstein," Lisa said, wondering if this twit was packing a tomahawk.

"Bear-Daughter, my sister."

"Uh. Right. And Ms.–mm, Bear-Daughter, your function here today is...?"

"I'm a leading expert in the voice of our friend the noble grizzly bear, my sister."

Perry studied the young woman. If Bear-Bimbo, here, calls fire-woman 'sister' one more time, we're gonna see teeth, hair and eyeballs all over this office, he thought.

I'll kill this moronic cunt if she calls me sister again, Lisa thought.

"Bear-Daughter has made a study of the vocal patterns of grizzly bears, Senator," Ermie said proudly. "She can distinguish the emotions expressed in every sound the noble grizzly bear makes. She's brought some of her extensive library of recorded grizzly bear sounds to enrich our program today!"

"No farts," Lisa said. "Abso—positively, no farts."

"Oh no!" Ermie said, "Of course not, no, we're speaking strictly of vocal sounds here, Senator." Can this amoeba possibly be a state senator? Ermie thought.

"No, no, no," Bear-Daughter said, rolling her eyes. "Strictly vocal emanations, my sister!"

Perry subtly grabbed Lisa by the arm she was drawing back. She was making those little squeaking noises she always made before she went Hannibal Lecter on somebody.

Lisa took a deep breath and thought about capital punishment.

"What's that?" Lisa said, pointing to a peculiar backpack apparatus by Lowenstein's feet.

"Ah!" Bear-Daughter said, brightly. "That is my very own invention. It's a portable sound system! It's a back-pack mounted stereo speaker pack with built in-CD player. I use it at outdoor demonstrations and protests to play the wonderful nurturing sounds of the noble grizzly sow. Today, of course, I will play it only at volume level two, but outdoors, at volume level eight, it sounds exactly like a live noble grizzly bear with full volume and resonance! And believe me, you don't want to hear it at volume level ten."

Hmm, Lisa thought. This goth reject may have a functioning synapse or two after all.

"Excellent," Lisa said.

"Yes! I designed it, and had it built by my boyfriend who builds car stereos!"

Perry said, "You mean, like those things that make cars go thump-a-bump loud enough to be heard blocks away?"

"Right, my brother!"

Do I look like your brother, chick-pea? Perry thought. He'd occasionally had pleasant dreams of dropping grenades into those cars driven about by inconsiderate little punks rattling windows for a quarter-mile around them with their over-priced sound systems.

"So..." Lisa said, "you could take this thing, say, anywhere?"

Like, duh, you primped-up capitalist oppressor. What

do you think I, like, invented it for? Bear-Daughter thought.

"Yes," she said. "It's all battery powered, and back-pack portable. It's like having your very own live grizzly bear right next to you! Listen!"

"That's OK, I–"

Bear-Daughter removed a remote device from her beaded belt purse and keyed it.

"OOOOHRAAAHHHHRRRGGH!" the back-pack roared like rolling thunder in a cave. The anteroom walls actually quivered.

Perry jumped, went for his gun, and said, "Holy shit!"

Lisa flinched, went bug-eyed, and nearly wet her panties.

The nearby receptionist screamed, and did wet hers.

Ermie beamed, proudly.

Some guy wearing headphones burst through the studio door and demanded "What the fuh–hell was *that*?"

"Oops!" Bear-Daughter said, keying other buttons quickly. "Sorry! I forgot I had it set on five! Sorry!"

"We're doing a live interview in here, Miss!" Headphones hissed indignantly. He stormed back through the door.

Lexie and Nerves were now mired in typical evening rush-hour traffic gridlock on southbound I-5 between Tacoma and Seattle. Manual-transmission sports cars were fun on the open road, but in inch-up gridlock they were a damned nuisance.

Nerves had grown bored of sulking over Lexie's having car-jacked him after the encounter with the trooper, so he switched on the FM radio. North West Public Radio was preset, and an interview with some local gay activist was concluding.

'Is that the best you can do?" Lexie said, jokingly, to break the chill that had frozen them since the troopergate incident.

"Hey," Nerves groused, 'I hate Neo-leftist Propaganda Radio too, but it's that or country music or rap."

"Point," Lexie said. "Country all sounds the same anymore. You can't tell one whiny, nasal, boot-scootin' boogie from another since Johnny Cash died. 'Iiiiii'm proud to beeee a Walmart gaaaaal', bash, bash, bash. The country music industry would improve ten times over if somebody would just take all the cymbals away from their ham-handed drummers."

"At least it qualifies as music. 'Rap music' is an oxymoron. Rap is what people who have no musical talent do when they want to pretend they do. It's primitive, stumbling, artless babble-noise. I'll see if I can find another–"

"Wait!" Lexie said holding up her hand. "Listen!"

Nerves turned up the volume.

"...Sawili Ogante, and this is Newest News. I'm thrilled to welcome Washington state senator Lisa Belle, UW professor Emintrude Windgate, and Professor Windgate's graduate research assistant, um, Bear...Daughter... Lowenstein. Welcome to Newest News, ladies!"

"Sawili, I'm so pleased–" Ermie immediately began.

"Peace, my sister," Bear-Daughter said flashing the forked fingers..

There was a moment of dead air.

We should have left Bear-Brains in the lobby, Lisa thought.

"Uh, right," the show host said, "um, peace to you too, Ms. Lowenstein."

It's going to be a long fifteen minute segment, Sawili Ogante thought grimly.

Ermie recovered. 'Sawili, we are so very pleased to be with you today, to share with you the wonderful news about our nature friends, the noble grizzly bear!"

Don't mind me you cackling hens, I'm just the fucking eight-hundred pound gorilla senator in the room! Lisa thought.

"So I hear," Sawili said, but first I want to recognize our

distinguished third guest, the Honorable Senator Lisa Belle of our own 34th district! Senator Belle, thanks for joining us!"

"Oh drat," Nerves said.

"Sssssh!" Lexie hissed. She was getting clutch knee from inching the Porsche southward, bumper-to-bumper, four lanes deep, toward Olympia.

"... and Sawili," Lisa concluded minutes later, "I want to thank my friends, Dr. Ermintrude Windgate, and Ms. Bear, um, Daughter Lowenstein for their expert assistance in today's presentation of the Belle Noble Grizzly Bear Restoration Act. In keeping with my tireless efforts on behalf of the 34th district and all citizens of the great state of Washington, Sawili, I just felt it was my duty—no, Sawili, it is our solemn duty—as responsible shepherds of our planet, to restore one of nature's grandest creatures, the noble grizzly bear to its rightful habitat!"

"Truly impress—" Sawili began.

Like a mortician, Bear-Daughter solemnly intoned, "Would that we could so nobly restore the native American to her rightful habitat as well, my sister."

Walk on my closing line, you little twat!? I'll kill you! Lisa thought.

Perry's huge hand clapped onto Lisa's shoulder which was all that kept her from going Mt. St. Helens on the spot. He knew those peeping noises, appropriately similar to the catastrophic blowout warning on a burger-joint french fry cooker.

Sawili Ogante couldn't wait to get rid of the weird Jewish Indian bear person.

"Yes, uh, well, I'm, I'm sure we all share that, um, worthy sentiment, Ms. Daughter. Now—"

"Lowenstein," Bear-Daughter said. Could it possibly be that this token-negro, info-aparatchik is making light of my sacred name? Bear-Daughter thought. "*Bear*-Daughter Lowenstein."

"Yessss..." Sawili said, gritting her teeth. "Excuse me. Now, Senator Belle, I'd be remiss in my duties as a journalist–"

You'd have to be blind as cave eel, Perry thought, since Lisa's holding up that pink sticky-note to remind you.

"Journalist, my ass!" Nerves roared in the closed car. "You're a leftist propaganda pimp!"

"Sssssh!" Lexie said, reaching to turn up the radio volume.

"–if I failed to ask you about the persistent rumors that you may be casting your proverbial bonnet in the ring for the Washington US Senate seat up for reelection next year. What do you say Senator, will you be trading our Washington statehouse for the US Capitol Senate chamber?"

"Well, Sawili," Lisa said, "I've been so busy looking after my wonderful constituents that haven't thought much about it–"

No more than twenty-five hours a day, Perry thought.

"–but, you know me, Sawili, I'm the perpetual public servant. So if the good citizens of Washington were to feel I could serve them best in the US Senate next year, I'd certainly give it some thought!"

You'd give it one of everything you've got two of, Perry mulled.

"Well, there you have it folks," Sawili said, "you heard it first here on Newest News with Sawili Ogante. Now as we close out this segment, Ms. Lowen–"

"Bear-Daughter, my sis–"

"Bear–fff–Daughter!" Sawili fairly shouted. "Uh, uh-hum, perhaps you would play a few more of those groundbreaking scientific recordings you've made of the noble Grizzly Bear, as we fade to the news."

"Ruuharrgh. Ooarghh. Awnh!" went Bear-Daughter's back-pack recorder, at a civilized volume, as Nerves and Lexie finally began to clear traffic on I-5.

CHAPTER THIRTEEN

All Over the Place

Loverly and Hogan roamed the fire trails of the Flathead National Forest in northwestern Montana, in the old Suburban.

Just as the nice ranger guy had told them, many bears were concentrated around fire trail C-6, high up the timber carpeted mountain. They'd seen a boar and three sows crossing the trail in separate places and they were able to photograph a half dozen bears fishing in a mountain stream. Loverly took pictures while Hogan held a death grip on the Remington shotgun with the slug shots in it. They'd been careful to come in from downwind and keep their distance, so if the bears ever knew of them they gave no sign.

Having determined where the grizzly were plentiful, Loverly and her Paw-paw went in search of a nearby site where the purloined trailer truck rig might be discretely parked long enough to trap a bear. They found four possibles, the best of which was a little concealed glade near the fishing stream. The rig could be parked in there for days and wouldn't be noticed by passing motorists unless someone got out and wandered into the woods to take a whiz.

Tired but satisfied and excited at their success, Loverly and Hogan returned to their camper. Hogan wearily built a fire to warm his bones, and sat down in a lawn chair to enjoy a cold beer. Inside the camper, Loverly got busy on their dinner.

Loverly was about to call Paw-paw in to eat, when she heard a car drawing near. She peered through the camper window to see a gorgeous red Lexus pull into the site. Two men got out. One was a tall, black man with lots of rings and bolts through his ears, lips and nose. The other man was shorter and also dark skinned, but looked more Arab than African. Both were heavily tattooed.

Neither looked like Mormon missionaries.

Blubbo had complained all the long way down to the highway. He trudged along in the darkness behind Runs's pickup, which followed Boot driving the late Sol Pickering's 'borrowed' cattle truck.

Laboriously, and for what seemed like eternity, Blubbo backed along scrubbing out the remnant tire tracks of both vehicles with a pine branch. He wore a headband secured flashlight.

Periodically Runs would stop, walk back with his own flashlight and point to a section he'd missed or hadn't scrubbed completely clean. Blubbo would sigh and rectify the shortfall in his performance.

Blubbo's arms and back ached when he finally reached the pavement, but he reckoned that he'd worked off another fifty pounds in the process, and he had to admit that a starving Comanche hunting party couldn't have tracked the FOCM outlaws on this road.

Runs stopped out on the road. Blubbo threw the pine branches in the woods, got in the truck and peeled off his gloves and hairnet. He was astonished to see something he'd never seen before. The hard-assed old Indian vet actually smiled at him. Blubbo was transfixed with amazement until Runs reached over to slap him on the shoulder.

"Nice work, son," Runs said. Then the smile disappeared and they drove off in pursuit of Boot.

Blubbo was embarrassed because for some unfathomable reason he had to fight back tears as they rolled along.

At Boot's ranch, Blubbo ran to slide open the massive doors to the barn. The outlaws pulled the cattle rig inside, and slid the heavy doors closed. Runs took Boot's guest room, and Blubbo flopped onto his couch. They slept the deep sleep of the just.

The next morning, after a breakfast that would keep
Boot's chickens busy for a week, they donned their hairnets
and gloves and went back to work on the cattle rig.

Blubbo handed pieces of scrap steel, hydraulic hose,
colored wire, and other odd parts to Boot who crawled
about beneath the axles with a welding torch, hammer and
face mask. Once, Boot sent Blubbo to the workshop for
a heavy commercial power drill and some half-inch bits.
Blubbo watched as Boot drilled the insides of the wheels,
then he averted his gaze as Boot would touch off the welder
which buzzed deeply and sprayed sparks on the dirt floor.
Occasionally, Boot would call for some odd compression
containers not unlike spray cans, but smaller and stouter.
These he retrieved from a box labeled Alleskleber Liquaweld.
The box had red capital lettering that said: WARNING!
READ INSTRUCTIONS FOR USE BEFORE
HANDLING!

In the meantime, Runs slowly and carefully went over the
rig, inside and out, looking for anything that could be traced
to the FOCM. He could find nothing, but just to be safe, he
took a shop vac to the whole cabin of the tractor, even under
the mattress in the double-bed sleeper.

Two hours later, Blubbo's exaggerated boredom finally
gave way to curiosity as to what Boot was up to.

"Man, what the hell are we doing?"

Boot slid out and sat up as Runs handed cold, bottled
water to the cowboy and the Indian boy.

"I don't think the kid understands what geniuses we are,
Boot," Runs said.

"Naw, you're right, Runs. In fact, I'd say he might not
actually think we are the smartest two outlaws in the Pacific
Northwest."

"I thought you said this rig was OK," Blubbo said. "So
how come we gotta rebuild the damned thing from bumper
to bumper?"

"It is OK," Boot said. "Old Sol kept his rolling stock
healthy. What I'm doing - what we're doing - is installing

compression bottles onto the exterior walls of the hubs."

Blubbo rolled his eyes as only teenagers can do.

"Oh thanks, Boot. That clears up everything."

"Son," Runs said, "what did we say we were going to do with the bear when we get to the capitol grounds?"

Blubbo sulked. He hated tests.

"Hell, I don't know. Leave it there for the news media to come see, right?"

"Right. So, let's say you're Senator Lisa Belle, whose pet grizzly restoration bill is about to be voted on—"

"Or the cops," Boot said.

Runs nodded.

"Or the state police commander in charge of the capitol security force. Are you going to just leave that truck with the grizzly bear in it sitting there at the capitol steps? Maybe break out some tea and crumpets for the press jackals?"

"Hell no," Blubbo said. "I'm gonna want to move it somewhere, anywhere but there, and fast."

"Bingo," Boot said.

"Behold," Runs said. "It lives."

Blubbo went back into the sulk mode.

"You're dead right, boy," Boot said. They're gonna want that bear out of there sooner than yesterday. So what's to stop them from moving the rig, asap?"

"Duh. We take the keys." Blubbo said.

"Sure we will," said Runs, "but what's to stop them from hot-wiring it and driving it off?"

Blubbo frowned. Runs had a point. Not having the keys had never even slowed Blubbo and his gang buddies down when they'd gone car shopping.

"Suppose we take something off the engine, like the fuel injector?"

"No time," Boot said. "And besides, they'd just call in a heavy truck wrecker and tow it."

"Blow the tires?"

"You're thinking, now," Runs said. "But they could still tow it away, just more slowly. Besides, leaking eighteen tires would take too much time. We got to remember, some cop is going to see us arrive, either in person or on a surveillance camera. We'll only have seconds to dump the truck, run to a getaway vehicle, and split."

"So..." Blubbo said, putting two and two together, "we're...what? Gonna lock the wheels?"

Boot and Runs smiled at each other, then at Blubbo.

"Elementary, my dear Watson," Runs said.

"Who?" Blubbo said.

"Sherlock Holmes had a sidekick named Watson," Boot said.

"Shylock who?"

"Never mind," Boot said. "What we're doing to ole Sol's truck is rigging threaded nipples to the inside of the wheel hubs. When we abandon the truck, I'll pull a switch in the cab which will trigger electrical solenoids that will release a half-quart of pressurized epoxy into all eight tandem brake drums."

Blubbo squinted as his cogs turned.

"Glue?"

"Not just glue, son," Boot said. He held up one of the small stainless steel canisters. "This stuff is wicked. It's a German-made super epoxy that bonds just about anything in about thirty seconds. This stuff will bond spark plugs into engine blocks, even with all that pressure and temperature. It'll glue the wheel drums to the brake shoes."

"Meaning, the wheels are frozen?"

"Better than that," Runs said. "They might replace the wheels, but the hubs will stay welded up. Towing the rig will be impossible in any quick sense. They'll have to replace four entire tandem axle assemblies, or take it apart, crane it onto flatbeds and cart it away."

"In other words," Boot said with a grin, "it'll take them hours just to figure out what's wrong and what to do, and hours more to move the truck, during which time the media will have a Mardi Gras."

"Then won't they just try to get the bear out and move it?"

"Maybe," said Runs. "But they'll have to dart it, get it out of the rig, and haul it. That'll take hours, and experts and equipment to coordinate and achieve, too. By then they can haul the bear anywhere they want to, for all we care. The damage will be done."

Blubbo's eyes suddenly got wide. "Runs, then they'll shoot him!"

"We doubt that," Runs said. "Look at it this way, this whole Lisa Belle bear restoration act thing swings on the preciousness of the 'noble' grizzly bear, so...what?...they're gonna just shoot one dead, right in front of the statehouse? Imagine the media coming to you live from the scene with that delightful item. The environazis would have a miscarriage. Belle's reputation couldn't get any deader any faster than by them shooting or euthanizing a grizz on live TV, and Belle will know it."

Boot said, "Not only that, but no cop is going to blast a caged bear on the capitol steps in front of the media unless he's hard-ordered to by higher authority, meaning the governor, and the governor wouldn't touch that with her worst enemy's finger. So killing it will be the last thing on earth they'll want to do. Not a chance. Not as long as he's safely locked up and no threat to anybody."

Blubbo mulled on all this, and as he did a smile slowly opened his broad, plump face. "You know," Blubbo said solemnly, "It makes me want to puke, but I gotta admit. You guys are pretty smart."

Boot and Runs looked ruefully at each other.

Boot said, "I'm afraid we can't claim a lick of credit for the engineering here, Blub. We just put it together, we didn't think it up."

"Then who did? Oh no...no...don't tell me it was–"
Both Runs and Boot nodded.
"That *Nerves* guy?"

That Nerves guy and Lexie were touring the Washington capitol 'campus,' as it was called.

They'd parked Nerves's conspicuous butt-rocket blocks

away and hiked in to avoid its being photographed on capitol campus surveillance cameras. Nerves wore a broad-brimmed hat and Groucho glasses, big black plastic clear spectacles that had bushy eyebrows, a fake Jewish nose, and a bushy moustache attached to them. Lexie said Nerves looked like a schoolyard weener wagger. He demanded Lexie wear a floppy hat and sunglasses, and both wore gloves. They'd left all watches and jewelry in the Porsche.

"I can't believe I'm dressed like Sophia Loren wearing a hat and gloves in June, and being seen in public with an escapee from the state creepo prison," Lexie complained.

"Hey!" Nerves said, "we have to guard against anybody making us later on surveillance cameras, or lifting our fingerprints, when the bear caper goes down! Do I need to remind you that carelessness can get us *all* locked up in creepo prison?"

"Yeah, yeah."

"And remember, write with your left hand and don't sign your real name to the guest register."

"I got it, I got it, already."

Like most state capitol complexes, Washington's was damned impressive, Nerves had to admit. Not only was the capitol itself, officially called the Washington Legislative Building, an imposing work of splendid domed architecture, but it was beautifully coordinated with the Washington Supreme Court Building across a narrow, grassy ellipse, and with the nearby office buildings.

It was all that was coordinated about government, Nerves considered.

The Washington capitol campus overlooked Capitol Lake, the southernmost extension of Budd Inlet, itself an extension of Puget Sound. The entire facility was suitably elegant, yet it retained a ruggedly Pacific Northwest persona unique among such facilities. Stunning trees of twenty varieties were in abundance, including towering firs and western cedars, enormously spreading maples and a giant oak. Lexie walked about beneath them staring up in awe.

Nearly concealed in a grove of such magnificent trees

just west of the statehouse, sat the brick governor's mansion. Nerves said it looked like Casa Del Dracula, but Lexie scolded him.

"It's Georgian style architecture," Lexie read from a brochure, "I think it's beautiful."

"Humbug. More Transylvanian style, if you ask me."

"I didn't."

From the gate, Nerves could see at least eighteen white columns on the governor's mansion. He smirked. "Did you know that Pat Conroy has a theory that there is an inverse relationship between the number of white columns on a house and the intelligence of the residents?"

"Pat who?"

"Pat Conroy, the famous writer, for Christ's sake! *South of Broad, Prince of Tides, The Great Santini, Lords of Discipline*?"

"*Lords of Discipline*...hmmm...sounds like some ex-clients of mine."

"Not that kind of discipline!"

"I had some pretty inverse relationships with those guys too."

"Pulleeeeze!"

Nerves was dumbfounded to learn that he could take pictures without restriction not only of the campus grounds, but in the tourist-accessible part of the statehouse as well, and he did. He made copious mental notes and measurements of the grassy ellipse and parking area between the statehouse and the supreme court building, the latter known, rather pretentiously Nerves thought, as The Temple of Justice.

Nerves looked for surveillance cameras but, while he was certain there were dozens of them, none were in obvious evidence. The capitol campus was the people's facility after all, and no one wanted a tour to feel like daddy-day at a federal penitentiary.

Earlier, Nerves and Lexie had noted that the rear, or south, entrance to the statehouse was at ground level, while the north entry facing onto the supreme court building across the ellipse had broad, high, multilevel steps similar to

106

those on the US capitol.

It was clear to Nerves and Lexie that the action side of the statehouse was the ersatz 'front', facing the ellipse and the supreme court building. The 'rear' was more of a service entrance, and the surrounding parking area was cramped by narrow access, while the ellipse side was far more open and accessible by a large stolen truck with a hijacked grizzly bear in it.

Moreover, there was much more open space between the two imposing granite buildings to accommodate news media microwave vans, and the expanse of unrestricted visibility was immensely greater.

It was clear that Operation Grizz would take place at the foot of the north capitol steps for all to see.

"OK!" Nerves, in his Groucho glasses, announced after an hour hiking the grounds and photographing. "I got what we need. Let's beat it out of here before somebody starts paying attention to us."

"Who'd pay attention to anybody in raving pervert glasses?" Lexie said. "Besides, we're not leaving until I tour the statehouse," Lexie said.

"What for? The whole deal goes down out here! No bear inside the statehouse, remember? Even if we could get one in there, which is impossible, the whole protest would blow up in our faces."

"We drove all the way over here to libby-land with its congestion, and traffic, and over-priced everything, and hordes of yatata-yatata neurotic zombies, and I'm going to see one of the few good things over here that happens to be free. Beside, it's our capitol, Nerves, it's our building too."

"Not on the planet Washington it's not. Libs rule over here. Did you know that clueless Belle woman actually sued the people of Washington to make it easier to raise their taxes?"

"Well I don't see any 'libs only' sign on the door. I want to tour it."

"Deliver me," Nerves wheezed. He trotted up the granite steps after Lexie.

Calvus Markus and Mogo Mawhani had been positively delighted when a drunk-driving, hockey-mom in a mini-van full of kids blew through a Boise red light and hammered the Crown Vic in which US Marshals were transporting them back to court.

They were also deeply indebted to the bleeding heart administrator who decided the marshals couldn't handcuff prisoners when they were riding in a vehicle prisoner cage, but the icing on the cake was that, while no one in the Vic was seriously hurt, the right rear door had popped open in the impact.

The van had spun and sprayed four unrestrained kids onto the intersection, and the marshals—thinking their prisoners were locked in the car-cage—bailed out to triage the children. Calvus and Mogo could have made the Olympics with the speed they split the scene with, before the marshals noted their empty car.

There was an upside and a downside to this, Calvus and Mogo knew. The upside was they were free, when a judge was about to bury them so far under a prison that a coal-mine rescue team couldn't find them.

The distinct downside, though, was that the US Marshals Service hated losing a prisoner worse than they hated Nancy Pelosi, which translated to them tearing Idaho and Montana apart molecule by molecule until they found these two bastards, with the motivated assistance of every other badge in the business.

As much as it pained them to have to do so, the marshals had disseminated descriptions of Calvus and Mogo all over the US, especially to Forest Service law enforcement, since the dastardly duo were known to rob and rape campers in isolated campsites.

This was exactly what Calvus and Mogo intended to do, as such soft targets were easy take-downs, and cops were few and far between in the national forests.

So it came to be that, about sundown, a stolen red Lexus

turned into a remote outback campsite in the Flathead
National Forest and stopped before a Suburban and a camp
trailer. Out climbed two of the ugliest guys the crusty old
goat in the lawn chair had ever seen.

Calvus and Mogo had been making jokes about how
their righteous living must have been behind their recent
good fortune. As they surveyed the only occupied campsite
they'd been able to find away from the forest headquarters,
they knew they were right.

The boys from Boise were thinking the old man in the
lawn chair by the campfire wouldn't have much money, but,
then, he'd be a pushover too.

And then, yes, Virginia, there is a Santa Claus, the
sweetest little piece of ass in six states came out of the
camper bearing a beer for the old man, and she couldn't be a
day over fourteen, maybe fifteen. Hooooooly shit. The boys
were already looking at life in supermax for armed robbery
and rape, so what did they have to lose by tapping this little
princess and ripping off her granddaddy? Truth be known,
since they were going down for the duration on the three-
strikes rule anyway if they were ever caught, what'd they
have to lose by leaving no witnesses behind?

Period.

Calvus and Mogo winked at each other and bumped fists
as they swaggered near.

"Evenin' gents", the old man said.

"Hi!" the titsy little girl said pleasantly.

Calvus and Mogo studied the girl. She wore sneakers,
tight jeans and a baggy, man's sweatshirt with the sleeves
rolled up, but they could tell she was ripe. When you've been
in the joint, wolverine pussy starts looking good, but both
men knew they'd had a real stroke of luck tonight.

"Welllll...hey there, hot stuff," Calvus said, his eyes
moving up and down the girl. He snatched the beer from
her hand. "Thanks for the beer."

"Why don't you trot in there and get me one of them
too, bitch?" Mogo said, with a raspy life-long-smoker's voice.

The girl paused briefly, but then she said "Sure!" and in a

moment she was back with another dew-covered can. She set it down on the concrete campsite table, rather than hand it to Mogo.

Calvus was irked because the old man had a smirk on his face, instead of being terrified as he'd expected. He should at least be pissed 'cause Mog just called his little ho a bitch.

"Whatchu laughin' at, you old fuck?" Calvus demanded.

The old man just held up open hands and shrugged as though swearing the whole scene off, but he kept that damned grin on his gray-bearded face.

Mogo sucked on his beer. He reached to the small of his back with his left hand and withdrew the 9mm Glock pistol they'd found in the Lexus when they'd carjacked it from a woman lawyer outside a Boise office park. He spun the gun around his finger, as no one but an idiot would do.

"How funny you thinkin' now, mothafuckah? Huh?"

To Mogo's and Calvus's surprise, the old man now began to wheeze with easy laughter, shaking his head.

Calvus was confused. White people didn't laugh when he and Mog made their acquaintance. Even the fine lookin' little ho didn't seem appropriately terrified. Calvus found this unsettling.

Mogo stuck the pistol toward the old man in the lawn chair.

"S'pose I cap you wrinkly ass, you old mothafuckah!" Mogo snarled. "See how funny you think it is then!"

Yeah, Calvus thought, this is more like it. "Yeah, Mog! Cap that laughy-assed old motha–"

This is where their good living began to fail Calvus and Mogo. There was a thunderous, boom and blinding yellow flash, followed by Mogo's stolen Glock disappearing in parts and Mogo jumping around holding his hand and yelling like he'd just been caught in the prison showers by the whole damned Aryan Brotherhood.

At the blast, Calvus jumped three feet straight up. He was baffled. He looked to see the sweet little girl sighting down the barrel of an automatic pistol with a bore like an uncovered man-hole. She shouted something, which was a little hard to make out with her high voice and his ears ringing so, but it sounded like: "Freeze! Or I'll blow your dangles to Minnesota!"

Minnesota? Calvus thought, struggling to order the scene. He crouched, unsure whether to run, go for his knife, or chill and hope the psycho ho didn't smoke his black ass too.

Mogo continued to howl and dance with agony, holding his bleeding hand, but what unnerved Calvus worse was that the old man was about to cry from laughing. He wheezed, gasped for breath, then wheezed in laughter again. Was he a nut?

"Minnesota?" the old man said with strain, then burst forth in another howl of laughter. "*Minnesota*!"

"Well Jane Austen wouldn't say the h-word, Paw-paw! And Minnesota was the first place that came to mind! Sue me!"

Totally clueless, Calvus smiled weakly and sought to break the ice a little. "Is Jane, like, Stone-Cold Steve Austin's wife?"

"No!" Loverly snarled.

"Not a problem, ma'am," Calvus said instantly.

Mogo sank to his knees and moaned, still clutching his left hand with his right.

"Mothafuck, that hurts! Aaaaah!"

"Minnesota!" the old man howled, slapping his knee rapidly and nearly choking with his laughter.

"Da fuck?" Calvus erupted. "Are y'all fuckin' crazy? Damn, old man, tell this kid to watch that mothafuckin' gun!"

The old man wiped his tears and sniffed. He tried to speak, but broke up in laughter again.

"Minne-goddamn-sota!" the crazy old geet wailed.

"*Enough* already, Paw-paw! It...it just came to mind!"

The little kid with the cannon was now angry, which didn't go very far to settle Calvus's nerves.

"Hey man, don't piss her off! And tell her about that mothafuckin' gun, man!"

"Aaaah heee..." the old man said, gasping. "Hell, son, I have told her, many times. What'd I tell you about shooting folks, little darlin'?"

"I know, I know!" the girl said. "Only that Mr. Rogers guy on stone-age TV—"

"Roy!" the old man said.

"OK! You said only Roy Rogers tries to shoot guns outta bad guys' hands. You always said I should aim center of mass, double-tap 'em, and then give 'em one up the nose, 'cause dead guys don't testify!"

"Whaaaat!?" Calvus said, his voice cracking. "You tol' her *that*? Up the mothafuckin' *nose*!? Man, what kind of parent tells a kid a thing like that? Are you fuckin' nuts?"

"But I was afraid if I double-tapped him, he'd do a death clench like you told me dead guys will do sometimes, and he might shoot you, Paw-paw! So I made judgement call like you always said!"

The old man thought this over while Calvus gaped in horror, completely struck for words.

"Hell, little darlin', now that you put it that way, you done good! That's my girl!"

The girl smiled for just a flash. "Thanks, Paw-paw!"

"You mothafuckahs are nuttier than a Georgia pecan patch!" Calvus squeaked.

"Shut up, Einstein," the old man said. "You boys are goddamn lucky me and little darlin' here are busy tonight, or we'd haul y'all into town and give you over to the damn sheriff. Now, you got about five seconds to get your sorry asses back in your Jap Cadillac and haul balls toward... *Minnesota*!" The old man blasted with laughter again and slapped his knee.

"Paw-paw!"

"Where your balls almost got to before you!" the old man howled at his guests.

Calvus could be counseled. He knew when to shut up and take three steps mister toward the door. He headed for the car.

"Hey!" the old man growled. "Take this sack of shit with

you. And listen to me, good, son! We see y'all again, and we'll give you both one in the gut. It'll take y'all three days to die out here if the bears don't get you first."

The red Lexus could have taken the NASCAR pole at Daytona as it left.

"Who the hell goes camping in a hundred-grand Jap Cadillac?" the old man groused, sipping his beer. "You done damn good, little girl! Let's eat. I'm hungry!"

"Me too, Paw-paw!"

What a fun trip this was turning into! the little girl thought.

CHAPTER FOURTEEN

Flathead National Forest

Tonny felt like hell. His left-front foot throbbed so badly he could barely put any weight on it. He felt hot all the time, and he couldn't even keep delicious maggot-infested elk guts down. He was hungry, sick, and in pain.

Bear, Tonny thought miserably, as he limped through the dark woods, I got a bear of a toothache all over my foot.

Then he stopped, stood up to a twelve foot observation level and sniffed. He'd been following a very slight sniff of food barely detectable, borne from a long way off on the night breeze. But now he heard a noise that didn't belong in the forest.

Tonny's huge leathery nose twitched.

Urngh? he thought.

Only the thought of drillin' that tight little ho could have gotten Calvus to agree to traipse through the sticks in the dark with Mogo. He'd told Mog he was nuts, that they should cover a couple of states fast, 'cause if the marshals found them it would be: 'Bang! Bang! Bang! Halt, or I'll shoot.'

But Mog was over the edge. He'd screamed in rage as they'd sped down the road from the campsite with the crazy old white man and the psycho bitch. He'd wrapped his bleeding thumb in his shirt tail but his hand still throbbed. Worse, what passed for his manhood had been dissed big-time.

"No mothafuckin little kid shoots me and lives!" Mogo had roared. "Turn this mothafuckin thing around! We gon' go back there, we gon' kill that old bastard and stick that little bitch 'til she squeals, and then we're mothafuckin gon' kill her too! Turn around!, mothafuckah!"

Calvus sighed and rolled his eyes as he slowed to turn.

"Ain't you been shot enough for one night?"

""Fuck that! Little bitch got the drop on me, or I'd a killed her! Let's get back up there! Move!"

"Tell you what, mothafuckah, let's see you go take the bullet bitch empty-handed. I'll watch from out in the woods. Kid shoots like Annie goddamn Oakley."

"Shut up! We'll stop a hundred yards short of the campsite, and make it through the mothafuckin' woods, come up behind 'em. They'll be going to sleep soon. We'll bust in, git that little bitch 'fore she knows what hit her. We'll tie her up, off the old man with her gun, and then we'll take our sweet time with Angie Oakie whatshername. Come morning, we'll shoot her too, dump 'em in that lake, run the Lexus in after 'em. We'll take the Suburban and the camper. Nobody will look for us in no infidel camping rig, and I'll bet there's at least one more gun in that camper!"

Calvus wasn't inspired, but he had to admit that he really wanted to slip the wonder wand to that kid. Besides, Mogo had a point about changing vehicles. Even Calvus knew a fire-engine red Lexus wasn't the ideal low-profile getaway car. And Mog was probably right about more guns in that camper.

More guns, and a new ride, Calvus thought. And that tight little ass too. Cool.

Forest Service law enforcement officer Packy Rudd had packed for the two weeks vacation his despised boss had insisted he take forthwith. Cleaning up a lot of pre-vacation loose ends had taken several hours longer than Packy had thought it would. There was one more thing he needed to check off his list before he got some sleep. In the morning, he'd split for Washington to see his latter-day hippie sister who lived in some clatch of Woodstock rejects way up in remote Okanogan County near the border.

Packy locked his Forest Service truck, climbed into his battered old Isuzu Trooper, and turned north out of the parking lot.

He had to drive up to that campsite north of Widow Creek, and warn that old man and his granddaughter about these two bad numbers who escaped the marshals in Boise. There wasn't much chance they'd come this way, and besides, they were probably already caught by now. The computer said these two criminal master minds had jacked a bright red Lexus.

But, just to be safe...

Tonny felt dizzy and sick, so he wasn't at his tracking prime, but he could swear he smelled two-legs on the cool night air. In spite of his miserable health, the idea of snarfing a warm two-leg had its uplifting effects. Unable to run like he normally could, Tonny had been reduced to stealing carrion, and, while he was a bear of broad and cultured tastes, he was tired of cold-cuts. The flavor of a hot, fresh meal was so much richer, especially when they wiggled as you swallowed them. It went a long way toward relieving a bear's depression.

With this pleasant distraction from his illness and aching foot, Tonny limped away through the moonlight with what passed for a smile on an eighteen-hundred-ninety-six pound grizzly bear.

"Listen, Daniel Boone," Calvus said in a tight whisper, "you make anymore goddamn noise bustin' this brush and we ain't gonna have a chance in hell of catching them two asleep! You gonna wake up the mothafuckin marshals in Boise!"

"Fuck you, twinkle toes, they'll probably smell your stink first! There it is!"

Mogo pointed through the thinning woods at the

moonlit campsite. The fire had been doused and the camper was dark.

"Listen," Mogo hissed, holding his hand up to reduce the throbbing. "We move up quiet, listen for a while, make sure mothafuckahs be asleep. Them campers are built real light for towing, so we'll take us a big log, slam the door right over the lock. You go in first and–"

"Fuck you. This crazy shit's your idea, so you gon' be the entry hero! If that little killer come on like the mothafuckin' US Marines again, she can warm up on *your* ass!"

"Alright! But that means I get her first, and you got to settle for sloppy seconds!"

"I'll take my chances, dude."

"Then I'll jump the little bitch, make sure she don't get to her gun. You land on that old man. We got to move fast, Cal! Hell, all these redneck crackers got more guns than the mothafuckin' 82nd Airborne Division. We'll tie 'em up with coat hangers or rope or whatever they got."

"Got cha."

"Shoot the old fart right in front of the kid to get him outta the way, and get her mind right. Then by God, we'll make that little cunt pay for what she done to me."

Calvus was getting stiff thinking about the kid when he thought he heard a stick snap behind them.

"Hey man," Calvus said to Mogo, "what the fuck was that?"

I must be living right! Tonny thought the bear equivalent of. He couldn't believe his luck. Even though the two-legs had tied their food up in one of those damnable bags hung from a tree limb, two of them were now all hunched over doing their squeaky thing right smack under the food bag! Party time!

"Oooooghhh," Tonny said, and stood up to get a better look.

"What?"

"*Listen*, mothafuckah! They's somethin' out there!"

Now Mogo heard it too. It was faint and hard to distinguish for the wind in the trees, but it had a deep resonance like a distant engine running.

Only it had a rising and falling rhythm, sort of like something...breathing.

"Man, what the fuck *is* that?" Calvus squeaked, spinning about.

Mogo whirled around like Calvus had, and emitted a small squeak in his throat.

Neither man had ever found it necessary to be afraid since they'd turned into ruthless thugs in their mid-teens, but it all came back now like riding a bicycle. The sheer shock of a massive, hairy animal of that bulk and height, silhouetted against the moonlight, that close, was as paralyzing as a taser hit in the nuts.

Bigfoot! Mogo scraped together enough sparking synapses to think. That *ain't* no mothafuckah' in no gorilla suit!

One of them wooly mastadongs! Calvus thought. Them reincarnation fools finally made one outta DNA!

Both men reflexively tried to suck enough breath to scream, but all either could manage was a sort of hoarse croaking version of *muth-a-fuuuuuuuck*!!!

Both men tried to use the other as a launch fulcrum for the panic-galvanized run of their lives. They emitted whimpering gasps as branches tore at their faces and sleeves. They fell, lurched to their feet and ran again.

They were not delighted by the crash and crack closing fast behind them, let alone that soul-numbing, hollow grunting.

Out on the fire road, Packy's Trooper was now parked in the darkness alongside an apparently abandoned red Lexus. It didn't take NCIS to put two and two together here. Packy drew his pistol from his bag and stuck it in his belt. He pulled out his cell phone and started punching numbers as he drove up the moonlit road with no headlights on, toward that site where the old man and the girl were camped. Safely, he hoped.

Mogo's mojo ran dry. On his wild bolt through the dark forest only slightly behind Calvus, he ran under a low limb that took him about eye level, snapped his neck, and flopped him on his back in the pine needles, deader than Lenin.

Calvus heard the two thumps of Mogo checking out behind him, but he also still heard that wooly mastadong grunting and busting timber, so he didn't even glance back. What a break, Calvus thought, inasmuch as he could think at the moment. Maybe that thing will eat Mog and let me go!

Tonny wallowed to a painful stop by the steaming two-leg under the tree. He sniffed it, and figured it wasn't even close to its use-by date. With his good front foot he crushed the very late Mogo Mawhani's head to hold him place while he opened wide and sank his steak-knife-sized teeth into Mog's tattooed midsection.

Ahhh! Tonny thought, munching contentedly, blood running down his jowls. The pause that refreshes!

Packy slammed on the Trooper's brakes, sliding in the fire-trail dirt. A tall black man whose dark face gleamed with sweat had just exploded out of the woods on the right at a dead run. He turned hard toward Packy without slowing a nanosecond.

Together with the red Lexus and the paucity of black people in northwest Montana, Packy didn't need to be a profiler to know he'd come upon one of the US Marshals' escapees, probably the Markus subject.

Packy ripped up on the hand brake lever and bailed out just as the black man sprinted by him. Packy crossed his wrists and sighted his flashlight and pistol on the subject now fleeing toward the red Lexus many yards away. He shouted: "Federal officer! Freeze!"

He got a somewhat atypical response. It was croaky, gasping, it broke keys as it faded fast down the road: "Fuuuuck you...mothafuckah! *Shoot* me!"

Packy's mind was racing to determine if he could justify to investigators his shooting even a fleeing felon in the back, particularly since the suspect didn't appear to be armed and wasn't exactly threatening him. At this moment, luckily for the still pedaling Calvus, Packy was distracted by a profoundly unsettling noise from behind him, somewhat into the woods he judged. It had sounded very odd, sort of like something very big...well...belching.

Hogan usually went outside the camper to take a whiz because he liked to watch the stars when he pissed. But he too was distracted by a host of really weird noises emanating from the dark woods beyond the campsite clearing: thumps, grunts, distant shouts, car doors whumping, strained car engines roaring. He hurried back inside.

"Wake up, little darlin'," Hogan said, shaking his beloved granddaughter gently.

"What it is it? What time is it?" Loverly said sleepily, then, wide awake and alarmed, "Are you OK, Paw-paw?"

"I'm fine, sweetheart, but we're packing outta here."

"What? Now?"

"Yep. Let's boogie. Some strange shit going on outside."

"What?"

"I don't know, but I got a hunch we don't need to be part of it. Let's roll."

"OK, Paw-paw!"

Packy got the Trooper turned around and stood on it,

but Calvus had made it to the Lexus. Now all Packy could see was a blinding cloud of dust refracting in his headlights. Furiously, while he drove as fast as he dared in the dust, he pegged 911 on his cell phone. "Damn!" he swore as the phone told him his call could not be completed as dialed.

Packy followed the dust at every fork or turn, and it was clear the Markus suspect was headed for the highway. The dust was slowing Packy's Trooper to a relative crawl, and he had to admit that if the suspect could drive at all, it wouldn't be hard to out run an SUV in a high-performance Lexus LS. Fortunately, Packy knew, most crooks couldn't drive worth a damn, and were typically hyped-up, drugged and/or drunk, hence a pursuing officer needed only stay with them until they wrecked.

This gospel proved correct yet again. When Packy got to the highway, and looked a hundred yards to his right down the pavement, he found a Volvo road tractor and a shipping container on a flatbed trailer stopped with a red Lexus LS wrapped tightly around and slightly under the big truck's front bumper and grill.

As Packy slid to a stop at the scene, he saw the white male trucker, obviously shaken, gaping at the steaming, red wreckage molded around his truck's front end.

"Are you OK?" Packy called, scrambling to the mangled Lexus.

"Ran out in front of me!" the driver said, gasping. "He just blew through the stop sign! I never even saw him!"

"I believe you, driver! Take it easy! Get 911 on the phone if you can. Tell them highway 93 at Border Mountain Road!"

Packy wrenched open the warped passenger door to find the suspect wadded up in the right seat.

The bloody Markus suspect looked blearily at Packy, and mumbled some odd word twice. Then he slumped. Though his eyes remained open, Packy had seen dead eyes before, and CPR was not a viable option even if it wouldn't require tools to extract the 'victim' first.

When the first of the Montana Highway Patrol arrived,

Packy was able to order his thoughts to a degree.

What had that animal noise in the woods been? Given its volume and resonance, recently discovered evidence of a monster grizzly, and a still missing escapee, Packy had a disturbing theory.

And what the hell was the Markus suspect trying to say as he died? Packy knew he must have misunderstood, for it had sounded like: "Mastadong! Mastadong!"

CHAPTER FIFTEEN

Olympia

"Washington State Patrol, Capitol Security Detachment. Trooper Mendez speaking, how may I help you?"

"Jesus Christ, Jose, they make you spout that whole goddamn mouthful every time you have to answer a phone?"

"Hey, super trooper Bruce Murtry, as I live and breathe. Yeah buddy, hell, we used to have to say 'Washington State Patrol, Capitol Security Detachment. Trooper Mendez speaking, how may I help you, *sir*?' 'til women starting crying sexism. It's all just one of the exciting bennies for getting assigned to the pious plenipotentiary palace of plump politician pigs perennially pissing on the proletarian plebiscites."

"Ah jeez, you really need to get back on the road..."

"Did you know Senator Lisa Belle, actually sued the very people who elected her, trying to overturn the super-majority for enacting tax measures so these clowns can soak the working taxpayers more easily? Is that a brain-sucking abortion of government or what?"

"Enough already. You're giving me a headache. You've been the governor's babysitter too long. You're starting to smell like a politician."

"Ooh, you're brutal, Brucie. How's life on the road, where the real troopers play?"

"Well, I'm out on the road, now that you mention it, and I'm looking at something I thought you might need to know about."

Trooper Mendez pulled a pen and scratch-pad near. "Oh yeah?"

"I pulled some shit-bird over for speeding, and now I'm watching a long string of horse trailers go by, with horses in 'em. I mean we're talking maybe twenty of 'em and they're all in a tight little convoy."

"So? It's a Monday, I grant you, but there're horse clubs all over the state. This time of year they could be going to any number of riding events. What's that got to do with me?"

"I'm getting there, Jose. Well, see, running right along with these horse freaks are about thirty bike freaks."

"Motorcyclists?"

"No, pedal-bikey types. Got their velocipedes on racks on their cars."

"That is odd. You sure they're running together, Bruce?"

"Sure looks like it, dude. Now I figure, you got your big-hat, eastside cowboy crowd in their giant-assed, dually pickup trucks and loaded horse haulers, running a happy little convoy with your westside Volvo, Jetta, Saab, Mercedes types racking their expensive bicycles. Only these are all fat-tired mountain bikes they're toting. Not a Lance Armstrong crotch-rocket in the bunch. Does that seem likely to you? I mean, generally the manure bombers and the pedaling path plowers are always bitching at each other for messing up the outback trails."

"No, it doesn't sound right. Where are they?"

"Southbound I-5, milepost 114."

"Shit. That clinches it, they're coming here. About twenty horse rigs and thirty pedalers, you say?'

"Rough guess. Have fun, crime fighter."

"Thanks for the heads-up, Bruce. Watch your ass out there."

"Who's your daddy, Jane!? Who's your daddy, Jane!?" Perry Dinwiddie grunted like a grizzly chasing escaped convicts through the woods.

From her position bent over the people's desk in her Cherberg Building office on the capitol campus, Lisa Belle answered "You are, Tarzan! Unh, unh, unh! You, oh Lord of the Apes!"

Lisa was a stone psycho for the Tarzan and Jane game. Perry wasn't so sure he liked being called an ape, but what the hell, sex and women were crazy to begin with, so, whatever turned fire-woman on.

The intercom dinged. Caroline's voice said "Excuse me, Senator Belle?"

"Aaaaah!" Lisa bellowed. She hit the speaker mode button. "I said–unh, unh–no calls, Caroline!"

In the outer office, Caroline's expression of disapproval at all the thumping and humping in the background would've puddled titanium. *I earned a master's in poly-sci to answer phones for an ill-tempered troop whore!?* she thought.

"Ah, I know, Senator, but Sergeant Gordon of the security detachment just called. He said you might want to look out your window. I looked, and I think he's right."

Lisa struggled to hike up her pantyhose as she perp-waddled to her third floor window which overlooked the treed lawn and the parking area between the Cherberg Building and the capitol dome.

"Ooooh shit. What the demented voter hell is this?"

Perry stowed Mr. Binkie, who was tuckered out anyway, and joined Lisa at the window. He looked down on a bunch of trucks and horse trailers and what appeared to be a John Wayne movie saddling up. On the other side of the parking lot there were dozens of bike freaks unracking bicycles from their foreign cars.

"Looks like round-up at the Tour De France to me," Perry said.

"It's that tight-assed mountain bike bunch, and the horse-shit hicks! There's only one reason they could be coming here together, they want to bitch about the bear bill!"

"Gee. Ya think?"

"Fuck you!"

"Again?" Perry chortled.

"Ooooooh!" Lisa groaned, watching the stupid horsey

fudds in jeans, gaudy, pearl-buttoned shirts and giant hats mount up, and the bikey bunch in their overpriced tight shorts, space-cadet helmets and safety-lime vests, striding their toys.

Shortly, the cowboys and cowgirls rode those stinking animals onto the lawn under her window, and the pedaling piss-ants started–oh, damn–unfurling big banners that read: NO GRIZZLIES IN THE OKANOGAN! and GRIZZLIES IN SEATTLE PARKS FIRST! and MOUNTAIN BIKERS DON'T TASTE GOOD! It was the smaller, hand-painted banner that read DOES A BELLE SHIT IN THE WOODS? that really bubbled Lisa's blood.

A few of the mounted men and women carried signs that said: NORTHWEST HORSEMEN DON'T WANT TO BE RIDING THE ENTREE! and RESTORE GRIZZLIES TO VASHON ISLAND FIRST! and the especially clever DON'T BE CARELESS, LEAVE US BEARLESS!

Lisa looked for what she dreaded and they were there, those fucking microwave trucks with TV logos emblazoned on them. Oh no!

The lunatic horsey freaks started trotting about in a circle, rearing their horses up, waving their hats and anything else they thought would draw media attention to their banners and signs. But most galling was the little chorus of bikies chanting "Belle, Belle, go to hell! Belle, Belle, go to hell!"

Why should such a dedicated public servant as me have to be treated with this disrespect? Lisa thought, incensed. She fondly recalled the touching scene in Dr. Zhivago where the czarist cavalry rides those punk Leninists down in the street and hacks them up with sabers. Oh what Lisa wouldn't give for a troop of Russian saber hackers right now.

Lisa stormed to the intercom and keyed it.

"Caroline! Get Sergeant–"

"Gordon on the phone and–"

"–tell him to–"

"Get the unwashed masses off the lawn. Yes ma'am, I already have. He says he can't, that it's the people's right as long as they don't damage state property."

"Screw that communist crap! Tell him they can't just show up like this, they need a demonstration permit or something! What are we paying him and his gunmen for anyway?"

"I told Sergeant Gordon you'd say that ma'am, but he says they don't need a permit. Something about that annoying First Amendment thingy."

"I don't believe this!"

"It gets better, ma'am. There's a butchy looking woman in black tights and a helmet, and a Wilford-Brimley-ringer cowboy in the waiting room. They say they represent the Pacific Northwest Mountain Pedalers, and something called Back Country Horsemen of Washington. In fact...ah, they're walking in here as I speak."

"Ah, shi–uh shoot."

"They want to deliver their petitions to you."

"Tell them I'm busy with prior appointments, so just leave them on–"

"I did, ma'am, but they say they aren't leaving until they deliver their petitions directly to you."

"Motherf–!" Lisa began to shriek, but Perry clapped a hand over her mouth, and Caroline flipped off the intercom.

CHAPTER SIXTEEN

East of the Cascades, West of the Rockies

Unaware that their case was being pleaded in a more conventional manner in Olympia, the Free Okanogan County Movement was doing mission planning for Operation Grizz. That name didn't have the pizazz of the 'Boston Tea Party,' but there were important things to be concerned about now.

Nerves had become an obnoxious General Patton wannabe since he and Lexie had returned from Olympia. He was getting on everybody's real nerves with his fanatic obsession to details, but the other six revolutionaries had to admit that he was the brains behind Operation Grizz, as scary as that thought was.

So, reluctantly, everyone suppressed the urge to choke the eyes out of Nerves.

Hogan and Loverly had come back with lots of photos, maps, brochures and adventures to relate. Everyone was excited to learn that there were bears out the wazoo in the Flathead National Forest, and a suitable trapping spot had been located.

There was concern over the strange activity Hogan and Loverly had experienced on the night they'd left, especially the not-so-trivial matter of Loverly having *shot* some stranger, albeit one who needed it.

Nerves was worried about the shooting, so he checked online for news reports in northwestern Montana on the night in question.

"My stars!" Nerves said, at Loverly's computer in the little room off the rear of Winslow's Gun and Pawn. "Those guys were escaped convicts!"

"Really?" Loverly said. "I don't feel so bad about shooting him a little bit."

"I knew they smelled," Hogan said. "Who goes *camping* in a Jap Cadillac? Nice shooting, little darlin'."

"Thanks Paw-paw!"

Lexie rolled her eyes.

"No kidding!" Nerves said. "They escaped while being transported to court for...damn...robbery, rape, and assault! Nice shooting indeed, Loverly."

Loverly beamed at the additional congratulation from the group, including Lexie. Even Blubbo, who would've given his left nut for a chance to shoot a white man, cracked a smile that Loverly did not overlook.

"One of them was found in that wreck you guys saw the night you left," Nerves continued. "The other one is 'still at large'."

"Good," Hogan said with enthusiasm. "Maybe we can plug his ass too, when we go back."

"You think, Paw-paw?" Loverly asked with excitement.

Nerves looked up from the computer, his temples pulsing. "*May* I suggest," he said with an edge, "that we might accomplish our mission...a little more discretely...if we don't leave...a trail littered with dead *bodies* behind us!"

"Well," Hogan said, his feelings bruised, "we could throw the body in that lake."

"No *bodies!*" Nerves snarled.

"Ditto," Lexie said.

"OK, OK. Long as he don't stick another gun in my face."

The FOCM kicked the shooting and the wreck and news around for several more minutes, but in the end they agreed that none of it was likely to be a factor when Operation Grizz arrived in the Flathead two days later.

"These bears look healthy to you, Loverly?" Dr. Runs With Rivers asked.

"Yeah, Runs, I guess so. I didn't, like, take their temperature, but none of them had the sniffles that I could tell."

"I mean, did they look starved, or mangy, or odd at all?"

"Not that I could tell, Runs. They were all fat, wooly and happy, that I could see."

"A bear's a bear!" Hogan said. "What's it matter if it's healthy?"

"Yeah," Blubbo said. "Maybe all those legislortive palefaces will catch whatever some sick bear's got."

Runs gave Blubbo a scathing look. Blubbo shrugged, clueless.

"Because," Runs said, "it isn't going to further our cause to show up on the capitol steps with a sick—let alone dead—grizzly in our trailer, gentlemen...and ladies. We let this bear get hurt, let alone if it dies on us for some reason, and we're all going to look like a bunch of eco-terrorists in the public eye!"

This sobered the group.

"Not to mention that we're not in this to hurt animals," Lexie said.

"Yeah!" said Loverly.

"I'm the one who's got to watch over this animal's welfare," Runs said. "Bears are omnivores, as we've discussed, but that doesn't mean they can't get sick or poisoned, or die if they've already got some kind of disease, and the woods are full of potentials. Ticks, fleas, worms–"

"Yuck," Loverly said.

"And bears are wild creatures. They're not made to haul in boxes on cross-country road trips. Our bear could get so dehydrated from motion sickness for instance, that we could lose him."

Blubbo was struggling. "Are you saying our bear could, like, puke to death?" he said.

"Yes...doctor. It's not likely, but it's conceivable. My point is, what we're going to do can put the animal at risk, and that puts us at risk, so we have to be careful."

"I'm more worried about the goddamn bear throwing *me* up!" Hogan said.

"Point," Boot said.

"Runs is right, guys," Nerves said. "I'm thinking,

worse case scenario, if we get caught, is we get suspended
sentences, maybe some fines. The adults might do some
time, but probably only a few months. Judges and juries put
a lot of stock in a noble motive, sometimes even for a serious
crime, which, as crimes go, we're not committing. But we
injure, God forbid kill this bear, and we're screwed in the
eyes of the court. Instead of working to our cause, the media
will eat us alive. The bear has to be healthy when the state
returns it to its habitat."

Lexie reported on the Olympia recon mission. Much
to Nerves's relief she omitted the trooper encounter. Lexie
spread out her own batch of drawings, brochures, and maps,
and Nerves displayed scores of photos he'd taken of the
capitol campus.

Pointing to the aerial photos, Nerves said "It's way
too crowded to try pull off Operation Grizz at the south
entrance to the dome. Worse, it's a much tougher approach,
and media access would be harder. Right here, at the foot
of the north steps is where we need to drop the truck with
the bear. Boot, you've fixed it so the truck won't be driven or
towed, right?"

"Blubbo and me have tested the epoxy system with the
wheels off, and it works fine They'll have to call in heavy
truck specialists to figure out why the damn thing won't
roll and they'll play hell doing that. They'll try to remove
the fused wheels, but they won't come off without cutting
torches. When they cut them off they won't be able to
remount new wheels without replacing four whole load
axles, which will take them hours—minimum—to find and
install. If they try to carry the rig out, they'll have to send for
a heavy crane, and some lowboy trucks. That'll take hours to
set up and pull off."

Runs said, "The capitol people won't want them pulling
multi-ton equipment onto that manicured ellipse, and it'll
be very difficult to manage any other way. Permissions will
have to be sought. Bureaucrats are going to have to do the
thing they hate most, make critical calls with their names on
them, under pressure, right in front of the media. It'll take

them forever. Meanwhile, the media will be having field day with the whole show.

"Suppose they cover up the trailer like we will?"

"I've considered that," Nerves said, "but the media will scream because it'll cost prime video. They'll demand to know what it is, if grizzlies are so benign, that the state is trying hide."

Lexie spoke. "OK, suppose they fall back on removing the bear?"

Runs again. "Well, that's another cast-iron bitch of a problem, see? As we've discussed, to avoid a PR disaster they won't hurt it, let alone kill it, as long as it stays contained and is no threat to people. They'll then have two choices: move the bear conscious, or move it doped out. Attempting to move it conscious would require some absolutely fool-proof way of docking a transportable cage to the trailer's rear or side door. That'll be damned tough to do and will almost certainly take hours to set up and bring off."

"And moving it unconscious?" Loverly said.

"It's risky," Runs said. "They'll have to get some veterinary expert to sign off on the correct dosage or they risk killing it. No politician is going to dare authorize what could turn into a colossal screw-up before the media, so, in turn, no vet is going to want to touch darting it. And what if they do successfully drop it in that trailer? Then what?"

"That's some tough hauling," Boot said, "human bodies are hard to lift and carry. A six-hunded pound grizz...man, we're talking hernia city here."

"Precisely," Nerves said. "And they'll have a limited time window before the sedative wears off and they have a waked-up, pissed-off grizzly asking some difficult questions."

"Yeah," Runs agreed. "I'd say they'd have maybe an hour at most, without having to redose him, and then they get into possible respiratory, possibly even cardiac and other problems."

"So they torch off the side panels and crane him out," Blubbo said.

Everyone stared at Blubbo, astonished that he too was

capable of abstract thought.

"You're thinking, son," Boot said, "but, again, we're talking probably hours to set up and bring off. That trailer is made to keep in a whole moving herd of thousand-pound cows, it's built tough and it don't cut easily or quickly."

Hogan said. "They can't try to torch the trailer panels with the bear conscious because the hairy son of a bitch will be right in their faces. If they dope-drop him first, they'll still have that dangerous time-window problem."

"There's no hatch in the trailer floor?" Blubbo said. He was on a scientific roll.

"No," Boot said, it's continuously heli-arced, half-inch aluminum."

"Yeah, but..." Loverly said. Everybody looked at her. "What if they just leave it there? What if they don't even try to move it for days?"

"That's fine with us," Nerves said. "It'll draw crowds and more media coverage every minute it's there."

"Plus," Lexie said, "then somebody's got to feed and water it, right?"

"And nobody's going to take responsibility for that," Runs said.

"Except..." Nerves mused, " maybe somebody like PETA, but if they show up, it just hyper-drives the media circus. Either way, we'll have gotten the public's attention—maybe even nationwide—to our objections to dumping grizzlies in Okanogan County."

Everyone looked at each other.

"By God, this calls for a drink!" Hogan announced, and the motion was roundly seconded.

Over beer, rum, Pepsi and pizza delivered by a leery kid in an old Honda Civic, the FOCM designed their convoy.

It was decided that the mission rolling stock would consist of Sol Pickering's 'temporarily loaned' Peterbilt long-nose truck tractor and the charred aluminum cattle trailer for the obvious reason of trapping, securing and safely transporting the bear.

Hogan said, "We can alter the license plates or muddy

them up, but Sol's name is painted on the door!"

"I thought if that," no one was surprised to hear Nerves say. "I had magnetic stick-on signs made to put on the trailer truck's doors, complete with fake ICC numbers. Three sets. We'll change them every few hours."

"Uh oh," Boot said. "Who made those signs?"

"I didn't come in on a beauty queen float!" Nerves said. "I ordered them, picked them up and paid for them in cash, in person from a Moses Lake sign maker. I parked my car blocks away, and I wore my Groucho glasses!"

"That handles that," Lexie said. "If the federalies trace those signs to the sign shop they'll just think their looking for a creepy sex offender."

Nerves throttled his temper.

After much animated discussion, It was further decided that the second vehicle in Operation Grizz would be Runs's quad-cab diesel pickup truck towing his thirty-foot aluminum livestock trailer, upon which would be carried bear food, water, diesel drums, tools, spare parts and whatever else became seen as necessary for a happy grizzly road trip. Moreover, in the event of an abort due to terminal breakdown of the trailer truck, Runs's trailer rig could be pressed into service as an emergency transport for the bear, back to the Flathead National Park. Nobody brought up exactly how they'd make that transfer, if required. Some brilliant plans can be over-thought.

"OK," Nerves said. "That leaves the scout car. I think it's obvious that should be me in my Porsche."

"Yeah!" Blubbo suddenly said, startling the group. "Man, that's some bitchin' wheels, man! I'll be your co-driver!"

"When Hillary Clinton gets caught in a Motel-6 with Rush Limbaugh," Nerves said, which sailed right over Blubbo's head.

"Forget it, hot-rod," Runs said. "That car is about as unnoticeable and unmemorable as a gay pride parade at Paris Island. Besides, we need something for a scout car that'll carry more than two people and a carry-on bag."

"How about our Chevy Suburban?" Loverly said. "I just

changed the oil, filter, and serpentine belt last month. New tires. It's thirsty but it runs great! Lots of room and extra seats."

"Not very fast," Nerves groused.

"Who needs fast?" Boot said. "The scout car will be scouting for two truck-and-trailer rigs."

"We might have to run from the cops!" Nerves said.

"Yeah!" Blubbo agreed. "We might have to lose whitey!"

"Balls," Boot said. "Nobody outruns radio."

"We're not in this to run from cops," Lexie said. "Runs is right, Nerves, a hundred-grand exotic car is way too eye-catching for Operation Grizz."

"Alright, alright, Hogan's Suburban can be the scout car, but don't blame me if we–"

"Nexxxxt!" everyone else chorused.

Nerves drained his Pink Lady. Loverly raced to refill.

Mostly at Nerves's instigation, the FOCM decided to alter license plates by using black electrical tape, creating eights and Bs out of threes, zeroes out of Cs, Ls out of ones. This they would do twice a day, when they changed the magnetic door signs on Sol's truck tractor.

Blubbo took mental notes. These were useful ideas.

"That way, we greatly reduce our liability of being spotted on any one of a million surveillance cameras in America these days, and traced by our tags," Nerves said. "The twentieth century was the death of chivalry. The twenty-first century is the death of privacy."

"What's chivalry?" Blubbo asked.

"It's the part of sexism that women like," Runs said, "like holding doors and chairs for ladies, letting them go first off sinking ships."

"Whaat!?" Blubbo said. Women were for cleaning, cooking and poking. Everybody knew that.

"Forget about chivalry," Lexie said. "Everybody else has."

Nerves asked Lexie, "Did you get that stuff I–"

"Of course, but I still don't know why we need twenty rolls of stick-on shelf lining in different colors."

"Satellites!" Blubbo said. "The CIA is always watching us

from satellites!"

"Bullcrap," Boot said.

Nerves was now watching Blubbo with new respect.

"The boy's right."

"I ain't no boy!"

"That remains to be seen. My point is, you're correct."

"What's that got to do with stick-on shelf-paper?" Lexie said.

"We need to alter our infrared and visible light signature," Nerves said, making Blubbo suspect Nerves was CIA. Satellite cameras see everything anymore. If you doubt that, look up one of the map services on the Internet. You can pull up a photo of the laundry drying on the line behind your house."

"Freaky," Loverly said.

"In more ways than one," Nerves agreed. "But we need to stick the shelf-paper to the roofs of the vehicles, changing the pattern every few hours, having no pattern some hours, anything to change a constant visual signature a computer might scan from satellite photos after the event."

Now Blubbo was convinced that Nerves was either a CIA agent or an ex-con.

"And another thing," Nerves said. "We always drive at least a quarter mile apart, never in tandem with each other. We never park within sight of each other. We use old fashioned CB radios to talk between vehicles, and prepaid cell phones as a back up. We don't even *carry* our own cell phones, people! We turn them off and leave them here. They give out a tracking signal anytime they're on.

"Listen up everybody. Loose lips sink ships. We get careless, and we get locked up, maybe worse. Keep quiet about Operation Grizz, especially no mention on emails or phones, including text messages. It's all traceable. We all have one person we trust who will never tell our secrets. I'm telling you right now that if you say anything about our operation to that person, you'll be seeing them as a state's witness, in a courtroom, pointing their finger at you. Nobody knows anything about Operation Grizz outside the seven of us, ever!"

What am I, chopped liver? Ronald Reagan thought.

This was all amazing to Blubbo, like that James Bond guy who works for England or Eldorado or one of those Europe places and kicks ass and gets laid all over the world. Maybe this Nerves guy wasn't a dumb Custer cracker like most white people, after all.

"So!" Nerves said with an air of finality. "If that's all for now, we all have preparations to make."

Only Blubbo spoke. "Hey dude, you ever been in the CIA?"

Nerves rolled his eyes. "Alright then. Remember, nobody goes near the bear truck without their surgical gloves, booties, masks and hair caps on, not even once. Just getting our bear to the statehouse is only half the job, people, we have to make sure we aren't caught afterward. A single strand of human hair found on that rig can be DNA'd to its owner."

"Ever done time?" Blubbo asked.

"No!" Nerves said with exasperation. "And I don't intend to start now!"

Boot raised his rum to the group. "Second that motion." Everyone raised their drinks.

"Yeah."

"Me too!"

"Amen."

"Bet your ass."

"Screw whitey!"

Chapter Seventeen

Flathead National Forest

Jesus Christ, what a night, Packy Rudd thought, staggering into his little office and cabin at four am.

A suspected giant bear. My neuron challenged boss. Nearly in a line-of-duty shooting. Escaped cons, one of whom might still be around. A car chase. A bloody wreck. A dying man's mysterious words, "mastodong!" Packy still didn't have a trace of a clue about that one. He collapsed onto his foldaway bunk.

And all this had been before two hours of statements to a grateful marshals service, a curious FBI, and the cheery Montana Highway Patrol. Dead convicts had a very low recidivism rate.

Packy had foregone mentioning that he'd seen Calvus Markus run out of the trees, or that he'd heard what could only have been interpreted as an enormous belch in the woods nearby. Packy had only said that Calvus had appeared in his headlights, and he'd bailed out and thrown down on the running suspect and announced himself, only to be asked by the suspect to shoot him.

Packy hadn't lied. The feds never asked him if Calvus had come out of the woods, and they never asked him if he'd heard a belch like a ship's horn. But he was still terribly conflicted. The Mahwani suspect, a dangerous violent felon, could still be out there, but Packy had a strong hunch he wasn't, at least not ambulatory, and Packy wanted to see what involvement a bear had, before suggesting there had been any such involvement. People got all hinky and Second Amendment on you when you started going on about man-eating bears.

Mercifully for Packy, low rainy clouds had come in, and the police helicopters summoned by authorities had to pull out. The plan then fell back to establishing a law enforcement perimeter about the area, including checkpoints on all the roads, and at first light, hopefully in better weather, a huge manhunt with dogs and helicopters would be launched for Mogo Mahwani.

Packy had driven back up to the scene to show the feds and the MHP where he'd encountered the Lexus and Calvus Markus. He'd then left them on the excuse that he needed to check on some campers.

At the campsite where the old man and the girl had been, Packy was surprised that they'd evidently left in the night. Maybe the nearby commotion had scared them off. Or maybe they were now the Mahwani suspect's hostages and new ride, Packy thought grimly.

He had shined his large, powerful LED flashlight about the now rainy campsite looking for a pathway which nearly all campsites in bear country had, leading away a hundred yards to some tree where a food bag could be suspended out of bear reach. His experienced eye sighted the path, and, carrying his rifle, Packy hiked along it through the woods.

Packy was as jittery as a lawyer at an ethics hearing, because, while there could be a dangerous thug out here, if his suspicions were right, there was also a world-class grizzly bear out here too. Packy's only slight consolation was that, if his hunch was good, that bear wouldn't be very hungry right now, and by extension, the escaped con would be a big black ball in the woods.

Packy found the suspended food bag swinging gently in the breeze. As best he could tell by flashlight, two different sizes of human footprints led away through the woods toward the road. He followed them, then stopped abubtly, and looked wildly around, now breathing hard.

The human footprints had suddenly been over-layed by swear-to-god gynormous bear tracks twenty inches wide!

Holy shit. Ho...ly...shit.

Packy shivered not only from the cold rain but from sheer saturating fear. With trembling hands he withdrew his cell phone and took pictures of the tracks. He pulled his coat up over his holstered pistol, rechecked his rifle for chambering, and followed the tracks.

He saw the fresh stobs of small limbs broken off as high as six feet above the ground which did little to calm his nerves, but soon he found something else, and answers began falling into place.

Packy found a patch of highly disturbed ground where pine needles and earth had been gouged and tossed about. He saw what looked in the raw, bluish LED glare from his flashlight like a black fluid, but Packy knew it was blood, and a lot of it.

There came an arc-light flash followed by the rolling rumble of thunder. Packy flinched. He saw nothing in the strong light but the gashed, bloody ground. Still, he kept raising the flashlight to sweep it around him for the short distance he could see through the woods. On one such sweep, he noticed what appeared to be a tuft of hair lodged in the bark of a limb about six feet above the spot. It was too fine to be animal fur.

The deep, wide, heavy bear tracks led away through the trees to the south, but now there were signs in the wet pine needles of something being dragged. Then Packy found all he needed. On the ground lay a dirty, size eleven, men's basketball sneaker trodden down at the heel as though it had been worn as a slip-on shoe. Slightly beyond, lay the second.

The proverbial other shoe had dropped.

Mogo sleeps with Jimmy Hoffa, Packy thought, breathing through his clenched teeth. And sister, I ain't hunting no grave in this mess. That's what dogs are for.

I am sooo outta here.

Jesus Christ, what a night, Tonny thought the bear equivalent of. My freaking foot is still killing me, but a nice warm, two-leg meal goes a long way. And I didn't even have to fight wolves for it.

Tonny regretted the escape of the second two-leg, but that home-boy had run faster than a cougar hitting a mountain sheep on open ground.

Tonny buried what was left of the very late Mogo Mahwani who was looking a little the worse for the wear. He would enjoy the leftovers in a couple of days, when they had aged properly.

Limping and weary, Tonny waddled pigeon-toed into a depression beneath a shallow cliff, and fell asleep. The sky flashed and thunder rumbled overhead, but Tonny snored like a hippo dying of a gunshot wound to the lungs. He dreamt blissfully of hot-babe sows in estrus.

Just another day in paradise.

Packy awoke about 7:30 am to the flapping sound of a helicopter circling the area. He rose stiffly and looked outside. The sky was still gray, but there was obviously enough ceiling to fly a search helicopter. They'd be tearing these woods up looking for the somewhat former Mogo. It wouldn't be long before their dogs found those shoes, and they'd arrive at the same conclusion that, wherever he was, ole Mogo could be scratched off the most-wanted list.

Many loud, amused toasts would be drank to the noble grizzly bear in US Marshal watering holes tonight.

Packy had turned off the ringers on his desk and cell phones. Predictably, there were several messages on both from special-agent-in-charge, Dr. Melony Gaynor, PhD.

Screw her, Packy thought. She'd railroaded him into vacation, so let her tap-dance solo before the feds and the press about a man-eater in the Flathead.

As his coffee went down sweet and hot, Packy considered the prevailing state of affairs.

It would probably take the feddies, the MHP and their hounds about an hour or so to locate those shoes and whatever the rain had left of the blood and hair. Maybe another hour to find the grave. It would take them another two hours or so to process the scene and then call everybody out of his forest. When the word got out about some escaped rapist getting grizzly justice, the media would tee off on it, but probably only for a day.

The gross effect would be that public enthusiasm for camping in the Flathead would flatten out for a while, and when Melony finally caught up with him she would want him to assemble a team to track and kill the bear.

That was the bad news. But there was a silver lining, Packy considered.

Uh oh, Tonny thought the bear equivalent of. Trouble in River City. Paradise lost. Atlas shrugged. The bell is tolling.

Dogs! And one of those giant, noisy birds flying around. Tonny heaved himself up with difficulty due to his burning, tender foot. He shook like a rotary, drive-thru car-wash swab, and sniffed the damp air. Just as he'd suspected, he smelled two-legs, lots of them, and he could hear those big, hard-skinned, hummy animals with the big bright eyes that two-legs got inside of to go fast.

Tonny had seen this kind of thing before, when the sting-sticks barked and the deer, moose, caribou and elk died. He had grown to look forward to it for all the gut piles left around like deserts. Only, then, there were not so many two-legs in one place as today, and there had not been any dogs and meganormous whoppy birds with them.

Based on his one tasting, two-legs were decent enough eating, Tonny considered, but they didn't have much meat on them for the bone ratio. They had two skins, the outer of which tasted like crap and was hard to chew. Two-legs were dodgy little critters to catch, they could climb trees like those nuisance cougars, and they made insufferably annoying bleating noises.

But worst of all, most two-legs in Tonny's experience had sting-sticks growing on them that hurt like a moose-sized hornet. His aching foot reminded him with every step what that was about.

Dogs were a bad sign too. Two-legs didn't bring their wolfie friends with them to go bird watching. Damn, I bet they steal my two-leg leftovers, Tonny thought.

There goes the neighborhood, Tonny sighed. Time to beat feet out of Dodge.

I am sooo outta here.

Chapter Eighteen

Okanogan County

A graceful looking Beech King Air 350, a twin-engined, corporate turbo-prop, droned in a lazy circle over north central Okanogan County. Inside it, there were two sets-of-four facing seats split by a narrow aisle.

Perry Dinwiddie slumped and slept, as there was little chance anyone would try to shoot Senator Lisa Belle at a thousand feet over the Pasayten Wilderness...he hoped.

Dr. Ermintrude Windgate was babbling on about how no one in Okanogan County would even notice a few noble grizzly bears in all that 'uncharted wilderness.'

Bear-Daughter Lowenstein enjoyed the view and a few minutes more life before Lisa wigged out and yoked the vacuous bimbo for calling her 'sister'.

Lisa, her standard badger persona aggravated by stalking air sickness, whined like a toddler. "Are we there yet!?"

"Almost, Senator!" said a three-piece suit with one of those trendy 3-day, lazy-ass beards under a shaved pate.

The suit's name was Avery Honstadt, a public relations consultant whom Lisa had hired at Perry's urging to help her push the grizzly bill through the legislature.

Avery said, "I just thought you'd like to actually see the territory you're going to restore the noble grizzly to!"

I just want to see the ground and a drink, you overpriced bandit, Lisa thought, before I puke like an entire Delta Chi chapter on Sunday morning.

"What do I need a PR firm for!?" Lisa had howled in her office, when Perry had brought it up, weeks earlier,

between ruttings,

"Because, Miss Congeniality, if your teddy bear treaty doesn't pass, you'll have about as much chance of winning a US senate seat next year as Muktadr Al Sadr."

"Who?"

"Never mind."

"And stop trivializing the Senator Lisa Belle Noble Grizzly Restoration Act with that misnomer before the press gets hold of it!"

"Miss what?"

"You know what I mean!"

"Look, Lisa, if you don't get some PR pros on this bill soonest," Perry had said, "it's gonna go over like your gun-ban bill did, and you'll be damned lucky to get reelected to your state senate seat next go-round."

"Says who? My bear bill is brilliant!"

"Says the polls, toots. Every state senator from east of the Cascade curtain is having a hell of a time explaining the loveliness of your lawn dwelling land sharks to their eastside constituencies."

"Don't call the noble grizzly a land–"

"Hey, that's mommy's own love compared to what a lot of eastsiders are calling your bear bill."

"Ah, they're all a bunch of knuckle-dragging, trailer-park, John Birch neanderthals like Joe Kirksey."

"I rest my case for a PR firm," Perry had muttered.

"Oh come on. The people are...well, they're like children, Perry! Get serious. The public needs someone to think for them. Why...that's the whole reason we *have* a Democratic Party!"

So Lisa had hired Honstadt and Associates, and buried their substantial fees into her state expense account as 'voter research'. Avery Honstadt wore a five-hundred dollar, imported silk neck-tie, paid for by one of the many Washington state taxes Lisa had helped instigate and pass by calling every mundane tax proposal an 'emergency' so as to circumvent the late voter mandated supermajority law for passing taxes.

Among many other moves to promote Lisa's grizzly bill, Avery had arranged this flight to Okanogan County 'for a little hands-on', he'd told Lisa. "I mean...from what I can tell, it's not like you've ever been to Okanogan County."

"I've driven through it," Lisa said, "about twelve years ago."

"Right," Avery said, wishing he'd become an architect like his mother had wanted him to. "But, see, that leaves you vulnerable to the Joe Kirksey types who claim you don't know shi–um, much about the area in which you propose to insert grizzly bears."

"Restore."

"Restore, right. But, see, there are strengths and weakness to all arguments—we've talked about that—and of course your bear bill has its positives–"

"Damn straight it does. It's break-through environmental legislation, Avery."

"–and you've lined up experts to back you like Dr. Windgate, here, and Ms. Bear, um–"

"Daughter, my brother, Bear-Daughter," the refugee from a goth redskin zombie movie said loudly, over the drone of the engines.

"Right." Avery said, dragging his mind back from wondering why anyone would put rivets in their face. He nervously fingered the gold ring pierced through his left earlobe. "But, see, nonetheless, this great effort has exploitable weaknesses, and we must offset them vigorously. The weakness that concerns me most is how our opponent's play upon the peoples' fear of...well...of a herd of six-hundred pound, meat-eating, wild animals in their backyar–, um, let's say in their vicinity."

"Come on!" Lisa grumbled, looking out her window at the seemingly endless square miles of steeply mountainous, heavily wooded, dedicated wilderness extending like wrinkled green carpet below them as far as they could see. "Nobody lives down there! There's not even a trailer park, let alone a civilized subdivision down there."

Actually there was a thriving meth and pot industry hidden in places down there, to say nothing of poachers, but Avery passed on highlighting this because the only thing the residents of Okanogan County would sweat worse than a black Democrat president was grizzly bears high on pot or sizzled on toot. Besides, grizzlies couldn't read the wilderness boundary signs, and would go anywhere there was food, which was likely to lead them down the mountains to places that generated upwind cooking and garbage fragrances by the cubic yard.

"Right, Senator, but see, the operative phrases we want to emphasize here are 'remote', and 'wilderness', and 'pristine'."

Professional bullshitter, Perry thought. This guy is a pig perfumer, a truth warper, a prevarication pimp. You know. Like a lawyer.

"Say," Perry said. "Dedicated wilderness is, like, federal, isn't it? So I thought we were dumping bears on -"

"Restoring!" Lisa snapped.

"Yeah, yeah. Restoring bears to just the Department of Natural Resources land that the state controls?"

Lisa rolled her eyes. With all his exposure to her advanced ways, and all her patient tutelage, Perry was still so annoyingly logical all the time. Thank god Mr. Binkie was quicker on the uptake. Intellectually, Perry was always so hung up on things...making sense! He wouldn't last a day in the ruling class, Lisa thought.

"Perry, we've been over and over this," Lisa said. "The Lisa Belle Noble Grizz—"

"'Senator' Lisa Belle," Avery said suddenly. Remember our goal here is next year's U.S. senate seat. 'Senator' Lisa Belle—"

"Right, right," Lisa said. "The Senator Lisa Belle Noble Grizzly Bear Restoration Act merely restores grizzlies to their historically natural habitat on state-owned land, Perry. Again, there's no risk to users of the dedicated wilderness! I've told you—"

"Yeah, I get it, Lis—, uh, Senator," Perry said, looking

out the airplane's window, "but I don't see a fence anywhere down there. What's to keep the lovable fur-balls from taking a hike anywhere they want after we dum–, mm, restore them?"

"We've accounted for that potential misconception," Avery said primly, thinking what on earth was this African-American bodyguard dude doing in a strategic discussion anyway?

"Yes!" Ermie said, leaning across the narrow aisle, a frown on her pancake-slathered, Helen Thomas, shi-tzu face. She too was thinking, why was this big...African-American... always with the Senator, and what made him think he could just butt into important business? "The noble grizzly is a territorial soul, Mr. Dimwitty, they–"

"Ah, that's Dinwiddie, Dr. Windgate," Perry said with an edge, rethinking all the statutory elements of a legal shooting. "Dinnnn-widdy."

"Of course. I was just saying, really, we know what we are doing. You'll just have to trust us."

You and Bernie Madoff and Joran van der Sloot, Perry thought.

"Yes, my brother!" Bear-Daughter said with a condescending smirk that almost got her strangled at eight-thousand feet. "Our friend the grizzly–"

"'Noble' grizzly," Avery said with a worried tone. "Let's remember our key talking points, Ms. Bear Butter, we–"

Perry aspirated the cola he was drinking at the moment. He snorted and put a hand beneath his chin.

"Daughter, Mr. Honstadt! *Bear-Daughter*! Let's remember our key names too!" Wasn't Honstadt one of those German Nazi names? I bet his grandfather gassed mine.

"Of course, Bear-Daughter," Avery said, "a mere slip of the tongue, I assure you. Right, see, I just–"

"Alright already! I'm not a child. Like, duh. I know what to say when we're on the ground, dude. I am a University of Washington *graduate* student after all. "

I wonder if my grandfather gassed hers? Perry thought. Not soon enough, evidently.

Bear-Daughter turned fiercely to Perry, who was choking back a grin. She said, "As Dr. Windgate has noted, the noble grizzly bear is a territorial creature by nature. They don't, like, roam over two-hundred square mile regions like wolf packs. They happily dwell on their own appointed turf to peacefully raise their adorable young." Bear-Daughter reached for the back-pack loudspeaker device in the seat next to her. "Listen, I'll play you some baby bear dialogue, and you'll–"

"Nuh-nuh-nuh-nuh-nuh!" Lisa said. "Not on the airplane!" Save it for the peasants, you ditsy freak, I'm about to puke already.

Bear-Daughter pouted, eyeing the dumb neo-Nazi PR guy in his expensive threads.

"Now, see," Avery Honstadt said, "here's the flow line we want to maintain at today's appearance, Senator: We don't discuss any potential hazard posed by grizzly bears. If we are challenged on this point, remember, noble grizzly bears are not dangerous unless shamefully intruded upon by man, they are a natural part of the environment, they are key to the proper function of the food chain, and–"

"How's that?" Perry said.

"Hmm?" Avery said.

"That 'key to the food chain' thing, what eats grizzlies?"

"Well, you know..."

"No."

"Wolf packs, and wild cougars, that sort of thing."

Perry thought, as opposed to what, *domestic* cougars who eat grizzlies? "Wolves and cougars kill and eat grizzlies?" he said.

"Well, not exactly, see. But they eat them after they're dead."

"You mean, after they *drop* dead?"

"Mr. Dinwiddie," Dr. Windgate said, eyeing the Senator's thug down the breadth of her squashed-cabbage nose. "The noble grizzly bear predates upon deer, caribou, moose, sheep, goat and other species, thereby maintaining the delicate balance of nature. Perhaps you would be more

comfortable if you leave these details to those of us qualified
to remark upon them?"

Perry thought, perhaps you'd be more comfortable if I
stuff your fat ass through that little door back there, you
patronizing sack of—

"Wait a minute," Lisa said, concerned for that born-
to-kill look that sometimes filled Perry's eyes. "It's the
'unqualified' ignorant we have to worry about here—namely
voters. After all, most, well, educated people are in our
corner here. It's that one cow-eyed country housewife with a
litter of rug-rats who—"

"Whoa-whoa-whoa!" Avery said, "Now, see, Senator,
we've talked about this. One, um, injudicious remark
can scuttle an entire legislative effort! It's 'traditional
homemaker,' 'dedicated mother,' Christ, anything but cow-
eyed—"

"OK, OK, it's just a figure of speech made in private. I—"

"Senator, do you have any idea what Senator Kirksey's
people would do with a remark like that if it's...leaked?"

Slowly, all heads in the aircraft's cabin rotated to fix
on Bear-Daughter Lowenstein. Fortunately, she lacked
the wattage to perceive the implication that she was the
missing-link in the security equation, even if she hadn't been
daydreaming about the bodyguard guy boning her over a
sofa.

"I get it, already!" Lisa said. "OK, still, what we have to
worry most about is some...traditional homemaker...with
four photogenic toddlers who steps out of nowhere when
I'm on camera, and asks me why I want to turn her kiddies
into bait!"

I should have quoted this disaster of a client a lot higher
fee, Avery mulled.

"Mmm-hm." Perry said.

"Now, see," Avery stuttered, "we've covered this too.
True, we have no control over the occasional unaccounted-
for private citizen, but, see, that's why we're doing today's
photo op and press conference in the largely liberal Methow
River Valley of Okanogan County instead of the Okanogan

River Valley to the east, where most of the population is...
less supportive. Today's event is the annual celebration-
of-wilderness bar-b-que dinner held by the Wilderness
Democrats Opposing Population Encroachment, so we
should be in friendly territory."

"Wilderness Democrats Opposing Population
Encroachment," Perry said, "WDOPE?"

"Well, see, that's another expression on our little do-not-
say list."

"You know…" Perry said. Avery and Ermie rolled their
eyes. The Senator's gunman was forgetting his place again.
"One thing I'm not quite clear on. The Methow Valley is
only 'liberal' because it's the closest valley in Okanogan
County to Seattle, and has thus been bought up by droves
of Seattle retirees and second-homers who can't stand living
in Seattle. So...if they're so...distressed about the effects of,
like...human encroachment...on the animals and wilderness
and all, then why don't they just return *to*, or stay in,
Seattle?"

"Uh that's a little off-topic for today, Mr. Dinwiddie. See,
we–"

"It's because the white man destroys everything he
touches!" Bear-Daughter suddenly said with such vehemence
that one of the pilots turned to look back through the
cockpit door. "I studied that in my White Male As The
Anathema of Society class!" Bear-Daughter scowled at
Avery. To Perry, she said, "You of all people should know
this, my brother, for the white American male did that, like,
genocidie thing, with your people just like he did with my
people!"

"The Jews?" Ermie said, perplexed.

"No! The noble American Indian of course!"

Balls, Perry thought, the American Indians are your
'people' like the Hmong tribes of outer Laos are mine.

Avery was getting a migraine. "Whoa-who-whoa!
We're getting way off-topic here people. We don't want
to go anywhere near this vein of discussion. Let's stick to
the game plan, here. We land, Senator Belle is introduced

to the county dignitaries and the guests of honor. The locals say a few words to put rice in their bowls, then Dr. Windgate speaks on the noble grizzly as key to the properly functioning food chain, and Ms. Bear, um, Daughter demonstrates a few grizzly calls with her, um, backpack audio device. Then the guest of honor makes his pitch for the Belle bill. Senator Belle gives her prepared remarks on behalf of the bill, we stage some fast photo ops, and we're outta here. Everybody got it? Nobody talks to the press but Senator Belle or me, and even then it's nothing but our pre-discussed positive talking points. Any questions that remotely bring up any danger from grizzlies are met with, what, Senator?"

"I know, I know," Lisa said, "More people are killed by lightning every year in the entire United States, than are killed by grizzlies. I got it."

"'Disturbed' by grizzlies, not killed!"

"Disturbed, right. And the guest of honor," Lisa read from a sheet of paper, "is one...Dr. Jerimiah Paschale, chief of the Nespelum tri–"

"Um, right, see, well, not exactly," Avery said. "I meant to bring that up earlier, see–"

"What?" Perry said, sitting up.

"Well, see, that's the thing. Dr. Paschale's office called yesterday to say that the Chief had read the entire Senator Lisa Belle Noble Grizzly Bear Restoration Act, and had been compelled to cancel his appearance in support of it."

"What?" Lisa said. "That son of a bitch loincloth PhD betrayed us? He was supposed to be our 'authentication,' you said!"

Avery winced and glanced to see if the pilots had overheard the senator.

"Well, Doctor Paschale's spokesperson said that the Nespelum people raise sheep, goats, cattle and horses—not to mention little Indians—on the Colville Confederated Tribes Reservation that occupies half of Okanogan County. He said that if he promoted more grizzlies in the region he'd be about as likely to get reelected Chief of the Nespelum as

Baghdad Bob."

"Who?" everybody but Perry said.

"Skip it," Avery said. "It's not a problem anyway. I was able to get a substitute, even on such short notice."

"Hold it, man," Perry said. "What substitute? Who is this new guy? How do I know he's not one of Lis, um, the senator's many enemies?"

"Oh, thanks a lot, Chief Silver Tongue," Lisa grumbled.

"Will you watch those ethnic references, Senator?" Avery said, glancing again at the cockpit door. "Everybody just chill out. I was lucky to have gotten anybody on this short a notice."

"Who, damn it?" Perry said.

"Dr. Ward Terdhill, the noted Native American Studies professor at Columbia University. He's–"

"Flaming Turtle!?" Bear-Daughter suddenly shrieked, wide-eyed. "You got Flaming Turtle, himself?"

The pilots both glanced rearward. The captain unsnapped the lid on his leather flight case to better reach his .40mm flipped-out-passenger tool if needed.

"Flaming who?" Lisa said.

"Wait a minute," Perry said, "Ward Terdhill, isn't he that Indian-wannabe, shit-bird white professor who's in deep dookie for saying American soldiers were storm troopers who caused 911!? The little fu–, um, guy who bombed Kentucky Fried restaurants in the seventies 'to save chickens from the white slaver.' *That* Ward Terdhill?"

"He was never convicted!" Avery said.

"His name-of-The-People is Flaming Turtle!" Bear-Daughter said, indignantly. "That other name is just the one forced on him by the white oppressor! Flaming Turtle celebrates his Indianhood as I do!"

"Yeah," Perry said, "well, the oppressors call him a whole lot more than a terrapin on fire, they call him a plagiarist, a liar and an imposter."

"Flaming Turtle is a proud warrior of the great Indian people in their four-hundred year struggle against the colonial white oppressor!" Bear-Daughter said. "Flaming

Turtle is one thirty-second Cherokee, three generations removed, on his mother's side. He has Indian blood!"

"He's a Scotch Irish pretender, for Christ's sake!" Perry said. "That very same mother said so to the press last year! He's no more a Native American than Sheik Winky whatshisname who blew up the Towers the first time!"

Lisa rubbed her eyes, then looked acidly at Avery. "You have me set to speak on the same forum with someone named...Flaming...Tur-tle?"

"Look, Senator, please, I had about thirty hours notice to find an Indian authority to lend authenticity to the bear bill at today's event! Besides, Dr. Terdhill's remarks were taken out of context. He–"

"Exactly what 'context' makes saying American soldiers are storm troopers who caused 911 smell any sweeter?" Perry said sourly. "I *was* one of those military men and I guaran-damn-tee you I didn't cause 911!"

Over the closed cockpit intercom system, on their headphones, the co-pilot said to the captain, "One'll get you five the big black dude dukes out the bald-headed nerd in the suit."

"My money's on him punching the lights out of that weird girl in the Pocahontas outfit," the captain said. "Call us visual on the Methow Valley Airport, and pull up the chart. Let's land this thing before there's a riot back there."

Dr. Ward Terdhill stood by the runway, near a podium constructed from a ribbon-draped flatbed truck trailer, among a gaggle of local officials and Democratic Party apparatchiks. He looked like a seriously hung-over Mick Jagger with a long, gray, braided pigtail, which is to say about as Native American as Justice Bader-Ginsberg.

"Dr. Terdhill," Lisa said on introduction by Avery. She was vastly underwhelmed with both men.

Avery nodded at Perry, avoiding eye contact. "And, Dr. Terdhill, this is Senator Belle's, um, associate, Perry Dinwiddie."

"Yeah hi," Perry said, making eye contact with Terdhill in a way that rendered a handshake unwise.

Another storm trooper military veteran, no doubt, Terdhill thought, leaning back out of right-cross range.

"And, Dr. Terdhill, may I introduce Dr. Ermintrude Windgate, of the University of Washington? Dr. Windgate chairs the ecology department."

"Dr. Terdhill," Ermie gushed, "what a thrill to meet you at last! I was one of the many professors who signed the academic petition last year to have you declared ipso facto distinguished professor emeritus. Can't have those wretched Republicans choking off our great academic right to free speech, eh?" Ermie winked at Terdhill.

Yech, Terdhill thought. "Ah yes, Dr. Windgate. Your, um, reputation precedes you my dear colleague."

Ermie blushed for the first time in the twenty-first century.

Bear-Daughter shouldered past Ermie, offered her hand to Dr. Terdhill and batted her eyelashes like Scarlette O'Hara in Taipei smog. "An honor to meet you, oh Flaming Turtle. I am Bear-Daughter. I too am of The People, my brother."

A match made in heaven, Perry thought.

Niiiiice...tits! Terdhill thought. "Why hello there, my, uh, sister!"

Incest within 48 hours, Avery thought, weighing the angles for his client. Avery knew a class III sex offender when he saw one.

"Actually, my sister, Flaming Turtle is a loose translation of, ah, our people's language," Terdhill said.

The American Indian people have a hundred languages, and you don't speak a lick of any of 'em, you calcified phoney, Perry thought.

"Really, my brother?" Bear-Daughter said, receiving incoming lech signals on her boobs. She held the antennas upward and outward.

And I left my airsick bag on the airplane, Lisa thought.

"Yes, my sister, the original Indian name given me is Mahurp-na-kay, Nin-wa-ep. It's literal translation is 'creeps-with-lust'. As you know, the turtle, which crawls of course, is a revered symbol of wisdom among our people, so it was natural that my name-of-The-People became Turtle-With-Fiery-Passion. The stupid conservative news media bastardized it into Flaming Turtle."

Bastard being the operative word here, Avery thought.

At that moment, the co-pilot walked up with Bear-Daughter's backpack stereo apparatus and handed it to the zombie princess.

"Oh no, no, no, my sister!" Terdhill said, snatching the backpack. "Allow me!"

Bear-Daughter beamed as she took Terdhill's free arm.

Boww-woww on the proww-wol, Perry thought.

God...*damn*, this thing is heavy! Terdhill thought, staring down into Bear-Daughter's cleavage.

The small audience of Wilderness Democrats Opposing Population Encroachment members wondered what could be more numbingly boring, this Windgate woman from UW, or the poet laureate of America.

"And as a special treat for you, today," Ermie was blowing on, "we have one of my brightest graduate assistants, Ms. Bear-Daughter Lowenstein, who has done extensive studies on our friend the noble grizzly bear, specializing in recording the audible communication of these wonderful animals. Bear-Daughter will play us some recordings she actually made of communicating grizzlies in the wild." Ermie managed to start a listless applause, which was more for her departure than for Bear-Daughter's introduction.

"Greetings my brothers and sisters!" Bear-Daughter said, setting her backpack on a folding chair next to the podium. "Before you, you see the latest development in the study of animal communications, my own invention, if I say so myself. I will now play for you the male grizzly crying out in hunger as he fishes for salmon."

Bear-Daughter keyed the volume display on her hand-held remote to seven, and pressed play.

OOOOREEEAAWWWWNNNNK! The audio device bellowed through its six speakers. The roar echoed across the valley and bounced back from the surrounding mountains.

Instantly, there were startled cries from the audience, and a fifty-four year old matron hit the pavement like a dropped elephant. Thirty-seven cell-phones were whipped out, there was a firestorm of mad electronic peeping like a chicken incubator, and the local emergency number maxed out. Then, thirty-seven text versions of 'OMG, woman here passed out!' flooded the local ethernet.

Simultaneously—albeit unknown to anyone in the preoccupied little airport crowd—every ranch dog within half a mile hackled up and sprang to its feet. Seventeen dogs curled their lips, bared their fangs, and headed for the Methow Valley Airport on a dead run.

Bear-Daughter had no firm idea what the motivation was of the bear growl she'd recorded two summers ago in the Flathead National Forest of western Montana, and she had wholly extrapolated what she thought it meant. In truth, it was the male grizzly's offensive warning cry to competitors to stay away from his food. Loosely translated, ooooreeeaawwwwnnnk was grizzly-speak for 'fuck-off, assholes!'

Ranch dogs spoke fluent grizzly.

"Thank you, Bear-Daughter!" Ermie said, re-assaulting the stage. "In a moment my friends, Bear-Daughter will play us another exciting natural bear call recorded live in the wild, but first, it is my great honor and profound privilege to introduce to you a man who needs no introduction, my colleague, Columbia University distinguished professor, Dr. Ward Terdhill!" Ermie backed away clapping her hands feverishly.

Dr. Terdhill made a few platitudinous remarks as inspiring as a sewer pump repair manual. He told of an "ancient legend of my people" lauding their brother the noble grizzly bear, and he pronounced that "the great Native American people were of one glad voice about the return of the grizzly to Okanogan County!" Luckily for Terdhill,

there were no real Native Americans among the Wilderness
Democrats Opposing Population Encroachment. He gave
Lisa a lukewarm introduction, and then sat down in a
different chair so as to better see up the skirt of a young
woman in the first row of seats below.

Seventeen dogs ranging from fat black labs to fit border
collies to frantic little corgis to boxer-rhodesian monster
mutts were now a quarter mile away and closing fast to
check out the rude grizzly invader they'd heard insulting
them.

Uncharacteristically, Lisa Belle kept her speech short and
sweet. She wanted to blow town before any photos could
be taken of her anywhere near the dimwit with a youth
history of bombing chicken joints, who had blamed 911 on
American soldiers. She would kill Avery just before she fired
him.

A woo-wooing ambulance arrived for the dropped-
elephant woman, interrupting Lisa's remarks, much to her
already pronounced agitation. Attention finally refocused on
her as the ambulance woo-wooed away.

Lawsuit, Avery thought, but he firmly felt he was out of
the loop, as he'd been against the bear noise machine from
the start and had said so in a letter to the Senator. Voters
didn't need anything to make them feel any closer to grizzly
bears, let alone frightened unconscious by them, but he'd
been overruled by the sorority from hell: Lisa, Ermie and
Bear-Daughter.

"And in conclusion," Lisa said, smiling at the small crowd
to its ecstatic relief, "I just want to reiterate my steadfast and
heartfelt alliance with the Wilderness Democrats Opposing
Population Encroachment, and all the fine work you're
doing! Give yourselves a hand!" Lisa clapped, and the crowd
joined in. A few women in the crowd went woooo-hooo,
and much self-congratulatory slappy-handing went about.

My God, the seventeen nearing dogs thought. The
humans are howling at the grizzly!

By now, many of the dogs had locked in on the smell
of the bar-b-qued ribs being grilled under a tent-like sun

shelter nearby. Tongues flapping, they kicked their throttles up to ramming speed.

Lisa reminded the WDOPE crowd that the very survival of the noble grizzly bear, indeed the entire Pacific Northwest animal ecosystem, depended on their support for the Senator Lisa Belle Noble Grizzly Bear Restoration Act. She also mentioned that she hoped to carry the hopes and dreams of the great people of central Washington all the way to the other Washington next year, as their United States senator! Faint applause.

For now, Lisa told the crowd, she would have to take some of that famous western bar-b-que with her, as her never ending crusade to meet the people's needs required her immediate return to Olympia.

The crowd clapped just long enough to retain the senator's good will in case she actually did make it to the US Senate next year, then they beat it for the bar-b-que line.

"Start the goddamned airplane," Lisa smile-snarled at the pilots, who were licking bar-b-que sauce from their fingers.

The expedition had gone fairly well, considering, but it wasn't over.

It wasn't just that the seventeen ranch dogs had arrived, now in packs, for they were now distracted toward the tent by the meat smells on the breeze. No. Greater forces of nature were at work.

One was that Ward Terdhill was still focused on his plans for inviting his newfound 'sister', Bear-Daughter Lowenstein, to dinner at nearby Sun Mountain Lodge where he had rented a suite courtesy of the tuition payers of Columbia University.

Toward this end, Terdhill lit up a cigarette which he imagined lent him a sort of Bogart/Casablanca cool, as opposed to the prehistoric, stinking, nicotine addict it actually portrayed him as.

The professor winked at Bear-Daughter, which she took as his eyes burning from the rancid smoke, as hers were. Terdhill was quick to seize Bear-Daughter's audio backpack, as he'd figured out it was her prized possession, but rather than struggle with its weight on one arm, he shrugged into the straps and bore it as a backpack. Bear-Daughter stepped back from the cancer cloud and forced a smile.

Terdhill and Bear-Daughter hadn't gone two steps toward the airplane when WDOPE purists pleaded to hear more bear vocals, and Bear-Daughter was only too happy to accommodate them.

Whereupon, just as the dogs were circling about the food tent, wagging their tails (but for the tailless corgis, of course) and sniffing each other, Bear-Daughter thumbed the play button on the remote.

OOOOREEEAWWWWNK! repeated the backpack, echoing yet again across the Methow Valley.

Instantly, seventeen sets of hackles sprang up, seventeen canine heads whipped about, seventeen sets of teeth were bared, and seventeen assorted ranch dogs went snarling for Ward Terdhill. That dick-head two-leg grizzly wannabe did it again! the dogs thought.

Women squealed and men shouted, which was universally taken by the dogs as a sort of cheerleading endorsement of their attack. After all, if the humans were barking too, the dogs thought, then they must really be onto something.

Ward Terdhill didn't have to be The Dog Whisperer to figure out why about a thousand snarling mini-wolves were coming his way with a vengeance. Nearly swallowing his cigarette, he shucked the backpack like the Falcons dropped Michael Vick, and ran for the airplane, now only a few feet away.

Understandably motivated, Terdhill set a pace that would've inspired pseudo-academic leches all over the world. He flipped his cigarette away just as he reached the small airplane stair in the tail section, half a chomp ahead of the lead dog, a laser-eyed border collie.

Terdhill dived through the door screaming, and scrambled up the narrow, carpeted aisle toward the cockpit on all fours, followed by seventeen hysterical dogs all snarling and snapping at each other to scramble through

160

the airplane door after the two-leg who had called them all assholes and told them to fuck off, in grizzly.

Both pilots had Christian upbringings, so, as one completed his preflight outside, he yelled "Holy shit!" at the invasion of the ranch dogs. The captain, in the cockpit, beheld Terdhill and the howling, barking dog pack churning up the aisle toward him. He yelled "Jesus, Mary and Joseph!" and went for the pistol in his flight bag.

The laser-eyed border collie nailed Terdhill square in the part of his anatomy presented by his retreat on all fours. The professor squawled, rolled onto his back and kicked wildly at the dogs, who were now clambering over the seats and each other, snarling and frothing to get at him.

The copilot, outside, ran to the nose of the aircraft, opened a panel and withdrew a fire extinguisher with the hope of using it to frighten off the dogs.

The captain, in the cockpit, gaped aghast at the swarming maelstrom before him replete with cacophonous snarls from the dogs, and howls of terror from the thrashing professor. The captain made a command decision that there were more dogs than he had bullets, even if he could have hit them without shooting the professor and damaging a multi-million dollar airplane. So, on the verge of panic, he slid back the cockpit side-window and fired a shot through it towards the tarmac, hoping the noise would frighten off the dogs. His plan was only partly successful.

At the boom of the .40mm pistol, painful inside the confines of the airplane, the dogs flinched, yelped and poured out the door in the tail, leaving a weeping Ward Terdhill gasping on the floor like a manatee marathon runner. This was the good news.

The bad news was that the captain's hasty gunshot actually blew the valve off the co-pilot's fire extinguisher, which thence emitted a foamy roar. The startled but momentarily unhurt copilot dropped the extinguisher which landed on his foot and then shot about in tight little circles like a released, unsealed balloon, discharging its contents in circles of cloud.

The bullet, meanwhile, had ricocheted off the extinguisher into the bottom of the left wing fuel tank, and aviation fuel now dribbled onto the runway as the copilot hopped about clutching one foot and making colloquial observations about his agony.

The crowd of onlookers, originally rushing across the tarmac at a dead run to rescue the professor and crew, now heard a gunshot, and they beheld seventeen yelping dogs pouring forth from the airplane. They screeched to a halt, stacking up on one another, some falling. The puddle of turbine fuel trickled over to Terdhill's still smouldering cigarette on the tarmac, and blue-edged, orange fire lit off like a five-million dollar, flying bar-b-que grill. This development sent the onlookers scrambling away from the airplane, texting with gusto as they ran. OMG! OMG! OMG!, etc.

The captain seized the cockpit fire bottle with one hand and Terdhill's shirt collar with the other. He fought and sprayed his way out of and away from the airplane, dragging the now blubbering and somewhat tattered professor.

The seventeen dogs retreated forthwith to their respective ranches, but not before taking advantage of the pandemonium to seize mouthfuls of abandoned but no less delicious bar-b-qued ribs on their way out.

All in all, it had been a great day to be a ranch dog, they reflected, gnawing bones and watching the plumes of roiling black smoke fill the sky over the distant airport.

One hour later, fire trucks and police vehicles were parked everywhere, their red, yellow and blue lights gaily flashing. The airplane was a lumpy, steaming black-spot on the tarmac.

Professor Terdhill was babbling under sedation, the co-pilot was on crutches, and Ermie was being treated for the vapors by paramedics.

The captain was being interviewed by copious news media who had helicoptered in upon the texted alert that

Senator Belle's airplane had 'crashed' in the Methow Valley.

Lisa was apoplectic because the media had eyes only for the 'brave captain who had single-handedly rescued the famous Professor Ward Terdhill!' She was thus forced to fail to capitalize on Rahm Emanuel's Democratic Party principle that no crisis should ever go politically unexploited.

Bear-Daughter had forgotten all about Flaming Turtle, and was now wondering how well hung the captain might be.

Avery Honstadt was out on Route 20, hitchhiking west with one hand, and cell phoning the UW College of Architecture with the other.

Perry was sitting on the flatbed truck trailer, toking a joint dropped in panic by some WDOPE when all the cops had started arriving. He was shaking his head.

Perry wagged his foot and softly sang: "'Momma saaaid there'd be daaaays like this, there'd be daaaaays like this, myyyyyy Momma saaaiid...'"

CHAPTER NINETEEN

Flathead National Forest, Western Montana

The FOCM was excited. Operation Grizz was underway. Loverly and Hogan arrived first at their former campsite, in Hogan's old Suburban. Hogan was disappointed that there were apparently no felons to gun down, but he knew the evening was young.

With a slight, out-of-sight lead, Hogan and Loverly had ridden scout for the stolen trailer truck driven by Boot with Blubbo riding shotgun, along back roads so the truck could circumvent truck inspection stations. It was not peculiar that a cattle rig should be plying isolated country trails, and everyone was careful to stick to the speed limits.

Ten minutes afterward, the pickup truck bearing Runs, Nerves and Lexie groaned up the park road, towing the thirty-foot aluminum gooseneck stock trailer full of bear-napping paraphernalia.

With great anticipation and some destruction of inconsequential trees, the FOCM revolutionaries placed the cattle rig in the remote clearing two miles away that Loverly and Hogan had reconnoitered on their recent felon-shooting expedition. Loverly led everyone on a hike down to the river to see a half-dozen grizzlies fishing in the distant rapids, which had the dual effect of raising moral and reminding everyone that they could become grizzly dung real fast if they got careless.

"Damn those things are huge!" Blubbo said.

"Not really," Runs said, looking through binoculars. "They're maybe five-hundred...maybe up to seven-hundred pounds on the one big boar. They all look healthy from here though."

"Good!" Nerves said.

"They're beautiful!" Lexie said.

"Yeah," Loverly affirmed. "Like big puppies!"

"Puppies, my ass," Hogan said, holding his shotgun and squinting nervously around at the brush behind them. "They're walking meat grinders."

Boot said, "We ain't got long 'til dark. Let's get set up."

At the trapping site, Hogan stood guard with his laser-sighted police twelve-gauge with the sabot slugs. Nerves barked orders like Mussolini reborn.

The cattle trailer was sited, it's metal gate slid up. Boot, Blubbo, Loverly, Lexie and Runs busied themselves hoisting the parts for Nerves's door-trigger mechanism to the roof with a block-and-tackle suspended from a tree limb. Nerves set about rigging it.

In an hour, they were ready to test the trap. All watched as Nerves used a long stick to break a thin, clear plastic fishing line stretched across the interior of the trailer a few feet inside the rear door. There was a dull, G-minor twang as the line parted, followed by a clank as the rusty brake disc, swinging beneath a tripod on the roof, struck the old jeep engine block, which tumbled off the roof and jerked the trailer door shut by means of a cable and pulley.

Everybody clapped, cheered and slappy-handed like the Oprah show on car giveaway day.

A hamhock was retrieved from a plastic container in Runs's truck and hung from the overhead of the cattle trailer for bait. This prompted Ronald Reagan to galumph up through the door and blunder through the trip line. Again, the door slammed shut, and had to be reset amidst much unflattering rhetoric by all at the dog.

Ronald Reagan's feelings were hurt, but dogs were good at rapidly forgetting this sort of human foible.

At last, they loaded into Runs's rig and departed the trapping site. With all those bruins down by the river, the group reasoned, they'd have the capture of a fine specimen for Operation Grizz by morning.

They retired to the campground and pitched their

tents. Lexie, Loverly and Boot set about preparing a
traditional camper's meal of grilled steak, foil-wrapped,
coal-buried potatoes, lettuce, tomatoes, and onions. This was
complimented by enough butter to plaque up a blue whale,
enough salt to cure a buffalo herd, and enough pepper to
make every illegal Mexican in America long for home. The
splendid meal was topped with apple-cinnamon pie and ice-
cream.

All of this was lubricated with enough beer, whiskey,
rum, scotch or diet-Pepsi to stock the average cruise ship.

Boot belched as he leaned back in his lawn chair and
toasted everyone staring glaze-eyed into the crackling, late-
evening campfire. "Now this is my idea of living off the
land!" he said.

"Yeah!" everyone said, exhausted. They all gulped their
drinks.

Nerves raised his bottle and shoveled meat leftovers to
Ronald Reagan. "To vegetarians the world over!" he said.

Everyone laughed and toasted yet again, while Ronald
Reagan schlorped down the scraps.

The FOCM policed up their campsite, bagged and hung
their food in the same clearing where Calvus and Mogo
had communed with nature a few nights earlier, and settled
down for the cold night.

Loverly and Lexie slept in the double-bed sleeper of the
truck tractor, and the men slept in sleeping bags on folding
cots in Runs's 30-foot aluminum gooseneck horse trailer.

Lexie dozed off thinking that surely they wouldn't get
more than a year or so in prison for this lunacy.

Loverly thought Blubbo was sooooo cute with his shaggy
black hair and dark handsome face; he wasn't really fat,
he was just...husky. As she plotted to get Blubbo to forget
his inconveniently racist outlook on white girls, she asked
herself, what would Jane Austen do?

Boot immediately snored like a drunk rhino, which
prompted Nerves to say he was going to sleep under the
stars, until he considered that the woods were full of big
furry dung processors. He moped with his sleeping bag to

Hogan's suburban and slept across the back seat.

Hogan dozed off in the trailer hugging his shotgun.

Dr. Runs With Rivers lay in his bag using a small flashlight to read several references on grizzly bears he'd downloaded from the Internet. Under Basic Studies Of Bear Nutrition And Foraging Ecology, he'd selected several such articles as Optimizing Protein Intake To Maximize Body Mass Gain In Omnivores, and Predicting Body Condition of Grizzly Bears Via Field Methods. At last he fell asleep with the articles on his chest, and the flashlight rolled to the floor, still on.

Blubbo frowned at Runs, turned off the flashlight and stowed the articles. As he drifted off to sleep he wrestled with a troubling thought. Was the awful plight of his people really because the white man was evil, as his brothers in the gang thought...or was Wasi'chu whitey just onto something with all that talk about 'education?'

CHAPTER TWENTY

Flathead National Forest, Western Montana

Dr. Rivers didn't know it of course, but maximizing body mass gain in Tonny was the least of his coming worries as nature had already maximized Tonny to more than twice the body mass of the average adult grizzly.

As the huge bear now cracked branches, grunting and waddle-hopping through the woods at dusk with his increasingly painful limp, he just wanted to kill something. His left forefoot had become swollen fat, tight and tender, and the throbbing pain now extended up his leg. As a result, he was not sleeping well and had a constant headache with occasional dizziness. Worse, he was now starving again.

The frigging noisy two-legs had indeed dug up the partially eaten two-leg he'd buried days ago and carried it off. Damn. And that partially eaten, dead two-leg would have cured out so tastily by now. Two-legs. What a sorry lot.

Tonny eased from the brush into the river as the evening light faded, and eyed the smaller grizz fishing on the rocks. The cold water lowered the temperature in his swollen foot, causing the gasses trapped within the tissue to contract, slightly relieving pressure on the nerves and temporarily reducing his pain.

"OOOOOOREEEEAAAWWWWWNNNK!" Tonny bellowed.

Oh shit, the other bears thought, snapping their heads up. Him again. Unlike Bear-Daughter Lowenstein, the other bears were not confused about Tonny's message. Even the testotesrone-amped young boars trying to interest the sows in a date decided they now heard their mothers calling. Time to haul fuzzy butt. 'Bad, bad, Leroy Brown, baddest dude in the whole damn town', was back.

As darkness settled over the rushing river, Tonny hobbled about from rock to rock sucking meat from what fish leftovers his intimidated neighbors had abandoned. He tried to turn over rocks to glean the crawfish and snails beneath them, but his foot hurt too much to hook two-hundred pound rocks with, or to stand on while hooking with his other forefoot.

After a time, Tonny struggled out of the river still hungry and feeling sicker by the minute.

Damn nuisance two-legs. He'd kill 'em all.

Enforcement officer Packy Rudd finished packing his ancient Isuzu Trooper. He would catch some much needed rest, then strike for Okanogan County at dawn.

He was baffled. *What the hell was going on? I got bear tracks the size of a Brontosaurus, and something ate a dirtbag federal escapee from Boise, then buried what was left until the feds found it. Grizzly grits.*

But the hell with it. His boss had demanded he withdraw from it all and take vacation, so he was outta here early tomorrow morning. Special-agent-in-charge Dr. Melony Gaynor, PhD. could handle the uncatalogued bear problem. She'd been right about one thing. Packy needed a vacation.

Color me gone fishin'.

Chapter Twenty-One

Olympia, Washington

For once, Caroline was actually glad that Senator 'Hell's' Belle hadn't promoted her from receptionist to staffer. Judging from what volcanic rant was penetrating the senator's closed, heavy wooden office door, Lisa Belle was making her staff wish they were burger flippers in Libya.

Ever since the airplane crash-that-wasn't, Senator Belle had been PMS on steroids. She'd have fired Avery Honstadt but he'd quit on the smouldering scene of the airplane fire. Since then, she was threatening to fire everyone from Caroline to the commander of the state police capitol security detail, the latter of whom who didn't even work for her.

Caroline shook her head. And then Ms. Hell's Belle rages in apoplectic mystery over how all four of the tires on her Cadillac Escalade had somehow gone flat in the capital garage on the evening she was running late for a speaking engagement. What goes around, comes around, those cops liked to say.

Caroline remembered how the senator had waxed all Jeffery Dahmer when she bought the emerald-colored Escalade and was told by the senate environmental committee chairman that that wasn't what he meant when he said 'buy green' in his memo.

The press had teed off on that one. 'Belle Buys Behemoth!' How the hell am I supposed to buy green and American at the same time? Lisa had squawled at Perry. Besides, I am a senator, after all. I am too important to the people to risk my life around psycho Seattle drivers in some tiny, tin-foil, electro-hybrid death-box!

Inside Senator Lisa Belle's office, Perry Dinwiddie leaned back in a chair in the corner and felt sorry for the table-full of mostly younger white kids whose self-esteem wasn't high on Lisa's priority list. Everyone pecked like crazy on their brain-babysitter toys, scribbled on yellow legal pads, and avoided eye-contact with battleaxe Belle.

If 'Jane' didn't calm down pretty soon, Perry ruefully considered, 'Tarzan' wasn't going to get any this evening before she went home to her doddering magnate husband on Vashon Island. At this rate, Lisa wouldn't be fit company until Wednesday.

"It's just two days until the Senator Lisa Belle Noble Grizzly Bear Restoration Act comes on the senate floor for a vote!" Lisa railed. "And what's in the news? My groundbreaking, historic ecological statement, that I paid so much to get ram-rodded through committee? Hell no! What are Washington voters reading about? What's all over the goddamn TV? That fucking 'heroic' airplane captain's new *book* contract!"

Lisa's voice cracked on the last syllable. Perry was trying to remember if there was any history of heart attack or stroke in her family.

"I can't believe it!" Lisa squeaked. "I write the most important bio-eco bill in the Pacific Northwest, I barely escape a burning aircraft in some Twilight Zone massed dog attack, and I'm upstaged by some gun slinging propeller jockey!" Lisa was panting and her jaw muscles flexed.

Ain't lookin' good for Mr. Binkie, Perry thought, and he's hungry. Lisa's so sexy when she's homicidal.

"Am I in the Seattle Times today laying the groundwork for my U.S. senate run next year? Noooooooo! I wake up this morning to a page two photo of Top Gun going into a nightclub with that pseudo-Indian JAP bimbo, Bear-Slaughter whats-her-name, on his goddamned *arm*!"

Lisa's face looked like she'd fallen asleep on the beach.

Perry sighed. Better forget about it tonight, Bink.

Lisa's black press guy, Lamont Gaylord, who occasionally daydreamed about Mr. Binkie, spoke up unwisely. "But, ma'am, we have no control over–"

"*Shut* up, Lamont!" Lisa blistered. "I have too much invested in this bear bill to let anything ffff...foul it up. Now I want results, not reasons. Action not alibis! I want a full court dress on–"

"Press," Perry said from his distant corner of the room.

"What!?" Lisa said.

"A full court *press* is the basketball term for when everybody goes balls-to-the-wall," Perry said. "A full court dress is...I don't know...what Whoopi Goldberg wears on TV."

"Thank you, Perry, for that priceless observation," Lisa said, acidly. "I want a full court press these last three days on the bear bill, people! Joe Kirksey is stirring the pot on the eastside trying to kill it, but we have our usual substantial support on this side of the Cascades, and we Democrats rule the state.

"But we can't take a chance on some last minute desperation stunt by the Republicans, some sudden gross-out photos of bear kills on the net or TV. We can't afford some podunk professor they hijack from some outer-galactic, eastside state college who starts mouthing off to the press about grizzlies being native to Seattle in the Stone Age, yada, yada, etcetera.

"Get on the horn to all our media friends across the state and have them watch out for such a stunt so we can stop it. Let it be known that you're willing to...be as 'green' as you need to be...to hear about any such move in time to cut it off at the knees!"

Lisa glared about the long conference table, making eye contact with each staffer, which, with Lisa Belle, could trigger bowel reflexes in an NHL goalie.

"Show me some hustle, here, people, because if anything happens to interfere with Thursday's vote on the Belle Noble Grizzly Bear Restoration Act, I'm gonna be doing some knee cutting of my *own*!"

Everyone double-thumbed their PDD's with frenzy.

"That's all. Now get out there and make things happen!"

Everyone but Perry sprang for the door. When it closed. Lisa stalked about collecting her papers. "That will be all this evening, Mr. Dinwiddie," she said primly.

Damn, Perry thought. I knew it. Down, boy, *down* big fella.

CHAPTER TWENTY-TWO

Flathead National Forest, Western Montana

The FOCM was bitterly disappointed.

They'd all shucked out of their sleeping bags in the chilly dawn, piled into Hogan's Suburban, and hurried to the hidden site of the grizzly bear trap.

Empty.

Worse than empty, it was wholly undisturbed. Not even any footprints outside it.

"Shit!" everybody said in unison.

"Nothing," Runs said, walking carefully about looking for tracks. "Not a single track."

Hogan safety'd the heavy shotgun and leaned it on the car. He limped over with the others to peer at the big cattle trailer.

"Bears on the Jenny Craig program or something?" Lexie said.

"Guess they're gettin' all the fish they need down at the river," Boot suggested.

"Wrong bait?" Loverly asked.

"This is absolutely unacceptable!" Nerves announced, his eyes popping as he glared up at the ham hock still swinging on its string from the trailer ceiling.

"Ain't even touched the trip string," Blubbo said, standing in the open rear doorway of the trailer and scratching his stubbly beard. He jumped down and walked to where the others were clustered in disappointment.

Stupid grizzlies.

Tonny had suffered a bad night. His foot had kept him

awake with a growing hot pain that now throbbed up from his tightly swollen foot through his whole left front leg. Putting any weight on the leg was searing agony. He hadn't slept a lick.

Tonny panted and grunted as he'd three-leg limped to the river before sunup, hoping for something to eat, but he'd not even had the strength to tell the other bears fishing there to fuck off. If there was one thing he didn't need right now, Tonny reflected, it was a poontang fight with some young, new-sheriff-in-town boar. Even soaking his foot in the frigid mountain river water no longer reduced the intense pain. He felt alternately hot and cold and dizzy, and his naturally limited vision was now fuzzy at the edges.

It was all because of two-legs, Tonny knew. They bang-stung his foot, putting the suffering in him. They'd tied his ditch-bitch to a tree, and then they'd come all around with their big noisy birds and big glowing-eye animals and their bang-stingers and they'd stolen his carefully cured, buried two-leg in its prime.

Two-legs were like black-flies, a scourge on the earth.

Coming out of the river, hungry, there came a shift in the breeze. Tonny stood up the length of his almost thirteen feet, breaking branches, and sniffed.

Hmmm. Smelled like two-legs with a trace of wart-hog.

Pay-back time, Tonny thought, limping toward the scent.

The FOCM held council at the trap site. Everyone was so frustrated they were now talking at once.

"I say a new site!" Boot said,

"Different bait!" Loverly said.

"Yeah," Blubbo said, "something still alive, man. Let's go snatch some farmer's goat and tie it in there."

"Exceptional!" Nerves said. "You might be onto something, Blubsie!"

"Yeah!" Hogan said.

"That'd work." Boot agreed.

Blubbo beamed.

"I ain't tying no little goat up in there to suffer in fear!" Lexie said.

"Me neither!" Loverly said.

"Pussies." Blubbo muttered. He promptly got slugged in both shoulders by both women. "Ow! Damn, woman! Ain't you heard of the first amendment?" Blubbo rubbed his arms.

"Oh, now the white man's rules *count*, huh?" Loverly said.

"Listen up!" Runs said. The revolutionaries quieted. "That's just what we need is to get blasted out of our shoes by some farm woman for goat rustling. We'll cover the ham hock in peanut butter. Peanut butter always works in my rat traps."

"Aw, peanut butter!" Blubbo said.

"Where we gonna get that much *peanut butter* out here?" Hogan said.

"I'm thinking another site," Nerves said.

"Not another site," Boot argued. "No pun, but we had a bear of time getting that trailer in here. Besides the more we drag a cattle rig around a national forest the more we risk getting noticed, even questioned."

"Point," Hogan said. "We'd stand out like a red Jap Cadillac."

"We don't have unlimited time, here, people!" Nerves said. "The bear bill comes to the floor of the senate in Olympia day after tomorrow. We need a grizzly bad, and now. Let's not lose sight of our mission, here. If we don't stop this stupid grizzly restoration act in its tracks, in Olympia, we are going to face the damn things all over our county for the duration. Once the meddling state has them in there, we'll never get them out!"

All would later consider the possibility of Nerves's latest edict as having moved the Great Spirits.

From the edge of the clearing, ten yards behind the trailer, there now emitted a stunning noise no FOCM revolutionary would ever forget.

"OOOOOOOREEEEAAWWWWNNNK!" Tonny thundered. He stood up for effect.

It worked, in spades.

Everyone whirled and gaped. Standing upright, over twelve feet high at the skull and five feet wide at its blubberous butt, was several times the grizzly bear anyone present had dreamed of. It was covered in shaggy brown and blondish fur. It was humped at the shoulders like a buffalo, and had paws like excavator buckets. It drooled from its truly scary open mouth. Think T-Rex with an endocrine problem. The beholders' pucker meters pegged.

"Ho-leee...jumpin'...Jesus Jones," Boot whispered. He reached for his .44 magnum S&W revolver stuck in his belt beneath his coat.

"Jesus in *sequins*, would you look at the *size* of that thing?" Nerves squeaked with difficulty.

It was notable how popular the Savior got at times like these.

"Oh...*shhhhhit*!" Blubbo observed, looking like he'd just swallowed a swamp leech.

Whoops, Ronald Reagan thought, time to keep a loooow profile.

"Oh...my...God," Lexie said.

"Somebody get the kids outta here," Runs said softly, slowly drawing his .45 auto from a hip-holster. "Walk...don't run. My Christ, that thing is huge."

"Biggest goddamn bear I ever heard of," Boot said, beginning to breathe hard through his nose. "Look at that thing. A ton, easy. This ain't good."

"I'm not leavin' my Paw-paw!" Loverly said, drawing the automatic pistol she'd impressed Mogo and Calvus with, a few nights earlier. She too couldn't drag her eyes from the creature.

As if things were not bizarre enough, Hogan broke into a croaking rendition of Junior Walker's, 1965 top 100 hit: "Shotguu-uh-unnn," he sang tightly, about eight octaves too high. Hogan did as close to Michael Jackson's moonwalk as a 72-year-old, terrified white man can get. He reverse shuffled toward the Suburban where the shotgun stood leaned. "Shoot 'im 'for he runs now. Shotgu-uh-un..."

Matter-of-factly, Nerves now whispered, "My fellow Americans...there are...no words...in the entire English language...for how totally fucked we are right now."

"Blubbo," Lexie said hotly. "Get Loverly to the car." From her coat pocket, Lexie drew the .357 she'd run off the rapist deer hunters with.

Blubbo immediately seized Loverly by her upper arms. Lexie took the pistol from her.

"No!" Loverly objected, jerking. "Not without my Paw-paw!" She shook, but Blubbo had her and outweighed her.

"Sssssh!" Boot said. "Lexie is right, Loverly!"

"Hogan's headed for the car," Blubbo said, breathing hard, clutching Loverly and twisting to see the godawful monster bear. "So are you."

"Shotgu-uhun..." Hogan sang, bug-eyed, backstepping for the shotgun.

"No! I'm staying! I can shoot too! Turn me loose, Blubbo!"

There were four handguns in the equation, but everyone present knew they were designed to drop maybe a three-hundred pound man at best. To have any short-term effect on a creature the size of the hairy giant now glaring down at them, its lower lip drooping to reveal finger-sized teeth, someone would have to land a brain shot through a solid inch of bone. Those odds with a handgun were somewhere around the lotto jackpot. Even with the shotgun, a vital hit would be required to so much as make this animal flinch.

"Fucked," Nerves said casually, "we are soooo...*amazingly* fucked."

"Y'all get to the truck!" Boot said, stepping toward the towering monster, thirty yards away. "Everybody move! Now!"

"Boot, no!" Lexie said.

"Boot!" Runs said. "Get back here!"

"We are completely, totally–"

"Shotgu-uh-un!" Hogan gasped, almost within reach of the weapon leaning against the Suburban.

Glancing quickly from the bear to the people behind

him, Boot snapped, "Somebody's gotta distract him, draw him off. Get 'em movin', Runs! Get 'em outta here!"

"No, Boot!" Lexie cried again.

Runs read the bones on the table. "Boot's right, everybody get to the car! Nerves! Wake up! You and Lexie get the kids to the car! Go! I'll back Boot!" Runs stepped off after Boot. Both men held their sidearms high, more in symbolism than any realistic threat to the bear.

What is it with these jabbering idiots? Tonny thought. Well, time to settle accounts. He dropped to his good forefoot and hobbled after the big two-leg nearest him. Chow time.

"Hey!" Blubbo suddenly called loudly. Everyone looked at the big Indian boy who easily held the struggling Loverly. "You're right Boot! Somebody got to draw this bear away or he'll get us all!"

Blubbo shoved Loverly hard. She staggered into the arms of Runs. Boot jumped to keep them both from falling.

"But not *you* old farts!" Blubbo said, now gasping for breath. "You nursing-home nerds couldn't outrun a slug!"

With that, Blubbo bolted past Boot toward the advancing bear, waving his hands and yelling, "Yaah! Yaah, bear! Yaaaaah, bear!"

"Blubbooooo!" Loverly screamed. "Nooooo!"

"Get back here, boy!" Runs commanded. He was ignored.

"Ah, *shit*!" Boot said, turning to the group. The die was cast. "Everybody to the car! Move, move, move!"

Boot and Runs sighted toward the bear, but Blubbo had run into the line of fire, still waving his hands and shouting "Yaaah! Yaaah! Yaaah, bear!" The men lifted their sights.

Hogan staggered forward. He sighted with the shotgun, rasping, "Get outta the way kid! Get outta the goddamn way!"

Tonny's foot was killing him and he held it up as he
hopped. Now what? A new two-leg was running right at
him, but so much the better. This one had a lot more meat
on it, and it came on like it wanted a fight, so he wouldn't
have to chase it. If it would just knock off all that infernal
noise and flapping! Why couldn't these stupid two-legs go
down without all the drama?

Tonny lunged as best he could on three legs, dizzy, sick,
with blurred vision, for the oncoming two-leg in the shiny
red skin. Food. Tonny knew he was a sick bear. He was
hungry. He hurt. He had to kill something.

Fuuuuuck *me*! Blubbo thought, sliding to a halt in the
pine needles. *What* was I *thinking*!? He whirled and rocketed
for the trailer doorway. The bear was too big to get through
the trailer door. If he could just get inside the trailer, he'd
trigger the door shut, then he'd be safe and the others could
get away! I shoulda lost some more pounds!

Boot, Runs and Hogan scrambled to be able to fire on
the enormous bear, so massive in its stride that it was closing
on the fleet-footed Blubbo, even on three legs. But no clear
shot presented without risk of hitting the big Indian kid.

Boot suddenly divined Blubbo's plan to gain refuge in
the trailer, and also assessed that the stunningly big bear
wouldn't pass the door designed for cows. "Hold your fire!"
he shouted, holding up his free hand.

The snorting, huffing, fat-wobbling monster humped
up behind Blubbo, who imagined he could feel its hideous
breath on his neck. He staggered, emitted a distressed nasal
squeal, then made the jump to warp speed. God, I hope
Nerves's door closer works!

Blubbo plunged through the rear door and made
sure to snag the trip string as he scrambled on all fours.
He dived through the rear partition doorway, and rolled
down a textured aluminum ramp into the central bay. To

his immense relief he heard the bang of the brake drum swinging into the jeep engine block. As he fell down onto the lower central floor of the trailer, desperate for air, he heard the falling motor block twang the slack out of the cable. Blubbo would've chanted praise for the Great Spirits if he'd known any.

But there was no resounding boom of the door slamming shut, only a blood-curdling, roar combined of pain, rage and surprise. It was ear-splitting at that range inside the cavernous trailer.

Blubbo leaped to his feet, spun, and hopped backward toward the ramp up to the open second partition, but then he froze in horror.

Twenty-five feet away, up on the rear entry level, Blubbo saw the giant bear had wedged its fat ass in the doorway and the door had slid down onto its voluminous rump. The behemoth beast bellowed and the trailer rocked with the animal's weight as it thrashed and clawed madly to free itself. Blubbo frantically tried to slide the second partition shut, but it was designed to be cranked shut from the outside. He shook it but it wouldn't budge.

Outside, Runs and Boot charged for the trailer followed by the hobbling Hogan. Lexie restrained Loverly.

Inside, Blubbo backed up, choking for breath, and his world shut down on him.

The bear pitched and lunged and struggled onto its side. It suddenly thrust through into the rear of the trailer, and clambered to its feet.

The rear entry door now slammed down, shutting the Indian boy in a forty-foot cage with eighteen-hundred-ninety-six pounds of enraged grizzly bear.

"Blubbooooooo!!" Loverly shrieked.

CHAPTER TWENTY-THREE

Whitefish, Montana

"Uh-huh?"

"Um...is this Lightfoot Upholstery and Tracking Service?"

"Uh-huh."

'Is this Ray Lightfoot?"

"Uh-huh. My native name actually means find-tracks-even-at-night, but the early trappers couldn't pronounce my real name so my gramma's gramma just let 'em call us Lightfoot. White man fucks everything up. You know."

"Um...yes, well, good morning, Mr. Lightfoot. This is Dr. Melony Gaynor, PhD. I'm the special-agent-in-charge for the Flathead National Forest?"

"Uh-huh. Heard a you."

"You're the friend of officer Packwood Rudd?"

"Uh-huh. But his name is Packy."

"Well...OK, well, what I'm calling about, see, is—"

"Gotta bear problem."

"Um - hmm? Well, yes. Actually it's a—"

"Big bear problem. Two-thousand pounder. Ate some convict."

"Um, well, not...all of the convict, but what I need, see, is—"

"Track da big boy down. Kill 'im."

Unh! Melony thought. No wonder this monosyllabic cretin is friends with that impudent Packwood Rudd! "Look, ah, Mr. Lightfoot—"

"Packy usually calls."

"I, ah—excuse me?"

"When you got a bad bear, Packy always calls me."

"Yes, well, uh, Packwood is–"

"Packy."

Melony gurgled like Old Faithful before its cyclical performance. "Officer Rudd is on vacation, see? So I need you to–"

"Packy, see, he pays me outta his own pocket. Then when the government check comes in, months later, I sign it back to him. That way I know I'm gettin' my money."

"Uh. Well, Mr. Lightfoot, I assure you that you will get paid. The government has very sound procedures for verifying–"

"You got three sort-of wives and eleven kids?"

"What? Of course not!"

"Well I do. And they eat like a logging camp. And I can't wait no six weeks to get paid. I can reupholster six truck seats and half a motor home in the time it takes me to track a grizz."

"Mr. Lightfoot, I personally guarantee the government will pay you."

"Uh-huh. Does that guarantee carry the full weight and honor of all the US Government's other promises to the Indian?"

Jesus Christ, Melony thought. This bone-headed Native American is just Packwood Rudd with feathers. "Alright! I...will advance you your normal fee out of discretionary operating funds, but–"

"Is that white-man-talk for I get paid pronto?"

"Yes! So will you—look, Mr. Lightfoot, I'm in a bit of a, well, an issue, here. See my superiors are placing exceptional pressure upon me to dispose of this, um–"

"Man-eater?"

"Well, uh, we don't actually like to use that term, Mr. Lightfoot."

"Me neither. When a grizz eats a white guy, I call it a public service."

Melony's arm trembled from the impulse to slam the phone down. "Mr. Lightfoot...may I assume I can count on you, now, to respond promptly to track and kill this...

animal?"

"Yes and no."

Melony groped through her purse for the Prozac. "What...ah...what...*exactly* does that mean, Mr.–"

"Means I'll track him down for you. But I won't kill him. Packy, he always does the shooting."

Oh no. "What?"

"Bear is my brother. He ain't tryin' to eat me, and I don't care to eat him. Got no reason to kill him. Packy, though, he can hit a running fart at a thousand yards."

Ten thousand bear poachers I could've called, Melony thought, and I get an aboriginal PETA freak. She rubbed her temples. "Right. OK. Wonderful. Well, come on out and find the bear. Meanwhile, I'll get someone else to go with you to...shoot it."

"Grizz huntin' dangerous. 'Specially dis big boy. I ain't goin' to da woods wit some panic-blastin' college-boy. Better wait 'til Packy gets back."

"That's not an option, Mr. Lightfoot! Packwood isn't answering his cell phone. I don't know his itinerary. He isn't due back for two weeks, and I can't wait that long. Now... there is another...local gentleman in Whitefish...who is proficient with a gun, who has done some work for us be–"

"Jeb Pullman."

"Yes! You know him?"

"Yep. He'll do. Ain't as good as Packy, but at least he won't shoot me in the ass."

"OK! Can you come right out?"

"Uh-huh."

"Good! Then–"

"Tell Jeb to bring his .458 WinMag, and a shitload of ammo."

Melony heard a click and a dial tone. Now I know why God invented testicular cancer, she thought.

CHAPTER TWENTY-FOUR

Western Montana

Special-agent-in-charge, Dr. Melony Gaynor, PhD.,
hung up her phone and leaned back in her office chair.
Thank God this Pullman guy was on his way with his rifle.
Now maybe he and that Lightfoot neanderthal could get her
little two-thousand pound problem handled before the story
got any bigger.

This bear disaster was just what she needed. This was just
fabulous. Not just an uncatalogued man-eater exactly like
that insipid Packwood Rudd had said, but to hear him tell
it, a very unusually big bear. Fortunately, all it ate was some
violent escaped convict. He'd had no family, ergo lawsuits
were unlikely, ergo the threat to Melony's job was reduced.

The biggest break was, nobody had seen the bear yet,
except the convicts of course, and even the one who escaped
the bear conveniently got himself killed by a trailer truck.
The downside, though, was that every cop in Montana had
been tramping on or flying over her forest for twenty-four
hours, and, even though the police were now gone, the
incident had drawn the news jackals.

So far it was all contained to the local rag and one of the
Kalispell papers. She'd received a call from a friend in Boise
who said the event had been on the radio station there,
but the emphasis was not on the bear but on relief that the
escaped rapists were no longer a threat to the public.

Cops hated news media people like ranchers hated
pasture gophers, Melony knew, so they'd managed to
minimize the details about the gore. Moreover, they had
allowed the media no access - read: no photos—of the
escapee's uncovered body...or what was left of it. The cops

were focused on the criminals. The bear was a forest law enforcement problem.

But she had a lid on it. Packwood Rudd wouldn't answer his cell phone, and was apparently taking the vacation she'd ordered him to take. That had complicated the bear destruction problem, but she had that handled, thus Packwood disappearing was a bonus. The last thing Melony needed was that right-wing jerkoff telling the press he'd warned her about the bear, let alone about it being some kind of monster.

Melony took a deep breath and let it out slowly. She congratulated herself. She had the Indian philosopher and the local Hawkeye coming to track and kill that damned bear. She had a backhoe lined up to bury it, and she'd left strict instructions that, if any photos were taken, nobody got paid.

Melony knew the drill with the media. No photos, no giant bear story. No photos, and it was just another monster bear yarn that got no more purchase than a fish-that-got-away tale.

Lightfoot, Pullman and the clod-kicker with the backhoe couldn't put that surprise bear in the ground fast enough. Shoot, shovel and shut up.

Thank heaven for drugs.

Then the phone rang.

"This is special-agent-in—"

"Yeah, yeah, uh-huh," Caroline of Olympia said, in a hurry. "Hold for Senator Lisa Belle please."

Melony was suddenly on a hold line wondering if she shouldn't drop a couple of the ole blood pressure pills too. Maybe an aspirin. Her fury at being put on hold was tempered somewhat by the shocking question: Senator *who*?

"Dr. Gaynor?" a brittle woman's voice suddenly said. Melony knew that PMSie tone intimately.

"Yes, um, Senator?"

"Dr. Gaynor, I am state senator Lisa Belle of Washington. Perhaps you're heard of me?"

Not a frigging clue, Melony thought, but at least she's

just some obscure state legislator, and not even in Montana. Melony didn't think she'd ever heard of a US senator named Belle. "Um, why...of course, Senator...uh–"

"Lisa Belle!"

"Belle! Of course, Senator! How nice to–"

"Yeah, yeah, listen up. You should have heard of me because I'm one of you."

Oh, Melony thought, I can't wait to hear–

"I am actually the sponsor of the Senator Lisa Belle Noble Grizzly Bear Restoration Act."

"I...um...well–" Melony was somewhere out beyond the ex planet Pluto.

"It's a pioneer ecological legislative milestone that will restore the noble grizzly bear to its historic habitat! I propose to seed sixty grizzly bears onto state lands in some outback central Washington county where nobody lives who matters."

Melony had a flash that maybe this was some kind of crank call. A setup by the media? Packwood Rudd getting even? "Um, uh, how...wonderful!"

"This visionary achievement could be the cornerstone of a run for the U.S. Senate for me next year, Dr. Gaynor."

Uh-oh. "Yes...ma'am?"

"That means I could soon be in a position to affect the funding for your forest, if you see what I mean."

Oh yeah. Uh-huh. You're threatening me with my job, essentially. "Why...yes, Senator, I can certainly see–"

"My bill comes to a vote on the Washington senate floor in two days. As you can imagine, I have my antennae, so to speak, up for anything that could derail this precedent setting legislation."

Sixty grizzly bears, Melony thought. The people of that county must be ready to lynch your uptight ass. Melony got a sudden premonition that this call was about her bear, which she hoped was seriously high on the endangered list at the moment. "Of course, Senator, how can I help?"

"You can help me like this: One of my staffers came across one of those bullshit scare lines on that right-wing

nutty FOX news website. Something about a grizzly bear...
um, contributing to the cause of a human death in your
forest?"

Oh sweet Jesus, Melony thought. It's on FOX! Melony
had heart-stopping visions of deer-in-the-headlights
ACORN officials doing the Tallahassee Two-step on camera,
trying to scuttle under a rock. "Excuse me, senator?"

"Now, so far, it's just a blurb line and a one paragraph
article gloating over a bear attacking some escaped felon.
No photos, thank Christ, so the story will be gone from the
website in an hour."

"Um...right."

"It better be. I don't need any photos of some dead
body that a rogue grizzly chewed up on the news, right
now, convict or no convict. Now I want to know what you
are doing about this...your...bear problem, and I better be
impressed, because I'm pretty well thought of in the...mmm,
forest world, over here, and I soon will be nationally. You get
my drift, Dr. Gaynor?"

No more than a hit threat from the Russian mafia,
Melony thought. "Certainly, Senator! Well you can rest
assured that I am right on top of—"

"I don't rest assured of anything until you tell me this
animal is shot dead and buried deep, and—"

"Absolutely no photos. I'm with you Senator. We are...
immensely compatible on this issue, believe me. Even as
we speak, I have the best Native American tracker and
Montana's most famous hunter hot on the trail of this...um,
problem animal. I fully expect this to be a former situation
in less than twenty-four hours, ma'am."

"No photos on the inter—"

"No photos, Senator. You have my word."

"It better be good, or what I'll have next is your ass!"

Melony found herself treated to another dial tone.

I know, Mother, I know, Melony thought, laying her
head on her arms upon her desk. Marry a doctor, settle
down, have kids and haul them to soccer games and
Girl Scout cookie sales. You're right, as always. I should

have listened.

As Melony enjoyed her chat with Senator Belle, officer Packy Rudd was eating lunch at a country roadhouse in northern Idaho, on his way to visit his hippie sister in some outback Okanogan County commune. He was feeling guilty about sticking Melony with the bear crisis to handle on her own, but then he remembered that Melony was...well, Melony.

To hell with it, Packy thought. She'll call Ray Lightfoot, and he'll get Pete or Jeb or Owl Nose to back him up.

The bear situation's under control.

Chapter Twenty-Five

Flathead National Forest, Western Montana

"Blubbooooo!" Loverly screamed again. She thrashed to free herself, but Lexie restrained her from running toward the big, rocking cattle trailer containing the giant grizzly just closed in with the giant Indian boy.

"Ooooooooh...*shit*!" Nerves said, aghast.

"Fuck *me*!" Blubbo squeaked again. He couldn't pull his bug-eyes from the biggest, scariest, smelliest, loudest, angriest and closest grizzly bear he'd ever seen.

Aiming their guns, Boot, Runs and Hogan rushed the trailer, but what to do? There were only narrow channels between the heavy, horizontal slats in the aluminum hull of the cattle trailer. A shot at the monster bear would likely only ricochet into someone else. Even if it went through, it might hit Blubbo. But even with a well landed hit on this nightmare animal, none of their weapons except Hogan's shotgun was likely to stop it in any time frame that included Blubbo's not becoming taco stuffing.

Blubbo himself was not at all confused about what to do. He leaped up the ramp and through the rear partition doorway to the slatted, forward side door of the trailer, locked by a latch bar from the outside. He shook it like a mad-man and howled: "Open the door open the door open the door open the door open the door open the door open the goddamned *doooooooor*!"

Tonny was having a bad day and he was not happy about it. He was starving, fatigued, in a bitch-load of pain all through his leg, and he'd just been whacked in his immense fuzzy butt with something hard and heavy which had shut him into this weird looking cave thing. Now he hurt on both ends. Two-legs, again. This had to be two-legs, the vermin.

"WHAAAAAWWWWNAAAHH!? Tonny roared, which was grizzly for: what...the Sam Hill...is *this*!? He bellowed again, and whirled about on the elevated rear floor of the trailer while holding up his swollen, searing, left-front foot. The trailer rocked and bounced violently.

The good news, Tonny considered, was that he had cornered the fat two-leg, and even with his bad foot he knew he could catch it, trapped as it was in this half-assed, light-leaking cave. The two-leg was rattling the cave wall and making those silly croaking noises two-legs made just before you ate them. He might be in too much pain to enjoy this plump two-leg, Tonny thought, but he'd sure kill it deader than a week-old ditch-bitch. He'd earned that.

Tonny opened his cavernous mouth bearing his drooling five-inch canines, and he squeezed through the rear partition doorway, dropping down the steep textured aluminum ramp onto the sunken center section of the trailer. The forty-foot, twelve-ton trailer, and the road tractor it was attached to, rocked again.

When the big grizzly's weight hit the floor, Tonny was forced to put some of it onto his agonized left-front foot, which hurt beyond even Tonny's vocabulary to describe. He stood up, waving the bloated, tender foot, and squawling like a ship's horn.

That is, he tried to stand up, for there were only 10 feet between the trailer floor and the roof above. His skull hit the latter with a resounding boom.

This development did not go a long way toward improving the situation. Tonny recoiled from the blow, dropping again to his forefeet, which once again made his injured foot feel like it was dipped in lava.

Tonny whirled again in agony and roared with the pain, rocking the rig. Clumsily, enraged, he went for the squeaky two-leg who'd retreated behind another wall with a passage in it. Painfully, Tonny inserted his head and front legs up the shallow ramp and through the forward partition doorway.

Terrified to the point of weeping, Blubbo now sank to his belly and shook the trailer side door with what little strength he had left. "Open the door! Open the door!" he sobbed.

Oddly, it was Nerves who shook off the horror and reacted fastest. He sprinted past Hogan, Boot and Runs to the trailer side door over the road-tractor axles, slid into it, and whipped back the locking bolt. Boot seized the door with his free hand, slammed a foot into a drive-axle wheel beneath the trailer floor and heaved the heavy sliding door back on its overhead track.

Runs stuck his pistol in his belt, shouldered past Boot and Nerves, and slapped both hands on the hysterical Blubbo. Runs pulled, but only dragged the heavy Blubbo's slick red-nylon basketball jersey up to a roll at his armpits.

Nerves pulled Runs, Boot pulled Nerves, Blubbo slid over the dusty aluminum, and then all four men landed in a heap in the pine needles beneath the door just as the bellowing bear clambered onto the elevated nose floor of the trailer.

"*Close* the door, unh! *Close* the door, unh! *Close* the door, unh!" Blubbo gasped, face down, puffing little dust clouds.

The big bear roared. The trailer rang.

Boot had already scrambled to his feet and slid the heavy door, yet it hit not with a satisfying clang but rather a dull thump as it smashed the bear's curiously swollen, extended forefoot into the door edge.

There was another earsplitting roar that would make a Klingon wet his battlesuit. The whole truck rig shook. The huge clawed paw, larger than a garden rake head, was snatched inside, allowing the door to slide shut.

The bear collapsed, briefly, grunting hoarsely, apparently in great pain. The trailer and tractor creaked and swayed. The heat, rank smell, and hot breath of the beast was all over the four frantic men.

Motivated, Boot shouldered at the heavy door with a grunt, his boots sliding in the pine needles. Runs frantically reached for the locking bar from his knees, but it was out of his grasp. Nerves clambered up and stood on poor Blubbo. He rotated the latch bar, and it dropped into place.

Hogan finally had a clear shot. The old man staggered forward and sighted through a sidewall groove with the shotgun. The bear was struggling to regain its footing, grunting in pain with each breath, slipping on the metal floor of trailer.

"Don't shoot!" Runs gasped. "Dooooooon't!"

"Nooooo!" Lexie shouted, releasing Loverly, who ran for Blubbo.

"Blubbo!" Loverly called.

"Gunhk!" Blubbo said.

"Hold your...fire, Hogan!" Boot struggled to say, struggling for breath.

"Don't kill it, Hogan!" Nerves said, heaving, bleeding from his wrist. "Don't kill it."

Breathing hard himself, Hogan paused, eyeing the thrashing grizzly down the shotgun's barrel. His trigger finger quivered. Then he withdrew the weapon from between the slats, raised it, and stepped back.

Blubbo still lay face down, making odd noises. Loverly, was on her knees by him, stroking his shiny black hair.

"Gunhk!" Blubbo repeated, inflating and deflating like a mating pond frog.

Lexie hurried to Nerves who had dropped to his own knees and now held his wrist, which dripped blood.

Runs stumbled back and dropped to his butt in the pine needles. He propped on his arms, and gasped to breathe.

Boot swayed, then lowered himself carefully to one knee.

All stared at the bear, the immense, unbelievable grizzly that now lay on its side, huffing loudly, in the front section of the cattle trailer. It was waving its left forefoot slowly, and grunting deep in its throat with each exhalation.

"Biggest...grizz...in history!' Boot said.

"Must run a ton!" Runs panted. "Jesus Christ, look at the size of that animal!"

Lexie returned with a first-aid kit she'd stowed in the suburban. Nerves had ripped his hand, somehow, closing the locking bolt.

Hogan stepped back again, and dropped the shotgun. "Better get them pills, darlin' girl," he said, and he collapsed.

"Paw-paw!" Loverly called, springing to her feet.

Runs crawled toward Hogan. "Get his prescriptions, Loverly!"

Loverly instantly diverted her scramble from Hogan toward the car. Boot raced to Hogan's side and cradled his head. Blubbo rose to all fours. "Hogaaan!" he yelled.

Runs held Hogan's wrist, gauging his pulse. Loverly slid in the pine needles with three of Hogan's pills, which she loaded in his gasping mouth.

"Paw-paw! Swallow, Paw-paw, swallow!"

Hogan choked the pills down. Loverly placed another under his tongue.

Blubbo stood, his feet apart, hands on his knees, still heaving. "Is Hogan OK?"

"Hogan!" Nerves yelled. "You homophobic old goat! Don't you dare die on me!"

Lexie held pressure on Nerves's bandaged hand, but watched the crowd around Hogan with worried eyes.

"Hogaaaaan!" Nerves cried.

"What!?" Hogan said. "It's just a heart attack. I have 'em all the goddamn time. I need a beer! And I ain't no homo!"

Paw-paw!" Loverly cried in relief, holding the old man.

Hogan patted Loverly's head. "Hush, little girl," he said. "Hush that cryin'. Old Paw-paw's just fine, darlin'."

A collective sigh passed through the group. Hogan was helped to his feet. "Jesus Christ," he said, grinning. "That is one big bear. I ain't even seen a picture of anything that big."

Nerves limped across the pine needles toward the trailer. "We did it! We did it! We got a bear!"

"And he's a beauty," Boot said, standing. He's a record-booker if I ever saw one."

"He's massive!" Nerves said.

"He's our whole cause!" Lexie said. "The media in Olympia will freak out over him. We'll get twice the air and ink!"

"He stinks," Blubbo said, as Loverly walked by him to take a cautious look at the recumbent monster.

"He's...hurt!" Loverly said. "Look at his foot!"

Runs strode near and peeped through the slats. "Or sick." Runs said, squinting at the mass of heaving hair. He turned to face the group wearing a grim expression no one wanted to see. "This animal may be dying."

Everyone cautiously crowded close.

"Dying?" Lexie said.

"How could he be dying?" Blubbo said, exasperated. "He damned near *ate* me!"

"Get me a flashlight, Blub," Runs said. Blubbo hurried to the Suburban.

"This is unacceptable!" Nerves said, melting down yet again. "Fifty-million fu–, grizzlies in the forest and we get a *sick* one!?"

"He don't look sick to me," Boot said. "He looks lame. See how that one foot is all swole up?"

Runs took a flashlight from Blubbo and the two circled the trailer to the other side. Runs peered through the slats with the light. They felt the animal's heat and smelled him.

"He hurts!" Loverly repeated. "He's in a lot of pain. Look how his eyes are glazed and how he's panting!"

"And, damn, I don't want to sound silly here, folks," Lexie said, "but I think he's crying. Listen to that whimper in his breaths."

"Get me a long stick," Runs said. "About six feet." Blubbo scampered for the wood line.

Nerves was now sweating. "We can't take a sick bear to Olympia! It'll kill the whole purpose! People will see it as a poor hurt teddy bear deserving of sympathy. PETA and the press will make us out as bear abusers! If he croaks on us, it'll be a PR disaster!"

Lexie sighed. "Give it a break, Nerves. Let Runs figure

out what we got."

"Infection is what we got," Runs said, still examining the panting bear. "Lots of inflamation in that left front foot, looks like he took some kind of slash wound across the top of his foot. Trap maybe. Possibly a bullet. Sealing up, but still supperating."

Blubbo returned with a stick. "Super what?" he said, peering with Runs.

"Means leaking pus," Runs said.

"Oh...*lovely!*" Nerves sneered.

"How bad?" Boot said.

"Depends on how much it's in his blood. Crank that partition door shut, Boot."

The grating of the compartment door roused the enormous bear, which grunted and clambered to its feet, still favoring the injured foot. It roared, hopped and slammed the partition with its good foot. All this made for a loud bang and more rocking of the rig.

The FOCM warriors took a step back, praying that the trailer was assembled by someone who knew what they were doing, but the bear just stood heaving, its swollen foot held up, its lip drooping, a guttural groan admitted with each breath. It began to swing its massive head from side to side.

Loverly took the Indian veterinarian by his arm. "Is he gonna die, Runs?"

"Not if I can help it, little girl," Runs answered. "Blubbo, get me some duct tape from the toolbox. Boot, build us a small campfire."

CHAPTER TWENTY-SIX

Flathead National Forest

Can't a bear get a break in this nutty country!? Tonny asked himself the bear equivalent of. He longed for his native British Columbia where this kind of insanity didn't happen, where a guy could just eat, fight and poke sows without all this theater.

Tonny limped, rotating about in a circle, looking for a way out of the damnable, unsteady two-leg cave thing. It had slots all in it, but none that were close to big enough for him to insert a paw, let alone pass through.

Speaking of paws, Tonny was about to start gnawing on his ailing foot. He had to relieve himself of this awful pain, whatever it took. The searing, throbbing tightness of his whole left front leg seemed to contain that scalding, sticky stuff that stuck to Tonny's feet in the summers when he crossed those hard paths the two-legs made for their big-eye creatures. The relentless pain had made him sick, crippled, woozy and fuzzy-eyed, none of which boded well for life in the forest. Tonny staggered against a sidewall. The pain spiked again, and he tried to growl and hit the cave wall, but he could barely stand on all fours in the shallow, forward compartment of the two-legs' cave.

If all this wasn't bad enough, his highly needed, fat, two-leg dinner had somehow escaped! Just when he'd almost had it, the two-legs had smashed his bulbous, swollen foot, raising his pain level beyond description. Tonny was still sweeping his head back and forth and grinding his teeth with the agony, between desperate, grunting breaths. It was torture to set his foot down, but his good leg hurt too much to keep holding the bad one up.

And that was just the upside, Tonny reflected, looking with foggy vision through a trailer sidewall slot at the pack of two-legs chirping about so near, yet so far away. The little critters had made flame like the forest fires, only tiny. They were clustered about it, cackling like prairie hens.

Tonny resumed swinging his head to dissipate the pain, but not with much success. Oh momma, the big bear thought, I am one hurtin' cubby.

Lexie glanced at the trailer with narrowed eyes. The giant bear had gone back to rocking side-to-side, making the trailer oscillate slightly. Hogan's faith in the cattle trailer was demonstrated by his tight grip on the shotgun.

"Are you sure about this, Runs?" Lexie said in a tone that confirmed she wasn't.

"Hell no!" Runs said, stooped by the fire with the others. "We didn't spend a lot of time on goddamned grizzly bear field surgery in vet school!"

"But Runs!" Loverly said, also glancing at the bear. "You're gonna stick a *knife* in Tonny? How's that gonna—"

"*Tonny*!?" everybody but Loverly said.

"Well! You guys said he weighs a ton! What *else* are we going to call him?"

"Why does he need a name?" Nerves said, exasperated. He was trying to dial down his state of mind, but he wasn't having any more success than the bear was.

"Well, *we* got names, don't we?" Loverly said.

Nerves opened his mouth to speak but locked up.

"Call him Blubbo," Blubbo said. "It was good enough for me, and don't look like he's passed on many meals either."

"Let Runs do his thing, guys," Boot said, eying the bear. The cowboy had seen several horses with infected feet, and he had a notion what the Indian veterinarian was up to. "We gotta get this show on the road, soon."

"I just don't see why we gotta stick Tonny with a knife you duct-taped to a stick!" Loverly protested.

"Yeah, me neither," Lexie said. "I can see why you're

turning it over a fire, to sterilize it, but damn, it's, like, red hot."

"He's gonna scream like a raped ape when you stick him," Hogan observed. "Hope that trailer's hung together well."

"Look, people!" Runs said. "Near as I can tell, this animal's got serious infection in his foot from some injury. It's making him lame and might be poisoning his blood. We got to—"

"Poisoning his blood?" Loverly said with distress.

"Sepsis," Nerves said.

"Septicemia, actually," Runs said, slowly turning the knife blade over the fire on the stick. "But you're close enough."

"How can you tell?" Loverly said.

"Runs sighed again. "Well, unless one of you wants to put a rectal thermometer in this animal—"

"I'll kiss Osama on the lips, first," Boot said.

"—I can't be certain, but I'm pretty sure the big guy's got a fever, and that's almost necessarily from the infection."

"Is it..." Lexie began.

"Deadly?" Loverly finished.

"I don't know," Runs said, eyeing the bear. "Could be. Depends on how much toxic bacteria's in his blood, how far it's invaded, and how healthy his immune system is. Either way, we have to drain the animal's infection—"

"Tonny!" Loverly said. "His name's Tonny."

Runs sighed and paused. "Loverly, it's gonna take me some time to get used to calling some colossal grizzly bear by its first *name!*"

"He's not some bear, Runs, he's *our* bear! And he's like a big puppy, and he's hurt."

"Puppy, hell," Hogan muttered.

Runs wondered how he'd let this bunch of certified whackos talk him into this calamity. "Alright, Loverly! Tonny it is. Now listen up. We have to drain...Tonny's infection immediately and do it without giving him more infection. Draining that festering foot wound will greatly reduce his pain, temporarily at least. With a little luck we'll beat back the invasion enough that his white blood cells will knock it out."

"And if we don't?" Nerves said.

"Let's just be sure we *do*, Mr. Sunshine!" Lexie said.

Loverly was still very concerned. "But Runs, why can't we sterilize the knife, then, like, let it cool before—"

"Cauterize the wound," Boot said.

"What?" Loverly said.

"He means to burn the area stuck by the knife to seal it, honey," Lexie said. She patted Loverly's shoulder.

"It's not just sterilization," Runs said, "the hide on this thing...on Tonny, is thick, tough and hairy. This old Buck knife is sharp, but we'll still need to burn our way in."

"Won't it hurt him?" Loverly said.

"No more than setting fire to his foot," Hogan said.

"Yes," Runs admitted. "It'll probably put him in orbit at first. But, if I'm right, the drainage should quickly relieve all that built-up pressure in his foot, and his pain should drop like a rock in about a minute. Regardless, we have to do it or he could die, even if we, say, turned him loose to stay here."

"If we show up in Olympia with a dead bear, the media will make us out like the Michael Vick kennel club." Nerves said.

Runs stood, and held the glowing hot knife on the stick close to examine it. "Alright," he said. "Let's do it."Uh oh, Tonny thought, I don't like the looks of this. He shook his wide head to try to clear his vision, but the best he could make out was that the two-legs were advancing on him in a pack, except for one who remained in the back with what looked like a sting stick.

The two-leg bull in the lead held a real stick that he poked through a gap in the cave wall, and its point had heat. Not a good sign, cubby, this could get ugly.

Tonny hopped forward and tried to generate an impressive roar, but his breath caught from his pain. He heaved, and grunted and bared his impressive maw, with his huge nose wrinkled upward to show his scary teeth. As he could not stand on his bad foot, he waved it as a threat.

And all hell broke loose.

The FOCM revolutionaries tensed as Runs inserted the spear with the scalding hot knife taped to it through a space between trailer slats. Runs spread his feet and wiggled them to burrow through the pine needle carpet for some leverage.

Nerves decided it really wasn't necessary for him to be this intimate with the prevailing situation. Someone should watch after Hogan and the shotgun.

"Don't hurt him!" Loverly said, wincing. "Don't, like, really hurt him!"

"Let's step back, honey," Lexie said.

Runs stood close enough to smell the dank, wet-dog stench of the great bear and feel it's warmth. It was angry and hopping about, causing the trailer to bang and jerk, affecting Runs's aim. Runs drew back with a double-handed grip on the dispatch end of his makeshift spear, and reflected that being this close to a ton of raging, drooling carnivore was not the spiritual communion he might have wished.

The bear hopped close and waved it's injured foot which at the moment looked like the upper jaw of an orca, only hairier.

Runs resisted a consuming urge to drop this crazy spear idea and run, like a sane human, but he struggled to swing the knife end of the stick in an attempt to aim. Then, for a brief moment, the bear lowered its paw, leaving a trajectory to the upper side. Runs heaved the spear toward the top of the enormous, bloated foot with all the strength he could muster.

There thence came the mother of all ship's horn bellows, the trailer shook and clanged with a boom, and the spear was levered so violently against the edge of the wall opening that Runs was hurled sideways by its butt into Boot, decking both.

At the sudden reaction of the enraged grizzly, everyone drew back several steps. Boot scrambled up and dragged

Runs back. Hogan lifted the shotgun to his shoulder.

Loverly cried, "Oh no!"

In his agonized, cacophonous squawl of searing pain, the bear had reared, slamming its head into the ceiling of the shorter nose compartment. It promptly dropped like it was turned off with a switch, in a big cloud of dust. It rolled onto its side, and lay frighteningly still.

From the top of its injured foot, a thick stream of bloody pus shot from the stab wound in a three foot arc lasting several seconds before it gradually dribbled off to a bubbling ooze.

"Bingo," Runs said.

"Eeeuuw!" Lexie said.

"Oh my god!" Loverly cried.

"Holy shit," Blubbo whispered.

"Nice shot, Runs!" Boot said.

"Oops," Hogan said.

Nerves gawked. "Is...that thing...*dead*?" he asked.

CHAPTER TWENTY-EIGHT

Spokane, Washington

'Vacationing' Packy Rudd hit the right-turn signal on his ancient Isuzu Trooper and began working his way across the westbound lanes of I-90 west of Spokane. The cell phone on his belt was playing Ode to the Common Man. Packy was not about to answer it if it was Melony Gaynor, but he needed to know.

Besides, Packy considered, since a blind, drunk, quadriplegic monkey that couldn't read or speak English could get a U.S. driver's license, and never have to requalify for it until he was a hundred-ten years old, traffic on American roads was exciting enough without trying to talk on a cell phone while driving.

Packy pulled well clear, onto the grass. He recognized the incoming call number as Ray Lightfoot's.

"Ray! What's up, buddy?"

"Hey Pack, where you at, man?"

"Ah, a little west of Spokane, brave. Stopped at the *Cabela's* in Post Falls for three hours. Bought a bunch of stuff a tree pig can't afford."

"I hear that, man. Say, man, you left town at the wrong time. We been havin' a saga here."

"Melony ordered me on vacation, bro. I'm gonna go look up my sister in Okanogan County. Melony call you to get that bear?"

"Yep. Me and Jeb."

Packy could tell by Ray's tone that something was in the wind. "So it's history, right? Did you get a chance to scale it before hiding it?"

"No, man."

"No scales?"

"No bear. We ain't got it."

"Couldn't track it?"

"No, man we tracked it just fine. Found the signs on the river bank, couple miles north of where he ate the convict, right where the big brownies fish, you know?"

"Yeah, I just sent some tourists up to that area last week who wanted to get bear photos."

"Brother, no mistaking this big boy. Print twenty inches wide, man. Four inches deep in places. Heavy mother. Go near a ton, my guess. We figger'd, we get him soon, you know? 'Cause he three-leggin' it."

"Lame?"

"Yep. Left front."

"Yeah, that meth tooter in the Whitefish trailer park, Arliss Bernall, said he got off a shot at him. Could be one of the cons shot him too, I guess, but the cops didn't find any guns on them. So...where is this big grizz, then?"

"Good question, man. Look like the spirits got him."

"Come on, Ray, I'm sitting on the side of the highway. I'm not in the mood for riddles."

"Not woofin' you, bro. Took us a couple hours to locate the prints on the riverbank, but then he was about as hard to track as a D-8 Caterpillar. We traced to him to that clearing about a thousand paces into the woods, you know, off that ole fire road?"

"Yeah."

"Then he disappeared man. Tracks lead right up to all that dirt and needles at the clearing, and flat disappear. But that ain't the half of it."

"I'm listening, Ray."

"Well, it look like somebody swept the clearing, man."

"What?"

"And, not just the clearing. Look like somebody dragged a big smoothie bundle made of spruce boughs all around the clearing. Wiped out all the signs there, and then clean down to the main road where the container truck got that other convict. I mean, no tracks of no kind, all the way from where the big bear disappear, down to the pavement. Must a used a vehicle to pull the smoothie bundle, was so big. Found the limbs scattered in the woods down by the highway."

Packy thought about this. Ray could track a chipmunk, and he wasn't prone to fantasy. "I don't get it, Ray. What am I missing?"

"It gets better, man. Me and Jeb, we hungry about sundown, you know? Ain't trackin' no ton grizz in the dark. So we drive into town to the Burger King?"

"And the bear was sitting there having a Whopper?"

"No, man. He already eat fifty of them."

"Come again?"

"The kid at the drive-through, man, he say some woman with biblical hooters come through about a hour earlier. Say she wants Whoppers. Kid says he's tempted to tell her she's already got some, but he asks her how many? Woman says *all* of them. Kid gets manager. Manager tells woman maybe they can make fifty Whoppers in ten minutes. Woman says I'll take 'em, get busy."

"With or without pickles, Ray?"

"Hey man, I'm just tellin' you what the kid said."

"Ray, think carefully now, did the kid notice a live grizzly in the car with the woman?"

"Kid didn't mention no bear man, but he said this woman a real MILF, have tits to die for, so he mighta overlooked–"

"OK, OK. So what do we have here, Ray? Are you suggesting somebody *stole* a two-thousand pound, killer grizzly?"

"Hey man, the tale ain't told yet."

"There's more?"

"We leave with our take-out. Jeb, he says drop by the Rite-Aid so he can pickup his prescription. I say OK, sure. Jeb, he goes in, comes back with his pills, says this is the night for weird."

"The grizzly's in the Rite-Aid reading magazines."

"Listen to me, man. Jeb says the girl at the checkout

tells him, some guy come in earlier, wanted two *cases* of nighttime, cold-and-flu medicine."

"Aw, come-on, Ray, what is this? *Twilight Zone*, redux?"

"You know, medicine got that dexter-morphine stuff in it?"

"I know! But what, that's...what, forty-eight bottles a case, that's...hell, Ray that's about eight *gallons* of the stuff!"

"I'm just tellin' you, man. You know, it's like, for aches and pains and–"

"Sleep! That much nighttime flu med would put an *elephant* to slee–" Pause. "Ho...lee shit."

"Uh-huh."

"Ray. Ray. Are you trying to tell me that somebody boosted a ton-weight grizzly outta my forest?"

"Hey man, I'm just tellin' you what's happenin' here."

"But, Ray, who'd want to capture a grizz that big—hell, any size—and transport it? Where? Why? If they were after the gall bladder, they'd just slaughter it in the woods. And ain't no zoo gonna buy a hot grizzly."

"Hey bro, you said you sent some tourists up there to take pictures. Ask them."

"Ray, that was some medicare case and his granddaughter! She was cute, but she probably wasn't as old as the burger kid, let alone a 'mom-he'd-like-to-f–, uh screw'. Besides, how does anyone...kidnap a grizzly?"

"Coulda pipe-trapped it, maybe."

"You ever see a pipe trap that could hold that big–"

"Hey, man, I'm just tellin–"

"I know. Thanks, Ray. What'd you tell Melony?"

"Same story, except for the burgers and the flu-med. We didn't go to those places 'til after I called Melony."

"What'd she say?"

"Ain't no telling that woman anything, Pack; I gotta tell you that? She say we incompetent, ask if we been drinking. You know what the term 'squaw' really means, man?"

"Point."

"Anyway, we tell Melony we try again tomorrow, but, dude, I been trackin' for thirty-three years; that bear ain't out there. We'll take another day of her money tomorrow, then I'll tell her, bear, he musta beat it back to Canada. She won't care, long as it's gone."

Gone where? Packy thought. "Thanks for the call, Ray. Hey, did the burger kid remember what this fifty-Whopper woman was driving?"

"I asked him that, Pack. He said it was dark, but when he walked five big bags of whoppers out to where she was waiting in the parking lot, she was in a big SUV."

"Brand? Color? Tag?"

"I asked him that, too. He said he didn't remember nothing but her–"

"MILF tits. Yeah, yeah."

"Said it was just a big ole SUV."

"What about the—what was it? A man?—the guy who bought eight gallons of nighttime cold-and-flu medicine?"

"I went in and asked the Rite-Aid girl too. Said she never saw what he was driving, but, get this bro, he was tribal."

"An Indian?"

"What she say, man. 'Bout fifty, Wes Studi looking guy, cowboy threads and hat."

Packy sat for a moment. He kept having visions of an old man and a young girl towing a camper trailer with an old Chevy Suburban. But what sense did that make? What sense did any of it make? That kid and her granddad were out of the camp ground the day after he saw them, which was before the bear...disappeared. No way they captured any grizzly, let alone this monster. The burgers might have just been for some blowout the woman and her crowd were throwing somewhere. Kids' sports team or something. Maybe the Indian guy was just stocking up medicine for his big family for a winter or two. Who knows? Could be no connections here at all.

But fifty Whoppers and eight gallons of flu-med? In one little western Montana outback town? At the same time a monster grizzly goes missing?

"This is too freaking weird, Ray."

"Hey, bro, you palefaces have done crazier shit.

Remember the guy who spray-painted a bull buffalo white, and sold spiritual seances with it to dumbass tourists?"

"Point, but what about the Indian?"

The phone was quiet for a moment.

"Point."

Tonny had lived all his adult life at the top of the food chain in his world, so fear was a new experience for him, but a little fear is what he felt, periodically, as he lay stiffly on his side, passing in and out of consciousness for hours.

When briefly awake, with his eyes narrowed and his leathery lips drooping, the massive, shaggy bear noted dimly that the slots in the sides of the crazy cave were now covered over with something, but worse, the cave was...moving, jarring up and down, rocking side to side.

What the Sam Hill is this? Tonny thought, wallowing blubberously with the moving cave, but then he would drift off to sleep again.

Before the cave had begun to move, Tonny could barely remember the two-legs coming with their hot stick. He remembered his throbbing, agonizing leg, and feeling like a giant yellow flash bang from the sky had suddenly hit it, and then going blank. Yet, when he regained consciousness, he couldn't believe his good fortune. The horrible pain was gone! At last, he didn't hurt. Finally, he could sleep.

Then the cave stopped moving, and the two legs entered from the passage he himself had entered through. Tonny had struggled to his feet, astonished and hugely pleased to find his hurt leg now only stung a little on top of the foot, even when he stood squarely on it. Tonny felt he could dance the Flamenco with a rose in his teeth.

Tonny had roared at the two-legs, but his pounding headache put an end to that nonsense. Besides, they didn't seem intent on harming him. They just dragged a big, dark object to the wall of the middle chamber of the cave and left, closing the hole in the rear compartment and the rear hole in the cave itself.

Suddenly, there was the most beautiful smell in the air. Meat! Warm meat! And lots of it. And something else... tangy smelling.

Shortly, the two legs cranked opened the forward compartment door from the outside. Tonny waddled stiffly down the steep, textured ramp into the lower, bigger, middle chamber of the cave, and ate voraciously from the night-colored container there. He started briefly as the two-legs closed the forward compartment door shut behind him somehow, but the big chunks of meat sloshing in an intoxicating sort of purple sauce were overpoweringly delicious, and he ate like a...well, like a starved grizzly.

Tonny had eaten meat like this before. It was like the huge, fat deer that lived in herds with the two-legs. But the sauce was *superb*! It was heavy and sweet, and it felt mellow and good all the way down. He'd never known anything like it.

When Tonny had eaten all the meat and slurped up the last of the sauce on the container bottom, the two-legs poured water from the river through a hole into the container, and he drank.

Damn, Tonny thought, rolling back in a corner belly-up, burping like the space-ship in *Close Encounters of the Third Kind*. I may have to rethink whole my position on two-legs.

For the moment, though, it didn't matter.

He was sooooooo...sleeeeeeeeeeeeepy...

CHAPTER TWENTY-NINE

Washington Senate Office Building, Olympia

"Go, big boy! Go! Hyaaah!" Senator Lisa Belle cried, waving one hand in the air and holding Perry's shirt collar as he pretended to buck Lisa off like a rodeo bull. As both were clad in mostly unbuttoned office clothing replete with a cowboy hat on Lisa, this would have made for a memorable photo op. "Buck me, big boy! Buck me!" Lisa cried.

In the adjoining receptionist office, Caroline rolled her eyes, read job ads online, and prayed no citizens or senate colleagues came walking through the hall door.

Inside Lisa's office on the taxpayer's plush carpet, Perry had had enough of this one. He'd always gone a long way to satiate Lisa's nutcake sexual fantasies, but Lisa wasn't exactly svelte.

A man did what he had to do to get laid, of course, but even Perry had drawn a line at the spurs Lisa had intended to use on him.

"But they're brand new spurs, Perry!" Lisa had said. "I just ordered them! Come on, they'll be fun. Mr. Binkie will love them!"

"Listen, 'Helga, She-wolf of Dodge City'," Perry said evenly, "Mr. Binkie remembers the roller-derby queen phase. Believe me, if you touch Mr. Binkie with any spurs, he'll recycle them and you with extreme prejudice."

They compromised, and now Perry hunched one more time, tossing Lisa to the carpet, whereupon he climbed astride her and held her arms to the floor. "Go, you raging bull! Have your revenge!" Lisa panted.

Fire-woman is crazier than a baboon on PCP, Perry thought.

That was when the intercom beeped.

Perry collapsed to the carpet, shaking his head. Lisa sprang up, spurs jingling, snatched the phone and snarled from the edge of sanity. "Caroline, I told you no inter–!"

"You also told me that anything about bears was to come to you immediately, Senator..."

"Aaaaaaaargggh!" Lisa said, flopping into her office chair. "Alright, who is it?"

"It's Dr. Melony Gaynor...PhD", Caroline replied in a stuffy royal tone, "special-agent-in–"

"Damn! I don't know who's more proud of themselves, that Windgate cow or this cackling hen. Put her through!"

Thus unprepared was Lisa to hear that the man-eating grizzly in Dr. Gaynor's national forest was not accounted for, let alone buried beyond the reach of any cameras. She took the news with her predictable grace. "If that ff–, animal eats anybody else, it had better be you!" Lisa slammed the phone down, the erotic ambience of the earlier moment somewhat diluted. She pulled her clothing together.

"Why is every *goddamn* public official *incompetent?*" Lisa growled.

Perry eyed the ceiling and let that opportunity go by. A paycheck was a paycheck. "What is it?"

"That man-eat–uh–cornered...desperate bear, got away from the two cowboy pretenders that Gaynor halfwit sent after it yesterday!"

"It's a big forest."

Lisa hopped about while taking off her spurs, something akin to Miss Piggy on a pogo stick. "Oh, that's not all! Gaynor says her flunkies told her somebody took it!"

"Somebody took what?"

"The goddamn bear!"

Perry stared. "Somebody...stole...the grizzly bear?"

"Yes! She says they're making it up to cover their failure, but I swear to God, if that animal turns up live on fucking *YouTube* between now and tomorrow morning, I will castrate that woman!"

Perry sighed. "Lisa, if somebody had the bear we'd know

it. They'd already have flashed pictures of the...'man-eating monster of justice!' online. We'd have heard about it by now. Relax."

"Relax? Do you have any idea what could happen to my bear bill—and by extension my career! And yours!—if somebody comes in here day-after-tomorrow with that killer bear, for a demonstration, as my colleagues prepare to vote on the bill? Reporters will flock out here with every microwave van in Washington to broadcast the...' monster of justice!' We'll have some slobbering, growling, famed man-eater outside our window, right where those horse freaks and bikey people were last week marching around with their signs! My career milestone bear bill will go down like the goddamn *Hindenberg*, Perry!"

"Come on. The Flathead Forest is like, what? Four-hundred miles away? Lisa, hauling horses in here for a demonstration is one thing. Hauling a jacked grizzly that far is another. You can't just go motoring clear across a state with a large, dangerous, wild animal, hell, I think it's an endangered species, even. And all this assumes anybody would think they could bring off such a stunt, let alone capture some specific killer bear, let alone some freak monster."

"Nonetheless, I didn't rise from poverty to where I am today—"

"You didn't rise from poverty to take a pee. Your daddy was a doctor, you went to private schools. Some reporter is gonna nail you for talking that crap."

"Everything is relative, Perry! The point is, I didn't work this hard on a breakthrough piece of legislation like the Belle bear bill to take any chances at the last moment. The house is looking to the senate on this one. If my bill is approved tomorrow morning, it's a cakewalk through the house. But if the senate kills it, it dies on the spot. And my chances at a U.S. senate seat next year die with it. I might not even get re-elected by the stupid Washington state voters! I can't take the chance that some inbred semi-sapiens from the eastside will try to scuttle my bill with a last minute protest, let alone with a scary bear. If that happens, no senator is going to vote on seeding 'man-eaters', anywhere in Washington, even in some insignificant backwater like Okanogan County!"

Perry sighed again. There was no reasoning with fire-woman when she was on a rant. "OK...so...what are you going to do?"

"What are *we* going to do! Get on the phone with your contacts in the state and local police. I don't know, call the forest service, park rangers, whoever you have to call. Just make sure they're looking out for some bear trick the morning of the vote. I'll talk to Lieutenant Gordon, here, myself. We're close, Perry. My ticket to the real Washington only is only hours away. And we aren't going to drop the goddamn ball now!"

"OK. But I still say you're getting all bent out of shape for nothing. Nobody's gonna show up here with some killer grizzly bear. It ain't like ordering in pizza. Besides, who'd be dumb enough to even try such a lunatic scheme?"

CHAPTER THIRTY

Okanogan County

Operation Grizz had arrived at Boot Colhane's ranch the previous evening at 11pm. They pulled the cattle semi into the main aisle of Boot's immense barn and closed the big wooden sliding doors. Nerves was making everyone crazy with his concerns about satellite surveillance. He'd been changing the truck door signs and the trailer roof panels at every opportunity.

Hogan, Loverly and Nerves had run scout in the Suburban, Nerves at the wheel. Boot and Lexie followed a quarter mile back in the cattle rig, which looked like a Barnum and Bailey Circus truck for its bright blue Korean tarps, secured by black rubber bungy cords. The magnetic ownership signs stuck to its cab doors, and the anti-infrared stick-ems on the roof helped disguise the rig's infrared image on satellite cameras, at least in Nerves's paranoid mind. Blubbo and Runs brought up the distant rear in Runs's crew-cab pickup truck towing its thirty-foot, gooseneck horse trailer loaded with equipment and fuel.

Most of the trip was after dark and they had stayed to back roads. It was decided that Boot and Lexie, in the big rig, wouldn't wear the surgical hairnets and masks - they felt conspicuous enough without looking like a rolling bio-hazard - but they would wear western hats, the booties and the rubber gloves. The group would have all the next day at Boot's ranch to sanitize the truck again, necessary because Blubbo had been all over the inside of the trailer, uncovered, and several of the group had put hands on it trying to rescue

Blubbo.

Plus, the trailer floor was caked with dried pus and blood, it held sections of gnawed cow bone, and stank to Mars from grizzly pee. It was not something one would wish to follow on their motorcycle.

It had been a nerve wracking trip, but one with only a single potentially catastrophic moment.

Just after dark, it became necessary to cross an isolated ferry over a section of Lake Roosevelt.

Crossing a small, country ferry no longer than the cattle rig and only three times wider, was hairy enough. The sixty-year old barge tilted precariously as Boot and Lexie pulled the big truck up the ramp, then it washed and wallowed wildly, leveling itself when the rig was aboard.

Nerves, Loverly and Hogan were also aboard with the Suburban. Runs and Blubbo with the horse trailer rig had to wait for the next trip. Fortune had ruled that, at this hour of night, there was no one else aboard but the two-man ferry crew.

As the ancient ferry labored on its ten minute voyage across Lake Roosevelt, Boot and Lexie pretended not to know Hogan, Loverly or Nerves as they stretched their legs in the cool night breeze. All stared at the beautiful, clear Pacific Northwest sky which gave one to feel they could reach out and touch the Big Dipper itself.

But then the snoozing Tonny broke wind.

Regrettably, this sounded like a loaded sixteen-wheel dump truck descending a grade on its compression brakes, and drew the alarmed reaction of the ferry's elderly deck hand standing at the bow.

"Whut the hayul wazzat?" the old deck hand said, moving aft, weaving against the roll of the ferry. "One a my engines musta blowed a exhaust manifold!"

The FOCM revolutionaries tensed when the deck hand paused by the trailer and reached to lift the edge of a side tarp.

"Dang, this thang stanks! What y'all carrying, pigs? I used to be a trucker. Nothing stanks like pigs. Smell 'em a mile behind."

Nerves drew a breath to yell at the deck hand not to raise
the tarp, but Lexie slipped her hand over his mouth. Loverly
hurried to the deck hand. "Evenin' sir!" she said with a
commanding smile.

It worked. "Well hey thur, little missy!" he said, releasing
the tarp to snatch off his greasy ballcap. "Yur a mighty pretty
young lady!"

Loverly slipped her hand about the old man's arm and led
him back forward. "I was just telling my Paw-paw," she said,
pointing skyward "I bet you can tell me what that big star
right up there is!"

The deck hand suddenly became Carl Sagan. "Well, ah,
why that's the Big Gripper, orbits around the moon, see,
and–"

Nerves let out his withheld breath as Hogan walked
by, chuckling and whispering, "Taught the little darlin'
everthang she knows..."

On arrival at boot's ranch, the FOCM was exhausted.
Everyone but Runs left the barn and staggered into Boot's
big log home for something to eat. In the barn, flashlight in
hand, Runs cautiously disconnected and raised a corner of
tarp to inspect his charge.

The immense bear was on its feet, walking ponderously
about the central chamber of the trailer, sniffing, examining,
but apparently not terribly concerned. The trailer jerked
minutely as the big animal moved. The bear strolled casually
over to Runs, its towering shoulders shuffling fore and aft
with its step, its great furry shoulder hump looming behind
its broad head. It walked pigeon-towed, and it's scythe-like
claws made a slight rattling noise on the metal floor of the
trailer.

The Indian veterinarian stepped back, but the creature
just stopped at the wall and stared at him through widely
separated, big, brown eyes on either side of a black, leathery
nose and jaw assembly the size and shape of a rural postal

box.

My God in Heaven, Runs thought, drawing a sharp breath. That is the biggest bear I've ever seen, in or out of a record book.

What the hell are we doing? Runs thought. But then he thought about distant, oblivious politicians making dangerous decisions about other people's homeland, as the invading whites had done to his people long ago. Some said they were still doing it to his people. Regardless, Runs thought, somehow, some time, some way, you have to fight back, or you become a slave, and are no longer a free man. No. Not here. Not in America.

Runs was startled to note that the giant bear was calmly staring him in the eyes through a slot in the side wall, it's lower lip drooping, immense front teeth showing.

Runs stared back at the wide brown eyes. Scary visions flashed of a horrifyingly gigantic monster, rearing, drooling, roaring, bearing a maw like a trac-hoe thumb-bucket. Runs remembered how his heart had leapt when the creature had dropped to all fours and limped hard after Blubbo, who had so foolishly rushed to distract the bear so the others might escape.

But, now, Runs saw no malice in the animal's gaze, rather just a gentle curiosity.

Runs flinched as the bear suddenly placed his formally injured foot against the trailer wall. Two claws on thick, shaggy stubs protruded through one of the slot, each looking like yellow-ivory ice-ax blades.

Runs took the opportunity to shine his flashlight on the left paw. He leaned closer to the wall, cautiously. The wound had sealed and was healing nicely. Neither the injury nor the bear's recent behavior suggested any lingering infection to speak of.

Runs glanced again at the bear's eyes and thirty-inch head. The lower lip was still drooped, giving Runs the impression of a smile.

Let's not get too silly here, Runs chided himself, but still, he was compelled to put out his own hand and pet the long, bristly hair of the bear's extended foot. He figured that as long as he didn't put more than a few inches of his hand through the sidewall, the bear couldn't get enough grip with his 'smile' to rip Runs's arm through the trailer wall and off at the shoulder.

Then Runs was startled and astonished. An enormous, thick, purplish-pink tongue slathered across the top of Runs's hand. His first instinct was to yank his hand back, because the heat and rough texture seemed so alien, but Runs didn't see the action as an attempt to make dinner of him. Again, the bear licked the top of Runs's hand. Runs petted the paw, five times the width of his own, and withdrew his hand.

Runs didn't want to think of the bacteria in the smelly slime all over his hand, but, as he wiped it on his jeans, he was dumbfounded again.

The bear rumbled softly from deep in its belly, as though in agreement with some proposal Runs might have made. The huge, furry head bobbed up and down several times.

What Tonny was actually conveying, of course, was: "Listen two-leg, that sauce y'all put on that meat was amazing stuff!"

Runs came away with a different impression of the bear's gesture.

In Boot's rustic dining room, everyone sat wolfing down spaghetti and garlic bread that Lexie and Boot had prepared. As they became filled, Runs surprised everyone by sternly issuing an order. "Blubbo, go out on Boot's deck and build a small fire on the hearth."

There was something about Runs's tone that caused everyone to stare at him. Blubbo wiped his mouth, stood, and exited through sliding glass doors feeling like he was being excluded for a reason, and the hurt it caused him showed. He could be seen stacking kindling on the raised rock hearth outside.

Lexie seemed to voice the group's collective weariness

and feeling. "Runs, it ain't my affair I know, but it wouldn't break my heart to see you cut that boy some slack. He's worked hard for all of us."

"Yeah," Loverly said with an edge.

"He's just a kid, Runs," Nerves said softly. "Sixteen."

Runs pushed his chair back and rose. "Everybody outside," he said. "Now."

Members of the FOCM stared briefly at each other, then followed Runs through sliding glass doors onto an expansive stone deck. It was cold at this hour, this high in the Okanogan highlands, so the warmth of the fire Blubbo was building on the raised bar-b-que hearth felt good.

Boot sensed what was coming, and turned off the outside lights. The FOCM stood in a half circle facing the hearth, firelight flickering on their faces, shadows dancing behind them. Blubbo tossed another split of wood on the growing fire and stepped back from the group, as though he sensed he was not and could never be accepted by the white world like Runs had. Who cares, Blubbo thought. Fuck 'em.

The fire popped, and a shower of sparks rose into the cloudy night.

Runs stepped before the group. "I–ah. I just had a talk with the bear," he said.

This announcement might have evoked surprise, even humorous derision at any other time, but the group knew Runs wasn't kidding.

"Tonny!" Loverly said.

"He seems like a nice guy," Runs continued, staring into the fire. "He doesn't seem to be a mean spirit, at least, not now, not since his pain is relieved."

Nerves raised his beer mug. "Here's to Dr. Runs With Rivers, DVM. Wilderness bear healer. Without your skills, Runs, we might have had a dead bear on our hands."

"Hear, hear," Lexie said raising her drink. "We didn't come to harm animals. We just don't want them helping themselves to our kids and livestock."

"So...what'd the damned bear say?" Hogan asked.

"Tonny! He's got a name, people!" Loverly said.

"Alright, what'd…Tonny…say, Runs?"

"Along with Blubbo, of course, I'm of the First Nation, an American native. Our people are supposed to have special spirit, including a unique capacity for communicating with the animals. Anybody who'd believe that stereotype would probably also buy a tomahawk made in China from some tourist hawker.

"Truth is we're as human as any other people and none of us are Dr. Doolittle. The bear…excuse me, Loverly—Tonny—might have asked me to play hockey with him, for all I know, but that wasn't the impression he gave me. He seemed to be telling me that the spirits in us all are subject to change with the winds that blow over us, and even though he was one bad-to-the-bone scary beary this morning, he's not any more, now that he can be himself."

"I could have told you that, Runs," Loverly said. "He's just like a big old pup—"!"

"He ain't no puppy, little darlin', and don't none of us forget it." Hogan said, looking toward the big barn where the cattle rig and it's cargo were sheltered. "If we're working up to a group hug with a ton of grizz, here, count me out."

Runs smiled. "My point is, we're all subject to changes born on the winds that blow through our lives. Sometimes these are gentle breezes that make life easy. Other times they're harsh, cutting gales that bring much hurt. Sometimes they're just steady, relentless winds that, in time, blow us off our courses. Some of us cope with the winds better than others. Some of us surrender to those winds of change and become the litter blown about in life. Others of us struggle to keep the winds from blowing us away from what we are or what we want to be."

"Yer gettin' a little windy yourself, compadre," Boot said. The group chuckled.

"You're right, Boot, so I'll come to the point. This morning we all saw something amazing and impressive and it wasn't twelve feet tall and covered with hair, it was more like six-feet-four and covered in one of those silly-assed, droopy-pants basketball outfits."

A brooding Blubbo was suddenly startled to note that everyone was looking at him. The basketball pants part was all he'd caught. So he hitched up his voluminous, red nylon basketball shorts, and assumed an indignant expression, still not aware of what had drawn the attention to him.

Dr. Runs With Rivers continued. "This morning we all saw a boy who, to date, had thought poorly of himself, yet thought of no one but himself. The winds in this boy's life have not all been gentle summer breezes. Tough shit. Life makes no promises of fairness, and we play the hands we're dealt. There are many fine adults today who got that way in the face of worse winds than our young friend has known. Blubbo that's you. Step up here, please."

Casting a wary eye about, Blubbo advanced to stand in the firelight by Runs, before the remaining FOCM.

"Tonight," Runs said, "we still see those dumb britches, but we no longer see that boy in them. Tonight we see a young man who this morning did a very brave and selfless thing on behalf of the rest of us, a young man who did not hesitate to put his life on the line for friends he cared more about than himself. Blubbo, I saw some combat in the Corps, but I never saw a man do a braver thing than you did when you ran to draw off that bear."

"Yea!" Loverly said.

Blubbo looked sheepishly at the ground and mumbled, "Wasn't brave, man. I musta been outta my mind. When I figgered that out, I was so scared I nearly wet these 'britches.' I ran like a rabbit."

Boot spoke up from the edge of the firelight. "Brave and stupid ain't the same thing, son. Brave ain't about having no fear. It's about having the fear, but not letting it rule you."

"Hear, hear," Nerves remarked.

Hogan said, "A man who knows no fear ain't brave, Blubbo, he's just ignorant. Brave is knowing them risks and facing them anyway."

"But I ran," Blubbo mumbled, looking at the ground.

"And you took the bear with you," Runs said, "exactly what we all needed. You captured the bear, Blubbo, not us.

221

Without you...without what you did for all of us, some of us could've been hurt bad, killed maybe. And there's little chance we'd have been able to get a bear in time for the vote."

"As it is," Nerves said, smirking toward the barn, "we have availed ourselves of a bruin that's going to make headlines and photo ops all over the news."

"Hold your head up, son," Runs said. "Come here." Runs unfastened his tooled leather belt and slid from it the buckskin scabbard containing the knife they'd used to drain Tonny's wound. It was a fine, hand-tooled, five-inch skinning blade with beautifully integrated elk-horn grips. The scabbard was tooled and heavily stitched.

"This knife is no trinket bought in a reservation tourist shop. My granddaddy—my momma's daddy, we called him Tree Of Many Rings, in English—he made this knife," Runs said, "from an old truck spring leaf. Smithed it himself in his own forge. Grips come from an elk he shot the year I was born. Carved them himself. There's not much means more to me than this old knife, but, son, I'd say you've earned it. I'd like you to have it." Run's handed the knife to a dumbfounded Blubbo and started a round of applause that lasted until Blubbo's lips began to quiver.

"Welcome to manhood," Runs said, offering his hand. "From this day of honor, we call you boy no more."

Blubbo was a softy. As he shook Runs's hand, his eyes watered and his lips trembled.

Lexie knew a lighter tone was in order. "Speaking of what we call you," she said to Blubbo, "surely we can do better than Blubbo! What's your given name?"

Let's not get carried away, here" Runs said. "Blubbo's still got 14 pounds to lose before the Corps'll take him."

"I like Blubbo OK," Blubbo said.

"Me too!" Loverly said, bobbing up and down on her toes.

"No way!" Lexie insisted. "You've already lost—what? Ten pounds? We can't go on calling you *Blubbo*! That's outrageous. What's your real name?"

"We don't want to go there," Runs said, rolling his eyes.

"Whitekill," Blubbo said. It was a family name that had long been among the tribes.

A pause hung in the air.

"Well...OK," Lexie said, not really thinking Blubbo would care to be called White, and Kill was even further out of the question for a name than Blubbo. "What's your first name?

"Just call me Blubbo, OK?" Blubbo said. "I've kinda got used to it, you know?"

"I like Blubbo!" Loverly said.

"Let it lie, Lexie," Runs said.

"Aw come on people! We can't call this fine...young man...'Blubbo'! What's the first name on your birth certificate?"

Blubbo sighed and rolled his eyes. "Barffarhdt."

"*Barf-fart*!?" went everyone but Blubbo and Runs.

"Aw come on!" Lexie said.

"He's not putting you on," Runs said. "B-a-r-f-f-a-r-h-d-t."

"My word!" Nerves said.

"*Barffarhdt Whitekill*?" Boot said.

"Any woman would name a kid that oughta have her nuts shot off," Hogan mumbled.

"My momma told me about the name before she died," Blubbo said. "Some South African German student guy who came to the rez to study tribal culture when she was a young woman."

Lexie was struggling. "Well...what did they call you in your gang?"

"*Ex*-gang," Runs said.

"Barf," Blubbo said.

Lexie sighed. She could put two and two together. "Blubbooooooo!" she said, walking the give the young Indian a hug he wouldn't soon forget.

"Barf-fart?" Nerves repeated. "What, was he, like, your father?"

"Naw. I think he was, like, my momma's first...you know,

but I wasn't born 'til a couple years after he went back to South Africa. I...I never had no father."

"Ancient history," Runs said, reaching up to tousle Blubbo's shaggy black hair, "besides, you got one now."

"I reckon that means you got a white uncle too, then!" Boot said, clapping Blubbo on the back. "Suck on that egg."

"And a Hispanic, sort-of auntie," Nerves said, crossing his ankles like a ballerina and shaking Blubbo's hand.

"Ah Jesus," Hogan grumbled. Loverly stuck him with her elbow.

"And you got another auntie with a...damned colorful... resume," Lexie said.

Loverly stepped forward. "Annnnd...you got a—"

"Sister!" Hogan growled. "*Best-case* scenario!"

"Not...exactly," Loverly said, standing on her tip-toes to hug Blubbo about his neck. She planted a long and not altogether sisterly kiss on his lips.

"Wuh-wow," Blubbo said, wide-eyed, when Loverly let him come up for air.

"Ahhhhhhh, *shit*." Hogan said. "There goes the neighborhood."

CHAPTER THIRTY-ONE

Eastern Washington

Normally when he visited his dizzy sister, Packy Rudd would drive from Spokane to Grand Coulee Dam and thence to Omak, the biggest town, such as it was, in immense, sparsely populated Okanogan County. From there he would usually drive north into the remote hills outside the tiny town of Tonasket. Packy's sister lived in some sort of fairy-worshiping, nature cult buried so far back off the grid that God couldn't find it with GPS.

Packy regarded his sister as sweet, but a couple of bulbs short of a chandelier.

Tonight, though, Packy decided to take the slightly longer but spectacularly scenic route through Ferry County, in part because he'd driven the faster route often, and in part because the longer route entailed a ten-minute cruise across the Lake Roosevelt ferry. Packy had hoped the clear weather would last this late in the evening, but cloudy weather had moved in. He'd heard snippets on NPR about a big storm system coming in off the distant Pacific.

The ferry ride broke up the trip at an opportune point, and allowed Packy to stretch his legs and breathe the cool night air. He was relieved to barely make the last ferry run for the evening at 11:15 pm, along with one other car, driven by a teen couple who walked to the blunt bow and laughingly pretended the Winslow-DiCaprio scene from *Titanic*. Packy set the brake on his Trooper, snatched a denim jacket, and bailed out as the old ferry began it's umptimillionth voyage across the expansive lake.

Before he reached the north landing, though, Packy wished he'd gone another way.

In driving, since Ray Lightfoot's cell phone call, Packy had almost wiped this crazy bear nonsense from his head. Maybe he'd been trekking the woods too long. How could anyone buy off on some set of peculiar circumstances and somehow come up with this nutty bear-napping scheme? He couldn't believe he'd been dumb enough to entertain such an idiotic fantasy, even in theory. Some Indian stocks up on nighttime cold-and-flu med. Some unconnected white woman with mega-boobs happens to buy out a Burger King full of Whoppers. So what?

There were perfectly ordinary reasons for these events, just, nobody knew what they were, which meant nothing. Damned sure didn't mean anybody stole a two-thousand-pound, man-eating grizzly bear.

And how?

For what?

Absurd.

Too silly to contemplate.

Still...Packy thought, looking at the waters of Lake Roosevelt slide by the groaning ferry...*fifty* Whoppers...and not one single order of *fries*?

An elderly deck hand limped up to Packy. "Kids!" he said, indicating the kissing couple at the bow with a tilt of his head. "You wouldn't believe it. I've had some of 'em go right at it, right in their cars, while making the crossing."

"My friend," Packy said. "I'd believe anything about people. That's why I make my living in the woods. The less people I see, the happier I am."

"Logger?"

"Forest Service officer."

"Oh yeah. I like animals too. 'Specially dogs. 'Specially old dogs. Old dogs just want to lay down by you on the porch while you smoke a cigar and drink a brewski."

"Or two or three," Packy said.

The old deck hand laughed. "Yeah! Old dogs ain't like women, they ain't gonna bitch about how much you drinkin'."

"Yep. Animals are cool."

There was a pause in the night breeze while the two men looked out over the dark lake.

"Not all animals, though," the old man said. "I ain't real fond a pigs."

"Aw, give 'em a break," Packy said. "Pigs are smart. Some say smarter than dogs."

"May be, but they the stankinist animals on earth. Next to maybe a skunk."

"Can't argue with that."

"Had a big semi full of pigs on the boat this evening just after sundown. Stank to high heaven."

More pause.

The trouble with me, Packy thought, is I can't just stop thinking and shut up my mind. Who'd be trucking pigs into isolated Ferry County? They didn't even truck pigs out of Ferry County, not a trailer-truck load anyway. Ferry County was like Okanogan County, it was cattle country. They didn't call the locals *pig*-boys, they called them cowboys for a reason. Ferry County was a couple thousand mountainous square miles with less population than an average eastern small town. If every citizen in the county raised pigs, they couldn't raise a trailer-truck load of them, and if they did, they'd be trucking them outbound to some slaughterhouse. There was no place in Ferry County that could slaughter that many hogs, and it was not a route to Canada any livestock trucker would use. Too slow, too long, too crooked and too steep.

It didn't make any sense. Packy was tired of things that didn't make sense.

"Full truckload of pigs?" Packy said.

"I reckon. Stank like a full truckload."

"So...what, you didn't actually see them?"

"Naw. Come to think of it, that was odd. They had covered over the sides with tarps, the middle bay, anyway."

Oh, no, no, no, Packy thought. Don't go making some off-the-wall remark that wakes up the whole bear-napping scenario. He sighed. I can't believe I'm saying this. "What, they had the sides of the trailer tarped over?"

"Yeah. Ain't that odd? I mean it's cool weather and all, but now that you mention it, I ain't never seen a livestock trucker tarp up his vents."

Oh, no. "Me neither."

"And that ain't all."

Oh no, no, no.

"Then, later in the crossing, I seen this little weasel-lookin' guy peel signs off the cab doors and put some other signs on them. Musta been them magnetic kinda signs."

"The trucker changed the signs on his doors?"

"Well, naw. It weren't the trucker. The trucker was a big ole cowboy guy, had this fine lookin' wife with tits out to here." The deck hand held a hand several inches before his chest. "Naw, see, that's the thing, the weasel-lookin' guy that changed the signs wasn't even on the truck. He was some duded up city-boy. I'm thinking he sways in the breeze if you know what I mean."

"Mm-hmm," Packy said.

"Wore them stupid Brickinshock shoes with socks, you know?"

"Birkenstocks?"

"Whatever. Who the hell wears sandals ain't at the goddamn beach or in the goddamn shower? Anyway, this weasel dude, he come aboard in another vehicle, with some other folks, and, funny thing is, none a them spoke to the trucker or his ole lady, even though they stood next to each other. Like they didn't know each other, you know?"

Packy rubbed his face and shook his head slowly. I can't believe this is happening.

"What was the weasel guy driving?"

"Aw, I don't know. I see three hundred vehicles a day on this job. They all look the same after a while. Old Chevy Suburban I think."

Oh no. "So...nice-tits...she was with the cowboy trucker on the big truck."

"Yep."

"And...you said there were some other folks with... Weasel?"

"Yep. Didn't see any of them but this one pretty little gal, come up to me, asked about the Big Flipper.'

"The big what?"

"You know, the star constitution." He pointed up.

"Oh."

"She were a pretty little thang."

Packy shook his head again. This can't be happening.

"So...the sides of this truck were tarped, right, so you never actually saw any of these...pigs?"

"Yep. I mean, nope."

"Did you, like, hear them moving around, grunting, that sort of thing?"

"Hmm. Well, naw, now that you ask, I didn't. But I did hear one a them pigs fart. Son...I tell you...sounded like a goddamn train at a crossing."

Packy hung his head, staring at the racing water.

"Man," the old deck hand said, "that musta been one big pig."

Tonny thought he'd died and gone to Heaven. Some time in the night, the two-legs showed up again, all chattering and scurrying about outside the movable cave. They'd put another thing of delicious cow parts with that special purple sauce in the adjoining cave chamber, and a second, like, movable puddle full of water. Then they'd slid open the wall passage. After he'd squirmed through the hole in the wall to eat, they'd closed the wall, and come in the old chamber to remove all his dumplings. And then damned if they didn't wash away all his pee with what smelled like clean river. Tonny felt like he'd stayed at a Holiday Inn Express.

Yes bear, Tonny thought, wolfing down his meal. I'm gonna have to reexamine my whole stance on two-legs. They didn't taste that good anyway, judging from the one Tonny had eaten. But, then, that one hadn't had this great sauce.

CHAPTER THIRTY-TWO

Both Sides of the Cascade Curtain

The day before the Washington senate vote on the Belle Noble Grizzly Bear Restoration Act was one of ominous portent.

Senator Lisa Belle was wired to the max with paranoia about someone, somehow, scuttling the senate vote on the bear bill.

The FOCM held a mission briefing that fairly squirted bad news.

Packy Rudd was wandering through Ferry County and then Okanogan County, stopping at every little town, road house, convenience market and fast-food joint he came to, asking if anyone had seen anything weird.

Tonny was the only player in the drama who thought the good times just kept on coming.

"So where do we stand?" Lisa demanded of Perry and Caroline, when Perry closed the door to her senate office.

"We're ready," Caroline said, shuffling her notes. "Dr. Ermintrude Windgate will be present in the rotunda during tomorrow morning's senate session, in case some technical question about grizzly bears should come up. That...Bear-Daughter...sister-woman person will be on the ellipse between the legislative building and the supreme court, in full Indian regalia, playing recorded grizzly sounds on her... back-pack loudspeaker thingy–"

"Mistaaaaake," Perry said.

"Oh, enough already!" Lisa said, flopping into her throne-like, gold-monogrammed office chair. "Lowenstein

has more than a few cracked tiles, we're agreed, but the
loudspeaker thing is a good idea. It'll set a positive tone for
the vote, but more importantly it'll act as a drown-out if we
get some silly-assed demonstration from the horse manure
crowd or those anal mountain-bike pedalers! I'm not taking
any chances on this bill!"

Perry rolled his eyes but kept his peace.

Caroline chimed on. "Like you said, no word goes out
to the media from here until the vote is final, then they all
get shotgunned with the announcement. None of the TV
stations are interested in showing up to interview you, but–"

"Ingrateful jackals!"

"Ah...right, but I did get one radio station to send
somebody, and the Tacoma paper will send a reporter."

"No TV?"

"No ma'am."

"Did you call *Animal Planet*, like I–"

"Yes ma'am, but they wanted crashes between whale
boats and protestors, that sort of–"

"Nobody from the *Times*?"

"Sort of. They said call if the bill passed and they'd run a
blurb on it."

"A blurb! I push a landmark ecological milestone bill
through the senate, and the Times won't even do a P.O.?"

"They said bears are sooo yesterday, unless they've eaten
anybody."

"Fuck the *Times*!"

"Yes ma'am. I suspect they're thinking of when you last
told them that on the day they wanted to interview you
about the horsey and bikey protestors."

Lisa smacked her hand on her desk, then rubbed her
eyes. "Alright. So we're all set, then?"

"Well, there's this weird weather thing," Perry said,
looking at a computer printout.

"What does that mean? Bad enough to close the regular
session? Bad enough to postpone the vote on my bill?"

"No, it's way too early for snow. According to the
Northwest Weather and Avalanche Center, we're just looking

at rain and wind, but a lot of it."

"Rain, shmain!"

Perry looked out an office window. "I don't like it. See how dark it's getting already? Some kinda colossal front is supposed to blow in off the ocean tonight or early tomorrow morning. The weather weenies are talking ark floating rain. The Coast Guard is warning small boats to stay in port tomorrow, but the schools aren't cancelling yet."

"Then we're alright on the vote, right? The goddamn senate can't exactly close for business if the screaming brats have to go to school."

"Yes...Senator," Perry said, tapping the readout in his other hand. "There's something else, though."

"What? Don't tell me a grizzly invaded Children's Hospital and ate up half the patients."

"NWAC is getting some disturbing seismic signals."

"*Tsunami*!?" Lisa squeaked, springing from her chair with impressive gusto. "Get the car! Charter an airplane!"

"Um, no ma'am," Caroline said. We're not at much Tsunami risk as far inland as Olympia. It's just that they're reporting some...peculiar seismographic indications, and–"

"*Volcano*!?" Lisa said at a higher octave. "Mount St. Helens again?"

"No, not Mount St. Helens!" Perry said. "Will you settle down a–"

"Baker? Adams? Glacier Peak? Oh my god! Not *Mount Rainier*?"

Perry fired an acidic look at Caroline, whom he'd urged not to tweak the eminently tweakable Senator Belle with any seismic voodoo. Volcanos were a dicey subject in western Washington, which had more of them than a teenager with acute acne. On a clear day, towering, snow-peaked Mount Rainer was a signature sight from Seattle. Mount St. Helens was almost visible from Olympia. Three other volcanos were uncomfortably close and also listed as 'potentially active.' Washington's 'ring-of-fire' volcanic faucets had rarely rumbled, but that was like saying nuclear explosions were rare when you lived on Bikini Atoll.

Lisa wasn't deathly paranoid for no reason. "What 'peculiar seismic indications'?" she demanded of Caroline.

"Oh it's probably nothing," Caroline said, wishing she'd taken Perry's advice. "It's just what NWAC calls 'atypical sine waves from some sensors'. I don't think–"

"Caroline!" Lisa said tightly, "I took algelus in high school. An atypical *wave*...is a *sign*...of a freaking *tsunami*!"

"Nobody's talking tsunami!" Perry said. He flopped onto a maroon leather couch and loosened his tie. "Lis–, Senator, we live on the edge on one of the world's major tectonic plates. The Juan de Fuca subduction is about ninety miles thataway." Perry pointed west.

"The wonder *what*? Sounds like a porn video!"

"Forget it. I'm just saying there hasn't been a day in fifty-thousand years when we didn't have 'seismographic indications'. It's gonna rain tomorrow. Big deal. It rains in northwest Washington damn near all year, but it never rains in the senate chamber. The vote on your bear bill will go off on schedule. If anything, the weather will discourage any... demonstrators who might be inclined to show up."

Lisa eyed both her secretary and her bodyguard suspiciously. Both tried to look as neutral as Buddha.

"Well, OK," Lisa said, "but, Caroline, you charter an airplane to stand-by anyway. If we go in the bug-out mode, for 'seismic' or any other reason, I want to be on the first thing that flies."

The Free Okanogan County Movement had spent the morning before G day at Boot's isolated cattle ranch in Okanogan County, marveling over their captive, who, as Loverly had predicted, behaved like a giant puppy.

Well, marveling might be too strong a word for the superfund job of cleaning up the bear's trailer, but the FOCM revolutionaries were impressed at how quickly Tonny picked up on the routine of being baited by food into one of the end chambers of the trailer, where he ate, while the two-legs cranked the door shut, then shoveled and hosed out the main middle compartment.

Tonnny would have figured out String Theory for the tub of hairless, boneless, delicious meat he was regularly offered. The smallest two-leg—a young sow, Tonny thought—had even taken to sliding him especially tasty side snacks of some kind he'd never known, through the slots in the cave walls. They were tiny but wonderfully sweet tidbits. One of the old boar two-legs, the crabby one with the sting stick, would growl at the little sow when he caught her. Still, she kept coming back when the old boar wasn't looking, cooing pleasant noises at Tonny and shoving the snacks through the holes.

"Loverly!" Hogan grumbled yet again, "Quit feeding that thing by hand!"

"But Tonny loves Snickers bars, Paw-paw!"

"Bullshit! He'll love your whole arm right through that trailer wall in a minute! Knock it off."

"Aw, Paw-paw, he's just a big puppy." Loverly had elected not to tell Hogan that for over an hour she'd had Tonny lapping M&Ms out of her hand with his plate-sized, purple-pink, warm, sand-paper tongue. Tonny's breath would deck a goat, but Loverly thought snacking him was fun anyway.

Tonny's attitude toward two-legs had undergone a sea-change in the last twenty-four hours.

The trouble not fully anticipated was that, at his record extraordinary size, Tonny consumed food like a Japanese excavator went through a coal mine. Even supplemented by the fifty Whoppers from Whitefish, Montana, with the buns, they'd already run through the meat they'd originally thought would sustain a captured bear until they dumped him on the state of Washington at the capitol building in Olympia tomorrow.

It was decided that, since they needed some feminine items anyway, Lexie and Loverly would drive the Suburban into the nearby town of Tonasket, where there was a sizable neighborhood grocery, and buy more meat. A collection was taken up and the two women disappeared down the rocky dirt trail in the old SUV.

In late afternoon, when the girls returned, the FOCM settled into what Nerves called a strategy review session.

Nerves wasn't happy at the weather forecast he'd pulled off Accuweather on his laptop.

"Screw the weather," Blubbo said, now wearing jeans, boots, a western shirt and a ball-cap that had 'You're in Indian Country!' emblazoned on it. Runs and Boot had left the new clothes by Blubbo's bed the previous evening after awarding him Runs's family knife. They'd been delighted to find his red basketball togs in the trash can this morning. "Weather changes all the time around here," Blubbo concluded.

"Thank you, Punxutawney Phil!" Nerves said.

"Who?" Blubbo said. He'd never heard of that tribe.

"Look! This is no cakewalk we're going on here, Blubbo. Every detail matters and this record storm they're predicting is more than a small detail!"

"I'm with the kid," Hogan rasped. "What's the big deal? So it rains. Bears are waterproof."

Nerves sighed, pecking at his laptop computer. He chewed a nail. "It's what the weather people aren't saying that bothers me more than what they are saying. They're making all those noises they always make when something big is in the works, but they can't figure out what. Near as I can figure they're expecting a massive low pressure area coming up from California and–"

"Piss on California!" Hogan said. "Buncha pot-sucking communist hippies, you ask me. Only thing in California worth a shit is the San Andreas Fault."

"Will you pay attention, Hogan? And there's a high pressure system coming down from the Bering Sea, too. They're still making a lot of 'ifs' and 'maybes' here, but the bottom line is we could be dealing with some major winds and rain late tonight and in the morning when we strike for Olympia. They're talking possible flooding, possible power outages, the whole nine yards. This could mean closed roads, traffic jams–"

"So maybe they'll postpone the vote on the bear bill,"

Lexie said.

"I doubt it," Nerves said. "These sneaky legislators always try to pick a key day to put their bills up for votes. They're always looking to match it up with some other more favorable bill, or the absence of legislators who might vote against it, or some way of avoiding negative demonstrations or other bad PR. Senator Belle chose tomorrow for a reason, and it's always possible that something could happen to negatively influence her bill if the vote is postponed."

"Like us," Boot said.

"Exactly. So she definitely won't want a postponement. Besides, the senate website still lists the vote for tomorrow, and they aren't likely to shut down for anything but cataclysmic weather. They'd take too much public heat from all the voters who have to go to work in bad weather."

"OK," Runs said, "so Operation Grizz is still a go, in your view, Nerves?"

"Absolutely, Runs. This bear bill is Senator Belle's best shot at a U.S. senate run next year and she knows it. She also knows this bill is a shoe-in in the house if she gets it through the senate. The governor is left of Lenin; she'll go for it just to posture green. Nobody in Okanogan County but a bunch of Seattle weekenders in the Methow Valley votes for her anyway, so what's she got to lose? The libs rule in Olympia because Washington voting is dominated by the big money west of the Cascade Curtain, so there's no way to defeat this bill through democratic means. The only thing that stands between Okanogan Countians and this crazy bear scheme is Operation Grizz. If we can bring it off, we'll call in enormous publicity at a key moment in the process. It'll keep dozens of also-ran senators, who Belle's bought off in some quid-pro-quo deal, from voting for the bear bill thinking no one in their home districts will know or care."

"*Will* they care?" Boot asked. "Why would some liberal voters from a westside democrat county give a damn whether some senator from some other liberal county sticks sixty grizz in the back yards of some conservative eastside county most of them never think about?"

"They *won't* as long as it's just some abstract, eco-fuzzy concept they don't even know much about! That's what makes Operation Grizz so critical, Boot. It's one thing to look the other way and miss a bill getting passed—hell, that's the way the vast majority of American legislation is done on the local, state and national levels—but it's another deal altogether to look right at a scary, dangerous animal about to get super-populated into anybody's back yard. This isn't the spotted owl we're talking about. A whole lot of soccer moms will wonder, hey, if the state can force grizzly bears into that county, what about the county where my kids play? A lot of people who jog, bike, camp, hunt, fish, and trail-ride horses will think about finding themselves face-to-face with a six-hundred pound, wind-up food processor and–"

"Two-thousand pounds," Hogan said.

"So we lucked out and captured a monster. So much the better for us! Most voters won't know our bear is an aberrant giant. The press can blab all they want discounting his size, but the viewers will think all grizzlies are the size of a Toyota Prius when you're looking at them in your own yard!"

"Besides," Lexie said, "the media is going to tee off on Tonny's record size, not downplay it."

"Exactly! The other senators are going to know all this, and they're going to take a different tack on voting for a bill they have that kind of public accountability for."

"I'll take that as a go for Operation Grizz," Runs said. "We better know what we're about, here, guys, because this could blow up in our faces."

"You're telling *me*?" Nerves said. "We're already indictable on everything from grand-theft-auto, to the endangered species act, to contributing to the delinquency of minors. And you can get more jail time for violating game laws in America than you get for murdering humans."

"Oh that's really great to hear, Nerves!" Blubbo said.

"Ah what are you worried about? You're a corrupted juvenile."

"May be, but I'm a ten-pound lighter corrupted

juvenile."

"Yea!" Loverly said.

"Look, as long as nobody—including our fuzzy friend in the barn out there, gets hurt—worst-case scenario in the final legal analysis, as is the kids will walk and we adults probably get off with fines and suspended sentences, but that's no guarantee. Not to mention that the whole point here is to stop the state from cozying us up to grizzlies in Okanogan County, not to cause them to do it because we got a bear shot or got some capitol janitor eaten alive."

"Tonny wouldn't eat anybody!" Loverly said.

"He's a bear, Loverly," Runs said, "an omnivore. That means he'll eat Osama if he's hungry enough."

"I'd like to see that," Hogan said.

"But ..." Blubbo said, puzzled, "I thought we're not going to turn him loose?"

"We're not!" Nerves said. "We just drop the truck off on the capitol ellipse with the bear in it, and call the news media. Boot, you're confident that you've fixed the truck so it can't be moved when we dump it, right?"

"It'll take them hours to figure out what the problem is, and hours more to get the equipment in there to move the rig. By that time, that monster will be on every front page and TV station in Washington."

"What's our exit plan?" Blubbo said, stunning everybody else.

"Our what?" Nerves said.

"I heard it on TV, man; we need a exit plan in case it all balls up on us."

Everybody stared at Blubbo. The idea of him as a thinking man hadn't occurred to anyone. "What?" Blubbo said at the perplexed looks.

"He's right," Runs said. "Anything from a traffic accident, to some stray cop in the wrong place, to a blocked highway and Christ knows what else could go wrong." Runs turned to Nerves. "The kid's right. What's our exit plan?"

Nerves considered thoughtfully. "OK. Legally, as long as we're not actually caught with the bear or the stolen truck, we're–"

"Borrowed!" Lexie said.

"OK, but 'borrowed' isn't how the law is going to look at this escapade, Lexie. If we run into a problem we can't handle, the important thing is to part company with the bear and the boosted truck, pronto. We'll wash the rig, wipe it down and vacuum it thoroughly before we leave tonight, and nobody will get near it without their surgical gear on. Beyond that, there're no witnesses or any evidence to connect us with anything illegal as long as no one talks. On that subject, if any or all of us are nabbed, we have absolutely nothing whatever to say to anybody until we talk to a lawyer. That's before or after they read us Miranda rights. Everybody got that?"

"Been there, done that," Lexie said.

"Me too," Blubbo said.

"Ditto," Hogan said.

Runs sighed. "OK, so we have an exit plan. Now here's what I want to know. Are we all sure we're in? Because when we're committed and something goes haywire, and it will, that won't be the time to wonder whether we need to be doing this. Nerves, we know where you stand. Boot?"

"Don't the constitution say something about how government's power comes from the governed, and when government forgets that, the governed have a right to take over?"

"Mmm," Nerves said, "that's the Declaration of Independence you're thinking about, and it doesn't exactly say that."

"Does it say it or not?" Boot demanded.

"Basically yes, but I wouldn't trust any modern judge to see what we're doing quite that way."

"I don't trust judges any damn way," Boot said. "I got no use for some bimbo in a Dracula robe who never served a day of combat in her life who wants me to call her 'your honor' any more than I do for some westsider witch trying to put grizzlies in my back yard. We ain't doing anything but defending our rights. I'm in."

"Hogan?"

"Hell, way I see it, it's this bear trick or we bomb the statehouse. I'm in."

"Lexie?"

"I was in from the beginning. I'm tired of being pushed around by government assholes who don't know or give a damn who they're putting at risk."

"Me too!" Loverly said. "And somebody's got to watch out for Tonny!"

"Blub?"

"I ain't no pussy. I'm in."

Loverly and Lexie slugged Blubbo in the arms again. "Ow!" Blubbo said, baffled. "What'd I say?" Lexie shook her head and Loverly scowled.

The FOCM now set to finalizing a tactical assault plan.

Nerves announced that there was good news and bad news about the forecast for heavy weather. The bad news was that the risk of traffic accident and blocked roads had worsened, and reporters might be somewhat less likely to turn out in force in the rain. The good news, though, outweighed the bad. Potentially troublesome tourist movement near the statehouse would likely be reduced, and, best of all, the thick, extensive, electrically active cloud cover virtually guaranteed that satellite photography and even satellite infrared surveillance were temporarily not a risk.

It was decided that G-hour would be 9 am. This was early enough to get Tonny in the day's major news flow, giving time for the event to hit even the eastern time zone TV stations before evening, but it was late enough in the morning that the incoming traffic would be light for a weekday. It would also allow escape before the afternoon rush hour.

They would drive through the night to arrive at a huge truck stop off I-5 near Olympia by dawn, well before the Seattle area rush hour gridlocked the roads. There they would repair to a distant, ergo lightly occupied corner of the parking area with the Tonny war-wagon and block any parking near it with the other two vehicles. At G-hour minus twenty minutes, they would put new taped misprints over all license plate numbers and pull the magnetic signs off the truck tractor. Nerves and Hogan would lead in the Suburban while they moved to the 14th Avenue Tunnel only a thousand or so yards from the state capitol building, keeping an interval unlikely to be seen from any one surveillance video camera on buildings. Runs, Loverly and Blubbo, bringing up the rear in the pickup and horse trailer, would block the westbound lanes of the east tunnel entrance, pretending a breakdown. Hogan and Nerves in the Suburban would block the west entrance. Both vehicles would fake breakdowns.

Boot and Lexie would halt the war-wagon in the four-lane tunnel. Nerves, Boot, Lexie, Blubbo and Loverly would converge on the war-wagon, wearing surgical caps, masks, gloves and booties. They would quickly un-bungy the trailer tarps, displaying Tonny in all his glory, roll up the tarps and stick them in the horse trailer. It was estimated that time in the tunnel would take two minutes, max, not enough to draw inordinate attention. By the time any cops responded to investigate a possibly reported traffic blockage, the FOCM would be on the move again.

Nerves and Hogan would proceed in the Suburban at a legal speed out of the tunnel and slightly right on South Diagonal Avenue toward the statehouse. They'd circumvent the traffic circle at the Winged Victory Memorial Statue, stopping shortly at the entrance to the long, grassy ellipse constituting the elliptical drive between the front entrances of the legislative building and the state supreme court.

Meanwhile Boot and Lexie would drive the war-wagon out of the tunnel and follow slowly and straight ahead along Sid Snyder Avenue past the Visitor Center building. It was not unusual for supply trucks to use these approaches to the capitol area, and Tonny would be hard to spot until the truck stopped, especially in rain. The FOCM would just have to take their chances with that smell, they decided. It did not occur to the strategic masterminds that the last time an actual cattle truck drove onto the Capitol Campus was probably a farmer protest in 1977.

Runs, Loverly and Blubbo would stow the tarps in the horse trailer, and transit the tunnel in the pickup, turning north on Capitol Way, well back from the statehouse complex. They would then turn back east on 11th Avenue, where they would pull tightly to the curb, and pretend another breakdown.

At precisely G-hour, assuming Nerves and Hogan found the entrance to the ellipse and the ellipse itself clear enough of traffic, Nerves would pick up his hand-held radio and say: "Tora! Tora! Tora!" which would be the final signal for Boot, Lexie and Tonny to turn right onto Cherry Lane, drive down the eastside of the statehouse and hook a hard left into the ellipse.

Immediately upon the approach of the war-wagon, Nerves and Hogan would drive the Suburban into the ellipse counter-clockwise, in accordance to the normal traffic flow between the statehouse and the supreme court. They would stop in the parking slots before the Temple of Justice.

Boot would drive the war-wagon into the ellipse but swing clockwise only a few yards until they were immediately before the statehouse front steps, whereupon they would stop in the roadway. Boot would trigger the compressed air bottles that squirted epoxy into the truck's wheels, then he and Lexie would bolt across the ellipse on foot and bail into the Suburban. Nerves, the Porsche ace, would escape-and-evade the Suburban out the other end of the ellipse, circling right, past the entrance to the Governor's mansion, and around the Temple of Justice. They would wind their way east on 12th Avenue and Water Street.

All parties would diabolically be dressed like 3rd-world surgeons, to prevent later identification on surveillance cameras, or fingerprint/DNA tracing.

When they passed Runs et. al. on 11th Avenue, all would proceed back to the nearby truckstop. There, they would drop the Suburban, which might be recognized if they went back to the capitol in it. They'd pile into the horse-trailer pickup truck, and return to the capitol campus. They'd park on South Diagonal Road and pretend to be tourists on foot as they observed and gloated over the greatest statement for independence and freedom since The Boston Tea Party.

It was brilliant if he said so himself, Nerves told the FOCM around Boot's dinner table. Foolproof.

"'Tore up' what?" Blubbo said, very confused.

"No!" Nerves said. "Pay attention! We'll maintain radio silence until Hogan and I check that the coast is clear, then–"

"The coast of *what*? Puget Sound?" Blubbo was lost.

"Never mind! Hogan and I will be sure the access of the Tonny truck onto the ellipse is clear, then I'll call over the radio, 'Tora! Tora! Tora!', like the Japanese did when they attacked Pearl Harbor. Boot and Lexie will know to proceed with the final approach of the war wagon."

Pearl Harbor was, like, Peloponnesian history as far as Blubbo could remember from school, but he figured that if Nerves was modeling the plan after a famous one to kill white people, it was probably OK.

Not so, Lexie. "We're gonna make like Japs attacking Pearl Harbor?" She asked in a frigid tone.

"Yeah," Boot said, "that sucks, Nerves."

"It's just a signal, people! One that's easy to remember and hard to get confused on the radio!"

"Hey, Nerves," Runs said. "I'm a United States *Marine*. We need a better signal."

Nerves sighed. Runs hadn't been an active duty Marine since disco was hot, but Nerves knew when Dr. Rivers had entered his nonnegotiable mode. "Alright, alright, what, then?"

"Why do we need a code, for Christ's sake?" Hogan said. "What's wrong with 'Bring on the goddamn bear'?"

Nerves rolled his eyes. "We must have codes in operations like this, Hogan! Who knows who's listening on the CB radio these days? We don't want to tip off the cops!"

"Well, we never had no jive-ass codes in Vietnam or Rhodesia. Our 'code' was, 'find the bastards and shoot 'em'."

"Thank you, General Sun Tzu! But we need a code word

so we don't leave anything indictable on some recorder, OK?"

"How about, 'Die motherfucker!'" Blubbo said helpfully. "That was our gang's motto."

"You ain't in no gang, anymore!" Runs said.

Loverly sniffed. "Jane Austen would never be in any operation with that codeword," she said. "Neither is Tonny."

Blubbo sighed. "What's some town in Texas got—"

"Jane Austen was not from *Texas*, you dummie!"

"Alright, alright, I got it," Boot said. "How about this, that great line right outta the movie Scarface. 'Say hello to my 'leetle friend'!"

"Yeah!"

"Works for me."

"Perfect!"

"Damn straight!"

"Ooh-rah!"

"I love it!"

So it was that Dr. Runs With Rivers, DVM, leaned his chair back and slowly looked everyone in the eyes. "OK, then," he said, "let's do it."

CHAPTER THIRTY-THREE

Tonasket, Washington

Federal officer Packy Rudd was learning that driving around the north central Washington outback asking if anyone had seen anything weird was a waste of time, because, as near as he could tell from the responses he received, no one up here ever saw anything else.

One aged waitress in a restaurant had seen Elvis only two days ago, and yeah he was bald and wrinkly and all, and riding in one a them Wal-Mart fat-broad scooters, but the curled lip was a giveaway. She was afraid to ask him, you know, security and all, but she was sure it was The King.

A Pakistani green-card in a Keller Lightning-Mart had seen Sasquatch, at night, a week before, behind his apartment. The giant ape had been "going through the dumpsters like they were a New Orleans CostCo after Katrina, dood!" the clerk had told Packy. "He was hairy as Khalid Sheikh Mohammed, but twice as ugly and much taller!"

Yet another convenience market attendant in Republic had seen unmarked black helicopters come over bearing what he was pretty sure was A-rabs or PETA or some other terrorist bunch. This clerk suspected that the raghead who worked for the rival convenience market in the previous town was behind it all, know what I mean, dude? I mean why else would some camel-kisser live up here and pretend to work for a Lightning-Mart in Keller?

Packy was pretty sure the clerk had his racial slur targets confused, but it didn't seem promising to try to enlighten him.

It was frustrating and Packy began to feel more than a

little silly. After all, he only had the flimsiest of suspicions that any grizzly bear had ever been stolen, or that it had come the route he was following even if it had. There were any number of explanations for the events that had occurred in Whitefish that didn't involve a bear-napping, and nothing the old ferry deck hand had said even meant that Packy wasn't doing a Sherlock Holmes number on some stock truck full of pigs. What was he doing on this crazy mission anyway? He was supposed to be on vacation!

But Packy struck paydirt of a sort, at a chainsaw shop in Wauconda. A huge-bellied guy who looked like roughly Charlie Daniels, replete with beard and enormous western hat, shouted over the clatter of an idling chainsaw he held in his workshop, "Onliest thing I seen weird...today that is...is somebody went by in a cattle rig had them blue, chink tarps all over it. Looked like a damn circus rig!"

Packy flashed out of his numbed boredom in a hurry. "Oh yeah?" he shouted over the saw.

"Yeah man. I mean, the truckers, they'll sometimes tarp the sides of a cattle box in, like you know, real cold winter when the air's, like, below zero. Slaughterhouses, they won't pay fer no frostbit steers, but hell, not in the middle of the summer, you know?"

"Yeah," Packy said, trying not to appear unduly interested, "who...ah...who do you suppose it was?"

"Ah, hell I give 'em just a quick look they go by, mostly for this blonde chick with outstanding wubbies in the passenger seat. Shoot, I thought the driver was Boot Colhane, but couldn't a been. It wadn't his rig. Looked like ol' Sol Pickering's rig, but wadn't his brand on the door, and 'sides, ol' Sol, he's been dead fer nigh a year. And Boot, he ain't got no wife since Coretta died from that infected wolf bite in 2000 trying to git back one a her lambs."

Packy assumed that if you made your living servicing chainsaws you didn't turn one off just because a stranger starts a conversation. "Boot...?"

"Colhane. Boot, he got a big ranch about half way here to Tonasket back up in the Aeneas Valley. But it weren't

246

his rig and he ain't got no old lady. I'd have me a old lady, though, if she looked like this rider. Wubbies clean out to–".

"Uh huh. You didn't, like, see a name on the truck or a license number?" Packy called over the chattering saw.

Charlie looks-like-Daniels suddenly got that feeling he always got when some one a them gubmint sumbitches showed up to make trouble. "Son," he said loudly, "you startin' to sound a awful lot like a cop!" Chainsaw Charlie's tone did not sound like he was terribly interested in making a contribution to the police memorial fund, which could have had something to do with his two priors, one for assault and the other for riding his horse drunk in a Cheyenne shopping mall in '05. Both Charlie and his horse had been under the influence. Charlie revved the chainsaw to a brief snarl. *Raaaaaaaad-na-na-na-na-naaaaa!*

Packy watched the chain whirl and got the message that a three-hundred pound cowboy with a running, chainsaw in his hands had just cooled about thirty degrees centigrade. Packy held up both palms and smiled. "Hey you're pretty sharp, sir, but you got me wrong. I'm just a tourist from over in Montana." he said. "See the tag?" Packy pointed through the window to his old Trooper.

Charlie looked and considered that though them rich Hollywood liberals had bought up a lot of Montana, none of 'em drove twenty-year-old Troopers. And no Montana cop or gubmint asshole would likely have any jurisdiction in Washington. Still...how come this little dude with the faggy New York goat beard wanted to know?

"It weren't Boot no ways!" the mechanic shouted. "Wadn't his rig and wadn't his old lady."

Packy said thanks and turned to leave.

"Side's," the mechanic added for good measure, "Boot wouldn't never wear one a them Frog hats!"

"Excuse me?"

"One them blue things like those UN troops wear. Barrette or something, I think."

"You mean a beret?"

"Yeah! That's the word. Both the driver and Miz Wubbies

was wearing blue berets. And come to think of it, the driver guy, he was, like, wearin' those blue rubber gloves a doctor wears. Up here? In the summer? Shit. Ain't no way it was Boot Colhane. Boot wouldn't be caught dead in no Frog lid. He won't even wear a Seahawks cap."

A few miles later in the little town of Tonasket, it was late afternoon and Packy had had enough excitement for one day, or at least he thought he had. He'd drive out to his sister's commune tomorrow. Staying overnight out there was out of the question. He'd get high just from the ambient air in the commune lodge, and he'd have to listen to a lot of self-anointed social geniuses explain what a lousy country America was.

So Packy took a room at a small motel with a horse trailer for sale by the office door, and walked a couple of blocks to a restaurant called the Battalion Burger Bunker. A pleasant young woman who, thankfully, had evidently *not* seen Elvis, brought him a fine steak and spud. Packy liked to read when he ate, so he bought a copy of the Seattle times from a machine. The paper was a day old since Seattle was five hours away by road.

Chomping his excellent steak, Packy began to turn from page eleven to page twelve of the newspaper when the printed word 'bear' caught his eye. At a lower corner of page eleven, the header over a two inch blurb read:

Belle Bear Bill Before Senate

The short text read:

Having expeditiously cleared the Senate Natural Resources, Ocean and Recreation Committee, SB 11-8862, The Senator Lisa Belle Noble Grizzly Bear Restoration Act, is due for vote in the Washington senate chamber on Thursday. SB 11-8862 provides for the restoration of sixty grizzly bears to ecologically suitable and historically appropriate areas of

248

Washington, by the Washington Dept. of Fish and Wildlife.

Packy froze in mid chomp, staring at the article, killer trans-fats dribbling innocently down his chin. No. No way.

Packy furiously pecked numbers into his cell phone. Information, press for English, say party number requested, press for connection, useless clutter recordings, hold for a representat–

"Thank you for calling Senator Lisa Belle's office, my name is Caroline, how may I help you today sir, ma'am or undeclared?"

"Uh, hi. My name is Packy Rudd. That uh, senate bill 8862 about bears, where will those sixty grizzlies be, um, restored?"

"Mmm, and are you a voter of the 34th district, sir?"

"What? No. I'm, I'm a US Forest Service officer, Flathead National Forest in Montana. I just–"

What Caroline called a Belle bell went off in her mind. Flathead National Forest, a name easily remembered. Oh yeah, that pretentious Gaynor woman who spelled and pronounced her name with her doctorate attached like a nose wart. Senator Belle had had Caroline called Gaynor recently. Was this forest guy was calling at Gaynor's direction? "Oh, nothing to worry about, sir. Senate bill 11-8862 will simply restore the noble grizzly bear to its historical habitat."

"Right. And that would be exactly...where?"

"Mmm, not to worry, sir. Senator Belle's bill doesn't affect Montana in any way. Um, may I ask why you're inquiring?" The area code showing on the caller ID display was not from Washington. Caroline typed 'flathead national forest, rud' into her computer search engine.

Packy heard the frantic keyboarding and got the drift. "Oh, yeah, well, see, the senator's bill is indeed noble, and we here in Montana are excited about it. We'll will want to track it so that we might possibly emulate the senator's progressive foresight here in Montana, ma'am."

"I see," Caroline said as the search engine came back indicating one Rudd, Packwood, law enforcement officer, listed under Flathead National Forest 'staff'. What a relief. "Didn't ah, didn't I read that you folks had a little bear... mmm, issue, over there recently?"

A bell now went off in Packy's mind. "Oh. Well, nothing important. Our investigation indicates that bear may be back in Canada now."

"Well, I'm sure glad to hear that. The senator was a little concerned about publicity, what with her bear bill coming before the senate in the morning, you know?"

"Sure. And we here in the Flathead are a hundred percent behind the senator. So, where was it again that those bears will be restored?"

"Oh, nowhere important. Just a few dozen breeding pairs, over a couple of years, on state lands in Okanogan County. It's just some remote, mountainous outback over on the eastside by the Canadian border. Mostly owned by the state and the federal governments. Nobody lives there...to speak of."

It was one of those days for Packy Rudd. As he talked to the senator's receptionist he gazed idly out of the Battalion Burger Bunker window at the grocery diagonally across the street. What seized his eye was not so much the notable chest on the older of the two women he saw by an old Suburban, but the fact that they were loading two entire shopping carts full of what appeared to be white-paper packaged meat into the SUV. The range was nearly a hundred yards, and the clothes were different, but Packy could swear the younger girl looked a little like that kid at the campground, with her grandpa, the day before the great convict consumption. And they'd been driving an old suburban!

"Uh! Gotta go, ma'am. You're breaking up! Thanks!"

In his haste, Packy dropped his cell phone, which bounced off his foot and slid under the booth table. He scrambled on all fours to retrieve it, and, by the time he stood, the old Suburban was chugging past the restaurant.

Packy put his hand on the table to pull himself up, but it came down on the edge of the plate and launched meat, steak sauce, ketchup and mashed potatoes all over his face, shirt and the floor. He spun about to run to the window, but stepped in the mess, slipped and fell into a nearby chair which upended the table next to it adding flatware, salt and pepper shakers, and napkins to the mess on the floor.

When Packy finally regained his feet and limped to the window, the Suburban was a block away and fading, way out of license plate reading range. He watched as it went two more blocks, turned east toward Republic, and disappeared.

Packy turned back to his booth to find customers and staff staring at him like he was Elvis.

"You OK, sir?" the waitress said, meaning mentally.

"Uh, sorry," Packy said, hurrying to help clean up the wreckage. "I uh, I thought I saw an old girlfriend!"

"I saw her too, son," a construction worker at another booth said, "up there by the IGA. Hell, I'd remember her too. She and that little lady she was with both had some healthy hooters on 'em!"

A grizzled old man in a white apron and a 101st Airborne ballcap, wearing a handgun on his belt said, "Hey... you with the gubmint, boy?"

Packy hurried to his car thinking, even for Sasquatch country, this was waaaaay too weird. He drove three blocks and turned east as he'd seen the Suburban do.

What would anybody do with that bear even if they had it? Packy wondered, turning on the Trooper's windshield wipers and having no idea where he was headed. And even if they intend to use it against this screwball bear bill before the senate tomorrow, how would they do it?

And *who*?

The chainsaw guy had said something about a Sol somebody, and a Boot Cocaine, or Colhane or...

CHAPTER THIRTY-FOUR
Twas the Night Before G-Day

The inside of Boot Colhane's barn looked like NASA meets the Beverly Hillbillies.

The war wagon stood cramped under bright lights in the cavernous center aisle of the big structure which bore a dull roar from the rainfall hitting its steel roofing. Blubbo went by Loverly with a borrowed raincoat on, pushing a wheelbarrow full of grizzly poop. The big Indian boy turned the raincoat hood up at the people-door built into one of the huge, sliding main barn doors, then he plunged into the pouring rain. He slogged with the wheelbarrow over the sandy Okanogan highlands soil to a distant manure dump Boot kept for his horses.

Inside, the rest of the FOCM wore their blue hairnets, booties, gloves and masks. Boot had the truck's hood tilted forward and was perched in the engine area doing a final preflight. Lexie was handing him tools, and considering that Boot had a pretty good butt for a forty-something cowboy.

Nerves was poring over maps spread out on a feed-bin next to his laptop. In his own surgical gear, he looked something like Dr. Frankenstein, his wide, blood-pressure bloated eyes scouring the data and rereading the increasingly troublesome weather reports on his laptop.

On the isolated side of the cattle trailer, Loverly surreptitiously slipped Tonny dog biscuits she purloined from a barrel in Boot's mud-room.

Tonny was head-over-furry-heels in love with the chirpy little two-leg. He swung his massive shaggy head with it's stubby, plate-sized ears back and forth, and he grunted lightly so little Chirpy would know he liked her. Tonny knew he had a way with the chicks.

He'd had two two-legs all wrong, Tonny decided. This cave was cramped, and these crunchy things Chirpy was feeding him tasted a little flat, but, on summation, it all beat the hell out of fighting wolves for a week-old ditch-bitch.

Speaking of bitches, Ronald Reagan sat patiently at Loverly's feet, content to eat every fourth biscuit or so. It was only proper that the giant fat dog in the cage should get more, Ronald Reagan reasoned, since it was about twenty-three times as big, and besides, what was she going to do, fight the thing over a biskie? Ronald Reagan had gotten to be an old dog by not being a bold dog.

Tonny licked Loverly's cheek through a slot in the trailer wall with his enormous leathery tongue, which activity would've given Hogan an MI if he'd seen it. Tonny's landfill breath would've given pause to a shark, too, but Loverly endured it because the gesture was soooo sweet. Besides, she had her surgical mask on. What could go wrong?

Loverly watched Blubbo disappear into the rain with the wheelbarrow, a hood over his hair net. She wished Blubbo would show her half as much attention as Tonny did. Maybe if she offered him a biskie...

Runs and Hogan were distracted, preparing Tonny's next meal, which would have to do him until they reached the truck-stop in Olympia at dawn, since the FOCM did not plan to stop once they hit the road at sundown.

Runs unwrapped bloody white paper from chunks of steak, hamburger, roast, ham, pork loin, sausage and boneless chicken breasts, dumping the meat into a muck tub. Lexie and Loverly had made quite a hit with the butcher at the Tonasket supermarket. "Big party," Lexie had explained.

"Right on, lady!" the butcher had said. "Vegans suck!

"Damn!" Hogan growled loudly to be heard over the rain on the barn roof. He was rummaging through a plastic storage container. "We're out of cold-and-flu stuff!"

"What?" Runs said with equal volume. "I thought the girls were going to get more in town."

"They was, but all the little pharmacy had left was the daytime shit–"

"That's no good to us."

"–and the grocery store just had four bottles of the nightime."

"Crap. We're about to do seven hours on the road with the biggest grizzly bear since the Pleistocene Era, and we got nothing to keep him calmed down! This is serious. If this animal starts raising hell because it's hungry or wants out or whatever, we could draw very unwanted attention from some motorist with a cell phone, not to mention the cops."

"Well," Hogan said, "there's always Jack and Johnnie."

"What?"

"Jack Daniels and Johnnie Walker."

"Are you talking about, whiskey, Hogan?"

"Yeah! Boot's a scotch man. He's got most of a case of the stuff up at the house. Me,

I'm a Tennessee kinda drinker, and I could spare... mmmm...coupla bottles of Jack. That oughtta do it huh?"

"Hogan, you brought *more* than two *bottles* of *whiskey* with you on this trip?"

"Well, they're not the party bottles, just quart-sizers!"

"Christ, you must have the liver of a goat if you have any liver at all. You know, a ton of inebriated grizzly might not be an improvement on this situation, Hogan."

"Well, we want to keep him happy, don't we? Hell, you're the vet, here!"

"I keep telling you people they don't teach much *grizzly* in veterinary schools! You know how humans are. Some get mellow when they drink, some get violent. Suppose we got a two-thousand pound biker-bar wrecker over there in that trailer?"

Hogan considered this. He shook his head. "Naw," he said loudly enough to be heard over the rain on the roof high above. "I've been drinking since I was ten. I'm about as experienced a drinker as they come, and it's my professional judgement that Tonny is a mellow kind of drinking bear."

Runs rolled his eyes, though he couldn't really argue with

Hogan's probable expertise here. He squinted at the tub
of greasy meat chunks and tried to call up what he knew
of bear digestive systems. They didn't call bears omnivores
for nothing. They could and did eat damn near anything
remotely qualifying as food, which meant they probably had
industrial-grade livers, bowels and kidneys. Runs considered
it vital to subdue the animal on the road, as they had been
doing with the flu meds, partly to keep it quiet, but also
partly to keep it from being afraid, which could lead to
it becoming sick. Bears were generally not accustomed to
being trucked, and tonight would be a long haul.

Still, Runs thought, while traveling sauced wasn't
medically recommended, hundreds of thousands of
American humans were doing it even as he was thinking
about it, many of them behind the wheel, regrettably.
Almost all of them tended to enjoy the trip more...if they
lived through it.

"How much?" Runs asked.

"How much hooch?" Hogan said. "Well, hell, I don't
know. I never tried to get a grizzly drunk, even a female."

"What's whiskey, about 80-proof?"

"You betcha,"

"So, forty percent alcohol. What? About 350 milliliters
per quart bottle? Average blood volume for a human is
about nine percent of body weight." Runs calculated in his
head as he often had to do in the treatment of cows and
horses, though he'd never needed to mellow one on whiskey.
"Jesus. That's something like eighty kilos of blood in a two-
thousand pound bear!"

"Will you speak English, not that Frog measurement
crap?" Hogan said.

"About a hundred-eighty pounds of blood. Figure
blood's mostly water, about eight pounds a gallon, that's...
Christ, that's over twenty-two *gallons* of blood. Drunk for
a human is legally point-oh-eight alcohol by static present
volume. Figure...about, I don't know, without a calculator or
a table, I'm thinking maybe a little over a gallon and a half
of alcohol, static present volume, so something like three,

maybe four gallons of whiskey. Sixteen bottles. He'd need several more bottles over an hour or two to raise his static present alcohol blood volume to that level."

"Sixteen bottles of scotch! Holy shit. This is getting to be one expensive operation."

Runs shook his head. "What the hell is the matter with me? I'm actually considering getting a monster grizzly bear intoxicated. I must be out of my mind. No. Absolutely not. It violates every ethic in veterinary medicine I haven't already broken. Forget it."

"How else we gonna keep him cool, then?"

"Good question."

"What if we just wing it?" Hogan said.

"I don't trust it. He's only been cool so far because we've kept him fed and sedated. A lot could go wrong if he gets frightened."

"Frightened! Him?"

"Of course. He's way out of his element, in a big, noisy, moving cage. Scents and noises he's never known. There's not a lot of accessible data on this, Hogan. He could wig out, raise hell, draw attention, maybe even hurt himself."

So what do we do?"

Runs sighed. "I guess we'll have to wing it. Nerves won't want us buying huge quantities of flu med this close to G-hour, even if we could find some Wal-Mart or an all-night pharmacy. Some clerk might remember it. We'll just have to give him the four bottles of nighttime that we have and hope it's enough. If he gets scared, freaks out or hurts himself, we'll just have to deal with it."

Runs and Hogan completed preparing Tonny's meal with the four bottles of nighttime cold-and-flu med, and together they struggled to carry the big plastic tub to the rear of the trailer.

Loverly had not been eavesdropping and had ignored the two men on the other side of the trailer. She was engrossed in hand-feeding M&Ms to her beloved new big puppy. But when Loverly heard the word frightened, she had cocked her head and listened. Now she was decidedly distressed.

Tonnikins…'freaking out?' *Hurting* himself?

Blubbo pushed the empty wheelbarrow back into the barn, rain glistening on his slicker in the harsh florescent lighting. Distant lightning backlit his bulk in the doorway with staccato flashes.

"I always wanted to haul manure in a ffff-rigging thunderstorm!" Blubbo said. "All my life I wanted grow up big and strong so I could haul grizzly crap in a downpour!"

Loverly seized her yellow, hooded raincoat from a stall gate and hurried to Blubbo. She looked about, then stood on her tiptoes to whisper to the young Indian man.

"We need to *talk*!"

CHAPTER THIRTY-FIVE

Premonitions

Perry Dinwiddie felt somewhat ridiculous standing in Lisa's senate office wearing only a Lone Ranger mask. And he didn't even want to think about Lisa in that beaded buckskin, bikini she'd also bought at a costume store in Seattle, replete with a pigtailed black wig and feathered headband. All this was before he even began to consider her insistence on applying what she called 'war paint' to her face and arms. "We're just gonna play hide-Mr.-Binkie, Lisa!" Perry had objected. "Not conquer the west!"

"Oh come on, don't be so provincial," Lisa had said, applying her war paint. "Good sex requires imagination!" She turned from the mirror looking roughly like Medusa of the Comanches.

Perry glanced over his shoulder again to check that the brass lock toggle on the big mahogany office door was in the horizontal position. If he should be seen boning a state senator on the people's sofa, even after work hours when everyone else had gone home, it could have disturbing ramifications for Lisa's rep and, by extension, his own paycheck.

Lisa had insisted that she and Perry spend the night before the most critical senate vote of her career at the office. She kept a fold-out bed in storage for this very purpose and Perry could use the couch. She was taking no chances in this weird weather on not making tomorrow's vote, and she was too nervous about it to sleep well anyway.

She'd explained on the phone to her doddering fourth husband that her unwavering sense of duty to the public demanded that she work through the night to ensure success of her historic bear bill, and she simply could not trek home to their white-columned, Vashon Island mansion in all this dreadful rain. He understood, she knew. Have Iselda prepare his favorite dinner and watch *Real Cathouses of Orange County* on TV like he loved. Lisa would call him tomorrow after the vote. Lovie, lovie. Click. Dial tone.

What the hell, Perry thought, naked in his Lone Ranger mask as thunder rolled over the Washington Legislative Campus. Unlike the white man, Perry hadn't known what it was like to stick it to the Indians, even in a hideously stereotypical sex farce.

"Now," Lisa said, waddling across the gray carpet to Perry with a sly leer, "let's talk about the Little Big Horn..."

The rain was getting scary, Packy Rudd decided. He was slogging along Rt. 20 east of Tonasket, and the old Trooper's wipers weren't getting the job done, even on the highest speed. He pulled well off the obscured roadway into a gravelly chain-up area, flipped on the SUV's interior lights, and unfolded an Okanogan County Map he'd bought in town. The drenching rain was so thick on the windows that it obscured what little fading daylight remained

Packy was very disturbed as he struggled with the bulky map. One the one hand, it seemed likely that his imagination was running away with him and making entirely too much out of a series of probably unconnected coincidences. He knew it was human nature, once a potential conspiracy suspicion invaded the common-sense realm, to begin to see everything that one experienced as some confirmation of the conspiracy. It had a name: Hysteria.

On the other hand, one didn't need to be a frustrated Hercule Poirot to start drawing conspiracy lines between the coincidences Packy had come across in the last forty-eight hours.

Packy had seen the signs and tracks of a record grizzly in his forest. It was almost undoubtedly the same creature that had shortly thereafter eaten a stray escaped convict, and scared another witless enough to get himself killed. Then there was Ray Lightfoot's incredible tale about a vanishing grizzly and some really peculiar local purchases. Next had come the ferry mariner's pig story, followed by the chainsaw weird-nik in Wauconda. Finally, he'd seen two women load enough meat into an old Suburban to feed Zhuong-Shwei Province.

As Packy studied the map, a set of headlights grew close on the road and passed by toward Tonasket. Packy glanced up, but descending darkness and sheets of rain reduced visibility to a blurry haze.

Returning his attention to the map, Packy hated to think what a fool he was going to feel like after he wasted vacation time and money trying to track down a nutty kidnaped grizzly conspiracy.

Another set of lights on a noisier vehicle loomed out of the rain going in the same direction as the previous vehicle, but Packy was absorbed in the map looking for something called the Anus Valley or Ameas Valley or something that sounded like it.

There were two overriding considerations for Packy, he thought as he read the map, and both were disturbing. One was, if this nightmare was actually underway, if these idiots really did have a bear and really did intend to make some kind of political demonstration with it, then it was more than a little possible people could get hurt or killed. He was, after all, a sworn law federal enforcement officer with the right of arrest and a duty to the public.

A third set of blinding headlights, this time with tiny yellow marker lights, hissed by in the downpour and disappeared to the west.

Packy pushed the map back, dropped the old Trooper in gear, and slogged back out onto the road eastbound. He had to find this Boob Coltrane guy's ranch, because Packy needed evidence a lot more real than what he now had to justify calling the State Patrol in Olympia and trying to convince them of some insane bear-napping scheme.

Besides, there was one far more important concern, Packy thought with a frown.

One of his bears could get hurt. Maybe killed.

Chapter Thirty-Six

G-Day

Dawn canceled its appearance on G-Day. The soggy blackness of the night gave way only grudgingly to a dull gray, foggy remnant of rain-soaked light as the Operation Grizz convoy groaned up the ramp from I-5 near Olympia and over the glistening pavement past an enormous lighted sign on a fifty-foot stanchion that read: Pacific Coastal Truckstop.

With Nerves at the wheel, the old Suburban led past the sea of parked trailer trucks, Loverly on the GPS, and Hogan on the radio. The gaily tarped war wagon with Boot, Lexie and Tonny swung wide off the highway and past the high-roofed fuel islands and terminal. Last came Runs and Blubbo in the pickup truck pulling the long, gooseneck horse trailer.

The transit had gone well, if one discounted the three state trooper cars that had raced up behind them on I-90, blue lights blazing. The FOCM had suffered collective cardiac arrhythmia until the troopers sped past them and disappeared into the rain and darkness.

As Boot geared the big cattle rig down for the retreat to the isolated rear of the asphalt parking ocean, he cocked his head and frowned. Lexie picked up on it immediately. "What's wrong, Boot?"

"I don't know, but I can feel that bear jerking around back there. We better check him out."

Lexie stared at the torrents of rain in the headlights. "Terrific."

Shrugging into their rain gear and hats, the FOCM conspirators hurried to join Boot and Lexie by the cattle

transporter. They'd been seven night hours on the road
without stopping. Everyone was stiff and bleary-eyed.
Ronald Reagan trotted at Hogan's heel wondering why these
idiots were out in the rain.

"What is it?" Nerves called as they joined up on the side
of the war wagon facing onto wooded land. He had insisted
there be no unnecessary discussion on the radio.

"Is Tonny OK?" Loverly said.

Boot stuffed his cowboy hat down on his bootie-clad
head against the growing wind, and began un-bungying a
tarp. "I'm feeling some jerking around back here! Wanta
check Tonny out."

Runs and Blubbo hurried to help hold the flapping tarp
as they pulled it back. Everyone crowded close to see within
by Boot's big flashlight.

Tonny was on his feet but it didn't take a veterinarian to
know that something was wrong. The massive, humped bear
stood with his feet widely spaced and his big head drooping
lower than usual. His lower jaw also drooped open, and he
drooled.

Tonny then startled everyone by staggering clumsily
backward and crashing butt-first into the wall, jiggling the
heavy trailer.

"Tonny!" Loverly cried, clenching the near trailer wall
with her fingers.

Chirpyyyyy! Tonny thought, as he waddled pigeon-toed
toward her, swinging his thick shaggy head and grunting
contentedly. Runs produced his own flashlight and began
shining it about within the trailer.

"He's hurt!" Loverly said shrilly. "He's hurt, Runs!"

"You OK, big boy?" Boot said.

"Is that animal, sick, Runs?" Nerves said.

"Yeah," Lexie said. "Something's wrong. Tonny's sick!"

"Bear's fucked up," was Blubbo's diagnosis.

"Tonny's *hurt*, Runs!" Loverly shrieked. "Do something!"

"He's *sick*!" Nerves cried. "Jesus Christ, we got a sick bear
on our hands after all!"

Iiiiiii don't think sooo, thought Ronald Reagan, sniffing

the wet air.

"Ahhhh, *bull...shit*!" Runs shouted angrily over the rain and distant thunder. "Heeeee's *drunk*!"

Everyone stared at Dr. Runs With Rivers, DVM.

"Uh oh," Blubbo muttered.

"Oops," Loverly said.

"Yeah!" Runs shouted. "Oh yeah!" He shined his light toward the rear of the interior illuminating a large, red and white plastic picnic cooler bungie-corded to the other side of the interior partition, on the rear chamber's elevated floor. On the cooler's near end was a white plastic butterfly valve that was intended to dispense liquids from the cooler. Duct-taped to the valve's spout was a one-foot section of garden hose leading through a partition hole into the center chamber. From the garden hose trickled a very small, slow stream of a clear golden liquid. It's expensively distilled bouquet could be smelled in spite of Tonny's fragrance.

Tonny now slurped enthusiastically from the hose for the bazzilionth time in seven hours. He waddled unsteadily toward Chirpy, convinced that he had her to thank for another one of these simply amazing two-leg sauces! He nodded his big furry head up and down at Loverly, and grunted with approval. " AWNK, AWNK, AWNK!" Tonny said.

"Drunk!?" Nerves said, maxing out on all circuits. "How could a grizzly bear in a truck get *drunk*!"

Runs shined his light through a slot at the cooler again. "Oh I don't know! Maybe because somebody set up an oral drip device with a picnic cooler! Maybe because I'll bet my soul that when we open that cooler it's going to smell like eighty-proof Johnnie Walker *scotch*!"

"*My* scotch?" Boot said.

Runs swung his flashlight to shine on a wide-eyed, strenuously innocent-looking Loverly staring out from her yellow raincoat hood like a deer in the headlights. "How *about* that, Loverly?" Runs asked.

All eyes were on Loverly. "Uh .. well...like..."

"Like *what*?" Hogan demanded.

Plead the fifth, little darlin', Ronald Reagan thought.

"It's my fault," Blubbo said, to Loverly's shock. "I–uh–I decided we needed to dope Tonny up for the trip. I did it."

Loverly was now distressed. She wiped rainwater from her face "Aw, that's not true! It was my decision! Blubbo only helped me because I begged him to!"

Nerves was still downloading. "Why...in the *world*...did either of you–"

"Because Runs said Tonny might get sick on the road!" Loverly cried.

"So you gave him freaking Johnnie Walker *scotch*!?"

"Well," Loverly said, "not exactly! We gave him the last three bottles of Paw-paw's Jack Daniels too!"

"What?" Nerves croaked.

"You...whaaat!?" Hogan said. "You gave that bear the rest of my Jack!?"

"Well, I heard Runs tell Paw-paw that Tonny would be frightened by the road trip because we didn't have enough nighttime cold-and-flu stuff! And–"

"And!" Runs said, "I also told him we weren't going to give *booze* to any animal I was responsible for!"

Loverly began to cry. "I know! I know, Runs! But you said Tonny would be scared at the strange sounds and smells and all, if we didn't give him something to...well, relax him!"

"Oh, he's relaxed, alright," Boot said, watching Tonny stagger over to nurse off the garden hose again.

"So, see? I was afraid, guys!" Loverly continued, tears welling in her eyes. "I was afraid Tonny would get all frightened on the trip with no flu med to make him sleepy! I was afraid he'd maybe get, like, really sick, or he might, like, freak out and hurt himself like Runs said!"

"Jesus Christ!" Nerves began, rainwater dripping from his nose. "I don't believe this!"

Can we get outta the goddamned rain, you geniuses? thought Ronald Reagan, sitting by Hogan.

Lexie grimaced and sighed, blowing rainwater from her lips. "OK! As far as I know there's no instant way to undrunk a grizzly bear. So where do we stand? How does this affect Operation Grizz?"

Nerves peeped at the exceedingly mellow Tonny through a wall slot. "Well, at least he's conscious...for a while."

"And he can walk!" Hogan grunted.

But now all watched as Tonny sat heavily on his blubberous butt, slid flat onto his belly, and placed his head between his mega-clawed front paws. He sighed and slurped scotch remnants off his big black nose. Quickly his eyes narrowed, then closed, and eighteen-hundred-ninety-six pounds of happy grizzly bear began to snore.

"Disregard," Hogan said.

"Oh great!" Nerves said, "the signature symbol of our whole movement has passed out!"

"Whadaya think, Runs?" Boot asked over the steady hiss of the rain.

Runs looked at his watch, then stared at Tonny. "I think he's just asleep, not drug-induced unconscious. How much scotch did you...veterinary wizards...give him, Blub?"

"All Boot had in the cabinet under his bar," Blubbo said.

"What?" Boot said. "You gave that bear my whole new case of JW? That's twelve quarts!"

"Plus...the half full one on the bar," Loverly said softly, looking at raindrops splashing on the wet pavement.

"Aaaah!" Boot said.

Hogan slapped his head. "And all three fifths of my Jack!? That bear's not coming out of orbit til Sunday!"

"Oh my god," Nerves said, shaking his head. "Runs, is there a way to CPR grizzlies?

"I'm sorry!" Loverly cried, her lower lip out.

"Well, I'm not!" Blubbo said. "We were afraid Tonny would go postal and hurt himself! We made a call and went with it, like a US marine would do!"

Runs now sighed. "Put the flag away, Sergeant Hardrocks. What's done is done." He looked at his watch. "We have a little time here til G-hour. Tonny is breathing normally and his nose is wet. My...completely ignorant guess is he'll wake up when we head over to the capitol campus."

"Alright!" Nerves said clapping his hands for attention.

"We've had a...possible setback, but, as long as Tonny is awake and looking dangerous when the press show up, he can sleep til then for all I care. At least he keeps a low profile in the meantime.

"Now, listen up! Let's take shifts getting breakfast in the truckstop restaurant and standing guard here. Then we'll put another tub of meat in for Tonny. Loverly, you and Blubbo put on your surgical duds and get every scrap of that lunatic cooler apparatus out of there. It's evidence that could be traced. Besides, we don't really want the news tonight to lead with: 'cretinous morons bring drunk bear to statehouse!'"

Packy bore through the rain on I-5 in his old SUV. Exit 105A, Olympia, State Capitol Campus - 3, the big green overhead sign said.

Packy had found the Colhane ranch the previous evening. He'd stumbled onto a rural route mail delivery person in a blue, right-drive, Jeep Cherokee with flashing yellow lights on its roof. The pretty, blonde postal woman cracked her window down when the guy in the forest service raincoat waved at her and pulled alongside.

Packy told the woman that he had come to go hunting with Mr. Coltraine, but was a little confused about the directions. "Sounded like...well...'Anus Valley!'" Packy yelled over rolling thunder.

"Oh! No! It's Aeneas Valley!" she replied with a lovely smile that said you must be a westsider, you dribbling dullard. "And you must mean Boot Colhane! Go a mile east, look for the Aeneas Valley Road sign. Turn right. Go six-point-three miles to a big green mailbox welded on top of a WWI howitzer with steer horns mounted on the top of the box. You can't miss it!"

No doubt in my mind, Packy thought. "Thanks!"

"Oh! And there'll be a sign on the fence that says: 'This property insured by Smith & Wesson.'"

Packy ascended the long narrow dirt fire trail leading from the road to the Colhane ranch. Jesus in a jumpsuit, he thought, the postal lady didn't tell him this Colhane place was miles along a cliff-side goat path back into the uncharted wilderness.

Packy looked for tracks, but it had been raining like Noah's worst nightmare for over an hour. The road revealed nothing but wet dirt.

No one was home at the big log house he eventually came to in the darkness after crossing a cattleguard. Packy tooted his horn, then knocked on the front door with his flashlight, and called hellooooo, forest serv–ah! Packy had initially and fervently hoped adding the last two words might keep him from getting shot for a burglar, but he cut himself off when he realized he would be marking himself as an even more hated gubmint asshole.

Packy got no response. There was a pickup truck and a large farm tractor standing in the rain, but there were no other vehicles around. This time of evening a rancher could be in his barn, Packy thought.

At the rancher's enormous barn, though, Packy found no one. What he did find was one more thread in the fabric. The floor of the long, wide barn aisle had obviously been raked throughout with a broad leaf rake, leaving tiny parallel ruts in the dirt.

But no tracks.

Packy tipped his old fedora hat down, rebuttoned his raincoat collar tight and walked back into the rain. He gazed around, swinging his flashlight, but saw nothing out of the ordinary for a cattle ranch.

Why would anyone rake the floor of a barn? Packy thought as he wandered about. I mean, horse people will rake stable floors sometimes, as part of cleaning them up, but why would you leaf-rake the floor of some cavernous old cattle barn?

But then Packy walked onto a sort of wooden loading ramp many yards away. At its end, he shone his light and gazed down about four feet into a long trough. Instantly it all became crystal clear to him. He gasped, and then bolted for his SUV.

No more reading the weird signs, no more ambiguity, no more confusion, Packy thought, hurrying back to the highway in the rain and darkness.

The Washington State Patrol officer on the capital security detail smirked, hung up the duty phone and let loose a suppressed laugh. "Man, I really have heard it all now. Jesus."

"What the hell was all that about?" his fellow night-shift trooper asked, looking up from a broad bank of surveillance monitors, and grinning.

"Ah, don't ask. It's some nut claims to be a Montana forest ranger or something. Get this. This mental case says he thinks somebody's bringing us a stolen grizzly bear for a demonstration tomorrow, reference some eco-bill that stupid Senator Cow Belle has in the works!"

"A stolen...*grizzly bear*!?" the other trooper howled. "Did your crime fighter get the tag number on this bear?"

Yaaaah-ha-ha-ha-ha! The troopers laughed.

"Yeah, and get this, Bobby, the guy says it's a 'really big grizzly bear!' And he, like, knows this because—I swear I'm not making this up—he saw *grizzly* shit in a *horse*-manure pile somewhere over on the eastside!"

"Yaaaaaaaaaaaaaha-ha-ha-ha-ha-ha-ha-ha-ha-ha-haaaaa!" the troopers howled, and resumed watching the boring monitors.

CHAPTER THIRTY-SEVEN

G-Hour

Still in her now somewhat disheveled Pocahontas outfit, Senator Lisa Belle had been wired all night. She got little sleep on her office rollaway, even snuggled up to Perry Dinwiddie with visions of Mr. Binkie dancing in her mind. She staggered off to the expansive bath and dressing room adjoining her office. "Wake up, Perry!" Lisa croaked. "We've got a bill to pass!"

Perry Dinwiddie jerked bolt upright, thinking he'd gone blind. But then he snatched off his slightly shifted Lone Ranger mask and slapped it on the mattress. I gotta get a better job, Perry thought, like Mumbai sewer diver.

Perry walked to the window of the senator's office, which should have been bright with sunlight. It wasn't. It was still nearly as dark outside as when he'd fallen asleep after midnight. He peered out at the pouring rain and some distant flashes of oddly reddish lightning barely visible through heavy fog. He'd never seen the sky this dark after what should have been dawn. He couldn't even see the rear portico of the statehouse barely two hundred yards away.

I got a bad feeling about today, Perry thought.

Though the shriek from the *Psycho* shower scene was yet to play, one could fairly hear the theme from *Jaws* in the wet gray morning air. Daa-dump, daa-dump, daa-dump...

The final phase of Operation Grizz was underway. The FOCM convoy descended into the 14th Avenue Tunnel and stopped. Dressed in the striking ensemble of surgical masks, gloves, booties and 'frog hats' over rain wear, the revolutionaries hurried to the war wagon and stripped the tarps from it.

Tonny squinted at the bright lights within the tunnel, but went back to his tub of meat. This tub had no sauce, but in his current state of inebriation, Tonny was still soundly in the party mode. He couldn't have tasted catagory-five Jalapeños.

Fortunately, traffic was light in the booming, flashing, increased downpour outside the tunnel. The FOCM agents raced back to their vehicles.

Nerves spun the Suburban's wet tires as he raced up out of the tunnel and crossed Capital Way with the light. Rain drummed loudly on the roof again. He and Hogan and bore slightly right toward the statehouse on South Diagonal Road.

Boot and Lexie climbed back into the big Peterbilt road tractor. The war wagon blew diesel smoke and roared forward, through the Capitol Way light and straight ahead on Sid Snyder Avenue past the nearly abandoned capitol visitor center building.

In the rear, Runs, Blubbo and Loverly proceeded out of the tunnel in the pickup truck with the horse trailer, and hooked a right to go north on Capitol Way.

An old brown Isuzu Trooper with a very tired little bearded guy in it exited I-5 and shortly plunged into the 14th Avenue Tunnel. Packy squinted at the bright tunnel lights as his overworked windshield wipers began to scrape on dry glass. Ahead of him was a large aluminum horse trailer, but it turned right once clear of the tunnel to reveal a sight that gave Packwood Rudd vindication at last. It was the lighted rear of a large cattle truck disappearing into the fog outside the west end of the tunnel.

Right for the capitol building.

Packy slowed as he came out of the tunnel back into the hammering torrential rain. He looked carefully, then blew the light at Capitol Way in pursuit of the cattle truck. If he drew the attention of cops, so much the better.

Packy's mind raced. What were these people planning to do? They couldn't be stupid, as they had somehow managed to capture a record-book grizzly bear and transport it about four-hundred miles, presumably keeping it alive, Packy hoped. Were they going to release it on the capitol grounds as a demonstration? Would the cops gun it down? Were these...people themselves going to...kill it? What do you *do* with a stolen live grizzly bear at a state legislative building?

Packy flinched at a seemingly near, peculiarly reddish lightening blast followed by a slam of rolling thunder. In the nano-flash, despite the fog, the enormous silhouette of the Washington State Capitol dome loomed beyond. Packy saw the cattle truck's brake lights come on.

And another thing, Packy now thought as the tree shrouded Washington Vietnam Veterans Memorial appeared out of the rain to his right...what the hell am I gonna *do* about *any* of this?

He would do whatever he could for the bear, Packy knew with conviction. That's my job. Fuck the people. They're all crazy anyway.

In the speeding Suburban, Nerves steered clockwise around the traffic circle at the towering Winged Victory Monument, giving a pair of Canadian retirees in a Buick a memory of their capitol visit they'd never forget.

"Wrong *waaay*, shit-for-brains!" Hogan bellowed. Nerves's elbows stirred the air like a paint-mixer as he frantically steered to avoid a head-on with the owl-eyed Canadians. He slid to a halt at Cherry Lane, immediately across from the entrance to the ellipse separating the statehouse and the supreme court building. Both men were about to code out.

"Fucking Nazis!" Bear-Daughter Lowenstein sputtered over her shoulder at the Washington state trooper in the little gray wooden guard-shack at the entrance to the ellipse. The trooper, wearing a long, safety-orange raincoat with iridescent stripes and his plastic covered Smokey The Bear hat, stepped back into the guard-shack, and jotted on a notepad.

Bear-Daughter was trudging toward the legislative building through the drenching rain. She wore yellow galoshes and was draped in a colorful 'indian blanket' style, hooded poncho made in Taiwan of synthetic membranes guaranteed to be waterproof. The oversized poncho encompassed to the ground all of Bear-Daughter and the audio back-pack she carried that had made such a hit at the Methow Valley Airport. She looked like the Hunchback of Notre Dame meets the Apaches.

"But I'm here to support passage of the Noble Grizzly Bear Restoration Act!" Bear-Daughter had said when the trooper asked her what she was carrying. It could have been a JDAM munition for all he knew. "This is my own invention, capable of reproducing the exciting natural communications of the noble grizzly bear in state-of-the-art fidelity, on an unprecedented level of stunning realism."

"I'm still going to have to take a look at it, ma'am," the trooper said with visible fascination. He'd never seen a woman with tattoos, scrap-metal and war paint, all on one white face at the same time.

"I am here at the personal request of Senator Lisa Belle, my brother!" Bear-Daughter huffed.

Then I should shoot your freak ass right where you stand, the trooper thought. "Yes ma'am, I'll still need to see what's in your back-pack, please."

The trooper wasn't sure whether he was looking at a glorified boom-box or a suitcase nuke. He called central control and explained the situation. His sergeant placed him on hold and radioed the senate chamber duty officer. The sergeant was irked that radio communications were broken and full of interference today, he assumed because of the horrible weather.

Shortly, Perry Dinwiddie walked half-way down the

gray carpeted aisle of the cavernous, marble-walled senate chamber, in session, then to his left to where Senator Lisa Belle sat in her large brown leather chair at her mahogany senate desk. He leaned over to whisper in her ear. She nodded vigorously with obvious aggravation. Perry rolled his eyes and left the chamber.

"Let her in," the police sergeant radioed to the trooper at the guard shack. "Cow–uh, Senator Belle confirms that she has some sound-effects person coming to demonstrate by the north entrance. Scare-daughter Sunscreen or somebody. Belle does have some bill about grizzlies on this morning's agenda."

Lightning flashed over nearby Capitol Lake, and thunder boomed again. A wind was building and the rain had taken a slant. The trooper struggled to make out the static-garbled message from his sergeant. He tugged Bear-Daughter's copious poncho down over the back-pack audio thing, and said "Have a good day ma'am."

Bear-Daughter made a show of examining the trooper's name tag, and writing it down. "P-A-K-O-O-T-A-S," she spelled out loud. "I'll be discussing *you* with Senator Belle, mein Fürher!"

As Bear-Daughter soldiered through the rain, she shouted another parting remark at the trooper in the guard-shack. "I'm of the Native People, you storm trooper! We were here centuries before...your kind!"

Eleven more years to retirement Trooper Richard Pakootas of Washington's Inchelium Tribe thought, I wonder what life in New Zealand is like.

Bear-Daughter Lowenstein made her way past cars parked nose-angled to the curb to the north entrance of the majestic Washington State Legislative Building which was sandstone and granite, and looked roughly like the US Capitol with a subtle Pacific Northwest flair. Its dome rose nearly three-hundred feet. Terraces of about fifty broad steps ascended from sidewalk level to the tall-columned front portico, beneath which were three pairs of magnificently sculpted bronze doors.

The Jewish Indian Goth princess was in a mood as foul as the weather. She had looked forward to receiving much attention from the television news networks today, but Professor Ermintrude Windgate had said on the phone last night that no TV stations had committed to appearing. Nonetheless, Dr. Windgate had emphasized, Bear-Daughter was to "do the UW department of ecology proud!"

Like, duh, Dog, Bear-daughter had thought. Don't I look like an exceptional scholar!?

Bear-daughter regretted that this driving rain required her to keep her beaded native wear and audio pack under this tent-like hooded poncho, but no matter. Bear-Daughter Lowenstein was a soldier for the cause of ecology, especially the noble grizzly bear. Besides, the audio-pack could be heard for blocks on its stronger volume settings, poncho or no poncho. Even the thunder and this damnable rain weren't likely to compete. Fuck weather.

Bear-Daughter would stoically pace back and forth on the sidewalk all morning playing her audio pack and thumping a small Indian ceremonial drum she carried, so all entering legislators and visitors would hear for themselves the moving cries of Ursus Arctos Horribilis, the noble grizzly.

The hearts of the people and corrupt political apparatchiks alike would be moved by her recordings to love this grand creature as she did, Bear-Daughter thought warmly. It would be a great day for the noble grizzly and the UW ecology department! The publicity wouldn't hurt her chances for grants either.

It was probably a good thing that Bear-Daughter didn't know that all the lawmakers trafficked through the south entrance of the great domed capitol, from the O'Brian and Cherberg office buildings. Virtually no one but tourists came in the north entrance.

She might even meet an eco-stud! Bear-Daughter thought. Love is eternal. Besides, she'd, like, worn out that airplane captain dude.

Speaking of love, Bear-daughter selected a set of recorded

bear calls she'd made in Canada three years ago that she thought were most impressive. She clicked methodically at the battery-powered remote-control device she held in her hand. It was fitting that she feature the female of the species, of course, so Bear-daughter chose a series of grunts and howls made by various grizzly sows as they sang to each other about the beauty of life in the wild.

Nerves and Hogan stared bug-eyed through the blowing rain as some squat hunchback in an Indian poncho walked away from the guard-shack toward the capitol. They were puzzled not so much that the Indian hunchback was flipping the bird at the trooper in the ellipse entry guardhouse, but that the Trooper wasn't breaking that finger off and stuffing it where the sun don't shine. Otherwise, the ellipse looked as normal as it had to Nerves on his recent recon mission with Lexie, except it was raining like freaking Victoria Falls.

"What do you think?" Nerves yelled over the rain noise on the roof of the Suburban.

Hogan was relieved that he hadn't had The Big One when Nerves nearly swapped grills with the Canadian Buick, but this wasn't Hogan Winslow's first war. "Fuck it! I say we go for it!" Hogan slapped the hand-held CB radio into Nerves's palm. "You engineered it; you do the honors!"

T. Larchmont Nuerves III, JD., PhD., took a deep breath, squeezed the transmit button, and began to make history.

"*Say hello to my leeedle fren'!*" he yelled.

Chapter Thirty-Eight

G

"Say hello to my leedle fren'!" Blubbo and Loverly repeated gleefully, with Runs in the pickup truck, blocks away. "Yeaaaaaa!" Loverly bounced up and down on the back seat and hugged Blubbo in the right front seat, then Runs behind the wheel. Runs seemed to be praying.

"Alright!" Boot said in the war wagon as it neared Cherry Street and the southeast corner of the capitol building. "Guess who's coming to dinnerrr!"

"FOCM!" Lexie cried, and she reached to place her hand on top of Boot's hand which was jamming the shift lever to the next gear. Boot swung the big cattle rig to the left, then widely hard right onto Cherry Street, jacking the clutch and snatching at new gears. The truck blew smoke and roared north past parked cars alongside the stone-columned east facade of the statehouse, but it could barely be heard for the thunder and rain.

Oh bear, the thoroughly drunk Tonny thought, watching the scenery flash by, his feet spread for tenuous balance. You got to hand it to two-legs, they make great sauces and they're never boring!

Nerves drove the Suburban west across Cherry Lane and counter-clockwise around the near end of the landscaped ellipse toward the temple of Justice.

In the guardhouse, Trooper Pakootas looked up as an old Chevy SUV churned into the loop toward the Temple of Justice, but this was not particularly curious as tourists came and went all day. He strained to see who was in the vehicle, but the fog and sheeting rain severely reduced visibility. What happened next was particularly curious beyond his wildest expectations.

Despite the thrum of rain on the guardhouse roof and the rumble of rolling thunder, Trooper Pakootas became aware of another roaring noise and movement from his right. He whirled to see a trailer-truck cattle hauler come into view from behind a huge tree. There were no reasons for any trailer truck to come this close into the capitol/supreme court complex, let alone a cattle truck. The driver must be lost, Trooper Pakootas thought.

Driving south on Cherry Lane approaching the ellipse entry at that moment was Dr. Ermintrude Windgate in her red Volvo, talking on her cell phone with one hand and doing her makeup with the other. She steered with one knee and squinted into the misadjusted rear-view mirror to apply her lipstick while she listened for her messages.

This too wasn't unusual for Washington drivers, Trooper Pakootas would have thought had he been watching Ermie instead of the big truck that had just appeared.

Boot had intended to swing the long Peterbilt wide enough on his entry turn that the forty-foot cattle trailer would not ride up over the curb before the guardhouse, but that was before an oncoming red Volvo strayed head-on into his lane.

"Watch out!" Lexie shouted.

Boot palmed the big steering wheel tight to the left and held down on the air-horn cord with his right. It was a day for multi-tasking.

At that range, the truck air horn sounded like a train, and Ermie went bug-eyed looking at bright headlights and a truck grill the size of Mt. Rushmore. She screamed, stomped on her brakes, and drew a streak of Parisian Rendezvous Carmine clear across her face into her left ear.

Boot managed to miss Ermie's little Volvo, but that was the good news. The bad news was he had to cut the left turn so tight so that, as the truck completed the swing into the ellipse, the rear end of the trailer climbed the curb and wiped out the guardhouse. Trooper Pakootas's last theologically related thought before being knocked temporarily unconscious was Jesus Christ, look at the size of that fucking bear.

"Oops!" Boot said, looking at the flying guardhouse wreckage in the big door mirror. "Well, darlin'," Boot yelled through his surgical mask to Lexie who was bracing against the heaving action of the road tractor, "I'd say they're gonna remember us in Olympia for a while!"

"Oooooooh *no*!" Nerves said looking over his shoulder in the Suburban before the supreme court.

"We're in the dookie, now, pardner," Hogan said. The two men's voices were only slightly muffled by the surgical masks they too wore.

"Holy shit!" Packy Rudd said, staring through his rainy windshield at the bouncing, rocking trailer truck disappearing from his view behind trees. "They just ran over a sentry shack!"

Yeeeeeeehaaaaaa! Tonny thought the bear equivalent of, peering through a trailer wall slot at airborne shack parts. Suck on *that*, two-legs!

Packy pulled his car to the curb and bailed out in his raincoat. A quick check determined the hysterical woman in the Volvo hadn't been hit in the face with an ax after all, but had merely smeared her lipstick. He raced to the pile of lumber where the guardhouse had been and helped a dazed Trooper Pakootas to his feet. "Buh!...Buh!...Buh!..." the trooper gasped.

"Bear!" Packy yelled over more thunder. "I know! Are you OK?"

"Ever been to New Zealand, Sarge?" Trooper Pakootas asked.

Boot steered the war wagon clockwise about the ellipse between bordering rows of parked cars until it came dead astraddle of the striped walkway that led between the statehouse and the supreme court. There he stopped the rig hard and killed the engine.

Oh shii-iit! Tonny thought as he slid forward over the wet floor into the front trailer partition with a crash.

Boot yanked out both air-brake valves and the electrical

circuit he'd added to trigger compressed air bottles that would inject industrial epoxy into all of the truck's wheels. There was a blast of hissing air.

"Go, go, go, go, go!" Boot shouted. He and Lexie jumped down and sprinted across the ellipse through the rain for the Suburban.

"Let's go, let's go, let's go!" Nerves was yelling, shaking the Suburban's steering wheel.

"Holy shit!" said the duty trooper at his surveillance monitor console in the capitol police control center. He watched two people abandon a trailer truck and run across the ellipse. In another screen it looked like someone had taken out the Cherry Lane guardhouse with a shoulder-fired missile.

In the dark rain and fog it was hard to see accurately on the monitors, but, to the duty trooper, the surgical gear and raincoats the fleeing terrorists wore looked on the monitor like hazmat clothing. They ran toward the Temple but entered a large SUV and fled. A lightning flash outside whited out the monitors for a second. When they cleared, the SUV was gone. "Truck bommmmb, Lieutenant!" the trooper roared on the radio, "a *dirty bomb*, sir!"

If all the cell phones and alarms that started going off could have been assembled together, it would have sounded like a plague of locusts in a video game arcade.

CHAPTER THIRTY-NINE

G Plus Thirty Minutes

Comparatively, it could be said that things were settling down on the Washington State Legislative Campus if one considered settling down to be merely a seemingly endless, blasting thunderstorm with fog, and a capitol ellipse choked with about twenty flashing police cars and an armored SWAT truck. More microwave-tower-sprouting news vans were arriving every minute.

There'd have been enough helicopters to fight Vietnam all over again, except nothing could fly in this weather.

To the astronomical relief of all concerned, authorities with bomb sniffing devices and radiation detectors had quickly ascertained that there was no bomb or hazardous material per se in the abandoned cattle truck. Rather it seemed to contain only some kind of mutant, steroidal grizzly bear. Jesus Christ, look at the size of that thing, everyone said. It was alive and sticking it's canoe-paddle tongue through holes in the trailer wall. It had something to do with a bill being voted on that pertained to bears, many people said. But it was apparently secure for the moment.

Alarms had been canceled. A security perimeter of troopers in safety-orange raincoats and Smokey hats had been set up around the cattle truck, and was in the process of warring with the news people to keep them back. Some of the jittery workers and legislators who hadn't fled at the alarm went back to work. Mobs of others gaped from the shelter of the capitol and supreme court porticos. What tourists had braved the rain were being kept back on the ellipse for the time being.

The giant grizzly in the truck was surprisingly mellow,

just striding calmly about, albeit a little clumsily, and the news people were thus angry yet again. They'd been promised a dirty nuke and were bitterly disappointed that it was only some bear that some flake demonstrators had brought in to contest some bear restoration bill Senator Lisa Belle was trying to push through the senate. They knew and loathed Senator "Cow" Belle, and they deeply suspected she'd set them up to promo this bill. But here they were, dragged out to the capitol in this unholy rain, thunder and lightning. The expensive equipment was deployed, and their editors didn't want to hear there was no story. So, of course, they would do what news professionals do. They'd contrive one.

For his part, Tonny was fascinated. He'd never seen so many two-legs in his life and they had colorful flashy things like the two-legs who'd been stirred up for some reason the night he ate that tough, stringy two-leg with no sauce on it. He was disappointed that he couldn't see or hear Chirpy out in the crowd. He had stuck his tongue through the cave holes, but no one else seemed have any M&Ms with them. No matter, Tonny was gut-busting full of his morning meal, not to mention having consumed a picnic cooler full of scotch.

Tonny sighed, cocked one rear leg in the air, and relieved himself of some aggravating gas pressure.

The huge animal hadn't smelled like daffodils to start with, but now an even more awful smell began to fill the wet air by the trailer. The nose-wrinkled troopers decided to move the perimeter back ten feet which set the impatient news media off yet again.

"Captain! Captain!" the newsies shouted over the troopers, trying to gain the attention of the uniformed district-1 state patrol commander on the sidewalk before the capitol.

But Captain Joanna Searcy had her own problems.

"Do something, goddamnit!" Senator Lisa Belle shrieked at Captain Searcy, a tall, handsome woman with short, reddish hair who wore an orange rain slicker and looked as though she too wondered what life in New Zealand might be like.

Lisa wore a Monaco Mauve designer raincoat and carried a large matching umbrella. She looked like a giant, pastel purple horseshoe crab in matching high heels.

Perry Dinwiddie hovered nearby under his own umbrella, watching fire-woman like a hawk.

"We're waiting on word from the governor, ma'am!" the beleaguered captain shouted over rain, thunder, and an idling SWAT team truck, the crew of which was packing up to leave.

"She's in *Belize* on a 'fact-finding tour', Captain!" Lisa bellowed back. "I want this, this, creature out of here! Now!"

"We've tried to drive the truck, Senator, but it won't run. We have–"

"The terrorists disabled the truck?"

Captain Searcy flinched and glanced at the reporters. "Ah, we don't actually use the T-word in situations like this, Senator. A memo came down from all Democrat governors when President Obama took office. We call 'em concerned dissidents if they're violent, demonstrators if nobody gets hurt."

"So you're saying you've been out-foxed by a bunch of bikey bums and horse-manure morons!" Lisa squalled, her face both wet and red. "Is that what you're telling me, Captain?"

Captain Searcy had no idea what the senator was referring to but, under the trying circumstances, her patience was fading rapidly toward the yoke-out range. "I'm telling you the engine won't start, Senator! I have my commercial vehicle enforcement guys on the problem. They're truck experts. We have a heavy truck wrecker on the way!"

"Well shoot that thing or something! Before it kills somebody!"

"I'm not capping some caged bear in front of half the news media in Washington, Senator! Not without a direct order from the governor! Case closed!"

"Well you better do something fast, Captain, or you'll be

writing parking tickets in Walla Walla!"

Sounds good to me right now, the captain thought. "Ma'am, I assure you that we are making every ef–"

"Captain! Look up there by the capitol doors! That's half my colleagues! I have a critical bear bill coming onto the floor in about a half-hour, and I can *feel* the votes evaporating! I demand you–"

"Excuse me, Senator," Captain Searcy said with an arctic smile, turning away, "I have some pressing–"

"Hey! I'm talking to you!" Lisa snapped, and she yanked on the turning Captain's raincoat.

Woops, Perry thought, hurrying forward. Fire-woman make baaad move.

Captain Searcy whirled on Senator Belle like an agitated Amazon sergeant-at-arms, and the two women went nose to nose.

"Senator!" Captain Searcy growled in a low hot voice. "Technically, you just committed assault! Trying some Cynthia McKinney number on me is not advisable!"

Perry wedged between the two women and pushed Lisa back. He smiled at Captain Searcy. "I'll take it from here, Jo," he said. "The senator's under a lot of stress."

Captain Searcy looked up. "You'd better get her outta my face, Perry, or she's gonna be under a lot of *arrest*!"

Legislators had immunity from arrest when the state legislature was in session, but that was waived if assault was the issue. "Gotcha," Perry said, "color us gone."

"Lemme go!" Lisa snarled.

Perry whipped around and towed Lisa toward the capitol steps, their umbrellas batting together.

"Will you listen to me?" Perry hissed in her ear. "Look at that bear! It's cool. It's just laying there asleep! So far it's backing up your notion that grizzlies are harmless. The press dimwits can barely even see the thing through those slats and so far they're using buzzwords like 'cute' and 'teddy bear'!"

"We have to get that thing out of here!" Lisa insisted, raindrops dripping from the tip of her nose. "We can't have the public knowing what their senators are voting on, Perry! It'll screw up the whole political system! Half my senate votes are now wondering how they're going to explain this to their constituents!"

"You only need the other half plus one! And they'll vote for your bill just to discourage citizens from muscling them with this kind of demonstration. But not if half of them are standing on the portico and you're out here picking fights with state patrol commanders! So get back inside and let the senate get back into session. You push the vote. Let me handle this. Go!"

Packy Rudd kept to the rear of the small, wet, tourist crowd, not sure how deep into all this he wanted to get. Ray Lightfoot had not exaggerated in his estimate of the size of the bear. Packy had known from the signs he'd found in the Flathead that it had to be big, but he still stared in awe at the gargantuan dark hump only loosely visible between the slats on the cattle trailer. Before the animal lay down to sleep, it had appeared to be not merely healthy but thoroughly pleased at all the attention. It walked a little shakily, Packy had noticed, but it did not appear to be sick or injured.

Bear-Daughter Lowenstein was ecstatic. In the Indian-pattern, hooded pancho, she humped the audio rig back and forth on the sidewalk peering at the magnificent grizzly through the slots. That fanged senator woman had snarled at the storm troopers that Bear-Daughter was present under her auspices so she'd been allowed to remain inside the trooper perimeter. Despite the continuing heavy rain and the briefly terrifying arrival of the bear truck and the initial pandemonium therewith, she was euphoric. At last the opportunity she'd never been able to obtain grants to research! At last she was in a position to test her ability to communicate with a real grizzly through her recordings. She would write a drop-dead master's thesis on this. Bear-Daughter fished in her Chinese beaded purse for the audio-pack's remote device.

As soon as Boot had shoved Lexie into the back seat of the Suburban and piled in behind her, Nerves pitched the radio to Hogan and stood on the accelerator. Hogan keyed the radio and said: "Do it!"

Blocks away, on 11th Avenue, Runs's crew-cab pickup and horse trailer sat by the curb with the flashers on. Blubbo and Runs were peering under the raised hood pretending to be nursing a breakdown. They had stowed the surgical accessories.

Inside the truck, Loverly heard Hogan's call and pressed the horn pad. She'd meant to just tap it, but she was so excited she caused a loud honk. Still leaning under the hood, Runs and Blubbo were deafened and jumped like they'd been stuck with cattle prods. It wasn't like they were not already somewhat over-torqued.

They slammed the hood and climbed in out of the rain.

Loverly had the Seattle and Olympia yellow-pages open to News - print, and News - broadcast. All three began punching numbers into their prepaid cell phones, which they covered with clear plastic to disguise their voices.

"KING-5 TV tip line, what is your—"

"Leesen carefully!" said a voice with a sadly faked French-redneck accent. "There ees a live, giant greeezzly bear at the Washington statehouse! If you theenk thees ees a hoax you're going to get scooped!"

Beep.

They need not have bothered, of course, for the whole legislative campus had already gone to defcon-one, condition red, this-is-not-a-drill status at the state patrol's truck bomb alert, and a thousand texts, tweets and frantic voice messages on the subject were already flooding the ether.

Almost all the papers and stations had been called when the Suburban steamed out of the fog behind the horse trailer rig and raced by.

As near as the editors at the news organizations could determine, Al Qaeda had sent a suicide grizzly bear into the Washington state capitol packing a dirty nuke. It sure as hell

286

topped the rain as the lead story.

Back at the truck stop, they FOCM stripped the tape off both vehicles' license plates, and tossed the surgical togs and their rubber boots down a gushing storm drain.

All seven piled into the truck, as there was the risk that the Suburban would be recognized if they drove it back to the capitol campus. As Blubbo and Boot were large men, the six-seat truck made for a cozy fit, but it was only necessary until they got back to the capitol campus. Lexie sat on Boot and Loverly perched in Blubbo's capacious lap. Ronald Reagan sat in Hogan's lap. No one seemed to be at all bothered with this arrangement.

Parking had ceased to be a problem near the capitol. Many motivated tourists and some of the workers in the five major campus buildings had staged a NASCAR race off the campus when the word got out about the suicide bomb grizzly. At least a hundred were miles away and still gaining speed by the time the alert was canceled.

The FOCM parked the horse rig on Sid Snyder Avenue, and hurried through the hissing rain past the Vietnam Veterans Memorial and the Winged Victory Monument circle to the decidedly busy entrance of the ellipse. All but Ronald Reagan wore moustachioed, heavy-browed, big nosed Groucho glasses at Nerves's insistence, out of his fear of surveillance camera recordings. Peering from under dripping hoods and western hats, the FOCM surveyed the remarkable scene.

Runs looked at the wrecked guardhouse. "What the hell went wrong?"

"Don't ask," Lexie said.

"Some woman in a Volvo nearly hit us," Boot said. "I had to cut that turn a little tight."

"I don't see Tonny moving!" Loverly cried. "They shot him!"

"Sssssssssssh!" Nerves hissed, looking about in the gray fog and rain. "They didn't shoot him, I promise you."

Blubbo said. "I can see him on the floor!"

"Oh God," Lexie said, craning her head. "He's passed

287

out."

"Again," said Hogan.

"Look at all the cops!" Blubbo said.

"And all those news vans," Nerves said with satisfaction.

"You...ran over a whole security building?" Runs said.

"It was just a shack!" Boot snapped.

"It is now," Runs muttered.

"Hey!" Loverly said, "who's that weirdo peeping in at Tonny?"

"Looks like some tribal hunchback," Blubbo said.

Lexie looked. "I'm thinking that's that college girl bear expert with a sound machine that plays grizzly calls. Nerves and I heard her on the radio on our recon trip."

"What's she doing with my bear?" Loverly said with a little heat.

"I don't like it," Hogan said, and everyone focused on him. "Check it out. The newsies are packing up. That tall woman trooper must be the commander, because she just spoke into her radio and now most of the troopers are headed for their cars!"

"Damn!" Nerves agreed. "Hogan's right. They're breaking down, going back to business as usual."

"It's the bear," Runs said, his shoulders hunched against the downpour. "Asleep or passed out like that, he's not news anymore. The news people have this record rain to cover, and the cops need that manpower back on the road."

"Yeah," Blubbo said, glumly. "If Tonny was growling and pounding his cage and all, the TV people would be tripping on themselves to film it. Who's afraid of a passed-out bear they can barely see in the trailer?"

"So...we've failed," Loverly said, her voice quavering, "because I got Tonny drunk!"

"No," Runs said, "I don't think he's drunk anymore, I think he's asleep. He's been out of his element for three days, and on the road for eight hours. He's just tired. He's resting."

Lexie squeezed Loverly's shoulder, "You meant well, honey, and even Runs said Tonny might have had problems on the trip if he hadn't been, well..."

"Drunk," Loverly said.

"Besides," Blubbo said, "you didn't do it alone."

Nerves sighed. "Operation Grizz hasn't been a complete failure. There's still a good chance the incident has made a lot of those senators in there rethink their vote. All we need is twenty-five of them to go our way, we can lose the other twenty-four of those idiots inside and still defeat the bear bill. We should know soon."

Those idiots inside were finally back in session in the majestic, cathedral-like senate chamber on the third floor of the statehouse. The towering walls were of a light gray and whitish German Formosa marble. The carpet was a matching gray with small, white flower patterns every few feet. Two elevated, steep visitor galleries were recessed into the walls near the domed ceiling.

A pair of tall mahogany doors at the rear of the chamber permitted entry from the rotunda hall of the capitol building. Two tall, curtain-draped doorways were midway along the immense room's sides.

The senators at their desks faced two broad mahogany judicial benches at which the Lt. Governor presided and various clerks, aides and officials sat. Behind these benches were the US flag and Washington state flag on poles, and another framed Washington flag was placed high on the rear wall.

It was altogether a fitting scene for the pending horrors no one could have guessed were to come.

One horror already present was tax-rabid, elitist Senator Lisa Belle, now on her feet speaking.

"...thus, Mr. President," Lisa droned on, "I say to my honorable colleagues, our duty to the great people of Washington requires that we make a statement against the sort of irresponsible...'demonstration'...we have seen before this capitol this very morning. We have a duty to render ineffectual the vandalism we have witnessed here today that recklessly endangers one of Mother Nature's most noble

natural gifts to the great state of Washington and her...
um, valiant citizens, the great grizzly bear! I submit that we
owe it to our treasures of nature like the grizzly, and to the
people we so devotedly serve, to carry forward with the great
cause of restoring this...ah, noble creature to our great free
Washington public lands...over there, on the eastside of the
great Cascade cur–, uh, mountains! I yield the remainder of
my time, Mr. President."

In other words, eastside Senator Joe Kirksey thought with
disgust, let's stick these monsters on the eastside where who
gives a shit if they eat somebody's kids or livestock, so you
can posture eco and green when you run for the U.S. Senate
next year. Sit down, Tubby.

The presiding Lt. Governor thanked the distinguished
senator from the 34th district, and recognized the honorable
senator from the 7th District. Joe Kirksey stood. Lisa
frowned at the heavy, gray-haired rancher.

"Thank you Mr. President. I will be brief, you will all be
relieved to hear. I would simply like to ask my honorable
colleagues about to cast their vote to consider the passion
of the free citizen that must have driven the effort by as yet
unknown persons to make this august body aware of the
full ramifications of the fine animal proposed to be seeded
in their midst. I ask each of my colleagues to consider
the...perfectly healthy and content...two-thousand pound
omnivore deposited this morning on our doorstep, and ask
yourselves this question: Since the grizzly bear was once
native to most of Washington, especially right here in her
great Pacific Northwest corner, shouldn't we *first* 'restore' it
to where it was *first* vanquished, in man's quest to conquer,
cut and construct? Namely, *Seattle*! I yield the remainder of
my time, Mr. President."

The Lt. Governor rose again. "There being no further
discussion on the docket regarding it, the senate will now
move to a vote on senate bill 11-8860, the Senator Lisa
Belle, Noble Grizzly Bear Restoration Act. The clerk will
prepare the vote."

Dr. Ermintrude Windgate was not to be denied her moment in the sun—so to speak—by some terrorist truck driver. She hobbled onto the ellipse through the rain and wind with her umbrella, having painstakingly restructured her makeup.

Ermie knew that the news media would let anyone say anything in an interview, no matter how biased, contrived or ignorant, as long as they could introduce the interviewee as "Dr." so-and-so, or say "PhD." after their name. This gave the illusion of actual responsible journalism.

"Excuse me!" Ermie said to a television news anchorwoman with her camera mule, "I am Dr. Ermintrude Windgate, chair of the department of ecology at the University of Washington, and I have a statement to make."

That was all it took. It instantly became irrelevant to the anchorwoman whether Ermie knew a nano-particle about what was going on or was remotely qualified or authorized by anyone to make a statement.

The seriously blonde anchorwoman snapped her fingers at her assistant who fiddled with the clear plastic cover on his shoulder-mounted camera. The news woman tilted her umbrella back and fluffed at her hair. The camera man held up a descending count of fingers.

"Good morning everyone, Olga Svednefson, KDZZ NEWZZ, coming to you live from the Washington state capitol in Olympia. With me is *Doctor* Ermincrude Windgate, PhD., chair of the UW department of economics. *Doctor* Windgate, I understand you have an urgent vital message for our audience?"

"Yes Olga! But first," Ermie gave Olga a narrow-eyed look, "that would be doctor Ermin*trude* Windgate, chair of the department of *ecology*." Ermie gave the camera her best send-me-endowments smile. "Olga, as a recognized authority on Washington wildlife, I feel it is my duty to inform your viewers that the noble grizzly bear is not a dangerous tool of terrorists as is being implied by the media here today. No, our gentle nature friend the grizzly is statistically harmless to the residents of the great Puget Sound community!"

Olga was surprised by the unexpected slight on the media, and she glanced again at the rank smelling mountain of hair, visible through slots in the cattle trailer, still snoozing. Tonny dreamt of comely if lewd young sows, of course, but Olga wasn't attuned to this.

"But...Doctor Ermingate, reliable sources are saying this meat-eating bear weighs ten-thousand pounds and measures twenty feet tall when standing. Isn't the term 'gentle' a bit misleading, here?"

"Windgate!" Ermie snapped.

Maintain focus and frame when these two get in a fistfight, the cameraman thought.

"And absolutely!" Ermie continued. "You have a better chance of being killed by lightning in Washington than by a grizzly bear."

Another blast of lightning flashed blocks away, and the thunder slammed past.

"But Doctor Windgate, there are rampant incidences of fatal bear maulings in the Pacific Northwest. Just this week, another giant grizzly bear attacked and devoured a hiker in the Flathead National Forest of Montana."

"Nonsense," Ermie said. "Such events are so aberrational as to be statistically meaningless!"

Olga was beginning to wish she'd checked this old battleaxe out before going on the air, but she wasn't going to be bitch-slapped on her own broadcast.

"With...all due respect...*Doctor* Windgate, when one is on a grizzly bear's *menu*, 'meaningless' isn't exactly what comes to—"

"I'll prove it!" Ermie said, staring down her snout at this impudent, blonde bimbo newsie. "Watch *this!*" And Ermie strode splashing toward the cattle trailer. Signaling the cameraman to follow her as she pursued the professor, Olga sensed she was onto a real story.

She had no idea.

At a nod from Captain Searcy, the troopers elected not to

get on TV blocking the fourth estate. They let Ermie and the news crew through. Other news organizations began to sense something was up and they moved in with their cameras as well.

On the sidewalk before the opposite, capitol side of the trailer, Bear-Daughter Lowenstein had located her audio remote device. She clicked up volume level eight, that the recorded bear calls be heard adequately over the rain and rolling thunder. Bear-Daughter was breathless. She was about to make academic history!

She too had not a vapor of a hint how right she was.

Ermie stopped by the sliding trailer side door and eyed Olga and her cameraman. "Our friend, the noble grizzly bear, is a peaceful, gentle natured beast, not to be slurred as an object of fear! Observe!"

With that, Ermie slammed the bolt back on the center trailer door, slid it wide open, and turned back to give that vacuous nordic news fluffy and her audience a wide-eyed, triumphant stare.

"Oh my God in Heaven!" Olga said, dropping her microphone. She stepped back, bumping into the camera man, and glanced about for trees to climb. Focus and frame the cameraman thought. The pros focus and frame when surprise photo ops occur. Jesus fucking Christ that thing is huge.

"Absolutely nothing to worry about, as your viewers at home can see for themselves!" Ermie said, pointing at the still zoned-out Tonny.

Bear-Daughter pressed 'select,' and the real fun started.

Bear-Daughter's studies of the grizzly had not yet progressed to a firm grasp of the more nuanced meanings of her recorded bear calls. The calls she had selected for today's demonstration were actually not of grizzly sows communicating with each other about the beauty of nature. They were recorded during the mating season.

WAHOOOOOORRROOONNNNK! blasted the audio pack.

Unbeknownst to Bear-Daughter Lowenstein, this was

grizzly girl-talk that translated literally to: Come and get it, big boy!

About two-hundred capitol employees, cops, news folk, tourists, seven FOCM revolutionaries and one wet ranch dog jumped twelve inches straight up and uttered some version or another of 'Fuck...*me*!'

Inside the cattle trailer, Tonny's eyes sprang wide open and he grunted sharply. He sounded battle stations on all systems and launched to his feet with a speed and agility that rocked and banged the trailer and caused widespread urinary incontinence in many of the nearby observers.

Poontang!? Tonny thought, swinging his huge skull about and sniffing with considerable interest. He called out a response to the sow wherever she was. AWWWWWGAAAWNNK? He roared with gusto, which meant 'Come here often?' in grizzly-speak.

Then he noticed a new hole in the cave wall and went for it.

Bear-Daughter had discovered her mental G-spot. It worked! She was actually communicating! She, Bear-Daughter Lowenstein, was exchanging real-time thoughts with an animal species! The audio-pack went WAOOOOOMMAAWWWWNH! which was basically grizz hussy for 'Got a light, sailor?'

Lightning hit nearby yet again, and the accompanying crash drowned out some two-hundred screams. Six troopers went for their guns. The KDZZ NEWZZ cameraman split so fast his camera hovered in mid-air briefly before falling to the watery grass. Olga and Ermie set new world land speed records for the high-heeled hundred-meter rain-dash.

The near crowd screamed and shouted anew, and spun off from the trailer area like water off a shaking dog. A departing news van ran into the rear of another with a loud thump.

Tonny hit the ground running and loped around the rear of the trailer to the capitol side, oblivious of the two-leg screams competing with the rolling thunder. Here, he stood up to his full height of twelve feet-plus, his huge forepaws dangling, and sniffed the air. Anyone in view who was still entertaining thoughts of gentility in grizzly bears cleaned the slate.

Two of the six troopers dropped their pistols on their panic-driven draw. The other four, together with Captain Searcy and Perry Dinwiddie, took moving stances and sighted on Godzilla in downtown Tokyo. Captain Searcy aimed with her right hand and keyed her lapel-mounted radio with the other.

MOOOOOOOOOOOAAWWNNNNKK! ('Let's party, handsome!') went Bear-Daughter's audio pack. She screamed on sight of Tonny, dropped the remote device and ran with several other people up the steps of the capitol to seek safety inside.

Tonny could hear this on-the-make sow's unmistakable calls, but he couldn't see her! As near as he could tell from her last invitation, she was moving toward the big gray rock at the top of the hill with about fifty chattering two-legs. Up the steps Tonny went in bounds. He was on a mission.

Bear-Daughter tore the poncho off over her head, tripping on it and falling to her knees on the granite steps. She was up without breaking stride, and shrugged frantically to shed the audio-pack's weight, but the fringe on her buckskin dress had jammed in the big plastic squeeze-buckle on the chest strap that held the shoulder straps together in front. "Aaaaaaannnhhhh!" Bear-Daughter sobbed, and kicked the yellow galoshes up to light speed.

Too many people! Perry and the troopers thought, scrambling up the steps, guns extended. Too many screaming, running people, everywhere! Trained shooters, all knew that a handgun shot was likely to be anywhere from useless to enraging in a twelve-foot grizzly, depending on whether it stopped in several inches of blubber or bounced off inch-thick skull bone.

Besides...if that damned thing turned on *them*, they'd need all the ammo they could muster.

In harmony and unison, the FOCM by the wrecked guardhouse collectively said "Ho-lee *shit*!"

Assorted panic-galvanized people of all descriptions swarmed past Bear-Daughter on the climb to the capitol entrance. The tall, cast bronze doors of the center entry were closed, but the left and right pairs were open except for heavy glass inner doors. These were now swung back and people fought and clawed to pass through. Discarded umbrellas, cell phones, Blackberries, hats, purses and shoes littered the steps and portico floor.

Bear-Daughter caught up, sprinted under the portico and slammed into the gasping, shouting crowd wedged in the right doorway. "Get the fuck outta my waaaaaay!" she screamed.

The glut of thrashing people jamming the left and right doorways screamed and pounded on each other. Tonny reached the portico as another blast of lightning lit off and banged. Dripping, he stood again and swung his head left and right, but he saw no hot little, eight-hundred pound tart anywhere. He only saw two groups of squeaky two-legs beating the tar out of each other, as near as he could tell. Tonny opened his impressive jaws and bellowed HOOOOOOOMAANGH? (Where *are* you, baby?)

OOOOOOOOOAAAWWWWWWGAH! (Git some!) the backpack roared, truly deafening in the rain covered portico.

Tonny looked to the choked right doorway. Well, he thought, at least he knew what hole in this new cave the little tease had disappeared through. He dropped to all-fours and ambled for the right door.

Tonny's memorable arrival on the portico landing caused the gluts of people in the doorways to dip down deep inside of themselves and find yet new reservoirs of strength they never knew they had. When the monster roared the second time, everyone in the right doorway could feel the sound rattle their breastbones.

People climbed over people, people pushed people, people carried people, but citizens flat cleared those doors with resolve. Some newcomers fled past the curved mahogany reception desk for the bathroom corridors. Those who knew those corridors were essentially dead-ends raced across the marble-floored vestibule and up the broad steps leading to the cavernous third floor rotunda, now echoing with much colorful outcry.

Just as the high glass entry doors, absent the people jam, began to swing shut, lots of inspired grizzly bear plunged through.

"Oh...my...god," Packy Rudd whispered on the capitol campus ellipse.

Chapter Forty

Vote On This

"Tonnyyyyy!" Loverly screamed, watching her big puppy disappear into the Washington Legislative Building.

"Oh *no*!" Lexie said.

"Uh ohhh," Blubbo said.

Two-legs, Ronald Reagan thought with disgust. No wonder God made 'em last.

"Good gawdamighty!" Boot said.

You pluperfect moron, Runs thought, his jaw muscles flexing. How did you ever let this happen?

"Kiss my ass!" Hogan muttered, figuratively, everyone hoped.

"This was not on my contingency list!" Nerves howled, about to pop a vein. "This is exactly what we planned *not* to do!"

"We gotta go get him!" Loverly sobbed.

"Say *what*?" Blubbo said.

Lexie said, "Honey, no, there's nothin–"

"What the hell are we gonna do?" Hogan said. "Call Orkin?"

"Ditto!" Nerves said. "We need to skunk the hell out of here, zippo, before we all wind up in prison or in bear guts! We exercised our right to political free speech in a um, unique, way. We may owe them for a guard shack, but what happened after that isn't our fault!"

Boot said, "I hate it, but Hogan and Nerves are right! What are going do in there to fix this mess?"

"Nooo!" Loverly protested, jumping up and down and shaking her fists. "We can't just leave Tonny in there! They'll kill him!"

The rain hissed down as Runs finally spoke. "You're right. You're all right." Runs tossed the keys to the pickup to Boot. "Get everybody out of here Boot. You too, Ronald Reagan."

"Hey! What does that mean?" Blubbo demanded. "What are you gonna do?"

"Just everybody beat it." Runs eyed everyone grimly. "I don't know what I can do, but what I definitely can't do is leave Tonny to kill somebody or get killed, or both, while I'm running down the road! I just can't do it! You guys get home fast. I...I'll make my way home later." Runs abruptly turned and trotted down the sidewalk toward the merry meltdown.

"No!" Blubbo said.

"Hey!" Boot yelled with an edge. Runs stopped and turned. Boot pitched the truck keys to Nerves who caught them in self-defense. "Get 'em outta here, Nerves. I'm going with Runs." Boot hurried to join Runs.

"If Runs goes, I go!" Blubbo announced and bolted for the men.

Nerves tossed the jingling keys to Lexie. "Take the kids and evacuate, Lexie. Runs is right. I planned this. I can't run out now." Nerves ran to join Boot and Runs.

"Bullshit!" Lexie said. "I'm no 'pussy.' You're not going without me!" Lexie tossed the keys to Hogan.

"And me!" Loverly said. "Tonny is *my* bear!"

All the FOCM but Hogan and Ronald Reagan ran down the wet sidewalk for the chaos around the capitol entrance.

Hogan watched them go. "Oh, Christ! Loverly, get back here!" He hunched his shoulders against the rain and limped after the rest of the group. "This is just goddamned *precious*! I *own* a fucking gun store and I'm going to a *bear* fight barehanded!"

Ronald Reagan sighed and trotted in pursuit. Where my old fool goes, I go, she thought. That's the rules.

The FOCM hurried up the capitol steps behind distracted troopers and some black guy in a suit with a gun. Passing them in double-step bounds was some short, bearded guy in a green raincoat bearing the US Forest

Service logo.

Despite the evolution in activity, barely one minute had elapsed since Ermie let the cat out of the bag.

In the senate chamber, despite its sturdy construction, it was becoming more difficult for the senators to ignore what sounded like multiple screaming and clatter coming from behind the tall, heavy, wooden chamber doors that opened onto the rotunda. Since there was a thousand-dollar fine for having one's cell-phone go off during senate sessions, the senators were unaware of the calamity outside. As yet.

Hearing the odd but still muffled noises, Senator Lisa Belle took alarm. She tapped her foot and shot quick glances over her shoulder at the closed chamber doors. Anything—anything—unusual at this juncture was likely to interrupt the pending vote on her bill, so whatever was going on outside the senate chamber could wait. After all, the bear demonstration was under control. How serious could it be?

By tradition, the senate eschewed the House's more modern computerized voting system in favor of vocal yeas and nays, or, barring a clear result, a show-count of hands. Regardless, a rigid, read: slow procedural protocol applied. Consequently, Lisa was beginning to emit little squeaks as she throttled the urge to yell *let's go, you geriatric sloths! Hurry up!*

The lieutenant governor, and president of the senate, said, "All honorable senators in favor of enacting senate bill 11-8860 will now signify by saying yea."

Lisa took a breath to–

The moment Tonny entered the second-floor vestibule, he stopped by a large bronze statue of Washington pioneer Marcus Whitman and the broad, curved reception desk next to it. The desk had been abandoned with vigor.

Again the mammoth bear stood to his towering full height, front paws dangling, and sniffed the air for the

300

coquettish sow who was eluding him. Still somewhat snockered, Tonny was largely oblivious of the swarm of fast-moving two-legs chirping and peeping and flooding either up the steps, or back out the very doors they'd just flooded in through. Two-legs were a strange bunch, Tonny thought, but he had more important concerns.

Bear-Daughter Lowenstein was now half way up the broad marble interior steps ascending to the rotunda floor when the cursed audio backpack she could not free herself from began to repeat its recorded cycle, as she had designed it to do.

WAHOOOOOORRROOONNNNK! rang in thunderous echoes under the rotunda, on volume level eight.

Hot damn! Tonny thought. He dropped to all paws and lunged up the stairway eight steps at a time.

What the *fffuck* was *that*!? was the general sentiment among the senators who whirled to look at the still closed rear senate chamber doors upon hearing that loud roar. Their curiosity was about to get handled.

On the rotunda floor, under the cavernous dome, some of the fleeing citizens went straight ahead and piled up in a heap when they tried to jump the velvet barrier ropes that surrounded the bronze Seal of the State of Washington imbedded in the floor. Some fled to their right up the second tier of steps toward the House of Representatives, and the remainder to their left up the short tier to the Senate Chamber.

The senate chamber doors blew open with a crash. First through them were the two security guys who normally stood watch over the chamber entry when the senate was in session. These gentlemen were going backward at a high rate of speed, propelled by an avalanche of howling citizens on their way to anywhere but where they'd come from.

The latter included one Bear-Daughter Lowenstein who shrieked and tore in vain at the straps of the audio pack.

"Order!" said the annoyed senate president, whacking his

gavel, but he was drowned out by another audio backpack announcement: WAOOOOOMMAAWWWWNH! which left almost all ears ringing. Bear-Daughter was whirling in a circle, decking senators right and left with the backpack. She clawed at the pack straps, screaming, "Get it off me! Get it off me!"

The two fuzzy ears that weren't ringing were promptly born into the State of Washington senate chamber by the largest, hairiest, smelliest, scariest creature anyone within had ever conceived of in their worst drug-warped, alcohol-fueled visions. This creature made divorce seem like fun. By comparison, Hell suddenly looked like an expensive Paris cathouse.

The apocalyptic animal could scarcely fit in the carpeted aisle between the party groups of mahogany desks being vacated forthwith. On all fours, it was as tall at the hump as anyone in the room. Now the great bear stood, raised its colossal head, and opened jaws that would impress Moby Dick. The creature made a life long grant to the therapy industry with a testicle-shrinking, scream-inducing bellow that everyone present would remember through infinity.

Tonny's slobbery drooling didn't help. He was thinking of sweeter things than eating two-legs, but that didn't occur to those present.

The only comfort to senators and citizens was that things couldn't possibly get any worse.

Then, overhead, enormous, complex, crystal chandeliers hanging from the high ceiling began to tremble, the glass in them began to tinkle, and the light they emitted began to flicker. If that were not a hint, the very floor itself jerked, the entire building groaned, and the high velvet curtains to the side exits shook with wrinkles. Dust and little pieces of chandelier glass settled from the ceilings.

All lights went out.

When Packy Rudd reached the rotunda floor, his first instinct was to help some of the downed people lying on the

302

Seal entangled in crimson velvet ropes and brass stanchions, but none seemed seriously hurt. The black man in the suit with the gun bounded by and leaped up the stair tier to Packy's left. State patrol troopers raced up, guns in hand, looked briefly at the rope roundup, then ran up steps to the left and right calling over the racket on their radios. Packy charged up the steps to his right toward the house chamber entry.

The FOCM, minus Hogan and Ronald Reagan, and wearing raingear and Groucho glasses, ran dripping up the steps to the rotunda floor just as Tonny had answered the seductive audio backpack in the senate chamber. They arrived at the open senate chamber doors just as the building began to groan and move, and everything went pitch dark.

In seconds that seemed like eternity, automatic emergency lighting kicked on. It was relatively dim, LED light that came from little battery boxes mounted on the walls and stairways. It left a lot of dark shadows everywhere, but it was a boatload better than darkness.

In the senate chamber, all the gasping two-legs were trying to absorb the horrifying reality that what they'd thought couldn't *possibly* get any worse...just had. When the lights came on, the building jerked again. All senators in the chamber within began to move like golf-balls teed off on a racquetball court.

Tonny couldn't have cared less about the earthquake, but he was beginning to get a little cranky about not being able to find that little vixen sow who was leading him on. Foreplay had its place, Tonny admitted to himself, but it was time to get down to business.

Lisa had crawled screaming down the carpeted aisle in the darkness, clunking into desks. When the emergency lights came on, she was laying on the floor between the senator desks and the wide judicial bench that was before them. She stumbled to her feet and turned toward the chamber doors only to find that, no, it wasn't just a nightmare, there was that hideous bear in the middle of the senate chamber.

Holy Mother of God! Lisa grunted, and went for the pink revolver she had velcroed to her inner thigh above the knee in case one of those crazy NRA gun nuts—or any of her other many enemies real and perceived—ever tried to do a Kennedy on her. She dropped the little gun on the carpet, then snatched it up.

Through the chamber doors Perry ran first, followed by the FOCM revolutionaries, fighting their way past an exhausted, howling ebb tide of emotionally wrecked citizens and limping senators.

Perry was scanning the room when the cacophony became punctuated by five loud, rapid pops. He flinched. A combat veteran, he knew the sound of a bullet going by his ear and ricocheting off the marble wall behind him. He also knew the report of a snub-nosed revolver. He couldn't see Lisa for a broad hairy grizzly ass in the aisle before him, but he didn't have to to know his very own self-anointed Annie Oakley had just opened up on nearly a ton of bear with a pop-gun.

Bear-Daughter Lowenstein thought she really knew what a heart attack was like, but she somehow still had the strength to stumble out the chamber doorway and zoom down the steps for the rotunda casualty zone, still locked in the embrace of her backpack.

Perry scrambled over and between desks until he could see around the bear, which looked at him with disinterest. He was dumbfounded to see Lisa spinning slowly about, swinging a young wet-haired person in a yellow raincoat and Groucho glasses who had Lisa yoked about the neck and was yelling: "Don't you shoot my bear, you witch!" Lisa was bug-eyed.

"Good Christ!" Perry said. He holstered his pistol and clambered forward. He slapped the empty pistol out of Lisa's hand and half a rotation later he yoked the yellow raincoat person. "Turn my woman loose!" Perry yelled.

Lisa was fading into unconsciousness from the choke-hold by the insane kid who'd attacked her, but she did so blissfully thinking: '*My* woman?'

Loverly was stunned to feel a strong arm encircle her neck, but damned if she would let the fat broad shoot her bear. She tightened her clutch and hung on.

As this trio rotated more slowly in their lockup. Blubbo bounded desks and grasped Perry in a choke-hold. "Turn loose a my girl, you son of a bitch!"

Perry went frog-eyed, thinking what new hell is this?

Loverly grew groggy from lack of oxygen, but with a slight smile as the words echoed in her mind: 'My *girl*.'

Truly inspired, Bear-Daughter Lowenstein made it all the way to the rotunda floor, down the left steps to the south vestibule and thence out into the pouring rain. She would not know for another hundred yards that one of Lisa's errant .38 caliber shots had killed the audio backpack, which probably saved her life.

Tonny had had enough of all this romance, besides, the little two-leg sow before him had just made noises not unlike the sting stick the day his foot had caught fire. He wondered if two-legs mated for life, and, if so, why?

That's it, Tonny decided. I'm outta here. He lumbered back up the aisle and out the chamber doors. As he descended the broad marble stair to the rotunda floor, people screamed anew and two troopers rushed up and sighted on him. Seen a nice sow go by here? Tonny grunted, but the good-for-nothing two-legs just cackled inanely.

Near the house chamber on the opposite side of the rotunda, Packy had heard grizzly roars coming from the senate chamber area. Then the floor moved and the awesome, brilliant, twenty-foot Tiffany chandelier began to swing slowly on its chain anchored to the rotunda dome. Jesus in a jumpsuit, Packy thought. *Earthquake!*

The lights went out, followed by emergency floods. Packy scrambled down the house steps and onto the rotunda floor only to find the immense bear coming down the senate steps to meet him, his great hump wobbling and his shoulders shuffling with each stride.

Packy slipped in all the rain and sweat drippings on the marble floor and fell, but his legs were working overtime before he even regained his feet. He turned to run toward the north vestibule stair, but the bear just calmly walked past a couple of gun pointing troopers and darting, screaming citizens, descended the south stairs, and shoved through the big glass doors into the downpour.

My God, that thing is big, Packy thought, watching Tonny waddle away. The huge building popped and jerked one way and back. Dust cascaded down. Lights flickered. The troopers holstered their guns as the bear appeared to be leaving. They began helping people toward exits. Packy hurried down the south steps and out into the rain after his bear. What else could he do? he thought.

The entire Legislative Building shuddered yet again. The emergency lights flickered on and off. Some fell from their mounts and broke on the Alaskan marble. In the dusty air, the troopers had decided that grabbing victims and dragging them away was more dutiful than wounding a giant grizzly who might then subdivide them.

In the senate chamber, it made for a genuine Kodak moment that Blubbo was yoking Perry who was yoking Loverly who was yoking Lisa. The mess of them toppled over. Runs and Boot seized Blubbo and dragged him off the black security guy. Nerves and Lexie pulled Loverly from the floor.

"Come on!" Boot yelled. "Elvis has left the building!"

When Perry could breathe again in the dim, flickering light, he saw the Groucho weirdos disappear out of the senate chamber. One of them was the size of an NFL offensive tackle, which explained a lot. He scooped his limp Lisa up and staggered for the rain.

"I gotta...get a better...job," Perry gasped.

CHAPTER FORTY-ONE

Don't Cry For Me, O-lym-pee-ah

Hogan in his Groucho glasses and Ronald Reagan read the shaking of the capitol building and the failure of the lights as a sign that they should go get the truck and horse trailer. They exited the north doors they'd come in through.

Tonny had ambled down the south steps and pushed through the heavy glass doors of the left entry into the rain. He snorted and sniffed and wandered south past the sundial plaza between the Cherberg and O'Brien office buildings, and into the narrow forest facing Lake Washington. Disgusted at the downpour and noisy skyflash-bangs, Tonny sighed and went looking for what were bacon and egg scents in the bordering, wooded residential neighborhood off Sylvester Street SW. Maybe he would find Chirpy, who might have M&Ms.

In the relative darkness and rain, and given the trees through which he wandered leaving the campus, not to mention the grave two-leg preoccupation with a trembling earth, few people actually got a good look at Tonny. They called only backed-up phone systems telling them their call was important and please hold for the next available call-taker, and their estimated wait time was two-hundred-seventy-four minutes. Even 911 was backed up until the next solar eclipse.

The Free Okanogan County Movement was moving.

Loverly made a difficult choice to go back into the capitol building to look for her Paw-paw, and let the others tend to her bear. It was quickly decided that Boot would go with Loverly, but, before they split up, Hogan and Ronald Reagan loomed out of the fog in the pickup-horse-trailer rig, albeit with a large uprooted hedge stuck in the grill guard. "Paw-paw!" Loverly cried.

"Let's get busy people!" Hogan rasped out the driver's window. "That state patrol SWAT truck is back here zipping around! My bet is they're after Tonny!"

Nerves, Boot, Loverly and Blubbo pursued Tonny on foot while the others wove the truck and trailer around the rainy streets to keep up.

Packy Rudd held back by the sundial plaza between the office buildings. He wondered, who are those tourists who seemed to be following the bear and why are they wearing those bizarre masks? Packy knew from grim experience that some witless tourists would try to be cell-phone-photographed feeding a Big Mac to a black bear, a bull elk or a buffalo cow with calf, but he'd never seen one try it with a giant grizz during an earthquake.

A stretch-cab, 4wd, dually pickup truck pulling a thirty-foot aluminum gooseneck horse trailer had just pulled up south on Water Street SW, and the group had run to meet it. Not your typical urban commuter wheels, Packy considered. The occupants conversed with the other...tourists.

Packy watched what appeared to be a young woman in a hooded, baggy yellow rain jacket with three men, one of them huge. They ran into the woods where the bear had gone. They had no cameras that Packy could see, but no rifles either. So, he thought, could these be the same people who captured the big bear and brought him here for their politics? But why would they be trying to chase him down now?

No, no, no, Packy thought. I don't believe it. These people are going to try to re-steal the bear! Packy ran for his car a block away. Five minutes later, his old Isuzu Trooper plowed through the rain south down Water Street where he'd last seen the horse trailer rig go. He took the first right towards the woods that he came to, 16th Avenue, which dead-ended at the spot where the grizz had disappeared into the woods. He backed up fifty yards, then turned south onto Sylvester Street, but stopped. He wiped the condensation off the inside of his windshield with a bandana and stared a block away in amazement.

The Groucho 'tourists' were moving things out of the trailer and dumping them in the pickup's bed when out of the woods behind some homes came a shaggy, ambling great grizzly bear, its massive hump swaying as it followed the young girl in the yellow-rain jacket. She was actually feeding the monster out of her hand as they walked! She led the bear into the rear of the rocking horse trailer. The others closed the big back door and opened the narrow side door, from which the girl emerged. She poured something that looked like pills into her hand and stuck it between the trailer slats. Thence, these crazy people piled into the truck, and the rig disappeared to the left on 17th Avenue.

Sweet Jesus, Packy thought. They did it.

The old SUV swayed slightly as the ground jerked yet again.

Time to beat it outta Dodge, Packy thought.

As he drove after his bear, the state patrol SWAT team van turned onto Sylvester and stopped. Black-clad men with big guns and small senses of humor leaped out. Some ham radio operator had radioed to say that the escaped al Qaeda bear just went by his back window and peed on his azaleas!

The rain had begun to taper off in the town of Sedro Woolley, seventy miles north of Seattle, by three pm as a McDonalds got a walk-in order for fifty Big Macs, hold the pickles, skip the fries, and hurry it up. A local Rite-Aid sold completely out of two brands of nighttime cold and flu syrup.

Some of the mystery cleared up for Packy when the bear people had hurried from the neighborhood by the capitol to a nearby big truck stop on I-5. There, they dumped the Groucho glasses down a storm drain. Packy recognized the two women from the grocery in Tonasket. Two of the men, a muscular one and an elderly one, and the young girl, retrieved the Suburban. The old man had to be helped to the SUV, Packy was concerned to note. They'd immediately hit the road.

Packy Rudd was running on junk food and energy drinks, which he loathed, but it was all he'd had time to snatch at a convenience market and fuel stop in Sedro Wooley while the bear people sent one of theirs to a McDonalds. He thought he'd lost the crazy bear people until he caught up with them refueling their rig from plastic diesel cans at a chain-up in the west foothills of the North Cascade mountain range. They could sleep somewhat, in shifts, in the vehicles, Packy thought, bleary eyed, but he hadn't slept in almost three days.

Packy consistently stayed well back to avoid being noticed, but as far as he could tell from frequently broken, distant views, the bear was traveling well.

Tonny too was exhausted by the time he finished his Big Mac and flu med meal. He slept the good sleep on the rubber floor of the horse trailer, assorted dropped M&Ms here and there. Two-legs were a never-ending source of entertainment, he thought as he dozed off, and, bear, could they make sauces.

By seven pm they had descended the east face of the Cascades onto now dry road in real sunlight, back in real Okanogan County. A few miles later, at the historic eastside town of Winthrop, near the scene of the torched airplane episode, Packy was alarmed to see the bear truck and the Suburban leave highway-20 northbound. As near as Packy could tell from the map, this secondary road would follow the Chewuch River north for twenty miles before dead-ending high up in the Pasayten Wilderness, in sight of Canada from high ground on a clear day.

Tonny was now back on his feet, feeling mellow and enjoying the passing scenery through aluminum slats at the tops of the horse trailer's four-foot high wall panels. He wondered what the kookie two-legs had planned next, but his belly was full, he'd been given plenty of water and the air was full of interesting scents, so life was good. Tonny was content to smell the rich scent of forest once again.

Up and up they climbed, past spectacular alpine vistas until they turned right on a twisty, dirt road that became a downright dangerous, ascending, cliff-side ledge. By 8pm, they were about as far into the middle of nowhere as one could get by a combination vehicle in the great Pacific Northwest, high in the Pasayten Wilderness.

At last, as the sun drew low, Packy rounded a tree shrouded section of road to see the truck and Suburban two-hundred yards around a hairpin bend, stopped in a clearing hacked out by loggers years ago, during a fire-fighting operation. He stopped on the road and watched. The setting sun split shades of crimson and lilac near the towering Cascades forty miles to the west. The air was cold and clean, even in June.

But we ain't in Montana, Toto, Packy thought.

Stiff and stumbling, the FOCM revolutionaries stretched their legs. Lexie and Loverly helped Hogan who was visibly feeling the strain of the last few days. No one spoke. It had all been said in nine hours on the road, in animated conversations and short snippets on the CB radios they communicated between vehicles with.

After a short time, they looked uneasily at each other. Boot Colhane and Dr. Runs With Rivers racked powerful, high-caliber rounds into the breaches of their big-game rifles. Hogan Winslow withdrew his sabot-slug loaded shotgun from the Suburban and racked it. Loverly cried, held by Blubbo. Lexie comforted Nerves and fought back her own tears. Ronald Reagan looked on impassively from within the Suburban.

From his distant vantage on the other side of the hairpin

in the fire road, Packy jumped when he saw the men the
pull weapons from their vehicles. Jesus Christ, they're gonna
shoot him! Packy jammed the Trooper in gear and its tires
sprayed gravel.

It was Nerves who'd planned Operation Grizz, and it
was Nerves who made the first move to generate it. It was
fitting that he be the one to end it. He walked to the trailer's
rear door, unlatched it and swung it wide. Runs, Boot and
Hogan held their guns cradled across one arm, forefingers on
the safeties.

Tonny stepped off the rocking trailer and shook. He
looked around, then at the setting sun. Ah, the big bear
thought, back in the 'hood. This is more like it.

Tonny looked at Chirpy, who was making odd noises
against the big two-leg, and he looked at the other two-legs
who'd led him on one hell of an adventure. He'd acquired a
non-culinary fondness for these particular two-legs at least,
and he loved their sauces, but dang it, it was the mating
season and he had deeply ingrained genetic imperatives
to meet. That teaser sow in two-leg land had gotten away
somehow, but he knew there were others in the forests, and
it was time to find them.

Never a bear to stand on ceremony, Tonny sat up, flapped
his fore paws and said AWNK. (Roughly: Thanks guys, it's
been special.) Then he dropped easily to all fours and headed
north. With every step, his hump swayed, his massive head
swung, his shoulders advanced, and his big shaggy butt
wobbled. He sniffed the air and drooled. It was a fine day to
go in search of poontang.

"Bye Tonnyyy!" Loverly sobbed, waving, smiling in spite
of herself. The men too smiled as they unloaded and stowed
their guns. Lexie dabbed at her cheeks, and held Nerves who
wept. Blubbo lifted his hand and said, "Take care, ole bear!"

Adios big dog, Ronald Reagan thought.

Returning to nature, Tonny was absorbed, embraced, by
the towering spruces.

Suddenly, all became aware of an approaching vehicle, decidedly not a good sign this far back in the wilderness. They turned to see an old Trooper slide to a halt, and a small bearded man emerge. "Jesus," the newcomer said. "I thought you guys were going to shoot him."

"Who are you?" Hogan grunted, breathing deeply, his hand on the shotgun that lay on the Suburban's front seat.

Packy said, "Oh, yeah." He held up his badge and ID. "Packwood Rudd, federal officer. I've been following you guys since Olympia. Since the Flathead, actually."

Houston, we have a problem, Ronald Reagan thought.

"Oh...shit," Blubbo said.

"We have the right to remain silent," Nerves recited rapidly, "anything we say can be used against us in a–"

"Oh relax," Packy said walking to join them, staring up the trail where the big bear had disappeared. "I'm not here to make any arrests. I'm just glad you didn't kill him." Packy looked at the people. "He was my bear too, see?"

Runs spoke. "We weren't going to kill him. The guns were just prudent precautions. Nature has a way of surprising us."

"Tell *me* about it," Packy muttered.

"Beside, if we wanted to kill him, why would haul him all the way up here in the middle of nowhere?" Boot said. "We coulda left him in Olympia for the state patrol SWAT guys."

Packy smiled and put his hands on his hips. "Exactly! Why *did* you haul him up *here*? Wasn't the whole...thing... about keeping grizz *out* of Okanogan County in the first place?"

Nerves said, "We...we all agreed that we had very poor chances of getting Tonny all the way back to the Flathead without getting caught. The rain and cloud cover and the earthquake were the only reasons we were able to get this far."

"We never wanted to hurt anybody," Lexie said, "including Tonny."

"We'd never kill *Tonny*," Loverly said, "we just wanted to

get him, like, to a safe place!"

"Tonny?" Packy asked. "You *named* him?"

"Why not, man?" Blubbo answered. "He was a cool bear."

"Why not indeed," Packy said.

"One bear high in the Pasayten ain't *sixty* on state lands in Okanogan County," Runs said. "Besides, there's a few grizzly already up here in the North Cascades region."

"None as big that son of a bitch, though," Hogan said, sitting on the seat, looking at the ground, breathing deeply.

"He was one for the record books," Packy agreed.

Then the inevitable happened. There was a groan and someone hit the dirt.

"Nerves!" Hogan yelled. "What's wrong?"

Lexie hurried to Nerves who lay on the ground rigid and trying to speak. Packy knelt by Nerves and studied his face.

"Ahhhm...ahhmmm!" Nerves said.

"What's his name?" Packy said. "What's his name?"

"Nerves."

"No, I mean his name!"

"Nerves. That's his name!"

Packy glanced up, then back at Nerves. "What's your name sir?"

"Nerves!" the FOCM yelled.

"I'm asking *him* now! What's your name, sir?"

"Naer...Naer..." Nerves groaned, his eyes wandering.

"Hey!" Packy said. "Smile at me, man! Smile at me!"

Nerves twitched one side of his mouth.

"Raise your arms! Both of them!"

Nerves lifted one arm.

"Both of them! Raise both arms!"

Nerves wagged one arm.

"Nerves!" Loverly cried.

"He's having a heart attack!" Boot said.

"He's having a *stroke*," Packy said. "Call 911."

"We're two hours from a hospital!" Runs said. "Four hours or more if we wait for an ambulance up here. Let's get him in the truck, quick. We'll start that way and meet an ambulance in route."

"It'll be faster on this jeep road in my car!" Packy said. Glances got exchanged. "People! If I was going to turn you in, I'd have done it hours ago! Now help me!"

Blubbo shoved his way in, slipped both arms under Nerves and hurried him to the Trooper where Packy was laying the passenger seat-back down. "Somebody come with me!" Packy said. "I don't know where I am."

"I'll go," Runs said. "Boot, you guys follow in the truck and the Sub. Mid-Valley Hospital in Omak."

As the Trooper departed, Boot hurried for Runs's truck. He stepped on a round rock which rolled, and he went down hard. He'd either broken or sprained his ankle.

Close on Boot at a run, Blubbo tripped over Boot and both men howled with pain.

"What the hell is this, an NFL scrimmage?" Hogan said as they loaded Boot in the truck, "Can we get out of this goddamned place? Before I turn up pregnant or something?"

I'd give a lot to see that, Ronald Reagan thought.

"I'll drive the Sub!" Loverly said.

"No cell phone!" Hogan bellowed.

They're at it again, Tonny thought, watching from the timber.

Epilogue

G-Day Plus Five Years

The earth under Olympia stopped quivering within hours. It was the biggest earthquake in the area since 2001, but it too was an 'incremental,' a relatively limited quake that scientists said helped avoid city-wrecking cataclysms. Glass got broken, groceries got tossed off shelves, some water mains broke, some pavement cracked, and some minor damage to older buildings occurred. No one was killed, but over a hundred-twenty people were injured at least slightly.

Communications, already heavily disturbed due to the massive electrical storm, got worse for days.

The tough, majestic, old Washington Legislative Building weathered the event better than initially thought. She took no structural damage, and none of her art treasures were damaged. It amounted to dust and some broken emergency lighting, if one discounted two bullet holes in senate chamber desks, and two chips in the walls. Four of the fired slugs were recovered by state patrol forensics. The fifth went to the bottom of Lake Washington with Bear-Daughter Lowenstein's audio backpack. Lisa Belle's marksmanship was rivaled only by her legislative acumen.

A state patrol guardhouse at the entrance to the ellipse was written off as not designed to be earthquake-proof and thus destroyed beyond recognition. The architects and contractors were sued.

Trooper Pakootas was promoted to Sergeant. He dreams of retiring to New Zealand.

It became very difficult to determine who was hurt at the capitol before or during the earthquake, and how. A few broken ankles, wrists and collarbones proved to be the worst of it. There was much tragic, negligent, reckless, irreparable damage to scores of expensive suits, designer dresses and panty-hose. Tort pirate lawyers sued everything with money.

At noon Pacific Standard Time on G-day, CNN.com ran with: '**Senator Defends Colleagues Against Giant Bear in Statehouse. Calls For Manufacture Of Bigger Guns.**'

FOXNews.com posted the bait line: '**Anti-gun Senator Shoots Up Statehouse In Earthquake.**'

Ratings soared.

On G-Day-plus-one-week, the WSP SWAT team, the aviation unit and the whole K-9 squad issued a televised public statement declaring that there were positively no grizzly bears in Olympia. With a nervous smile, the governor strolled the neighborhood before cameras to put all fears to rest. Residents of Sylvester St. still go to pucker-factor ten when anything goes bump in the night.

There ensued investigations of everything, including investigations, so that officials, elected and hired, could look dutiful. The WSP tracked Sol Pickering's cattle rig to his ranch, of course, but the trail went cold there. Sol's sister in California got the truck and a four-thousand dollar heavy-wrecker towing bill.

State patrol detectives made a show of looking around, but their hearts weren't in it, since they loved 'Cow' Belle like a butt boil. Further, they were covering their own who had ignored a call the night before the earthquake, from some Montana forest ranger they thought, who warned them the bear was coming. Inquiry with a Montana forest service LEO on vacation at the time was unproductive.

The WSP asked some enormous Charlie-Daniels-looking chainsaw repairman in Wauconda if he'd seen anything unusual before the bear incident, but his sum testimony was: "I ain't seen...*shit!*"

As investigators returned to their cars, Chainsaw Charlie revved a logger saw and grunted, "Gubmint assholes."

The Washington State Senate tried to impeach Senator Lisa Belle despite her immediate introduction of emergency legislation calling for the total eradication of grizzly bears in Washington. In the end, the senate settled for censure, a payment of costs to repair the senate chamber desks and walls, and an unwritten promise that Lisa wouldn't run for so much as Sudanese meter reader the following year.

Lisa's many friends at the Washington State Patrol and state attorney general's office charged her with carrying a concealed firearm without a permit, reckless discharge of a firearm, destruction of public property, and possession of a firearm in the legislative building during session. The United States Attorney's office for the District of Western Washington brought a federal charge against Lisa for attempted poaching of a threatened wildlife species.

Lisa's battalion of lawyers plea-bargained her down to fines and suspended sentences on the charges. As Perry dragged her out of court, she screamed that anti-gun laws were unconstitutional and she had a second amendment right to carry one.

The National Rifle Association went orgasmic over the incident for months.

Lisa divorced her husband because he wouldn't buy the rest of Vashon Island and sink the ferries. She sold her story for a TV show called Real Senators of the Pacific Northwest, and wrote the national best seller *How I Faced Death In The Senate In more Ways Than One*.

Perry is negotiating the movie rights.

Lisa and Perry now live on the south Pacific island of Pongo Pua, off Sumatra, where Perry fishes from his new boat, smokes cigars, and drinks tequila with salt and lime. Lisa studies the migratory habits of the North American grizzly bear, online, to assure herself that they do not swim. Lisa and Perry still do Pocahontas meets the Lone Ranger every week or so.

Dr. Ermintrude Windgate was charged with reckless disregard for human safety for deliberately releasing a dangerous animal from confinement. The WSP all but threatened to waterboard her to give up "her fellow conspirators." Ermie will be in litigation until the Second Coming of Christ.

To her parents' eternal relief, Bear-Daughter had her name changed back to Aleah Golda Lowenstein. She finally completed her masters, but in women's studies, of course. Appropriately, Aleah now runs a small tropical fish shop in Tel Aviv. That grizzlies are not native to Israel is not coincidental. She'd rather face Hamas any day.

Lexie came over to Boot's ranch with some pizza one night to look in on his sprained ankle, and she never left.

Blubbo lost the other fourteen pounds in four months and joined the United States Marine Corps when he turned seventeen. Two years later he married Loverly. Runs was best man, and the maid of honor was Ronald Reagan.

They are currently stationed at Marine Corps Air Station New River, in North Carolina, where Lance Corporal Barffarhdt Whitekill is a helicopter mechanic. The last guy who smarted off about Blubbo's name is recovering nicely, but is still on light duty. Hogan's great-grandson's name is Winslow Rivers Whitekill, but they call the baby Blubby.

Mrs. Whitekill is assistant sales manager for a large Jacksonville gun store, and is pregnant with Hogan's great-granddaughter. She reads Jane Austen novels.

Dr. Runs With Rivers bought out a retiring veterinarian's large-animal practice in Omak, but he still treats animals on the rez and mentors tribal high-schoolers. The Whitekill family stays with him when they're in town.

Hogan hired Lexie to run the gun and pawn shop, and she's a hit with the clientele. Wubbies out to here, etc. Hogan hangs out in the shop and brags about his great-grandkids present and pending. His ears and back are failing him, but he is researching the theory that geriatric hearing loss can be restored with liberal consumption of Jack Daniels, the only remotely liberal thing he's ever done. Hogan conned a doctor into certifying Ronald Reagan as service dog, so they can go into bars and restaurants together, which they are both quite pleased with. Boot and Lexie look after them.

Hogan has two other self-anointed caretakers who stop by occasionally to play cards. Nerves recovered from his stroke. He does well on medications and has gone back to teaching high school and working out at the health club. Packy Rudd kept driving over from the Flathead to see if Nerves was OK until one month he announced his retirement from the U.S. Forest Service and moved in.

Nerves says he has retired from any interest in politics for the duration.

When Hogan learned of Nerves's and Packy's arrangement he said "Ah, what the hell, they're everywhere. Wives are dangerous anyway."

The Senator Lisa Belle Noble Grizzly Bear Restoration Act was defeated in a unanimous senate vote that took all of twenty-three seconds. Bang went the gavel. Next!

Three days after the quake, Tonny came upon a Rubenesque but lovely grizzly sow fishing in a river near Canada. *WAHOOOOOORRROOONNNNK*! she said.

Tonny thought the bear equivalent of...hot...*damn*!

THE END

WILLIAM SLUSHER is the author of *Shepherd of the Wolves*, and its sequel, *Butcher of the Noble*. He has also written *Talon Force - Meltdown*, as 'Cliff Garnett'.

Mr. Slusher's latest novel, *For Whom To Die* (CMP Publishing Group, LLC - 2009), is a finalist selection in the Next Generation Indie Book Awards in New York for 2010.

Other work by William Slusher has been a finalist selection in the Pacific Northwest Writers' Association 2009 Literary Competition. He is currently assembling a short story collection and working on another novel.

A Vietnam veteran and retired police/medevac pilot, Mr. Slusher now enjoys six horses, four dogs, and three cats with his beloved wife, Dr. Linda Shields, on a ranch along the Okanogan River in North Central Washington.

Mr. Slusher deeply appreciates the investment of your hard-earned money and priceless time in his novel. He hopes it earns both.